Territory

S

SCEPTRE

Also by Elspeth Sandys

Catch a Falling Star
The Broken Tree
Love and War
Finding Out
Best Friends
River Lines

Enemy Territory

ELSPETH SANDYS

SCEPTRE

Copyright © 1997 Elspeth Sandys

First published in 1997 by Hodder and Stoughton
A division of Hodder Headline PLC
A Sceptre book

The right of Elspeth Sandys to be identified as the Author of
the Work has been asserted by her in accordance with the
Copyright, Designs and Patents Act 1988.

10 9 8 7 6 5 4 3 2 1

All rights reserved. No part of this publication may be
reproduced, stored in a retrieval system or transmitted
in any form or by any means without the prior written
permission of the publisher, nor be otherwise circulated
in any form of binding or cover other than that in which
it is published and without a similar condition being
imposed on the subsequent purchaser.

All characters in this publication are fictitious and any
resemblance to real persons, living or dead, is purely coincidental.

A CIP catalogue record for this title is available
from the British Library.

ISBN 0 340 68492 5

Typeset by Palimpsest Book Production Limited,
Polmont, Stirlingshire
Printed and bound in Great Britain by
Mackays of Chatham PLC, Chatham, Kent

Hodder and Stoughton
A division of Hodder Headline PLC
338 Euston Road
London NW1 3BH

For Diana Tyler

ACKNOWLEDGEMENTS

I am indebted to a number of people for help in writing this story, but to no one more than Judge Oke Blaikie, whose patience in leading me through the intricacies of family court law made the task of research such a pleasure. My heartfelt thanks are due to Judge Blaikie. If there are any legal errors in the text the fault is entirely mine.

I was also assisted in my legal researches by Roy Somerville, Judith Medlicott, and Professor Bernard Brown. To each I offer my thanks.

Most of the research for the novel was undertaken, and some of the first draft written, while I was Burns Fellow at Otago University. To that institution, to my colleagues in the English Department in particular, I acknowledge my continuing gratitude.

The Glossary was checked by my daughter, Josie Harbutt. For her support and encouragement I am grateful every day of my life.

That the painting chosen for the jacket is the work of my good friend, Jacqueline Fahey, is a source of deep satisfaction to me. My thanks go to Jacqui for permission to use her wonderful painting.

Enemy Territory was completed with the help of a grant from Creative New Zealand. I thank them for their assistance.

GLOSSARY

Hongi	A traditional greeting. Noses pressed together.
Jandals	Thonged sandals.
Kuia	A respected old lady.
Kia ora	Hello! Or thanks.
Karakia	A prayer or chant.
Mana	Power or influence.
Mokopuna	Grandchildren.
Pakeha	Non-Maori, usually of European origin.
Taonga	Treasure, property, artifact.
Tapu	Sacred: forbidden.
Tangi	To mourn. Or a funeral.
Tena Koutou Katoa	Greetings to us all.
Waiata	Song or chant.
Whanau	Family.

'We live our lives in enemy territory'—
Stevie Smith

The Hearing

1

Imagine a rectangular room with no softening domestic features, unless portraits of Judges in wigs and robes can be considered *domestic*. A room better described as a theatre, for it is in this forum that the dramas of 'real life' are played out.

At one end of the room is a stage, furnished with a throne-like chair placed under a central awning. Here the lead actor in the drama shortly to be enacted – one Justice Barrett – will sit for the duration of the play. The less imposing chairs on the level immediately below are intended for two minor but nonetheless vital players, the Registrar and the typist.

Now let the eye of imagination move from the stage to the auditorium, or *pit*. Those rows of seats to stage right are where the jury usually sit; but for today the seats will remain empty. The same will be true for the two rows opposite, where members of that unruly chorus, the press, customarily take their place. Grieve v. Grieve, as this particular drama is titled, is not to be acted out for the benefit of a jury. That is a matter of law. The presence or absence of journalists is a matter for the Judge's discretion. Justice Barrett, who holds a dim view of the press (far too keen on bringing good men down, in his opinion), has ruled against the inclusion of reporters. If he had his way that ruling would be extended to cover the entire judicial system.

The centre of the pit is occupied by two long tables, with chairs. At one of these the applicant and his solicitor will be seated: at the other, the respondent and her solicitor. A third legal player – counsel for the child – will sit to one side.

Now step back a few paces to the dock. Though this position will not be occupied today, it nevertheless casts a potent spell over the as yet empty courtroom. Stairs lead from the dock to the cells below, a reminder, should one be needed, of the awesome power exercised in this place.

Forward of the dock is the witness box, which *will* be occupied today. A plain black bible awaits use as an essential prop in the drama.

At the back of the room are the seats set aside for the audience, referred to, in this particular forum, as the 'general public'. But Justice Barrett's ban on the press has been extended to include that chorus too. The delicate nature of the case, and the prominence of the family involved, have convinced him this performance must be played out in private.

The room is eerie with silence. The clock on the wall above the public entrance informs us it is 9.45. Fifteen minutes to go to the start of the play.

The date is Monday, 12 March 1970.

'What d'ya reckon?' Greville King, counsel for the respondent, enquires of his colleague, Wesley Gorman. They'd exchanged stiff greetings earlier in the robing room, but formality is difficult to maintain in a urinal. 'Over by lunchtime?'

'Earlier. It's an open and shut case.'

'Reckon you've got it all sewn up, do you?'

'Look, she only got custody at the time of the divorce because the facts didn't come out.'

'She's the child's mother, Wesley.'

'She's a drug addict.' Wesley pulls up his zip, runs his hands under the tap, dries them and marches to the door. 'See you in court,' he says, over his shoulder.

Moments later Greville King is sitting with his client awaiting Justice Barrett's summons. They are in a small, sparsely furnished room adjoining the courtroom.

The client's name is Kay Grieve. She is twenty-seven years old. Were it not for the tension in her face she might be described as pretty, but for many months now Kay has been variously reported as having lost her looks.

The circumstances under which Greville has come to take this case are unusual to say the least. Three months ago his client's ex-husband, Geoffrey Grieve, contacted the senior partner in Greville's firm to request that someone represent his estranged wife in his forthcoming action against her. All fees and costs, an astonished Walter Talboys was assured, would be covered by Grieve personally.

When the file landed on Greville's desk, his instinct was to say no. He knew Geoffrey Grieve, though he wouldn't have described him as a friend. They were members of the same profession. They belonged to the same ski club. But what really bothered him was the unorthodox nature of the chap's request. What was he playing at, arranging his wife's defence in a case *he* had initiated?

'Look,' Walter admitted, 'I don't like it much either. But there's nothing irregular about it.'

'What about Grieve's old man?'

'Lionel, QC? I wouldn't worry about him.'

'He'll make Judge one day. If I were to win this case . . .'

'Lionel Grieve will never make Judge,' Walter stated firmly.

'Why ever not?'

'Just take the case, there's a good fellow.'

Greville had puzzled about it all the rest of that day. In the end he'd broken his rule about not bringing work home, and confided in his wife. She'd listened to what he had to say, then in that quiet, superior voice of hers suggested, 'Perhaps the child's father – what was his name? Geoffrey?—doesn't really want to win? Perhaps he's been put up to it.'

The trouble, Greville thinks now, glancing at his client, is that she doesn't seem to have grasped what she's up against. Geoffrey Grieve may be a decent human being, anxious to play fair, but he has all the big guns on his side.

Kay Grieve, who has spent the intervening minutes gingerly fingering her scalp, smiles, as if to reassure him. But you look as if you've lost already, he thinks.

Meanwhile, in a similar room on the other side of the corridor, a slightly built man of thirty-one years of age sits nervously smoking. Wesley Gorman, a man of bulky proportions, whose hirsute fists betoken a generous covering of hair elsewhere on his body, sits, or rather slumps, next to him. He whistles under his breath.

'Relax, Geoff,' he encourages. 'We're in luck. We've got Barrett. You know his reputation. It's all over bar the shouting.'

'He'll be hard on *her*, won't he?'

'Isn't that what you want?'

Geoffrey draws deeply on his cigarette. The second and third fingers of his right hand are orange with nicotine. When he can get no more from the butt he grinds it into the ash tray and lights another.

'King will cross-examine,' Wesley reminds, through the cloud of smoke encircling his client, 'but you've nothing to worry about. Our witnesses are water-tight.'

'Are they both here?'

'I've just been talking to them.'

'What about hers?'

'Haven't clapped eyes on either of them. That Polish broad she hung out with at university . . .'

'Sandra Grajawaska.'

'Wouldn't surprise me if she didn't show at all.'

'I never did understand what Kay saw in her.'

'You've read her affidavit. There's no way it'll stand up.'

'What about her Professor? He'll make a good impression, won't he?'

'Doctor Nathan Bute. Hmm . . . If I was King I'd be worried. You've seen what Bute has to say. Testifying to your wife's intelligence is one thing. Proving her a good mother is an altogether different kettle of fish.'

Geoffrey takes off his glasses and wipes them on his handkerchief. A humid autumn day, but it's not that which is causing him to sweat. Nina, his daughter, is at home with his mother. Kay, rather surprisingly, agreed to the arrangement. Winifred has not so far shown herself to be a willing grandmother. 'You might as well both know,' she said, at the time of the birth, 'I've spent half my life bringing up children. I don't intend to prolong the process by offering my services as your baby sitter.'

Wesley gives his client a quick once-over. Sober suit and tie. Neat haircut. Those fine cheekbones. His name. A walk-over, he thinks. Kay Grieve, whom he caught a glimpse of outside the court, could be anyone. She didn't exactly look 'cheap', but she didn't look much like a mother either.

'That was a good move of yours, shifting back in with your parents,' he confirms, listing, for his own satisfaction, the many advantages his client has over the opposition.

Geoffrey hooks the sides of his glasses round his ears. If Nina comes to live with his parents she'll turn out like his sisters, won't she? They were enchanting little girls once. Now they're merely vacuous.

'Time to go,' Wesley announces.

Geoffrey takes a last draw on his cigarette and stubs it out. How many times has *he* said those words, and failed to notice their effect?

He straightens his tie, adjusts his glasses, and follows Wesley into court.

'Time to go, Kay,' Greville King says softly.
'What?'
'It's ten o'clock.'
'But Sandra's not here.'
'We can't wait for her, I'm afraid.'
'I should phone. See if Nina's all right.'
'She'll be fine. She's with her grandmother, isn't she?'
'She hardly knows her.'
'She'll be fine.'
At the door of the courtroom Kay freezes.
'What is it?' Greville asks, turning back to her.
'I can't do this,' she whispers.
Greville puts a hand on her arm. 'There's nothing to be afraid of,' he reassures.

2

Mr Justice Barrett places his fob watch on the table in front of him, and opens the file which the Registrar has just handed him. Grieve v. Grieve. An unfortunate business. A good family, dogged by ill luck.

He peers over the top of his lenses at the estranged couple. Geoffrey Grieve, by all accounts, is destined to rise high. His recent performance as counsel for Flannagan and Rennie, the construction firm, earned him significant plaudits. If he stays out of trouble, he should outstrip his father. That's the prediction. Not that the poor chap looks like Bench material today. A serious error of judgement, marrying as he did.

As for the wife, the *mother*, well, she looks pretty wretched too, as who would not? No doubt she regrets the error of her ways. But a woman once fallen will almost certainly fall again. That's been his experience. And in the meantime there's a child – the Judge glances at his file – a three-year-old girl, to consider.

It's Justice Barrett's private opinion that the best guide in these matters is the old common-law principle which gives the father, as head of the household, paramount rights over the child. Not that he can cite those principles today. They've long since been eroded. In these enlightened times it's the child's interests, not those of either parent, which must prevail. But for once he anticipates no real conflict between his deepest instincts and the facts of the case. Nina Grieve turned three in January. The 'mother principle', so often used to undermine the rights of the father, becomes increasingly irrelevant as the child grows older. Especially, as in today's case, when the mother is a proven adulterer and probable drug addict.

His eye lingers on Kay Grieve. Someone should have told her not to wear that cheap-looking jacket. Fun fur, is that what it's called? She looks like something off the cover of an Elinor Glyn novel.

'Wesley Gorman,' a voice from the floor announces. 'I appear for the applicant.'

'Greville King,' a second voice follows. 'I appear for the respondent.'

The third voice is female. Justice Barrett frowns. He doesn't approve of women in court. This one, with wig perched on top of tightly permed hair, looks a fright.

'Yes, Mr Gorman?' he invites, when the formalities are over. His scowl is intended as a warning. Gorman has a reputation for loquaciousness.

Why is it so quiet? Kay wonders, as she struggles to comprehend what Geoffrey's lawyer is saying. She'd travelled in this morning on a crowded bus. The boy standing next to her kept humming the opening bars of 'It's All Over Now'. Kay can't get the tune out of her head.

'I refer you to paragraph thirteen of my client's affidavit . . .'

Kay looks down at her skirt. A brown leather mini. She's worn it hundreds of times before. So what's wrong? People have been staring at her all morning as if she were naked.

Now it's *her* lawyer who's talking. He's asking Geoffrey to go to the witness box. Kay, remembering Nina's happy face as she ran to her father's car this morning, wants to tell Mr King to stop. Geoffrey's shoulders are hunched with tension.

'. . . the truth, the whole truth, and nothing but the truth.'

She won't listen. It's better if she doesn't. She's read Geoffrey's affidavit. Her own can't hope to compete. But she has to believe she's the right person to raise Nina. If *she* doesn't believe it, no one else will.

The minutes crawl by. Every time Kay looks at the clock on the wall the hands don't seem to have moved.

Geoffrey's face is a map of anxiety. When counsel for the child begins her cross-examination his answer is lost in a fit of coughing. A concerned Judge calls for a glass of water.

'Thank you, Mr Grieve,' Justice Barrett says, when the time comes for Geoffrey to step down. Kay's audible sigh of relief puzzles her lawyer.

Now a new player is called to the box: Kay's former neighbour, Bettina Cantwell.

'It struck me every time I visited,' Mrs Cantwell says, in response to Mr Gorman's prompting, 'that Kay – Mrs Grieve – was really too young to have the responsibility of a child. I don't mean she was young in years. I had three children at her age, and nothing like her comfortable income to live on. What I mean is, she didn't seem to have a clue how to go about things. For instance, she'd let little Nina run around that patio of theirs with not a stitch of clothing on. In full view of the road. Not to mention the neighbours on the other side.'

Greville King's cross-examination is scathing. 'The things you accuse my client of could be said of thousands of mothers up and down the country,' he claims.

But Mrs Cantwell is not deterred. 'That poor wee mite had no regularity in her life at all,' she retaliates. 'Mealtimes, well, there *were* no mealtimes. Food was consumed whenever and wherever, as the child demanded. As for bedtime' – she snorts her disgust – 'many's the night, till gone ten or later, I heard their record player booming out that ghastly noise they call music nowadays. No child could sleep through that racket. In fact, I happen to know the wee madam was encouraged to sing and dance whenever the record player was on. No wonder I found her hard to settle the one time they asked me to baby sit.'

Mrs Cantwell is not easily silenced, but eventually, after cross-examination from counsel for the child, her place is taken by the Reverend Theodore Meddings, vicar of one of the city's most fashionable churches. Justice Barrett begins to look interested again. The vicar's affidavit is the one he's marked for special attention. Nevertheless he hopes the chap won't labour the point. The best part of an hour has gone already.

'It was my pleasure and privilege,' the Reverend Meddings begins, when asked by Mr Gorman to describe his relationship to the applicant, 'to be invited by Mr Lionel Grieve, QC, to officiate at the baptism of his first grandchild, Nina Joy.'

His voice, Justice Barrett observes, has that irritating measured quality, common to some priests. As if every word he utters comes straight from Holy Scripture.

'Though I knew Geoffrey only slightly at the time, I subsequently got to know both him and his wife well.'

Encouraged to elaborate, the vicar goes on, 'When, some weeks after the baptism, the young couple stopped attending church, I took it upon myself to pay them a visit. Despite the fact that I was expected, I found only Geoffrey at home. His wife, he informed me, was out with a girlfriend.

'I made the usual polite noises, only to be interrupted by a somewhat startling confession. "My wife," Geoffrey announced, "has declared herself an agnostic."'

Justice Barrett slides his spectacles down the bridge of his nose. 'This is all in your affidavit, Mr Meddings,' he reminds, glaring at the witness.

The priest smiles. 'The point I wish to make, Your Honour, is that it's only with hindsight I've come to realise what was going on. Geoffrey, I'm now convinced, was struggling to come to terms with the kind of change that would ultimately destroy his marriage. For my sake he tried to make light of his difficulty. As I recall, he blamed the study of Anthropology for his wife's loss of faith.'

Greville King's strangled laugh prompts a look from Geoffrey that could be interpreted as a plea. Distaste for the proceedings is written all over his face.

'So it came as no surprise,' the Reverend Meddings continues, 'when I learned from my friend, Lionel Grieve, that young Mrs Grieve had been seen frequenting places I can only describe as *unsavoury*. I refer in particular to The Devil's Kitchen, described in my affidavit, a so-called coffee bar, regularly raided by police in search of drugs.'

Justice Barrett scribbles a note on his pad. Now we're getting somewhere, he's thinking. So long as that fool King doesn't go on flogging a dead horse.

But Greville King is not about to win favour with Mr Justice Barrett. Rising to the challenge he puts it to the vicar that being seen in a place associated with drugs cannot be taken as proof of drug use.

'Indeed not,' Mr Meddings agrees, 'but being twice apprehended on suspicion tells us something, surely?'

To the Judge's dismay, a battle ensues. Mr Meddings has the

word of a member of his congregation, a high-ranking police officer, to back up his allegations. Mrs Grieve may have been released on both occasions, but so far as the police are concerned, she is still under suspicion.

Victory, to the Judge's undisguised relief, does finally go to the priest. Recreating a conversation he had with the respondent, mentioned but not elaborated on in his affidavit, he describes Kay's reaction when asked if she took drugs. 'She laughed,' he reports indignantly. 'Then had the audacity to ask *me* if I drank alcohol. I knew where that was headed. I've heard the argument before. Marijuana – grass, or pot as I believe it's called – is claimed to be no worse than alcohol. Better even since it seldom, so the theory goes, leads to violence.

'I let her have her say,' he concludes, 'then I warned her I would be informing both her husband and her father-in-law of the facts, as I understood them. There was no more laughter after that. As far as I was concerned she had condemned herself.'

The Reverend Meddings's testimony brings the case for the applicant to an end. It is now 11.15. Justice Barrett winds his watch conspicuously. He trusts Mr King will get the message.

Kay, listening to her lawyer's opening address, struggles to control her anxiety about Nina. If she breaks one of Winifred's precious pieces of china, there will be hell to pay. But how can a three year old be expected to know the difference between a Meissen figure and an ordinary doll? Geoffrey has always been protective of his mother, but Kay has heard things. A telephone hurled in anger. His favourite books burned.

'Unfortunately,' Kay hears, 'Miss Grajawaska appears to have been delayed. I would therefore like to call Dr Nathan Bute to the stand.'

This won't take long, Justice Barrett thinks, glancing at the relevant affidavit. There's nothing worth cross-examining here.

And so it proves. The embarrassed Professor, subpoenaed to speak on behalf of a woman he'd much rather, for all her brilliance, never have had anything to do with, is in and out of the witness box in six minutes flat.

That leaves only the respondent. But Greville King wants to delay calling his client in the hope that Sandra Grajawaska will turn up. Justice Barrett, approached for permission, refuses at first, but is persuaded when Maria Cargill, counsel for the child, offers to present *her* testimony. It's a decision he quickly regrets. Miss Cargill, he should have realised from the thrust of her cross-examinations, has come to court determined to throw a spanner in the works.

'As stated in my affidavit,' she begins, 'I visited the respondent at her flat on six separate occasions. In the course of those visits I was able to observe the relationship of mother and daughter, and assess the well-being of the child and the ability of the mother to take care of her. I also took the opportunity to speak alone with the child.'

Asked by Mr Gorman to clarify the statement in paragraph three of her affidavit, she has this to say.

'Yes, I did see signs of strain. It would have been remarkable if I had not. I doubt if any of the gentlemen present here today could hold down a job, *and* raise a pre-school infant. But I saw no evidence this strain was being taken out on the child. On the contrary, everything I saw pointed to the existence of a warm and loving bond between mother and daughter.'

A further question wins from her the concession that the respondent's flat is small, and could be described as untidy, but she categorically denies there is any evidence to suggest the child is neglected. 'There was always food in the fridge,' she asserts. 'And Nina was never less than adequately clothed. If I could refer you to paragraph seven, you will see I describe the flat as colourfully decorated, with a profusion of books and toys scattered about. Nina's room, with its mobiles and alphabet friezes, was as attractive as any I've seen.'

In answer to a question from Mr King, Miss Cargill reiterates her belief that Kay Grieve's first priority is the welfare of her child. 'May I remind you,' she says, looking at the Judge, 'that her job on *The Herald* is part-time.'

Ten to twelve, Justice Barrett observes gloomily. This will go beyond lunch.

What am I doing here? Geoffrey despairs, as Kay's solicitor launches into another round of questions. Kay and I were going to be so different. When did it start to go wrong?

I shouldn't have agreed, Kay worries, her mind blocked to the words flying around her. Winifred hardly knows Nina. She'll make her sit up at the table. She'll complain about her manners. It would help if the girls were home, but they seldom are these days. Auntie Sue and Auntie Belinda. Nina insists on calling them that, even though they've asked her not to.

'So,' the Judge says, when King's cross-examination has finished, 'you saw no evidence, on these visits of yours, of drug use?'

'None whatsoever, Your Honour,' Miss Cargill answers.

'But you accept, we cannot conclude from that, that the respondent does *not* take drugs?'

'I couldn't say, Your Honour.'

'Exactly. You can't say.'

Eleven minutes past twelve. Wesley is trying to decide whether to grab a quick lunch in the cafe, or take Geoffrey down to that new Italian place in Queen Street. A bottle of Frascati and a plate of pasta will help the time to pass.

'Don't panic,' he whispers in his client's ear. 'This is only a hiccup.'

'Think before you speak,' Greville urges, when he can no longer delay putting his client in the box.

Only Geoffrey notices the quick plunge of finger into mouth; the frantic tearing of the skin around the quick of the nail. Did Kay always bite her nails? Why can't he remember?

Justice Barrett looks up from his notes. Oh, yes. He can see now why the poor chap married her. Pale, porcelain face; large, doe-like eyes. A bit skinny for his taste, and too much of that black muck around her eyes, but attractive, no doubt about that.

She won't tell the truth, of course, despite her oath. If she does, she's finished. But he'll get to the bottom of this if it takes the rest of the day. All that Cargill woman has done is stir things up.

'Now, Mrs Grieve, your solicitor will no doubt have advised you to think very carefully before answering questions, but I must remind you, this is a court of law. Lying to the court is a punishable offence. So we will have the truth, please. The whole and nothing but. Do you understand?'

The woman nods.

'Over to you, Mr King,' the Judge sighs.

Of course the man won't ask anything pertinent. That will

have to wait for Mr Gorman. It's not love that's the issue here, it's responsibility.

When, at last, it's Gorman's turn to cross-examine, Justice Barrett makes a note to congratulate the man, privately, on his technique. Loquacious he may be, but he knows how to corner his prey. First he uses charm – 'We all know what an ordeal this must be for you, Kay' – then he attacks – 'I've only one question for you, Mrs Grieve. It's a simple one, requiring a yes or no answer. Have you at any time taken drugs?'

The woman throws back her head. It's as if, Wesley thinks, watching her with interest, someone has just grabbed her by the throat.

'Mrs Grieve?'

Don't answer, Geoffrey wills. Say no. Lie. Oh, Christ . . .

Bastard, Greville hurls silently at his opponent. You bastard.

'Yes.'

'Speak up, please.'

'Yes. In the past. Before . . .'

'Before what, Mrs Grieve? Before your husband brought this action against you?'

'I haven't taken drugs of any kind for almost a year.'

In the pause that follows Kay tries to work out what's different about the silence in the room: till she realises the typist has stopped typing. She looks at the Judge. He's busy consulting his file. She turns to her solicitor. He has his head in his hands. Geoffrey's solicitor is smiling. That's bad, isn't it? As for Geoffrey, he's preoccupied with wiping his brow.

'Perhaps I can help?' the Judge says at last. His voice, Greville registers with despair, is friendly. 'These drugs you talk about, Mrs Grieve. I take it you mean marijuana?'

'Yes, Your Honour. Mostly that. It's easy to get, you see. And people enjoy it. It helps them relax.'

'Quite. And the other drugs?'

'Sorry?'

'You said *mostly* marijuana.'

'Oh, you mean speed, things like that?'

'You tell me, Mrs Grieve.'

'Well, yes, if you can get it. Benzedrine. Some doctors will give you that on prescription. It helps keep you awake when you're studying.'

'Did you find it helpful?'

'I . . .'

'Answer the question, Mrs Grieve.'

'It didn't seem to do anything for me.'

'And what else did you try, besides Benzedrine?'

Kay turns her head so fast it makes her dizzy. She's heard something. A child crying. Has Winifred brought Nina to the court?

'Who's out there?' she whispers.

'I asked you a question, Mrs Grieve.'

Her parents offered to come, but she dissuaded them. The last person she wanted to see today was her father.

There it is again, that cry.

'Geoffrey!'

Greville jumps to his feet. 'Your Honour,' he pleads.

'Quite, Mr King. Your client is distressed. We will continue after lunch.'

The typewriter, which had mysteriously sprung to life again, falls silent. Wesley whistles under his breath. 'You can sit down,' Greville says softly to Kay.

'No!'

It's as if a gun has gone off. Justice Barrett rearranges his spectacles. The woman still looks alarmingly pale, but there was no denying the authority of that 'No'.

'My reasons for stopping,' Kay says, addressing herself to the Judge, 'were nothing to do with Geoffrey. I stopped because something awful happened to me.'

'More awful than your present predicament?'

'I was persuaded . . .' Here the respondent hesitates, tilting her head as if listening for something.

'You were saying?' the Judge prompts.

'I was persuaded to take a purple heart,' the woman finishes.

The Judge consults his papers again. Wesley flexes the muscles of his arms. 'Home and hosed,' he mouths to his client.

'Purple heart,' the Judge muses. 'Ah, yes.' He pulls a paper from his file, and holds it up to the light. '"A highly addictive drug known to increase sexual appetite,"' he reads. '"It has the qualities of immediate sensory gratification, setting up a craving for pleasure which the user finds difficult if not impossible to resist. Can lead to sexual perversion."'

He returns the paper to the file. 'Is that what you were *persuaded* to try, Mrs Grieve?' he asks.

3

'Dad! What are you doing here?'

Geoffrey has just emerged, with his solicitor, into the public waiting area, which everyone must pass through on their way to court. Recognising his father among the people clustered round the edges of the room, he quickly rearranges his expression. His father is not the person he wants to see right now.

Father and son shake hands. To an onlooker they would not appear to be related. Lionel Grieve, QC, is a bear of a man, not tall, but seeming so. His large, balding head, a gift to cartoonists when his name hits the headlines, puts him in a different physical category from his son, whose fine bones and shock of fair hair give him the look of a poet.

'Thought you might need some moral support,' Grieve Senior says.

'I'll leave you two to chat,' Wesley offers. He's already decided to eat Italian.

'No need,' Geoffrey protests. 'I don't imagine you can stay, Dad, can you?'

Lionel grins. 'Just between ourselves, son, I think we've turned the tables. Not that the opposition didn't put up a fight. They're clever, those Jew-boys. But it's going our way, no doubt about that. My client should walk out of here a free man.'

Geoffrey glances over his shoulder. His view of the door he's just come through is obscured by a group of Maori, talking agitatedly to a tall young man with tattooed arms. Kay must have gone out the back way. He should be relieved, but what he feels is an obscure disappointment.

'There's a new Italian place five minutes from here,' Wesley volunteers. 'If you'd care to join us, sir?'

Lionel looks at his son. 'Can't, I'm afraid. Geoff's right. I'm in conference in fifteen minutes. I take it things are going all right?'

'Foregone conclusion,' Wesley reassures.

'Good man,' Lionel says, though whether he means the words for his son, or his son's counsel, is difficult to tell.

'See you this evening then,' Geoffrey says, as they move to go their separate ways.

'I say.' Lionel's clipped 'English' voice, which so often strikes people as at odds with his appearance, causes heads to turn. 'Isn't that Kay's parents? Over there.' He nods at the row of seats against the opposite wall. 'They must have been here all this time.'

Geoffrey only needs to tilt his head a fraction to identify his in-laws. Both are looking steadily in the other direction. But of course they must have seen him. They would have been watching the door for Kay.

'At the risk of seeming rude, I don't see this as an occasion for exchanging pleasantries, do you?' Lionel quizzes his son.

'You might be surprised,' Geoffrey answers curtly. 'You might find you were on the same side.'

'How's that?'

'If you'd ever taken the trouble to talk to them . . .'

Lionel gives a throaty chuckle. 'You were none too keen on them yourself, as I remember.'

'I didn't like their prejudices, no. But I didn't see that as a reason to give them the cold shoulder.'

'Are you listening to this, Gorman? My son wants to understand everyone, even his ex-wife's unfortunate parents. Tell him from me, will you, he should save his breath for his clients. That is, if he wants to get on in the world.' He puts a hand on his son's shoulder. 'You're a good man, Geoff,' he says kindly, 'but you're too soft. The Dyers aren't our sort. Never were, never will be. The sooner you get Nina away from them the better.'

Kay has managed to lose her solicitor. It wasn't intentional. She needed to go to the lavatory. Mr King had said he'd meet her in the public waiting area.

But when Kay comes out of the lavatory, she hears the crying again. It *is* Nina. She's certain of it now. What's not certain is the direction the sound's coming from.

She takes off in panic, running down one corridor and into another, pushing doors open at random, seeing startled faces, empty rooms; hearing voices that aren't Nina's. She doesn't stop till she finds herself outside. Then, breathing painfully, she forces herself to listen.

The noise of a large city explodes in her ears. She registers the boats on the harbour, the black hump of Rangitoto Island, the couple sharing a picnic lunch on the bank below her. A tui shrills from the tall tree on her right. Seagulls circle the enchanted couple. A mother and child chase each other across the grass. 'Ho, Ho, Ho Chi Minh,' the mother chants. 'Ho Chi, Ho Chi, Ho Chi,' the child laughs back.

Kay puts a hand over her eyes. There's no one here; no one to ask about Nina.

She retraces her steps. When she reaches the courthouse door she has to lean on it to get it to open. Even the act of walking requires an effort of will.

She stares at the bare walls stretching ahead of her. She has no idea where to go. There's no crying now to guide her. Somewhere in this maze women are laughing. Their cheerful voices rise above the sounds of water running, and dishes clattering.

A few minutes later she finds herself outside Justice Barrett's courtroom. When she sees the room is empty she decides to go no further. Nina will find her here.

She sits down, and closes her eyes. How silent it is, she thinks. Like night-time.

Wesley Gorman was right. When the court reconvenes just after two o'clock it's clear to everyone but Kay that it's all over bar the shouting.

'All rise for His Honour the Judge,' the Registrar intones.

Kay, whom a distraught Greville King has only just located, has to be helped to her feet.

'We won't necessarily get a decision today,' he whispers, as they take their seats again.

But Justice Barrett is anxious to be shot of this case. His summary of the evidence is brief. 'As counsel will be aware,' he states, 'this court is not bound by strict rules of evidence. Hearsay evidence, such as we have heard this morning, is admissible. As are sworn affidavits without benefit of cross-examination of the deponents. I have therefore decided to deny Mr King's request for an adjournment. His missing witness, I am convinced, would add nothing to our understanding of this unhappy situation.

'I will now proceed to give my judgement. My reasons will be available in written form at the end of the week.'

In the pause that follows Justice Barrett adjusts his spectacles, rearranges his papers, and clears his throat. Kay measures each second in thumping heartbeats.

'Under the Guardianship Act of 1968,' the Judge begins, 'it is my clear duty to put the welfare of the child above the rights of either of the parents involved here today. That both parents feel deep affection for their child is not in dispute. But there are more important things than affection. There is moral example. There is education and training for life. There is the question of fitting the child for a place in our society, a society which condemns the taking of illegal drugs, and deplores the moral degeneracy associated with that pernicious habit.

'At a time when we are witnessing a serious decline in traditional standards of morality it's important the public should know precisely where the courts stand.

'I have therefore decided that both guardianship and custody should go to the father, Geoffrey Ayrton Grieve . . .'

The Judge stops. It's not unusual for him to pause at this point. A gasp, a cry, even a dead faint have been known to greet his pronouncements. But though he senses a change in the atmosphere, there are no visible manifestations. Geoffrey Grieve is staring at his feet, and his wife, his ex-wife, is sitting bolt upright, staring straight ahead.

I should point out, he continues, 'that under the Act adultery is not considered a bar to custody, but, and here I quote: "the commissioning of a matrimonial offence by one of the parents is extremely relevant in determining whether giving that parent custody is in the child's best interests."'

The Judge pauses again. He still has the question of access to address. Then he must decide about costs. Normally costs would be borne by the respondent, but perhaps there's room for compassion here. Mrs Grieve will have more than enough to reflect on without adding a financial dimension to her burden.

He clears his throat. 'In the matter of access,' he continues, 'I want to say two things. First, I have ordered that this matter be looked at again in a year's time when the lifestyle and habits of the respondent can be re-evaluated. Second, I have set access at one day a month, on condition a suitable chaperone can be found, someone acceptable to both the applicant and the respondent. On the basis of the testimony I've heard today I would suggest Miss Pauline Grieve, the applicant's aunt, whom both parties seem to hold in high regard . . .'

Kay has to be told when it's over. She appears not to have heard what the Judge has been saying. She watches him pocket his fob watch, tie the ribbon on his file, and remove his spectacles. When the Registrar instructs the court to rise, she has again to be helped to her feet.

She looks across at Geoffrey. His shoulders are hunched; his arms clasped in front of him. But you shouldn't sit like that, she thinks. Geoffrey, a man with almost no personal vanity, has been exercising for years in an effort to build up his chest. Kay isn't supposed to know about the chest expander hidden in his desk. Or question why he takes so long in the bathroom each morning.

She looks back at the Bench. The Judge has gone.

'Come along,' a kind voice says.

'You musn't take this too much to heart,' Greville encourages, as they walk into the public area. 'You heard the Judge. It'll all be reviewed again in a year.'

'Mummy, Mummy, Mummy . . .'

Kay drops to her knees, opening her arms wide to receive her daughter. 'Are you all right, darling?' she whispers. 'Did you have a nice time at Grannie's?'

'I not to say Grannie,' Nina lisps. 'I not allowed.'

• Elspeth Sandys

Suddenly there are people everywhere. Winifred Grieve, in a blue linen suit, her fingers weighted down with rings, her face a mask of make-up. Geoffrey, looking as he did after the divorce, like a hunted animal. Mr King, looking uncomfortable. The other lawyer, whose name Kay has forgotten. Her mother, in a hideous print dress and white straw hat. Her father, in his best suit.

'Now now, Nina,' Winifred scolds. 'Leave Mummy alone. You're going to be living with Daddy now.'

The child frowns. Her grip on her mother's hand tightens.

'Geoffrey!' Winifred commands.

Geoffrey sidles up to his daughter. He won't look at Kay. Tomorrow he'll write to her. Expressing what? Regrets? Sympathy? Her face, which he sees out of the corner of his eye, is like sand; colourless, expressionless. 'Come on, darling,' he urges.

'Mummy come too,' Nina says firmly.

'You'll see Mummy very soon, darling.'

'See Mummy *now*,' the child insists.

'That's right, sweetheart. You can see Mummy now, and you can see her again in a few days. You can talk to her too. You like talking on the phone, don't you?'

Nina screws up her nose. Auntie Bet, who looks after her and the other boys and girls when Mummy is at work, says not all children have mummies and daddies. Sometimes daddies go away and never come back. But her daddy hasn't gone away. He's standing right here. So why does she have to go to Grannie's house? Why can't she go to the house they used to live in? The one with Mummy and Daddy in it.

'We really must go, Geoffrey,' Winifred chides.

Geoffrey shoots his mother a warning look. 'Will the girls be home?' he asks.

'Your guess is as good as mine,' his mother sighs.

Geoffrey puts his hands on his daughter's shoulders. Tries, gently, to pull her free. 'We can get out the Lego,' he encourages. 'I might even manage to make that train you wanted. That'd be fun, wouldn't it?' He inches closer. His voice rises and falls, erratic as his heartbeat. 'And if you're very good,' he goes on desperately, 'Grannie Winnie might make you some play dough.'

'Did you hear me, Geoffrey?'

'Just leave it, will you, Mother?'

'I don't have all day.'

'Come along, sweetheart,' Geoffrey pleads. 'Auntie Sue and Auntie Belinda will be waiting.'

'Oh, for heaven's sake!' The voice is Kay's father's. As is the hand yanking on Kay's arm. 'Let go of the child! You're only making matters worse.'

Kay looks up at him. The words rush into her mouth. *Who are you to talk?*

'You can't muck about as you have, young lady, and expect to get away with it.'

'Cut it out,' Geoffrey mutters, glaring at his father-in-law.

'Your mother and I feel sympathy for you, naturally,' Harold Dyer goes on. 'But I have to tell you, we consider the punishment just.'

Nina's face begins to pucker. She hasn't understood all the words, but she understands that people are being mean to her mother. They mustn't do that. Sometimes when people are mean, her mother cries. Other times, she sleeps, and Nina has to shake and shake her to get her to wake. *I'll look after you,* she vows at these times. *I won't let people be mean.*

'I'll see you in the car,' Winifred hisses at her son.

'Come along, darling,' Geoffrey entreats again.

Nina looks at her father, then at her mother, then at the faces of the other people, two of whom she recognises, but not to say their names. Grannie Winnie has gone. Does that mean it's all better?

She takes her father's hand, but doesn't let go of her mother's.

'It's all right, little one,' her mother says, her voice all funny and crackly. 'You're going to be my big brave girl, aren't you?'

That's when Nina knows it isn't all right. So she opens her mouth, and howls.

Kay doesn't remember how she got home. What she remembers is the cold. The walls of her flat felt like ice.

The phone rang twice, but she didn't answer it.

'I'm sorry,' Geoffrey had said, as he pulled Nina from her arms. 'I'll call for her things tomorrow, shall I?'

At University

4

1964 was not a year that began auspiciously. Perhaps, Geoffrey Grieve thought, as he joined the straggle of revellers at the foot of the Robbie Burns statue, we're still in shock over Kennedy's assassination. A crowd had gathered in the city centre that day too. A sombre crowd, too stunned to weep, seeking from strangers some kind of explanation, some sort of comfort.

Which is what we're doing tonight, more or less, Geoffrey decided, as the first stroke of midnight rang out from the Town Hall clock, and beer bottles were raised in salutation: making sense of time; comforting ourselves in the face of mortality.

'Happy New Year, you son-of-a-bitch,' a familiar voice boomed. Alistair Glendinning, his room-mate.

'Where the hell have you been?'

'Getting the lie of the land. Observing the talent.'

'And?'

Alistair downed what was left of his beer. '"Should Auld Acquaintance be forgot . . ."' he crooned.

'Happy New Year, mate!'

'"And never brought to mind . . ."'

By the time the twelve chimes had sounded everyone was singing. Geoffrey, never much of a joiner, linked hands with his neighbours and let himself be tossed about in the wave of goodwill breaking round Robbie Burns's statue. Somewhere behind him fireworks were exploding. Elsewhere in the city church bells rang and car horns blared. A ship let off its siren. Alistair, Geoffrey realised, when he looked around, had disappeared again. The people surrounding him were strangers.

Ten minutes later it was all over. The crowd, its ritual acted out, began to disperse. Geoffrey, still searching in a vague way for Alistair, saw a man being sick in the flower bed. His companion, a woman with a foot-high hairdo and a cigarette hanging out of her mouth, hung on to his rump, as if afraid he might fall face-down among the marigolds.

As he made his way round the back of the statue Geoffrey had the impression the lights were being turned off, one by one. The Cathedral to his left was the first to go dark. Then the Town Hall, next door to it, grew dim. The street lamps still burned, but less effectively, as if their wattage had been turned down. By the time he'd rounded the statue only the lights from the department store on the corner blazed as before. Even the cinemas looked shadowy. He had to squint to read the signs: 'NORMAN WISDOM IN ON THE BEAT'; 'THE ALAMO WITH JOHN WAYNE'.

'Happy New Year!'

Geoffrey stepped back in embarrassment. He'd been staring into the face of a young woman. Searching for Alistair, ostensibly. 'Sorry,' he apologised. 'Sorry. I thought you were someone else.'

'That's OK,' she answered.

'I'm a bit blind,' he explained. He had the feeling she was smiling, but it could have been wishful thinking. 'Don't I know you?' he hazarded, moving close again. He wished he could see her properly. If her voice were anything to go by she should be attractive. 'You're a student?' he guessed.

'Right,' she confirmed.

'I knew I'd seen you.'

'And I've seen *you*,' she told him. 'You're Geoffrey Grieve, President of the Union.'

Geoffrey couldn't account for the feeling he had then. It was as if he'd just been ordered not to let this girl out of his sight.

He glanced around him. A hazy form lurched across his field of vision. Where had everyone got to?

'Which way are you headed?' he asked his anonymous companion. It was mid-summer, but the night was far from warm. He was beginning to wish he'd brought his car. It would be a long cold walk back to college.

'I'm supposed to be at a party,' she informed him.

'Whereabouts?'

'My place.'

Geoffrey raised an eyebrow, a trick he'd taught himself at boarding school. 'Won't people be wondering where you are?' he asked.

'Doubt anyone'll notice.'

'*I'd* notice.'

'No, you wouldn't. You wouldn't be able to see. Not with the lights out, and you not wearing your glasses.'

Geoffrey laughed; then frowned as he remembered Alistair, and wondered where the hell he'd got to. The two of them had set out tonight in search of excitement. Most of the student population was absent so there was a dearth of good parties to go to. Perhaps, they'd encouraged each other, the town would yield some thrills. Though Dunedin without its students was a sombre place, akin in atmosphere, Geoffrey had once gloomily observed, to the post-nuclear-holocaust town of *On the Beach*.

'Would you like to come to the party?' the girl with no name suggested.

Geoffrey hoisted his duffel coat higher on to his shoulders. He was slight of build, for all his efforts to increase his bulk by means of 'Mr Sandford's Chest Expander'. He blamed the years he'd spent at boarding school in England. His father was a robust man, and his mother, though slim (a condition she worked very hard to maintain), could never be described as 'slight'.

'I'd love to,' he answered, grinning.

'What about your friend?'

'Who?'

'The person you were looking for.'

'Oh, he'll be all right. He's probably picked someone up by now.'

'Is that what you're doing?'

Geoffrey laughed. She was a tease, this girl. He liked that.

'It's this way,' she said, pointing up the hill.

He wondered if he should offer her his coat. She wasn't wearing one herself. Just a straight skirt, and a cardigan buttoned up at the back.

'My name's Kay,' she announced, as they crossed the street. 'Kay Dyer.'

5

Kay hadn't consciously decided to abandon her own party. It just happened that way. She was doing the twist with Duncan when someone switched off the lights. Next thing she knew she and Duncan were wrestling on the floor. It was all perfectly good-natured. There was no need to run off. But that, joking she was not a sheep about to be shorn (Duncan's home was a sheep station in Central Otago), was exactly what she did.

She wasn't the only escapee. Mercia Bagent was being sick under the clothesline. Mercia was always sick at parties. 'Leave me alone,' she whimpered when Kay went to help.

'Where d'you think *you're* off to?' a voice demanded, as she took off down the path.

Kay laughed. It was getting to be as noisy out here as inside the house. Peering into the darkness she made out a figure sitting on the steps of the wash-house. 'Lynne?' she called.

'I've drunk too much sherry,' her flatmate answered.

Kay moved to join her. 'Has Brian been up to his tricks again?' she asked.

'What would you say, Kay? Am I the jealous type? *Possessive* was his actual word, but he meant jealous.'

'You should ditch him, Lynne. He's a louse.'

'Did you see him in there? Did you see who he was with?'

'You can't see anything in there.'

'That bitch Sue Holland! Her bloke's out of town so she has a go at mine. "Don't get your knickers in a twist. It's just a bit of fun." Bastard was grinning when he said that. *Grinning.*'

Kay took the scarf from her shoulders and draped it round Lynne's neck. The outfit she was wearing – a sun dress and bolero – she'd made specially for tonight. Her arms were covered in goose pimples.

'Cheer up, pal. I mean, it's not as if you're in love with him or anything, are you?'

'Hell, no!'

'Then why . . . ?'

Lynne's face, turned up to hers, was a ghastly shade of yellow. 'Wait till it happens to you,' she said bleakly. 'Then you'll know.'

As Kay walked out of the gate, the noise of the party followed her. The thought of Duncan hunting for her in the dark almost persuaded her to turn back. Lynne had already rejoined the fray. But somehow her feet kept moving, carrying her away from the house.

She and Duncan had been 'going out' for a year, but she could count the number of times they'd actually gone anywhere on the fingers of her hands. A couple of trips to the movies; half a dozen freezing expeditions to provincial rugby matches; and once, at the beginning, when he was trying to impress her, dinner at The Left Bank, the town's one French restaurant. Their only other entertainment, apart from what Duncan called 'getting friendly', was the regular Saturday night bash, held in one of the honeycomb of flats surrounding the University.

Sometimes, when Kay thought about Duncan, she wasn't even sure she liked him. Which hadn't, so far, stopped her from allowing him to take what her mother would call 'liberties'. ('Your father and I don't understand why you have to go and study at the other end of the country,' Esme Dyer had complained, when her daughter announced she was moving to Dunedin. 'Is it because you want your freedom? Because if that's the reason, let me tell you, no one respects a girl who allows a man to take liberties.')

Kay had never talked to Duncan about her family. Not that he'd asked. And not that she'd have told him anything if he had. But she was curious about his. Almost any family that wasn't hers had an aura of attraction about it. She sometimes wondered if she stayed with Duncan not for his charms, which were limited, but for the glowing picture she had of his father, handsome in the saddle, and his mother, smiling and pink-faced, presiding over a kitchen smelling of roast lamb, and filled with willow-pattern china.

It was pleasant walking down the hill. The evening was cool, but there was a hint of that aurora light in the sky which had so enchanted Kay when she first moved south. The flat she shared with Lynne and Judy (a fellow Arts student) was on a hill overlooking the city. They'd had to move into it at the end of last term to be sure of getting it. Judy hadn't wanted to be so far from the University, but both Lynne and Kay had had enough of life on the flat. Quite apart from the view which, in addition to the town, took in the harbour and the distant ocean, you could get to sleep up here. Parties like tonight's were rare.

The flat was on the ground floor of an old wooden house that had seen better days. There were several of these mansions in their street, most of them converted for student accommodation, but still bearing the marks of the gold rush money that had built them.

I love this town, Kay surprised herself by thinking, as she stopped to watch a rocket flare over the harbour. It was as far, within New Zealand, as she could get from her parents. That was part of it. But it was more than that. In the two years she'd been here she'd almost managed to forget.

She stopped at the corner and looked back at her house. It may have been a rich man's castle once, but that was history. The rooms were large and draughty, with open fireplaces that belched smoke into the air and sucked all the heat into the chimneys. The bathroom was antediluvian; the kitchen likewise. The furniture in the communal living room looked as if it had been attacked by dogs. But Kay loved it. After two years in a student hostel she felt as if she'd been released from prison. ('No daughter of mine will ever go flatting,' her father had said, in that even tone he used when he wasn't prepared to argue. The fact that she was flatting now was due to her good fortune in landing a waitressing job halfway through last year. 'I don't need your money, Dad,' she'd been able to retaliate, when he threatened to cut off her funds. 'I can support myself.')

Tonight's party was as much to celebrate Kay's unexpectedly early return as to welcome the New Year. She was supposed to have spent the whole of the vacation with her family in Auckland. 'There wasn't any work,' she'd told Lynne, when she'd turned up three nights ago on the doorstep. It was a lame sort of explanation, but it was the only one she could think of.

'Thought you had a job in a vineyard?'

'I did. It finished at Christmas.'

'Your parents must have been hosed off. They hardly ever see you.'

Duncan had been even more taken aback. He too was supposed to be at home. Bumping into each other outside the Hawaiian Coffee Bar they'd both looked embarrassed. 'Doing a bit of shopping for Dad,' he'd said.

She hoped Duncan would have stopped looking for her by now. It wasn't him she was running away from. Least she didn't think it was.

A brisk walk down the hill and she was part of the crowd surrounding Robbie Burns's statue. A woman grabbed her hand and pulled her into the line snaking round the Octagon.

'Happy New Year!' Kay shouted over the singing. She looked up at the sky and saw a flash of orange. As it faded, the stars came back into focus, brighter, it seemed to her, than before. She wished she knew their names. The Southern Cross must be there. And the Milky Way. But it was all milky. And warm. Fresh from the cow, Kay thought; then laughed. If God made the world, then God must be a cow. So what does that make me? A Buddhist?

When the singing came to an end, she lifted her hands high above her head. Her palms tingled, as if heat were being radiated directly to her from those countless small suns. 1964 is going to be *good*, she promised herself.

'Happy New Year,' she said, smiling at the young man who'd been staring at her now for several seconds.

'Sorry,' he mumbled. 'Sorry. I thought you were someone else.'

She recognised him then. She'd heard that voice before, over the campus loudspeaker. Geoffrey Grieve. President of the Socialist Club. Leader of last year's anti-nuclear protests. President of the Union. 'A stirrer,' her father would have called him. 'Standing on street corners spouting communist slogans at the tax payer's expense.'

'I'm a bit blind,' Geoffrey explained.

Kay grinned. The skin under his eyes was paler than the rest of his face, from wearing glasses, she imagined. He had a nice face. *Sensitive*, was the word that came to mind. All she knew about him was what everyone knew, more or less. He was a final-year law student. He was said to be clever but lazy. He was very political. He wrote most of the sketches for last year's graduation concert. He smoked Turkish cigarettes. He drove a car, a Morris Minor, so his parents must be rich. He'd been going out with Amanda Pitt-Forbes for the last two years.

She told him about the party, then asked him if he wanted to come. She knew he'd say yes. But then something happened which she wasn't prepared for. Geoffrey grinned at her, and her stomach gave the most alarming lurch.

As they crossed the street their hands brushed, and it happened again, that lurch. By the time they'd climbed to the top of the hill, Kay was willing him to kiss her.

6

'Tell me about your family,' Geoffrey said when they'd made themselves comfortable.

They were sitting on the sand at Kay's favourite beach. It wasn't exactly tropical, but in the shelter of the cliffs it was warm enough to justify the swimming togs they'd brought with them. Kay had made a picnic: fresh scones and jam; peanut brownies; a thermos of tea. Geoffrey had brought the rug they were sitting on, and the cushions he'd placed suggestively side by side.

'Nothing to tell,' she answered. 'My father works for the Automobile Association. He wears a uniform and answers calls in the middle of the night from distressed motorists. My mother, who stays at home and has no known vices, does voluntary work for the Plunket Society, and makes tapestry cushion covers and fireguard panels, which she gives away at Christmas. We, or rather they, live in West Auckland.'

'Funny that, that we should both come from Auckland.'

'Don't tell me you live in the outer suburbs too?'

'Well, no. Remuera actually.'

'Thought as much.'

'What's that supposed to mean?'

'You don't have a suburban manner.'

'Neither do you.'

'Ah' – Kay leaned towards him – 'but then I've run away. And I don't intend to go back.'

Geoffrey laughed. This was only their second date, but already they were at ease with one another. Kay Dyer had struck him from the beginning as a sensible sort of girl. Sexy and sensible. Marvellous combination!

He resisted the temptation, with her mouth so close to his, to kiss her. He wanted to find out more about her.

'What made you decide to come to Otago?' he asked.

'I told you, I ran away.'

'Long way to run.'

'I could say the same of you.'

'Oh, but my reasons weren't nearly so dramatic. I was practically enrolled at birth. My father studied law here before the war. Best years of his life, he reckons.'

'Do you always do what your father wants?'

Geoffrey plunged his hand into the sand, and let the grains trickle through his fingers. How come she was finding out so much about him while he still knew almost nothing about her?

'We're a close family,' he lied. 'I guess that's something to do with it. But I *wanted* to come to Otago,' he added quickly. 'And I wanted to study law.'

That silenced her. He glanced at her profile, and decided this might be a good moment to kiss her after all. She was an enthusiastic kisser. She'd demonstrated that after the party the other night. It had surprised him. Especially as there'd been another chap hovering who seemed to have a claim on her.

'Who is he?' Geoffrey had asked, in a quiet moment between records.

'Duncan Proudfoot,' she'd told him.

'Look, if I'm in the way or anything . . .'

'He's just a friend,' she'd insisted.

'So,' he said now, jettisoning for the moment the prospect of a kiss, 'you're a refugee from the suburbs, you're a third-year Arts student, you share a flat with two other girls, and you're looking for a job. Anything else I should know about you?'

'I think that about sums it up.'

'No brothers or sisters?'

'One brother.'

'And?'

'You wouldn't approve.'

'Try me.'

'He's in the Army.'

Geoffrey let his eye roam lazily along the beach. At the far end was a sheer white cliff which Kay had told him was called

Lovers' Leap. When he asked her how it got its name she said she didn't know. Waves churned over the rocks at its base.

Kay was wrong about his relationship with his father. It was full of conflict. 'Campaign for Nuclear Disarmament? What the hell's this?' he'd demanded, when the literature started arriving. 'You're not becoming a pinko, are you?'

If the difficulties Geoffrey saw ahead could be overcome, and he got to know Kay better, he'd be tempted to tell her things like that. The thought of her sympathy gave him a warm feeling in his gut.

He turned back to her. '*I've* only got sisters,' he told her. 'Twins. Younger than me. Spoiled brats, the pair of them.' He fished in his pocket for his cigarettes. 'Sure you won't?' he said, holding the packet out to her.

Kay shook her head. Watching him light up she experienced another of those lurches that had so disconcerted her on New Year's Eve. He was handsome in profile. It was his cheekbones you noticed, and his patrician nose, not his rather pasty complexion. He reminded her of someone she'd seen in films, but she couldn't put a name to the face. Leslie Howard was the nearest she could get.

While he puffed elegantly on his cigarette, and she inhaled the exotic fumes, she debated whether or not to tell him she'd broken up with Duncan. The trouble was, if she did confess it, it would mean acknowledging there'd been something to break in the first place.

Duncan had come round to the flat late on New Year's Day. He was on his way back to the farm, and wanted to sort things out with her. When she told him she didn't want to go out with him anymore she hadn't expected him to mind too much. She'd always suspected he had a girl back home.

'Why?' he'd asked humbly. 'What have I done?'

'You haven't done anything,' she'd answered. 'It's not your fault.'

'It has to be. You're the one who wants out.'

The catch in his voice had upset her. She'd never thought of herself as someone who would inflict pain. 'But it's not as if . . .' she'd said, searching for a way to defend herself. 'I mean, we weren't . . . in love or anything.'

'How do you know?'

'Oh, come on, Duncan.'

'Just because I didn't say anything.'

It was those words she'd been trying to forget. And the lie she'd told about Geoffrey. 'He's nothing to do with it,' she'd retorted, when asked if *he* was the reason for her decision.

She looked at Geoffrey now. His cigarette had burned low. She wanted to touch the nicotine stains on his fingers. Inexplicably, since she disliked the taste of tobacco, she wanted to put those fingers in her mouth. 'How old are your sisters?' she asked.

'Twelve,' he answered, stubbing out his cigarette. 'My mother calls them her after-thoughts.'

Kay followed the progress of a piece of thistledown fluttering past her face. It must have blown from the cliffs behind her. There were caves in those cliffs. People held parties there. They lit fires and drank beer. They probably did other things too, on the damp sand.

'What are their names?' she persisted.

'Susan and Belinda,' Geoffrey said. He was beginning to revise his earlier assesment. He wasn't sure he was at ease with Kay at all. 'But I call them both "Sub". "Sub-one" and "Sub-two". Fortunately you can tell them apart. They're not alike.'

'Shall we go for our swim?'

Geoffrey grinned his relief. The interrogation was over. 'What's happened to the sun?' he complained, scanning the bank of cloud that had built up over the water.

'This is one of the few occasions I wish I was in Auckland,' Kay admitted.

'You don't like Auckland?'

'Not the part I live in.'

'I used to tell the guys at my school it was the most beautiful city in the world.'

Kay eyed him warily. The more she found out about him, the more alarming – or did she mean *alluring*? – he became. 'Where did you go to school?' she asked.

'More questions.'

'You don't have to answer if you don't want to.'

'Well, it's not a secret. I went to school in England.'

'Why? Were your parents over there or something?'

'No. Well, not all the time.'

'So why . . . ?'

'Tradition,' Geoffrey answered curtly. 'Both my father and my grandfather attended the school. When you're eleven years old you don't argue.'

Kay watched him as he ran his fingers through his hair. It was straight and fair, not unlike hers in its natural state. Was she going to have to tell him hers was permed? Kay was self-conscious about her hair.

'Turn your back,' she instructed.

'What?'

'I'm going to put on my togs.'

'Oh, right you are. 'You know, I've never been to this beach before.'

'Not many people know about it.'

'It reminds me of a Norfolk beach. Minus the crowds and the gravel. Is that a lagoon further along?'

'Pretty, isn't it? Not nice to swim in though. Full of sheep shit.'

'I'm glad you suggested a picnic.'

'You can turn round now.'

'Wow!'

'I'm freezing.'

Geoffrey's grin convinced Kay it was 'alluring' she'd meant, not 'alarming'. When he untied the jersey knotted round his waist and draped it across her shoulders, the word 'gentleman' sprang to mind. Duncan would never have made a gesture like that.

Suddenly she felt his hand on her back. 'Will anyone see if I kiss you?' he whispered.

'Do you care?' she answered recklessly.

His fingers crept under the strap of her swimsuit. The jersey dropped to the ground. He was wearing shorts and a shirt, almost as little as her. They were the same height, near enough. He had an inch on her, no more.

She looked into his eyes: cool, grey eyes which looked back at her with – what? Intensity? Passion? The truth, she acknowledged later, when she couldn't get the scene out of her mind, was probably much more mundane. He was curious. He was amused.

Which didn't stop her experiencing what felt like a series of small electric shocks when his lips closed over hers. It had been the same after the party, kissing him goodnight. She hadn't wanted it to end. She had no idea kissing could be so exciting. When Duncan kissed her, when his hands strayed, as often as not all she felt was irritation.

Geoffrey, she shouted, in her head. Geoffrey.

'I think we'd better cool off,' he said.

7

Over the next three weeks Kay thought about Geoffrey almost all the time, and heard nothing from him.

'Perhaps he's gone home?' Lynne comforted. 'I mean, you have only just met. There must be a million things you don't know about him.'

'Most of them to do with Amanda Pitt-Forbes,' Kay responded gloomily.

'You don't know that.'

'He won't have gone home, Lynne. He's a law clerk. He doesn't have university holidays.'

'From what I know of Geoffrey Grieve he's quite capable of swinging whatever holidays he wants. People like him make me sick, if you must know.'

Confiding in Lynne was becoming something of a gamble, Kay decided. Ever since the party she'd been prone to these irritable outbursts.

At the beginning of the third week in January Kay landed a job. Her obsession with Geoffrey hadn't blinded her to the reality of her situation. Unless she found work quickly she'd be unable to pay her rent.

The job was at the Public Library. Looking back over the last three weeks Kay realised how close she'd come to scuppering her chances of a degree. She'd had a good job at Lassmann's Vineyard. She knew the risk she was taking when she gave it up. But there was a greater risk in staying any longer in the same house as her parents.

Arriving in Dunedin, discovering her old job at the Hawaiian

Coffee Bar gone, she'd started scouring newspapers and public notice boards for work. She hadn't been too worried. Lynne had found a job easily enough. Lynne didn't have to work – her parents were happy to support her – but she'd wanted to stay on in Dunedin to be near Brian.

The Library job came in the nick of time. Fifteen hours a week shelving and cataloguing. A vast improvement on carrying cups of coffee and washing dishes. Better still, she could do the work in her own time. 'So long as it all gets done,' Miss Ridley, the Head Librarian, had told her. Last year, working a fixed rota at the Hawaiian, Kay had sometimes missed as many as four lectures a week.

'Good for you,' Lynne congratulated, on hearing her news.

'You all right?' Kay asked. Lynne had just come in from work. Her employer, an elderly spinster, rumoured to be worth a fortune, was one of the town's personalities.

'Fagged out actually,' Lynne answered. 'The old girl had me cleaning brass all day. In between telling me how wicked the British are. Sometimes I don't think she's Jewish at all, I think she's Irish.'

'Why don't you crash on the sofa? I'll cook.'

'You cooked last night.'

'I won't tell if you don't.'

'I'm glad about your job, Kay,' Lynne said.

When Geoffrey finally did ring, Kay was at the Library.

'Don't panic,' Lynne laughed when her report was rudely interrupted. 'He said he'd ring back.'

'When? What if I'm not here? Did you tell him about the job?'

'Thought you weren't going to have anything more to do with him?'

'Only if he's still seeing Amanda. And I don't know that, do I?'

'You could ask.'

'Do you ask Brian?'

'What's that supposed to mean?'

'You know.'

'You think he's two-timing me?'

'Lynne . . .'

'You do, don't you?'

'All I meant was, it's a while since you've heard from him.'

'He's swotting. I told you. He has to re-take Anatomy.'

Looking at her friend's pinched face, her enviably curly hair hanging limply to her shoulders, Kay felt a twinge of shame. She and Lynne weren't in competition. If they couldn't support one another, what chance did either of them have? It was a jungle out there. Having a boyfriend, not having a boyfriend . . . there were times when Kay thought one as bad as the other.

All next day Kay waited for the phone to ring. She'd decided not to go into the Library. She would make up the lost hours later in the week.

For most of the time she sat at the desk in her bedroom, struggling with Gide's *Les Faux-Monnayeurs*, wondering if she'd been wise to go on with French just because she liked French writers.

It was mad to stay indoors on a day like this. Each time she turned to the window the sun, bouncing off the roofs on the hill opposite, drove splinters into her eye. If she stood up and pressed her nose to the glass, light boomeranged from the city's numerous church spires. Even the water sent off sparks. The harbour was a plane of crystals; the ships tied up at the wharf tossed diamonds into the air.

By five o'clock, when the phone still hadn't rung, Kay's mood began to sour. If she'd known where Geoffrey worked she'd have phoned him herself. There was nothing wrong with returning a call. But the truth was she knew almost nothing about him, as he, she conceded, acknowledging her reluctance to answer questions, knew almost nothing about her.

At ten past nine the phone rang. 'I'll get it,' Kay yelled.

'Hullo. This is Geoffrey Grieve. May I speak to Kay Dyer, please?'

'Hullo, Geoffrey.'

'Kay? I didn't recognise your voice.'

'I don't think I'd have recognised yours. You sound so formal.'

'I'm not much good on the phone.'

'Is that why . . . ?'

'Listen, I can't talk long, there's a queue of chaps waiting. Are you free this weekend?'

'Yes. Well, I have to work but . . .'

'I was thinking of dinner, Saturday night. There's a French place down by the waterfront . . .'

'The Left Bank.'

'Would you like to eat there? I could pick you up in the car.'

'Sounds lovely.'

'I'm sorry I haven't been in touch.'

'Oh, that's all right. I didn't expect . . .'

'I've been a bit caught up.'

'I've been pretty busy myself, actually.'

'I've got a fair bit to get through on Saturday. Would eight-thirty be too late for you?'

'That'd be fine.'

It was all over so quickly Kay had difficulty recreating it for Lynne. But the facts were not in doubt: Geoffrey Grieve was taking her to dinner.

8

The car reached the top of the hill, let out a slow hiss, and stopped. 'Blast!' Geoffrey swore. 'Not again.'

His car, he decided, was becoming as temperamental as an opera star. Not that he knew any opera stars, but it helped to think of his car, of which he was both proud and fond, as a difficult but rewarding female.

'She's overheating, right enough,' the mechanic had told him.

'What can I do about it?'

'I take it you're a student?'

'That's right.'

'In that case what I'd do, assuming you haven't got cash to throw around, is chuck a bottle of water in the back seat. Either that, or stay off hills.'

The only thing wrong with that advice, Geoffrey brooded now, was the time it took for the engine to cool down. According to his watch he was already fifteen minutes late.

He'd been in two minds about contacting Kay again. With Amanda no longer in Dunedin, seeing Kay at all smacked of disloyalty. But after last weekend he felt differently. Amanda had invited him to her parents' place. It wasn't the first time he'd visited, but he'd had the feeling, as he drove away, it could well be the last.

Amanda's home was in Canterbury. Her parents owned a sheep station in the hill country. As it happened, Timothy Pitt-Forbes was an old friend of his father's, but that wasn't how he'd met Amanda. He first saw her at a wool store hop during graduation week the year before last. Having succeeded in winkling her away from her date, he spent the rest of the evening dancing with her. At the time it had seemed the most incredible stroke of luck. Almost every bloke he knew was after Amanda. She was tall, blonde, leggy, with a smile you could warm your hands at. 'God knows what she sees in a weed like you,' his friend Alistair had taunted.

'She likes me for my mind,' Geoffrey had answered back.

When, a month after that wool store hop, Amanda offered to sleep with him, Geoffrey began to believe his luck was made in heaven.

He leaned over the bonnet of his car and placed a tentative finger on the radiator cap. Still as hot as Hades. Might as well enjoy a fag, he decided, turning back to face the harbour. It was a cool evening, with a brooding, overcast sky. Normally there would still be a lot of light around, but tonight the sky seemed drained of life.

The weather in Canterbury had been superb. This was the nor'-wester season, but for the whole of his stay the skies had remained clear. To make the trip worthwhile he'd taken Friday and Monday off, giving him two full days to enjoy the many delights on offer at Glengarry Station.

On the first day he and Amanda had gone riding, returning to one of Mrs Pitt-Forbes's exquisite lunches. In the afternoon there'd been tennis with Amanda's two young brothers, followed by a swim in the river. Geoffrey liked Amanda's brothers. They made him wish he had a brother of his own.

But it was what happened on the Sunday that changed the way he felt. Over breakfast Mr Pitt-Forbes suggested a visit to Cheyney Grange, a neighbouring property. Amanda's response was less than enthusiastic. For some reason that had made Geoffrey all the more keen to go.

'They're old,' Amanda had complained. 'And they're depressing.'

'They're not as old as us,' her mother had pointed out.

'You know what I mean.'

For Geoffrey's benefit it was explained that the people they were going to visit were not husband and wife, but brother and sister. 'Not that you'll meet the brother,' Timothy Pitt-Forbes had divulged. 'He was shot down in the war. Horribly burned, poor chap. His sister's the only person he lets near him.'

'And that other woman,' Amanda had put in sulkily. 'Daisy what's-her-name.'

Geoffrey, chewing his toast, had felt decidedly uneasy. He was squeamish by nature. Deformities, particularly of the facial kind, made him feel physically sick. It was not a weakness he'd ever confessed to anyone. Experiencing disgust where there should only be pity was not something to be proud of.

Cheyney Grange had turned out to be a long, dusty thirty miles from Glengarry. 'It was one of the great houses of the district in its heyday,' Mr Pitt-Forbes had disclosed, as they turned off the road on to a weed-choked drive. 'It's run as a guest house now.'

A curious place, Geoffrey had found it: a mixture of the colonial and the Gothic. Exactly right, he'd thought gloomily, for a meeting with a burned hero. Because he was certain, despite Mr Pitt-Forbes's denials, that they *would* meet. Why come all this way if not to cheer the unfortunate fellow?

But Amanda's father had spoken the truth. Richard could not be persuaded from his room. 'Please don't be offended,' his sister Sarah had apologised. 'He's been this way for years now.'

Standing on the side of the road, taking the smoke from his cigarette deep into his lungs, Geoffrey shook his head as he recalled the visit. Amanda could not have been more wrong about Cheyney Grange. There was nothing depressing about it. On the contrary, the atmosphere in those shabby, semi-public rooms, was one Geoffrey would have described, if pressed, as 'cheerful'. Amanda's impatience, the kindness of her parents, his own shameful apprehensions, dwindled into insignificance alongside what was being lived out in those faded rooms.

Puzzled by his reactions he'd tried, on the way back to Glengarry, to imagine himself a stranger visiting his parents' home in Auckland. It had proved a depressing exercise. There were no spontaneous gestures in his house, no reassuring hugs or understanding hands. The twins occasionally horse-played together, creating a ripple of disorder in that museum of good taste, but any resemblance to Cheyney Grange, where people listened to one another as if what was being said mattered, stopped there.

Since the weekend Geoffrey had thought a lot about that day. At one stage in the afternoon he'd found himself alone with the woman Amanda had dismissed as 'Daisy what's-her-name'.

They couldn't have spent more than half an hour together, but in that time she made a considerable impression. 'Her name's Daisy Mountford,' he'd informed Amanda on the way home. 'She's divorced.'

'Well of course I knew that, stupid,' Amanda had replied.

'Then you'd know she's in love with Richard Dutton.'

'Don't be daft. Who'd be in love with him?'

'You should talk to her sometime.'

That exchange was one of the reasons Geoffrey was standing on the side of the road now, waiting for his car to take him to Kay Dyer.

'I've loved Richard all my life,' Daisy Mountford had confessed, during their brief exchange. 'He was a glorious young man. A gifted artist, did you know that? I absolutely worshipped him.'

'And now?' Geoffrey had been bold enough to ask.

Mrs Mountford had smiled: a slow, thoughtful smile that had quite transformed her rather conventional face. 'Oh, now,' she'd said. 'Now is different, and the same. I certainly wouldn't use the word "worship".' Her laugh, and the nervous way she touched her hair, had reminded him of Kay. 'Young men can be very cruel,' she'd gone on. 'I imagine they don't mean to be.'

'Was Richard cruel?'

'Oh horribly. I suffered for *years*.'

'But you're not suffering now?'

'I live in hope now. No one who has hope can be said to suffer.'

'What is it you hope for?'

'I'm a free woman. Richard's a free man. What do you think I hope for?'

Geoffrey had no idea why Mrs Mountford should have chosen to confide in him. Perhaps she found it easier to talk to a stranger. Whatever the reason, he had her to thank, or blame, that for the rest of that weekend, and since, the woman on his mind was not Amanda, but Kay Dyer.

He tested the radiator again, decided it was cool enough, took out a handkerchief, and unscrewed the cap. A cloud of steam sent him reeling backwards. Blast these hills, he thought, trying to read his watch through his misted glasses. Is it going to be like this every time I take Kay out?

The question, once asked, posed another. So he *was* going to take Kay out, was he? Tonight was the start of something. The thought frankly terrified him. How did he get into this position? He'd always assumed he would marry Amanda.

Ten minutes later he was parked outside Kay's place. He tooted the horn, jumped out of the car, and ran up the path.

Kay was waiting for him on the porch. 'Hello,' she said shyly.

'Sorry I'm late.'

'Do you want to come in, or ought we to . . . ?'

'The car broke down.'

'Oh.'

'It's becoming something of a habit.'

'We can easily walk.'

'It's OK. I know how to fix it.'

Kay's hand strayed to her hair, patting it as if to make sure it was all in place. He'd noticed that about her on the beach, that she touched her hair a lot. 'Brian's here,' she said.

'Brian?'

'You met him at the party. Lynne, my flatmate's, boyfriend.'

'You look great,' Geoffrey pronounced. 'You remind me . . .'

A look of panic crossed Kay's face. 'Don't say it, please,' she pleaded, disguising her alarm behind a shrill laugh. 'I'm always reminding people of someone else.'

'It's not the way you look. It's . . .' He reached out for her hand. 'It was someone I met at the weekend,' he said. 'I'll tell you about it over dinner.'

9

Kay couldn't believe her luck. Here she was, barely a month after her bitter departure from Auckland, sitting in the passenger seat of Geoffrey Grieve's Morris Minor, listening to him talk about the law, and how it wasn't his father's career as a criminal lawyer which inspired him to take up the profession, but the film, *Witness for the Prosecution*. If she turned her head to the left she'd see the CND sticker on the back window. If she turned it to the right she'd see the words, 'CENSORSHIP IS A CRIME AGAINST FREEDOM. LIFT THE BAN ON JAMES BALDWIN'S *ANOTHER COUNTRY*'.

'Of course I know it doesn't happen the way they show it in the movies,' Geoffrey said, pulling the kind of face Kay found especially endearing. 'I've sat through enough cases to know how tedious even a murder trial can be. But there's always the chance of something unexpected happening. A surprise witness. A sudden confession. A dramatic reversal.'

'Sounds to me as if you should have been an actor.'

Geoffrey grinned. 'No money in it,' he said.

Kay snuggled down in her seat. It had started to rain. She had the pleasant sensation of being gently rocked between earth and sky. Every time a car approached its headlights wavered, creating the impression that the length of a watery beam was all that separated her from the stars.

She'd told Geoffrey she'd not been to The Left Bank before. She didn't know why she'd lied. Unless it was because of her growing feeling that everything, with him, must be for the first time.

'You're a good actor,' she said. 'I've seen you.'

'The concert? That's just a bit of fun.'
'Packs the theatre every night for a week. That's serious.'
'You're right. It's bloody hard work, actually. You should try it sometime.'
'Not really a girl's thing, is it?'
'What d'you mean? There are girls in it.'

Kay smiled evasively. She didn't want to argue. But it was true, what she'd tried, and failed, to say. The graduation celebrations, known to everyone as 'capping', were male creations. Women were needed to do the donkey work, but they seldom occupied the spotlight.

'Will you be involved again this year?' she asked.

Geoffrey slowed to let a car pass, then sped across the main street on to the waterfront road. 'My last year,' he said, gesturing his powerlessness against the passage of time. 'Last chance, you could say.'

Over dinner Kay talked animatedly, and thought about the only other time she'd eaten here, and how utterly different that experience had been. And she thought about what Geoffrey had said in the car, about this being his last year. It was *her* last year too. She would have a BA at the end of it. After which . . .

('You'd better decide what you're going to do with your life, young lady,' had been her father's parting shot. 'All this book reading you do, what's it supposed to be in aid of?')

'That's a very pensive stare,' Geoffrey remarked.
'Sorry. I was miles away.'
'Is my conversation so boring?'
'No!' To Kay's consternation she felt her cheeks flame. Why did that always happen? She'd bet five quid Amanda Pitt-Forbes *never* blushed. 'I was thinking about what you said earlier,' she admitted. 'About this being your last year.'
'Yours too, I imagine.'
'Yup.'
'What will you do? Do you have any plans?'

Put on the spot like that, Kay couldn't be sure whether the answer she gave was true or not. 'I'd like to travel,' she said.

'Still running away, eh?'

'Pardon?'

'You told me you'd run away from the suburbs.'

'Oh, that. Yes. Absolutely. As far away as possible.'

'Other places have suburbs. You can't escape them altogether.'

'It's just the one I want to escape from,' Kay said. 'The rest don't bother me.'

They were the last to leave the restaurant. Dunedin, circa 1964, was not accustomed to late diners. The waitress, hovering at the door of the kitchen, eyeing them with hostility, made Kay feel guilty.

On the way up the hill ('Fingers crossed,' Geoffrey had said, at the start of their journey) Kay surprised herself by asking about Amanda. It was the last thing she'd intended.

He didn't hear her question, so she had to repeat it. 'Do you still see Amanda?'

Waiting for him to answer was like waiting for the dentist to start drilling. She even wondered if he might be deaf. She'd had to repeat herself several times in the restaurant.

'She's not in Dunedin,' he said eventually. 'She graduated last year.'

'She did Home Science, didn't she?'

'Hmmm.'

'So she's got a job . . .'

'Not to my knowledge.'

There was no mistaking the chill in his voice. I've gone too far, Kay thought. He'll do what my father used to do, and put me out on the side of the road.

'As a matter of fact, I saw her at the weekend,' Geoffrey admitted.

'Oh . . .'

'I went to see her to tell her it was over.'

'Pardon?'

'It's over with Amanda.'

Kay looked out of the window. They were almost at the top of the hill. She should be feeling something. At the very least her stomach should have lurched.

'I'm sorry,' she muttered.

'What for?'

'You and Amanda. It must have been . . . You can come in, if you like?' she offered, when they reached the house.

'What about your friend?'

'Lynne? She'll be round at Brian's place.'

His hand went to the door. When she saw it open her stomach gave an obliging lurch.

'Sorry about the mess,' she apologised, as they walked inside. 'It's not usually this bad.'

She switched off the record player, and returned the cushions to the sofa. 'I'll put the kettle on,' she said.

Geoffrey nodded. He looked as if he was regretting the decision to come in. Perhaps it was the room. Empty beer bottles; unwashed coffee cups; that hideous plastic light shade she kept meaning to throw out.

'Is the person I remind you of Amanda?' Kay asked.

Geoffrey didn't answer. He still hadn't taken his coat off. If he didn't say something soon she'd . . . 'It's not very flattering, being compared with other people.'

Geoffrey threw off his coat, tossed it over the sofa, and moved to stand beside her. 'No one in their right mind would compare you with Amanda,' he said.

Kay hunched her shoulders. She still wasn't satisfied. Perhaps if he kissed her she'd feel better?

'Look . . .' Geoffrey dragged his fingers through his hair. 'I don't know what's happening here,' he confessed. 'I can't say where you and I are headed. But I do want to kiss you. I want to kiss you very much.'

'I want to kiss you too.'

'Then why the hell are we arguing?'

10

With rivals out of the way, and time pressing (last years, last chances), it was not long before Geoffrey and Kay began to talk of love.

Geoffrey was the first to say the word. He'd said it before, to Amanda, out of gratitude mainly, but in recent weeks he'd found himself thinking about love in ways that involved the few poems he knew on the subject, the many songs, and Daisy Mountford, whose love for the wounded hero, Richard Dutton, he'd elevated to the heights of Romeo and Juliet, or Tristram and Isolde.

There were many things Geoffrey was unsure of in life, but one thing he did know: he didn't want a marriage that resembled in any way the one his parents had. Perhaps their relationship had been good once – they must at least have liked each other – but all that was left now (it seemed to him) was their mutual determination to enjoy in perpetuity the lifestyle paid for by his father's high fees.

Looked at coldly he could see what was in it for both of them. His mother had accounts at all the best dress shops. She got to travel to law conferences all over the world. She had daily help in the house, and friends, whose husbands enjoyed equally high incomes, with whom she could lunch on a regular basis. His father had a wife whom women envied, and other men admired. The temper she occasionally exhibited in private was never seen in public. He came home each evening to a house that had been featured in a book of *Fine New Zealand Homes*, and a meal prepared by a woman who'd been an eager pupil, in the early days of her marriage, at the Robert Carrier Cooking School.

His parents still shared a room, but it was Geoffrey's belief the birth of the twins twelve years ago had brought the sexual side of their marriage to an end. His father had once hinted at something of the sort. 'Sex isn't the same for women,' he'd said. 'Once they have their quota of babies . . .' He'd shrugged, and poured himself another whisky. 'Maybe you'll have more luck than me,' he'd concluded gloomily.

When Geoffrey discovered, on one of his holidays from school in England, that his father had a mistress, he was saddened, but not shocked. From that day, whenever his father claimed to be working late at the office, or when he chose to sail his yacht alone, insisting he needed time to think, Geoffrey would picture him in the company of a buxom woman of thirty-plus years, with dyed blonde hair, and clothes that invariably included stiletto-heeled shoes, low-cut blouses, and tight skirts.

Love, Geoffrey was certain, had nothing to do with the relationship.

It was during a particularly passionate moment this afternoon that the word had slipped out. Kay, at such times, would sigh a lot, and urgently whisper his name, but he'd managed till now to resist the temptation to respond verbally. He'd gone down that road with Amanda, and was still suffering the consequences. 'You lied!' she'd screamed down the telephone at him. 'I thought we were engaged.'

He'd been tempted to remind her it was she who'd initiated their sleeping together, but that would have been ungentlemanly.

'You led me on,' she wrote, in one of the many bitter letters he'd received. 'What am I supposed to do with my life now?'

But it was not Amanda who'd gazed up at him from the sand this afternoon, it was Kay. Her flushed cheeks, tangled hair, parted lips, had moved him in ways he couldn't help but associate with the word 'love'. 'I think I'm in love with you,' he'd muttered.

Her response was not what he'd expected. She gulped, and her eyes filled with tears. 'I love you too, Geoffrey,' she blurted out. 'I love you so much.' No qualifying clause for her, more like a sworn statement. He didn't mind admitting it scared him.

Now he was in his room, drinking coffee with Alistair,

acknowledging, reluctantly, that Kay Dyer might very well be the person who would become his wife. Not that he said so out loud. The most he and Alistair had ever confided about their personal lives was the admission that Amanda, or Kay, or Alistair's current lady, Gail, was 'a bit of a raver', which would be rephrased, if the relationship lasted, as, 'Actually, Kay (or Gail or Amanda) is a real good sort.'

'Yeah,' Geoffrey conceded. 'Kay's a real good sort.'

'You and Amanda called it a day then?' Alistair asked.

'You could say that.'

Wife, Geoffrey thought, rolling the word round on his tongue. He was twenty-three years old. Quite old enough to marry, some people would say. But he didn't *feel* old enough. Ask me about the war in Vietnam and I'll tell you exactly what I think, he answered his imagined critics, but ask me about marriage, about Kay Dyer . . .

'Do you know that the chances of war breaking out in any one year, nuclear war that is, are one in twenty?' he said, in an abrupt change of subject.

'You know what your trouble is, don't you, mate?' Alistair drawled. 'You spend too much time reading that seditious bloody rag you get from England. What's it called? The *New Statesman*? Beats me how you get it past customs.'

'So you think the Cold War is a good thing?' Geoffrey retaliated.

'Better than a hot one.'

'You're just an old Tory, Glendinning. Like your father.'

'You'll be one too, mate. When you come to your senses.'

Was he in love with Kay? It had certainly felt that way on the Peninsula this afternoon. A glorious autumn day; a sheltered sand dune at the back of a beach so inacccessible hardly anyone ever went there. Kay had let him undress her. That had never happened before. He'd been too shy to stare at her as he'd wanted, but his fingers had looked. The problem was, he couldn't be sure whether she meant him to carry right on or not. With Amanda the matter had been taken care of when she announced, on that still memorable night after the college ball, that she'd had a diaphragm fitted.

'So,' Alistair went on, 'you and Kay are serious then?'

• Elspeth Sandys

'She's going to help with the costumes for the capping concert,' Geoffrey replied. 'Had to lean on her a bit, but . . .'

If Kay and I married, he thought, we could travel. She's always saying she'd like to go to England. Not that I'd want to stay there longer than a year . . .

'She going to help you ban the bomb too?' Alistair quizzed. 'I can just see you both marching up the main street, holding hands round a banner. Touching, really.'

Geoffrey laughed. 'God knows why I like you, Glendinning. Must be something wrong with me.'

Yes, he thought, as Alistair wandered off to the bathroom, a year would be quite long enough. Seven years in boarding school had destroyed any romance England might have had for him. Though he did owe the experience one thing. He'd come away convinced his only chance of happiness was to decide who he was, and where he belonged. No one at his school had wanted to be English (though most were). They'd claimed Welsh, Scots, Irish, French, even German ancestry. Anything rather than confess themselves Englishmen. It had puzzled Geoffrey – why live in a country you didn't want to belong to? – but in the end it had set him free. In the loneliness created by his own less acceptable accent and ancestry, he'd resolved to live and die a New Zealander.

With Alistair out of the room Geoffrey could think more clearly. He'd make a list. At boarding school list-making had proved a comforting alternative to conversation. He'd made lists (short) of people he liked; others (long) of people he didn't like. He'd listed the books he'd read; countries he'd visited; countries he wanted to visit. He'd laboured for hours over a list of possible professions . . .

'KAY DYER', he wrote at the top of the page.
'POSITIVE QUALITIES
1. Cheerful
2. Attractive
3. Sexy
4. Intelligent
5. Kind'
He drew a line under 5, then wrote,

'NEGATIVE QUALITIES
1. Family? Don't know much about them.
2. Friends? Don't much like the ones I've met.
3. Truthful? Not sure. Could be inclined to tell lies.
4. A worrier. Definitely.'

He paused, chewing the end of his pen as he considered what else he might add. Five positive to four negative qualities. Not bad. And when you took into account the briefness of their acquaintance . . .

'Once you decide to love her, you will,' he wrote.

5

Kay piled one more book on top of her already over-burdened trolley, stretched out an arm to hold the load in place, and headed for the stacks at the far end of the room. She would have to work all day to make up yesterday's lost hours. Miss Ridley, who'd been all smiles for the first few weeks, had taken to frowning and glancing at her watch whenever she encountered her newest employee.

'It'll all get done, Miss Ridley,' Kay had assured her this morning. 'I've had a load of essays to write. That's why I haven't been in.'

'Indeed,' Miss Ridley had retorted.

'Three, actually.'

'Then might I suggest you take another look at how you organise your time? Some judicious pruning of your social engagements would seem to be in order.'

Kay's response was to poke her tongue at Miss Ridley's retreating back.

'I can't make you out sometimes,' Geoffrey had said, on their way down the Peninsula yesterday. 'You never talk about your family.'

'Nothing to talk about.'

'Do you write to them?'

'Occasionally . . . Look,' she'd said, when conversation stalled, 'I don't talk about my family for the simple reason they're not interesting. Your typical New Zealand household, that's us. Suburban. Boring.'

'Why is it I don't believe you?'

'Because you're a lawyer. You want to dig the dirt.'

'Is there any to dig?'

'We have a quarter-acre section, with a Hills Hoist clothes line, a small greenhouse, and a vegetable patch. At the front there's a lawn, a flower border, and half a dozen symmetrically arranged rose bushes, for show. You can dig all you like but I doubt you'll find any weeds. My father is a meticulous gardener. My mother, likewise, is a meticulous housekeeper. My brother is being sent to Borneo to kill communists, so he must be a meticulous soldier. Does that satisfy you?'

'When you've finished daydreaming,' Miss Ridley's voice intruded, 'there are the new books to catalogue.'

'Right,' Kay answered. 'Big Sister is Watching You,' she scribbled on a piece of paper.

'I think I'm in love with you,' Geoffrey had said.

What did that mean? I *think* . . . Didn't he know? Weren't you supposed to know about things like that?

I love you so much. Those were *her* words. Was she telling the truth?

FLAUBERT, GUSTAVE; Kay wrote across the top of a blank card. *MADAME BOVARY*.

We were both naked, she answered herself. It seemed the right thing to say.

Taking liberties, was he? Not that you tried to stop him.

It's different with Geoffrey.

That so?

He's in love with me.

And you're in love with him. Fine. That makes everything OK.

Yes.

How do you know it's love?

Same way anyone knows.

Which is?

Wanting to be with him. Wanting him to . . .

Put his hands where he shouldn't?

Kay lowered her head. 'You know, don't you, Emma?' she breathed on *Madame Bovary*'s card. 'Thinking always spoils things . . .'

It was after nine when Kay finished at the Library. Walking up the hill she had the curious feeling she was alone in the city. It had rained all day, which may have accounted for the stillness. But it didn't account for the surges of excitement she felt as she continued her solitary climb.

Halfway up the hill she stopped and looked out over the shiny roofs and stabbing spires to the grey sheen of the sea in the distance. Something caught her eye: the glint of the clock-face on the University tower. The law firm where Geoffrey worked was in walking distance of that tower. Sometimes, when the weather was fine, they'd arrange to meet under the clock. They'd eat their sandwiches on the banks of the Leith, and talk about the end of the world, which some people were predicting, or the end of their university life, which was more certain.

A few minutes later, turning into her street, Kay had a vision. Geoffrey was standing by the gate of her house. He was waiting to ask her to marry him.

She rubbed her eyes, and the vision disappeared. But the conviction remained. *That's* what I'm going to do with my life, she answered the persistent voice of her father. Marry Geoffrey.

'You're late!' Lynne snapped, as she walked in the door.

'Big Sister was on the warpath,' Kay responded cheerfully. 'Is there anything to eat?' Her eye took in the mess surrounding the sofa where Lynne was sprawled. These days mess and Lynne seemed synonymous.

'Judy said to remind you it was your turn to wash up.'

'As if I could forget,' Kay groaned. 'With rosters stuck up all over the place. Where is she, by the way?'

Lynne gestured at the closed door of Judy's bedroom.

Kay pulled a face. Judy's diligence – no essays handed in late from that quarter – she regarded as a personal affront. 'You don't look too hot, you know,' she said, as she headed for the kitchen. 'Not getting 'flu, are you?'

'I'm pregnant.'

Kay laughed. It was a joke, wasn't it? She turned to look at her friend. Of course it was a joke.

'Oh, don't be so stupid,' Lynne flung at her. 'You knew what was going on.'

'No . . .'
'So much for french letters!'
This isn't happening, Kay told herself. Things like this don't happen to people you know. 'When?' she said.
'When what?'
'You and Brian, when did you . . . ?'
'What difference does that make? We've been doing it for six months, if you must know.'
Kay shook her head. Lynne was her best friend. How could she not have known?
'What am I going to do?' Lynne wailed.
The question snapped Kay out of her paralysis. She ran to the sofa, and threw her arms round her friend. So this is why you've been so irritable, she thought. 'Have you told Brian?'
'No.'
'Why not?'
'He'll hit the roof. He's a second-year medical student, for God's sake.'
Only because he keeps failing, Kay answered her silently.
'How far . . . ?' The words rose to the surface like scum. *How far on are you*? If she spoke them aloud they would make not just Lynne's predicament, but the baby, real.
'Two and a half months,' Lynne said. She sounded as though she were speaking underwater.
'You've seen a doctor?'
Lynne nodded. 'I picked one out of the phone book.'
'And it's certain?'
'Creep told me I had only myself to blame.'
A rogue thought momentarily distracted Kay. This was going to change everything, wasn't it? The flat. Geoffrey. Everything.
'He gave me this,' Lynne said, pressing a pamphlet into Kay's hand.
The words, 'How To Have Your Baby Adopted' flashed up at Kay. 'Some doctor you chose,' she said sourly.
'They're all the same.'
'D'you want *me* to tell Brian?'
'He'll run a mile.'
'You have to tell him, Lynne.'
'I'd rather have an abortion.'

Abortion. Kay had never heard the word spoken aloud before. That she was hearing it now, from the lips of her friend, meant something had ended. Maybe not the world, but something.

She swallowed painfully. Her mouth felt as if it were packed with stones. Geoffrey didn't like Lynne. He'd never said anything, but she could tell. What would he think now?

'If you won't tell Brian, then I will.' Something had to be done. Last year a girl in Lynne's position hung herself from a tree in the Botanical Gardens. The University tried to hush it up, but the story got around. People were still trying to guess the identity of the man involved.

'No!' Lynne shouted, as Kay made for the phone.

'You can't *not* tell him.'

'No . . .'

'What on earth's going on?' It was Judy, emerging, frowning, from her bedroom.

Kay and Lynne exchanged a glance. 'I'll do it,' Kay said.

'Do what?'

'Sit down,' Kay instructed.

12

The marriage of Brian Tippings and Lynette Allum took place on Wednesday, 17 April in the Registry Office in Edinburgh House. A drearier building could hardly be imagined. Kay had walked past it dozens of times and never noticed its existence.

Present at the ceremony were Lynne's parents, who'd driven up from Balclutha; Frank Herniman, a flatmate of Brian's, who was to act as a witness; Kay, the other witness; and Judy. Geoffrey should have been there but he'd cried off at the last moment, claiming urgent business in connection with an anti-nuclear rally he was organising.

The ceremony was held in a room hung with a portrait of the Queen and decorated with artificial flowers. A single-bar electric heater, aimed at the ankles of the bride and groom, provided the sole source of warmth.

Kay, who'd been instructed to stand on the bride's right, checked that the piece of velvet tied round her head to disguise her lack of a suitable hat was firmly in place. Now that the moment had come, the last three weeks were beginning to seem like a bad dream. With each new twist in Lynne's drama had come a corresponding crisis in her own life: a telling-off from her French Professor; a disaster with the capping costumes; an ultimatum from Miss Ridley. Looking back, Kay doubted whether she'd once managed more than five hours sleep a night. But it's over now, she consoled herself, as the little man with the wart on his nose began to speak. Life will go back to normal. Whatever that is.

'Good morning and welcome. It falls to me, on this happy occasion . . .'

That Geoffrey would fail to show up had been predictable from the beginning. What Kay hadn't anticipated was how angry she would feel.

Geoffrey was a liberal. A radical. Everyone said so. He could quote from Karl Marx. He could talk at length about the economics of socialism, and the reasons for the collapse of the Third Communist International. At Socialist Club meetings he advocated the abolition of private schools, inherited wealth, and non-taxable profits. The accumulation of personal or corporate fortunes he viewed as *prima facie* evidence of crime. 'You read Balzac,' he'd said to Kay. '"Behind every great fortune stands a crime."'

He hadn't gone so far as to say he believed in free love, but he included the family in his list of institutions ripe for reorganisation. 'Our divorce laws, for example, are draconian,' he'd complained. 'They enshrine the medieval concept of blame. Divorce should be available on agreement. Where there's no agreement it should become automatic after a year. The idea that two people can decide to get married, but not decide to get *un* married, is insane.'

Yet when Kay told Geoffrey about Lynne his reaction was not so very different from what she imagined her father's would have been. 'A shotgun wedding, eh?' he'd mused. 'Well, you reap what you sow. Isn't that what the Good Book says?'

'Lynne is my best friend,' Kay had reminded him. 'Doesn't that mean anything to you?'

'I'm sorry for *you*, Kay,' he'd responded. 'I can see you're upset.'

'They would have married eventually anyway. They love each other.'

'That so?'

'There's no need to sound so cynical.'

'I hope they'll be very happy,' Geoffrey had said.

'I solemnly declare that I do not know of any lawful impediment to this marriage between me, Brian Ronald Tippings, and Lynette Valerie Allum . . .'

Was a baby a *lawful impediment*? Brian had seemed to think so when the news was first broken to him. Three days had passed before he'd even speak to Lynne. Four more before he'd got round to suggesting marriage. Kay had been afraid to leave Lynne alone.

'I solemnly declare . . .'

Now it was the bride's turn. Look at her, you bastard, Kay willed, as Lynne's eyes flicked back and forth to Brian's face.

She glanced over her shoulder. Judy, looking like a married woman herself, in her wool dress and hat, flashed her a sympathetic smile. To Kay's surprise Judy had thrown herself whole-heartedly into the preparations for the wedding. It was she who'd persuaded Lynne to buy the pale blue frock-coat and matching petal hat she was wearing; she who'd baked a wedding cake, and instructed Kay in the mysteries of club sandwiches.

'I call upon these persons here present to witness that I, Brian Ronald Tippings, take you, Lynette Valerie Allum, to be my lawful wedded wife . . .'

Then it was over. Kay signed her name on the document; the Registrar offered his congratulations; the bride and groom kissed; Lynne hugged her parents; Kay dried her eyes; Judy blew her nose; and Frank, hands plunged deep in his pockets, grinned and nodded like a trained dog.

'No Geoffrey?' Brian asked, as they headed for the door.

'He had to be in court,' Kay lied.

When they were all outside Lynne's mother insisted they line up for a photograph. Kay quickly readjusted her 'hat', and tried not to notice the trickle of pedestrians, stopping to observe the proceedings. As soon as the photo session was over they climbed into Mr Allum's station wagon, and headed back to the flat.

Once inside, the atmosphere began to brighten. Judy had made the living room look positively festive. The tattered furniture had been transformed by a judicious scattering of shawls and cushions. Peeling paint and discoloured wallpaper had been disguised with streamers and balloons. While in the centre of the room stood the *pièce de résistance*: the kitchen table, covered with tea towels, laden with plates of sandwiches, jugs of cordial, and Judy's thickly iced cake.

If you could see Lynne now you might think differently about her, Kay thought, addressing the absent Geoffrey. The look of hurt defiance she'd been wearing for the last three weeks had given way to something Kay was tempted to call radiance. When

Brian stooped to whisper something in his wife's ear, Kay felt her heart contract with relief and envy.

After today Lynne's place in the flat would be taken by Phil Muir, a theological student from the overcrowded flat upstairs. Kay was uneasy about the arrangement – Phil was unlikely to be as sensitive to her need to be alone with Geoffrey as Lynne had been – but she didn't have the heart to disappoint Judy, who'd confessed to being seriously attracted to Phil.

'They'll be all right, won't they?' Judy whispered in Kay's ear.

'It won't be your fault if they're not,' Kay answered. 'This cake is delicious.'

Later, when it was all over and Kay was hurrying down the hill to the Library, Judy's question returned to haunt her. 'In my beginning is my end.' 'What begins in fear ends in folly.' Something about the day – the language of the ceremony perhaps?—had filled her mind with quotes.

Tomorrow Geoffrey would lead a march from the Town Hall to the Dunedin Wharf, where the American nuclear submarine, *Thomas Jefferson*, was berthed. Kay had said she'd walk with him, but as she pushed her trolley in and out of the stacks of books, a petulant voice was persuading her not to. He didn't support you, the voice argued. Why should you support him?

At the concert rehearsal that evening Kay sewed furiously and avoided Geoffrey's eye. When he asked her what was wrong, she answered, 'What d'you think?'

'We must never quarrel,' he'd said to her, the day they so nearly did, over Lynne. 'I can't stand quarrels.'

'Everyone quarrels sometimes,' Kay had argued.

'My parents fight,' he'd admitted. 'You can hear them all over the house.'

Kay's confusion – he'd told her his parents never quarrelled – must have shown in her face because he quickly changed his tune. 'I don't mean they fight *now*,' he revised. 'They used to, is what I'm saying.'

'But I thought . . .'

'All quiet on the western front these days.'

'Geoffrey rang,' Judy announced, when she got back to the flat.

'What did he want?'

'Didn't say. He sounded a bit upset.'

Kay threw herself on the sofa. Brian and Lynne would be at their new flat now. What would they be doing? When making love was expected of you, did you still want to do it? Lynne had said she didn't care about finishing her degree. She hated the thought of going to lectures and having people stare at her belly. So what would she do all day? Knit for the baby?

'Fancy a cup of tea?' Judy called from the kitchen.

'I'll make it,' Kay called back.

'I've invited Phil,' Judy explained, ducking her head round the door.

'Phil?'

'Don't be dozey. He'll be living here after tomorrow.'

'Oh, *Phil*.'

'There's some cake left. And a few of your scrummy sandwiches.'

'Just the tea, thanks. I'm not hungry.'

Kay dropped her head on to one of Judy's multi-coloured shawls. Her hair was tied up in a scarf. She'd had it re-permed for the wedding, but something had gone wrong. Instead of curls she had a frizz. Just touching it made her feel sick.

'Poor Kay,' her mother had said to her, the day she started school, 'you've inherited your father's hair. Such a pity. Clive now, he has the Maddock locks. You'll be jealous of your brother's curls when you're older.'

'You going on the march tomorrow?' Judy called out.

Kay pulled the shawl around her shoulders. She could see Geoffrey clearly: see the mark on his nose where his glasses sat; his hair tumbling into his eyes; those stains on his fingers. He wasn't the fortunate young man he made himself out to be. His parents fought. His sisters were strangers to him. He'd had a miserable time at school. The reason he wanted to change the world was because the world made so many people unhappy. Like me, Kay thought.

'Yes,' she called back. 'I'll be there. It's important to make a stand.'

13

'It's fascinating stuff,' Geoffrey enthused, beaming at Kay over the top of his cappuccino. 'Reopening a case that was last heard in 1903.'

'I didn't know you could do that.'

'Well, there has to be a certain amount of public demand. A petition as the result of new evidence coming to light, something of that sort. In this particular instance it's the Tuwharetoa people who are making the fuss.'

'Who are they?'

'A central North Island tribe. They deeded a vast acreage of land to the Crown in 1886. Then, in 1903, they tried to get it back, claiming that the Crown was planning to sell it. They didn't succeed, but they did manage to stop the sale, if indeed one was pending. That's never been proved. Now, however . . .'

Kay adjusted the scarf around her head, and smiled at the man she was suddenly quite certain she was in love with. She adored the way he used his hands when he talked. She adored the way he turned his head when smoking, exposing his marvellous profile. She adored his public-school voice, and his habit of making jokes whenever the conversation got serious. She adored *him*, and couldn't wait to meet his mysterious family.

It was the end of term. The Hawaiian Coffee Bar was crowded. The capping concert had been a great success. Likewise the procession which accompanied it. The local paper, attributing these twin triumphs to the organisational and creative skills of Geoffrey Grieve, had speculated as to his possible future. 'Otago University has sent many important men into the world,' the editor had written. 'Scientists, surgeons, lawyers, politicians.

At the risk of sounding grandiloquent, I would like to predict that Geoffrey Grieve will one day be Prime Minister of this country.'

Kay, as Geoffrey's now officially recognised girlfriend, had been basking in his reflected glory.

'I'm glad you'll be around over the holidays,' he said when his analysis of the Tuwharetoa case had come to an end. 'We could go up to Queenstown, if you like. Get in a bit of skiing.'

'I can't ski.'

'You'll soon learn.'

'It took me three months to learn to ride a bike.'

He leaned across the table. 'Bit unbalanced, are we?' he teased. 'We'll have to do something about that.'

Dear Mum and Dad,
Great to hear you're coming down. You don't say how long you think the case will last, Dad, but I hope it won't be over too quickly. It'll be good to see you in action again.

I should tell you I have a new girlfriend. I know you were upset about things coming to an end with Amanda, but *c'est la vie*, as they say. She's just got herself engaged, did you know? Some Aussie diplomat she's been going round with.

The new girlfriend's called Kay Dyer. She's a third-year Arts student. I know you'll like her. She's bright as a button and pretty as a picture. Which doesn't tell you anything, but happens to be true! She's from Auckland, somewhere out west. I don't know much about her family to be honest. She has a brother in the Army.

Incidentally, when I say she's bright, I mean she's *very* bright. Straight As last year, a hat trick she'll repeat again this year if I'm not mistaken. I'll have to watch my back!

It was a difficult letter to write. Geoffrey couldn't explain why, except that he felt this compulsion to present Kay, in advance of his parents' visit, in the best possible light. It didn't make sense. She hadn't done anything that required him to defend her. Six months into their relationship he'd only found one more negative quality to add to his list: she was inclined to sulk.

'But I don't want to ski,' she'd kept insisting, all the way up to Queenstown. 'I'll be perfectly happy reading.'
'You can't be in Queenstown and not ski.'
'Who says?'
'It's not natural.'
'Well then, I'll climb a mountain. Will that satisfy you?'
In the end she'd agreed to give it a try. He was still not convinced the injury she sustained on that first, ill-tempered day was accidental. Fortunately it was only a sprained ankle, but it brought her brief career as a skier to an end.

With the start of the new term, Geoffrey had become aware of a change in his feelings towards Kay. For the first time in his life he began experiencing pangs of jealousy. That what he was feeling was irrational was as obvious to him as it would have been to anyone else. Not that he discussed it with anyone else. Jealousy was definitely not a subject he would choose to raise with Alistair.

The person he was jealous of was Phil Muir. According to Kay it was Judy who fancied him, but Geoffrey couldn't help noticing how animated Kay was whenever Phil was around.

'He's a really nice guy,' she'd replied, when he asked her what she saw in him. 'I could almost be persuaded to go to church if he was the minister.'

'So what's going on then?' he'd demanded, on another occasion.

'What do you mean?'

'The Reverend and Judy. Are they going out together, or not?'

'Why the sudden interest? And he's not a Reverend, not yet.'

'So what's the story?'

'There isn't one. Judy's still interested, but Phil seems wary. Probably because they're living under the same roof.'

'I would have thought that was an incentive,' Geoffrey had observed gloomily.

Now, with his parents' arrival imminent, jealousy was uncomfortably mixed with the desire to protect.

'You'll like my dad,' he'd told Kay. 'He's a bit of a rogue, but charming. He'll probably flirt with you.'

'Will he like me? That's more to the point.'

'Course. They both will. Mum's a bit more formal than Dad, but don't let that worry you. She'll probably want to take you shopping.'

'What for?'

'Clothes. She never misses an opportunity. You can show her where to go.'

'I wouldn't have a clue.'

'Then ask Judy. She's keen on that sort of thing, isn't she?'

The last thing Geoffrey wanted was to make Kay nervous, but the fact was he was nervous himself. Dunedin was *his* territory. Apart from a couple of visits in his first year his parents had left him alone. Now they'd be poking their noses in, asking questions about his love life, his politics, his career prospects. He could imagine what his father would say if he told him he was thinking about taking a year off to travel. Kay was right, he'd decided. Travel was not a means to an end, it was an end in itself. Living at the bottom of the world made you appreciate that.

'Will your sisters be coming?' she'd asked him last night.

When he told her they'd be staying on in Auckland with his Aunt Pauline she'd seemed disappointed.

'Who's Aunt Pauline?'

'Dad's older sister. She's a weird old body, the archetypal spinster aunt, but I like her. She collects birds.'

'Live ones, I hope,' Kay had said.

14

'The French Revolution can only be understood in the context of the intellectual ferment which preceded it. Writers like Voltaire, de Sade, Rousseau, Diderot, sewed the seeds of what would become the single most significant political act in European history. "In the beginning was the word..."'

'Voltaire et al,' Kay wrote. '"In the beginning was the word".' The last sentence she underlined.

'History', she wrote next. 'What has happened in the past, what will have repercussions in the future.'

This morning, in the paper, there was a report on the recent trial in South Africa of Nelson Mandela, the Black Pimpernel. He too had been sewing seeds. And planting bombs, if the prosecution was to be believed. In the beginning was the word.

'I have decided,' Geoffrey said last night (the eve of his parents' visit: was that significant?), 'I have decided to love you.'

His manner, and the care with which he chose his words, had irritated Kay. 'I thought we loved each other?' she'd retorted.

'Being *in* love, that's easy.'

'I don't think I follow.'

'It's what comes after that's difficult. *Commitment*. That's what I'm talking about, Kay.'

In the beginning was the word.

Tomorrow, Saturday, she was to have dinner with Geoffrey and his parents at their hotel. The occasion had already caused a quarrel. They should have been having dinner with Lynne and Brian.

'Your parents are here for a while, aren't they?' Kay had argued. 'Can't we have dinner another night?'

81 •

'It's all been arranged.'
'So has dinner with Lynne.'
'His Royal Highness up to his old tricks again?' Lynne had scoffed when Kay phoned to make their apologies.

That she hardly ever saw her friend these days only added to her guilt.

'Mum, Dad, this is Kay.'
'How do you do?'

It was Geoffrey's father who took Kay's hand. She registered the look in his eye, and the fact that he held on to her a fraction longer than was necessary. Then it was the turn of Geoffrey's mother. The look in *her* eye was several degrees colder. 'How nice,' she murmured.

'Geoff didn't do you justice,' Lionel Grieve joked, as they settled into their chairs. 'Now, what'll it be?' He flicked his fingers at the waiter. 'Pimms for the young lady, if I'm not mistaken.'

Kay smiled. She'd never heard of Pimms.

While the drinks were being ordered Kay took the chance to examine her surroundings (though what she really wanted to do was study Geoffrey's parents). The room had a musty feel to it. Too much velvet and brocade. Not enough sunlight.

'So, Kay, tell us about yourself,' Winifred Grieve prompted. 'Geoffrey informs us you're from Auckland.'

'That's right.'
'Whereabouts?'
'My parents live in Astley.'

'Astley,' Geoffrey repeated. The name had taken him by surprise. Kay's reluctance to talk about her background had led him to believe she must come from somewhere outlandish. A predominantly Maori suburb was what he'd imagined. Not that Astley was a place to win any architectural prizes, but nor was it a slum. An average suburb, with the status of an independent town, blighted by secondhand car yards, was what it amounted to.

'Astley,' Winifred mused. 'Isn't that where they make wine?'

Geoffrey nodded. The way Kay was worrying at her hair warned him he should try and change the subject.

'And what does your father do, Kay?' Winifred sailed on.

'He works for the AA.'

'The AA. Is that . . . ?'

'It's the Automobile Association, Mother,' Geoffrey interjected. 'Not Alcoholics Anonymous.'

'Don't be clever, dear.'

In the pause that followed, Geoffrey groped for his cigarettes.

'No, thanks, son,' his father responded, when he proffered the packet. 'Only smoke cigars these days. Easier on the throat.'

'The twins send their love,' Winifred announced into the vacuum.

'How are the little devils?' Geoffrey enquired.

'Not so little, thank you,' his mother countered sourly.

'Kids don't seem to want to be kids anymore,' Lionel remarked. 'Not like my day.'

'Here we go,' Winifred muttered.

'Now, when I was a nipper . . .'

Kay listened with half an ear only. There were too many other things to think about: like the number of diamonds on Mrs Grieve's fingers, and the speed with which she'd downed her gin.

'Of course it all came to an end when I went away to boarding school,' Lionel concluded.

By the time dinner was announced Kay was feeling dizzy. One drink, when she was nervous, was more than enough to make her light-headed.

'You must call me Lionel,' Geoffrey's father insisted, over the soup.

She hardly dared look at Geoffrey. Alongside his father he seemed to shrink in size.

The meal was interminable. Soup, fish, roast meat and vegetables, assorted puddings. Geoffrey's father did most of the talking, for which Kay was grateful. Geoffrey himself hardly said a word.

'I think you might call me Winifred,' Geoffrey's mother pouted towards the end of the evening. 'Since you're already on first name terms with my husband.'

At last Geoffrey declared it was time to go. Kay leapt to her feet. She'd drunk three glasses of wine, more than enough to explain her burning cheeks.

'We'll see you tomorrow then?' Winifred enquired of her son.

'I have to be at a meeting in the evening,' Geoffrey replied, 'but we could do something during the day.'

'Perhaps Kay could join us?' Lionel suggested.

'I think it would be nice for us to see something of our son, Lionel,' Winifred cut in. 'What is this meeting anyway?'

'The Socialist Club.'

Winifred's immaculate eyebrows rose. She glanced at her husband, who responded by drawing deeply on his cigar. Kay, who'd spent the evening identifying signs of marital discord, was forced to revise her opinion. Geoffrey's parents might be unhappy, but they were not estranged. On the subject of their son's politics they were in complete agreement.

'And do you go to these meetings too?' Winifred asked Kay.

'Sometimes,' she answered.

Winifred looked down at her hands, spreading the fingers in a fan of diamonds. It was a gesture Kay had seen her make several times during the evening. 'Well, I suppose you'll grow out of it,' she said, raising her eyes to her son. 'Your father did.'

Driving back along the almost deserted main street, Kay let her hand rest on Geoffrey's thigh. 'I liked your father,' she said. 'I liked that story he told about . . .'

'The old bastard!' Geoffrey interrupted fiercely. 'His childhood was as miserable as mine. But do you think he'll admit it?'

'Will I see you tomorrow?' Kay asked, as they pulled up outside her house. She knew there was no point asking him in. Since Phil had taken up residence he could hardly be persuaded through the door.

'You heard my mother,' Geoffrey answered. 'I'm summoned.'

'I don't think your mother liked me.'

'Nonsense. It's me she gets ratty with.'

'I'll see you Monday then,' Kay said. She opened the door and swung her legs on to the pavement.

'Don't I get a kiss?'

Kay laughed, Perhaps the evening hadn't been such a disaster after all?

She leaned into the car, and kissed Geoffrey on the mouth. To her surprise he reacted passionately. She hesitated only a moment before climbing back in. She wondered if her breath tasted of wine. His tasted of tobacco, and the brandy he'd drunk with his father.

Lionel and Winifred Grieve's stay in Dunedin lasted ten days. Winifred, when approached by Geoffrey, expressed dismay at the prospect of going shopping with Kay. 'The girl has no dress sense at all,' she complained.

Lionel's objections to his son's new girlfriend were less frivolous. 'She's got a brain in her head,' he conceded, when Geoffrey, bruised from the encounter with his mother, sought his opinion. 'Which isn't the first thing you'd say of young Amanda. But there's a problem with clever women, you know. They expect too much.'

'But you liked her,' Geoffrey persisted.

'Oh, I liked her well enough. But I'm not sure about her, if you see what I mean.'

'Just because you don't know her family . . .'

'Now come on, son. You know me better than that.'

Two days later the subject of Kay came up again.

'Have you thought what you'll do when you graduate?' Lionel asked, over drinks in the hotel bar.

Geoffrey hesitated. He'd been asked this question before. It usually led to an argument. 'I've been putting feelers out here actually,' he lied. 'There are a couple of possibilities.'

'You'd do better in Auckland. A man tipped as a future Prime Minister doesn't rusticate in Dunedin. Would you like me to ask around? See what's cooking?'

'Actually, I've been thinking of taking a year off.'

'What for?'

'To travel.'

'You can do that when you're established. Your mother and I get away most years.'

'I thought I might go to England.'

'You hate England. That's what you're always telling me.'

'I hated school. I hardly know England.'

'This isn't anything to do with Kay, is it?'

'Not really, no.'

'Are you sure?'

'It's my own idea.'

'Because I'd be unhappy, son, if I thought this friendship was serious. Sew your wild oats, by all means, but don't confuse that with the real business of life.'

The *coup de grâce* was saved for the last day. Lionel, having lost his case, was not in the best of moods. 'Chap's a Rotarian, for God's sake,' he complained, as Geoffrey heaved Winifred's huge suitcase into the boot of his car. 'Rotarians don't go round raping young girls.'

'Seems this one did.'

'Can't tell me she didn't ask for it. You saw her in court. Provocative little devil, if ever I saw one.'

'She's only fourteen, Dad.'

'Juliet was only twelve.'

Geoffrey slammed the boot shut. 'I'll get Mum,' he said.

'Hang on a minute, there's something I have to say to you. I promised your mother . . .'

'If it's about Kay . . .'

'Oh, don't get me wrong. We both like her. She a lovely-looking young woman. And bright, as you say. But your mother and I would be distressed if we thought the friendship was likely to develop.'

'Is that all?' Geoffrey muttered.

'Shrewd judge of character, your mother. I've seldom known her to be wrong.'

'She doesn't know Kay. She's hardly even talked to her.'

'A word of advice,' Lionel said, locking his hand on to his son's shoulder. 'Keep off the subject of marriage. Women are the very devil once they think they've hooked you.'

15

If only I had someone to talk to, Kay thought. Once she would have confided in Lynne, but Lynne had other things on her mind these days. As for Judy, she was in a state of permanent misery about Phil. Bemoaning the difficulties of requited love to someone suffering from its opposite would be cruel.

I love Geoffrey, Kay reasoned. I'm in love with him. I want to make love to him. So why do I have these doubts? Is it normal to feel this way? One minute euphoric, the next sick with panic . . .

Geoffrey had given her a photo of himself. It was taken in England just before his return to New Zealand. He was smoking in the photograph, his long, elegant fingers curled around the cigarette, his profile rendered mysterious by drifts of smoke. When the panic hit, Kay would take out the photo and stare at it. How handsome he is, she would affirm; how romantic the expression in his eyes.

Three weeks had passed since the visit of Geoffrey's parents. For a while after their departure Geoffrey was sullen and uncommunicative, but now, with the snow gone from the hills, and the first crocuses showing in the Botanical Gardens, he was his old self again. Soon they would be in their last term. Their days, and nights, would be taken up swotting for exams. When Kay thought about what lay ahead, known and unknown, her panic increased. To the question, 'What are you going to do when you leave university?' she invariably answered, 'You tell me and we'll both know.'

My dear Geoffrey,
Well, here we are back in the City of Sails. Enough briefs

waiting to keep me busy to the end of the decade. This is a demanding profession you've chosen!

On that subject, I got into conversation with Bunce Goodbody at the club last night, and he was most interested to hear what you've been up to. He asked me for your address, so I'm really just writing to tell you to expect a letter from him. Bunce, as you know, is a first-class lawyer, and his firm, Goodbody and Sutch, one of the country's best. They don't of course have a high profile as criminal lawyers, but that could be to your advantage. If, as I suspect, Bunce is going to offer you a position (with a view to a Junior Partnership in a year or two's time), you could make it a condition of acceptance that you be allowed to build up a criminal practice of your own.

Geoffrey put the page down, and took out a cigarette. His father was an erratic correspondent. That this letter had been written at all was ominous.

'By the way,' he read, 'we had a visit from the Pitt-Forbeses at the weekend. Amanda's engagement is off. Thought you might like to know.'

Geoffrey glanced at his watch: 8.30. Kay was working late at the Library. If he set off now he'd be in time to pick her up.

'Geoffrey!' Kay's smile, on finding him waiting for her, convinced him he'd made the right decision.

'Where are we going?' she asked, as they got into the car.

'Wait and see.'

He drove past the Robbie Burns statue and headed for the southern end of town. When he turned the car on to the Bay Road, Kay giggled.

'Funny time to be going to the beach,' she said.

Geoffrey glanced at her. She was patting her hair, a habit which usually irritated him. But tonight he had resolved to feel nothing but love.

'Shall I bring the rug?' Kay asked, when he'd parked the car.

Geoffrey shook his head.

'Have you noticed,' she remarked, as they set off across the sand, 'how sinister seaweed looks at night? That piece over there, beside the log, look! It could be a cat-o-nine-tails.'

'Kay,' Geoffrey said, 'I've something to say to you.'

She pulled her hand free. From the look on her face he'd say she was scared.

'It's not an impulsive thing. I've been thinking about it for weeks.'

'You want us to make love . . .'

'What?'

'That's why you've brought me here. It's all right. *I've* been thinking about it too.'

'I want us to get engaged,' Geoffrey said.

'Engaged . . .'

'To be married.'

'You're asking me to marry you?'

'Yes.' Geoffrey laughed. Kay's face really was a study. Fancy her thinking . . . 'I'd like us to get married as soon as exams are over,' he said impulsively. 'Well, come on, say something?'

'You're sure?'

'One hundred per cent.'

'What about your parents?'

'I'm over twenty-one, Kay.'

She gave an odd little laugh. Then her arms reached out to him. 'Thank you,' she said. 'I mean, yes, of course I'll marry you. I'll marry you tomorrow if you want.'

16

Dear Mum and Dad,
I'm writing to tell you Kay and I are engaged . . .

The reply, in the form of a telephone call, came two days later. 'I'm coming down,' Winifred announced.
'What for?'
'I'm booked on a plane tomorrow.'
'But she's only just been here,' Kay protested when Geoffrey broke the news to her.
'She says she wants to get to know you better.'
'We'll fail our exams,' Kay predicted miserably.
On the day of Winifred's arrival Kay received a letter, the first in weeks, from her parents.
'So, you're making something of yourself at last,' her father wrote. 'Congratulations! This young man of yours sounds an excellent prospect. I know his father – by reputation only, of course. They're a fine family . . .'
'We're looking forward so much to meeting your fiancé,' her mother wrote. 'And his family, of course. Goodness, what a busy time you're going to have . . .'
Kay never showed these letters to Geoffrey, just as he never confided the nature of his exchanges with his mother.
'Why the rush?' Winifred demanded, on the way in from the airport. 'You're both so young.'
'We're sure of each other, Mother. What's the point of waiting?'
'You know so little about her.'
'I know enough to want to marry her.'

'She's not like your other girlfriends, Geoffrey, that's what worries your father and me.'

'You mean, she's not like Amanda.'

It was the same the next day, and the day after.

'You didn't tell me Kay had a job,' Winifred complained.

'Not everyone has such generous parents as I do,' Geoffrey replied.

Eventually Winifred was forced to concede that since her son was over twenty-one there was nothing she could do to stop the engagement. 'But can't that be enough for the moment?' she pleaded. 'If you wait till next year you can be married in Auckland. I would have thought Kay'd want that. It's *her* home too.'

'Kay wants to be married in Dunedin, Mother, and so do I.'

Winifred's face flamed beneath her face powder. 'I might have known that would be your response,' she snapped. 'My wishes, the wishes of your father, mean nothing to you, do they? You really are a very selfish young man.'

The day after that conversation Winifred took Kay shopping. Kay, who was having one of her panic days, trailed behind her future mother-in-law, and tried not to think about her hair, which she'd convinced herself was falling out. Winifred had dyed auburn hair. Unlike most women her age she seldom wore a hat. She must have known how young and pretty she looked, with her bouffant curls framing her face.

'That's it!' Winifred declared, at the end of what had been, for both women, a wretched afternoon. The shop assistant had just produced a cream satin dress with a scooped neckline and a small, scalloped train. 'That's the one. What did I tell you?' she crowed when Kay had been induced to try it on. 'Perfect.'

Kay, too numbed to protest, agreed the dress suited her, and allowed Winifred to pay the bill. 'It's very kind of you,' she murmured.

'I hope your mother won't think I'm interfering,' Winifred simpered.

'My mother isn't interested in clothes,' Kay replied.

Winifred's eyebrows shot up. 'You know, dear,' she said, exchanging a glance with the woman behind the counter, 'you can look quite attractive when you try. You must let me help you. I don't imagine you've built up much of a trousseau? No? I thought not. We'll make a start tomorrow then. And while we're about it, I think we should do something about your hair.'

That night Kay lay in bed in a state of terror. She'd made a terrible mistake. The engagement must be called off. In the two weeks since Geoffrey's proposal she'd only been on her own with him twice. These days, when her stomach lurched, it was from panic, not desire.

'Judy! Judy, are you awake?'

Standing at Judy's door Kay was already ashamed of what she was about to say. 'I can't go through with it, I can't,' she was going to confess.

But those weren't the words that came out. 'I'm sorry,' she apologised. 'I shouldn't have woken you.'

'Trouble with Ma-in-law?' Judy asked sleepily.

'How did you guess?'

'She'll be gone soon.'

'It's just that . . . oh God, Judy, I don't know – I don't know what I feel anymore.'

'Geoffrey's probably desperate you two should get on.'

'I think he's scared of her. I certainly am.'

'All the more reason.'

'What if I *can't* like her? What if she doesn't like me?'

Judy stifled a yawn. 'It wouldn't be the first time in history,' she said.

'What a lucky girl you are,' her mother wrote, in the letter that arrived a week later. 'There can't be many women who'd go to all that trouble for their future daughter-in-law.'

With Winifred's departure, Kay's panic began to recede. The engagement was now official. Kay wore a small solitaire on the third finger of her left hand, an object of awe and envy to her female friends. 'Very classy,' Lynne pronounced. 'Did the mother choose that too?'

Six weeks into the third term Kay received a guest list from Winifred. There were eighty-five names on it. She stared at it in horror. She'd been reading about Robespierre and the start of the Terror. On her page of notes she'd written, 'Cycle of revolution. The oppressed become the oppressors.' She and

Geoffrey had agreed on a small wedding. Close friends and family only.

'Shit!' Geoffrey swore when Kay showed him the letter.

'You did tell her what we wanted?'

'Of course.'

'Then why . . . ?'

'Because she's a spoiled child, that's why. She's doing this to get back at me.'

'For what? Marrying me?'

Geoffrey didn't answer.

'We could just ignore it,' Kay suggested.

But that, of course, was impossible.

'Never mind,' Kay comforted. 'Once we're married we can do what we want.'

In the end she convinced herself it didn't really matter. Let Winifred do the organising. She had exams to think about. As for *her* parents, relieved of both responsibility and expense, they couldn't speak highly enough of the Grieves. 'We've conveyed our appreciation of all they're doing,' her father had written. 'I suggested we might meet in Auckland before the happy day, but they haven't taken me up on it. Quite enough on their plates, I should imagine.'

Kay even agreed to having Geoffrey's sisters as bridesmaids.

'We don't much like the colour you've chosen,' Susan Grieve wrote, in her loping, childish hand, 'but Mum says we're not to make a fuss. However, if you could change it to apricot or teal blue, my sister and I would be ever so chuffed.

'By the way, Mum says your first name is Elizabeth. Does anyone ever call you that? It's a neat name. Better than Kay. When we talk about you we call you Lilibet.'

The day exams finished Geoffrey took Kay out for a meal. Over coffee he announced he'd accepted a position in an Auckland law firm. 'There's nothing binding about it,' he was quick to reassure her. 'We can still travel.'

'But we're staying on here, aren't we? That's what we agreed. I've already arranged with Miss Ridley to work full-time.'

'You'll get a job in Auckland. Better paid probably. It's only a temporary thing.'

Kay trawled her spoon through the sugar. Something was

wrong. Geoffrey wasn't telling her the truth. 'I don't understand,' she said. 'You were going to get a casual job. Nothing to do with law. You said you'd enquire at the wool store, remember? We'd work for six months, then go overseas. That was the plan.'

'I can make more money this way. They're offering a good deal.'

'Why didn't you tell me you were applying for a law job?'

'There was nothing to tell. Not till I got the offer.'

'And now you've accepted it?'

'They wanted my answer by return post.'

'So you said yes without even discussing it.'

'It's only a job, Kay.'

'It's a job in a law firm in Auckland,' she retorted angrily.

Geoffrey plunged his hand into his pocket, and pulled out his cigarettes. When he was upset, as he was now, his hands shook slightly. 'Do you want me to back out of it then?' he said, through the first wave of smoke.

'And be blamed by your parents? No, thank you,' Kay answered.

Three weeks later the following notice appeared in the *Otago Daily Times*.

> A wedding of particular interest in university circles took place yesterday in the University Chapel. The bridegroom, Geoffrey Ayrton Grieve, is a past president of the Student Association, and organiser of the Graduation celebrations. The bride, Elizabeth Kay Dyer, is this year's winner of the French and History Prizes.
>
> The bride, who wore a classic gown of cream satin edged with lace, was attended by Misses Susan and Belinda Grieve, twin sisters of the groom. Their gowns of apricot satin were styled on the same lines as the bride's.
>
> The bride wore a veil of fine tulle, falling from a wide satin bow. She carried a bouquet of roses and lily-of-the-valley.
>
> The best man was Alistair Glendinning.
>
> Among the many guests who'd travelled from outside Dunedin were the bridegroom's parents, Mr Lionel Grieve,

- Elspeth Sandys

QC, and Mrs Grieve; the bride's parents, Mr and Mrs Harold Dyer; and their son, Lieutenant Clive Dyer.

The reception was held at Wains Hotel.

Mr and Mrs Geoffrey Grieve will make their home in Auckland.

17

'You're very quiet,' Geoffrey observed, after they'd been driving in silence for several minutes.

Kay put her hand on her husband's thigh. They were coasting down the hill that separated Dunedin from the north. It was just after five. A trickle of commuter traffic accompanied them. 'I'm glad it's over,' she said.

'Went off pretty well, I thought.'

'I'm sorry about my brother. He doesn't usually get drunk.'

The place they were headed for was so small it didn't appear on most maps, but its one hotel listed among its attractions a honeymoon suite. Their booking was for one night only, after which they would be camping, first in Queenstown, then in Wanaka. At the end of that time the long trek north would begin. Geoffrey's car, complete with new radiator, was packed to the roof.

'You were very patient with Mother,' Geoffrey acknowledged. 'I'm afraid she likes to take charge.'

'Darling?'

'Yes, sweetheart?'

'We are going to travel, aren't we? This job in Auckland is only temporary?'

Geoffrey swerved to avoid a rabbit. 'We'll go to the ends of the earth, if that's what you want,' he promised.

One hundred and fourteen people had come to the wedding, most of them friends of the Grieves. Kay, who'd not slept the night before, had drunk two glasses of brandy before setting off for the chapel. Her hair, cut and permed by 'Anton', the only hairdresser worth consulting in Dunedin, according to Winifred, had foamed around her face like cream on a cake.

'Gee!' the twins had gasped, when she made her appearance. 'Wow!'

'You look like the Queen or something,' Belinda had pronounced.

'Is that why you keep calling me Lilibet?'

'Well, you don't look like a Kay, does she, Sue?'

'I don't look like myself,' Kay had asserted miserably.

Thank God for brandy, she thought now. Otherwise I might have stayed in that foul mood all day. Fact is – she glanced at her new husband – I can't remember much about the ceremony. Lynne's baby howling, no one could forget that. And Geoffrey stepping on my veil every time we moved. But what we said, what we promised, that's vague. Perhaps we're not married at all.

Which, as it happened, was the view of the proprietors of the hotel. Geoffrey had forgotten to confirm the booking in writing, with the result that the honeymoon suite had been given to a family of four from Nelson.

'Grieve?' the woman behind the desk repeated, her eye lazing over the pages of a large exercise book. 'Not down here.'

'But I phoned weeks ago.'

'I'll ask my husband,' she said. 'Not that *he'll* know. He can't remember what happened yesterday. Les!' she yelled over her shoulder. 'There's a party here say they booked the honeymoon suite. Name of Grieve.'

'It would have been about three weeks ago,' Geoffrey advised.

There was a shuffling sound from the other side of the door, then a man appeared: red cheeks, mottled nose, greasy hair, unshaven chin. 'What's up?' he grunted.

Geoffrey grinned. 'It was you I spoke to,' he affirmed.

Les exchanged a glance with his wife. 'And how long have you two been wed?' he drawled.

Geoffrey's grin widened. 'About six hours.'

Les's wife looked down at Kay's left hand; then, raising her eyes, she peered through the open front door, at their crammed car.

'It's too late to drive on,' Geoffrey pointed out reasonably. 'If you have another room we'll take that.'

A second glance was exchanged. Les nodded curtly. 'There's a twin room at the back,' his wife conceded.

Kay's face, when Geoffrey turned to her, was stony.

'Will you be wanting tea?' Les's wife asked, as she led them down a corridor that smelt of cats.

'Just dinner, thanks,' Geoffrey replied. 'What time . . . ?'

'Dinner's in the middle of the day,' he was informed. 'Tea's in the dining room at six o'clock sharp.'

Geoffrey reached for Kay's hand. They were outside the door of their room now. There was no key. 'You'll have to sign the register,' Les's wife muttered over her shoulder.

The door opened on brown walls, a stained brown carpet, and curtains of similar hue, minus most of their hooks. Two narrow beds covered with faded candlewick bedspreads stood either side of a small cabinet. Geoffrey's eye went to the bible lying on top of the cabinet. Then, through its partly open door, he spied a large white chamber pot.

'I'll get the cases,' he said.

There was no reaction from Kay.

When he came back she didn't appear to have moved. 'Did you notice where the bathroom was?' she asked.

'It's at the end of the corridor,' he told her. 'But I'm afraid we can't have baths, if that's what you're thinking. They have to be booked ahead.'

Kay's shoulders rose stiffly. Watching her, Geoffrey had the feeling she was grinding her teeth.

'How could you have let this happen?' she accused.

'I'm sorry, sweetheart. Please don't be angry. I feel bad enough as it is.' He moved to her side, grabbed her hands, and held them tightly. 'I'll make up for it,' he promised. 'A slap-up dinner in Queenstown. Champagne. The works. What d'you say?'

Her mouth twitched. Was she going to smile?

'At least we're on our own,' he encouraged. 'And we have not just one bed, but two.'

'Why can I never stay angry with you?' Kay said.

Over tea – cold mutton, sliced white bread, a salad of shredded lettuce and soggy tomato, topped with thick yellow mayonnaise – Kay tried to explain her anger to herself. It wasn't an emotion she experienced very often. Blaming it on the room brought her no comfort at all.

'I wish the wedding could have been different,' she said, between mouthfuls of drowned lettuce.

'Me too,' Geoffrey agreed.

'The only people *I'd* have invited would have been Lynne and Brian, and Judy and Phil.'

'Not your parents?'

'Especially not them.'

Geoffrey frowned. He'd only just met Kay's mother and father. He didn't want to begin his marriage by thinking badly of them.

'What do you think of your new mother-in-law?' Winifred had hissed in his ear when the photographs were being taken. She hadn't waited for his answer. 'Just as well I took Kay in hand,' she'd gone on. 'That outfit her mother's wearing looks like something from the Salvation Army.'

'I'm sorry I didn't have more of a chance to talk to your father,' Geoffrey said. He was struggling to remove a piece of mutton from his teeth. His tongue felt raw with the effort. 'I did manage a chat with your mother.'

'Poor Mum.'

'Why do you say that?'

'No reason.'

'Shame they couldn't have got down earlier. Given us all a chance to get to know each other.'

'Can you see your mother and mine chatting over a Pimms? I can't.'

'Ah . . .' Geoffrey put his hand to his mouth, and discreetly disposed of the offending matter.

'Don't think much of Kay's folks,' his father had stated bluntly. 'The brother might make something of himself, I suppose. If he survives Malaya.'

Though Geoffrey would never say so to Kay, he could see her point about not wanting to live in Auckland. Occasions involving both families could hardly fail to be embarrassing.

'More tea?' Les's wife boomed across the dining room. The only other guests, the family from Nelson, had already vacated their table.

'No, thank you,' Kay and Geoffrey chorused.

'Breakfast's at eight o'clock.'

Kay pushed her plate aside. Geoffrey had hated her family. She'd seen it in his face. He'd 'specially hated Clive, who'd drunk too much, and gone on *ad nauseam* about communists. 'You didn't tell me he was a redneck,' he'd said when Kay foolishly probed.

'What do we do now?' she asked. Through the window she could see the family from Nelson playing football on the lawn. The youngest child, a girl, was screaming with excitement.

'I can think of a few things,' Geoffrey answered.

'I suppose we could go for a walk.'

'Don't know about you,' Geoffrey said, raising a quizzical eyebrow, a gesture Kay had told him made him look like an owl, 'but I'd like to go to bed.'

'It's still daylight.'

'So?'

Kay laughed. Even to her ears it sounded unnatural: as if someone were pressing a finger to her windpipe.

'We're going to be married for the rest of our lives,' Geoffrey had said, the day he presented her with a copy of Havelock Ellis's *Psychology of Sex*. 'It's important we understand how things work.' She'd thought it was a joke, till she saw the expression on his face. She blamed Havelock Ellis for the fact that she was still a virgin.

'I love you, Mrs Grieve,' Geoffrey whispered across the table. 'I love you very much.'

'Then let's go to bed,' Kay said.

Marriage

18

To approach Auckland by air is to be startled by its beauty. The twin harbours, Waitemata and Manukau, press caressing fingers into the land, making of the narrow isthmus on which the city stands, a vivid Pacific Venice. No soft golds or faded browns here, but an edgeless canvas of blues and greens, intricately webbed with light.

The islands, scattered randomly over the water, seem uninhabited from the air. Some, by reason of their volcanic history, or their designation as *tapu*, are. But the eye doesn't make such distinctions till the descent is almost over. Then, as scattered farmhouses give way to sprawling suburbs, the conviction that this is a city quite different from any other begins to take hold. A stranger could be forgiven for thinking he was dropping into paradise.

It's only later, driving into town from the airport, that different words spring to mind. Auckland, circa 1965, is called in the tourist brochures the City of Sails. Publications of a more scientific nature refer to it as the City of Volcanoes. But for those whose houses look out on neither sea nor hill, their view being limited to the backyards of their neighbours, there are other, less flattering names.

For Kay Grieve, approaching Auckland by road, it's the unflattering epithets that dominate her thoughts. City of Swamps. City of Slums. City of Traps. She and Geoffrey have just driven across the fertile plains of the Waikato: a rich land, studded with tree-shaded farmhouses and prosperous dairy towns. But what Kay sees, travelling through the dreary suburbs of South Auckland, is poverty. It's in the faces of the people on the streets;

in their paint-starved houses, and the old cars that litter their neglected front gardens. It's in the rows of run-down factories and car yards: dreary corrugated-iron buildings, enlivened with sudden splashes of colour – a scarlet roof; a fence smothered with purple convolvulus; a convocation of pink-faced gnomes, wearing green jerkins and orange breeches, occupying pride of place in Sam Choy's Garden Centre. Only a few miles separate South Auckland from the gilded homes of Remuera, but it might just as well, Kay thinks, glancing at Geoffrey, be an ocean that divides them.

The honeymoon has not been a success. The wedding night, in the room that smelled of cats, was a disaster which husband and wife have agreed, albeit tacitly, not to talk about.

The problem was not the room, nor the hotel, but something neither Kay nor Geoffrey had thought about. Kay had her period.

'Hope you don't mind?' she'd giggled, as she and Geoffrey climbed into the narrow bed.

There was no answer.

'It'll make a mess of the sheets.'

'Perhaps we should wait?' he had muttered.

'What?'

'Till you're OK again.'

'I'm OK now.'

'Till you feel better, I mean.'

If she'd known this was to be the start of a pattern, she might have said something. She might even have suggested they consult Havelock Ellis! But his reluctance to engage in anything more than a cursory goodnight kiss was so obvious, she turned her back and feigned sleep.

Six days later they were camping beside the lake at Queenstown. It was colder than it should have been. Unable to swim, or make love, they'd spent the intervening days reading, hiking, and cooking meals over a primus. Behind them loomed the mighty ranges of the Remarkables, still capped with snow, reminding Kay of their abortive skiing weekend.

'You haven't changed your mind then?' she'd asked that night, over the promised champagne dinner. 'We will still be going overseas at the end of the year?'

'Something like that,' Geoffrey had agreed.

'And we will find our own place to live? We're not moving in with your parents or anything?'

'Hell, no!' Geoffrey had grinned at her over his hovering fork. 'A week's the most I could stand.'

As always, when they talked of the future, Kay had felt reassured. She hated doubting Geoffrey. It made her feel like a traitor.

That night they'd lain under their outspread sleeping bags, and Geoffrey's goodnight kiss, fuelled by the champagne, had quickly turned to something else. Kay, eagerly co-operating, had waited for the expected lurch, but it had failed to materialise. She was nervous. That was how she'd explained it to herself later. Suddenly what they were about to do had seemed difficult; impossible even. And Geoffrey was nervous too. His breathing was ragged: his hands, usually so sensitive, groped and plunged as if uncertain of their purpose. She knew he was afraid of hurting her, and she knew he was afraid of failing. She wished she didn't know these things. The knowledge was like a third person lying between them. All she could do, to make it easier for them both, was whisper and pretend, and sob out her love when it was all, painfully and bloodily, over.

'I've made you bleed,' Geoffrey had observed with horror.

'Yes,' she'd said.

'Oh God . . .'

'It's all right. That's what's supposed to happen.'

'I didn't know.'

'Shame on you! You haven't read your Havelock Ellis. Aren't you glad I was a virgin?'

He hadn't answered.

'I thought men were supposed to want that? See it as proof or something.'

'You sound like my father.'

'What? Don't tell me you two talked about . . .'

'He wanted you to see a gynaecologist, a friend of his . . . I know, I know. He's a shocking old patriach. But he meant well.'

'So you did talk about it?'

'I told him it was immaterial to me whether you were a virgin or not. I told him he was living in the Dark Ages.'

'I can't believe I'm hearing this.'

'It wasn't my idea, Kay.'

'So what would you have done if I wasn't a virgin? If this gynaecologist person had told you that?'

'It wouldn't have made any difference.'

'Oh, really?'

'Look, can we drop this? I was a fool to bring it up at all.'

'What about you? Were *you* a virgin? Or aren't I supposed to ask?'

'Yes, if you must know,' Geoffrey had answered, a little too quickly, Kay had thought. 'It was the first time for me too.'

'I don't believe you.'

'Suit yourself.'

'Not that it matters . . .'

'Exactly.' Geoffrey's agreement had been emphatic. Not for him the hesitation of a lie. He'd already dismissed *that* as insignificant. 'We're arguing about nothing,' he'd insisted.

Which brought the subject to an end for him, but not for Kay. How did she know he was telling the truth? If it had been Amanda he'd married, would his father have wanted *her* to see a gynaecologist?

As the pattern of her thoughts grew more obsessive, Kay took to drinking sherry, on the sly. 'You don't want an inhibited wife, do you?' she'd joked when Geoffrey caught her in the act.

'You never used to be inhibited.'

'We never used to be married.'

'Why should that change things?'

'I don't know, Geoffrey. I just know that it has.'

It'll be better once we have our own place, Kay had told herself, as they drove from Queenstown to Wanaka, then, a week later, began the long journey north. It'll be better once we have a decent bed!

'Nervous?' Geoffrey asked, as he turned the car off the Great South Road. His hand reached out and grasped her thigh. Kay returned the pressure gratefully. She was Geoffrey's wife. It was pointless to wish anything different.

'Yoo-hoo! Here they come. I saw them first. Yoo-hoo, Lilibet!'

Kay poked her head out the window. 'Hi, Belinda!' she called.

'Hullo you two Subs,' Geoffrey shouted.

'What's it like to be married?' Belinda yelled, as the car skidded to a halt. 'Do you stay in bed all day? I bet you do,' she said, grinning over her shoulder at her sister.

'Are you having a baby?' Sue, the quieter of the two, asked Kay.

'I heard that,' Geoffrey said, as he climbed out of the car. 'We'll have no more talk like that, thank you very much.'

'Spoil-sport,' Belinda snarled.

'You look just the same, Lilibet,' Sue complained, linking her arm in Kay's. 'I thought you'd be different.'

'She's browner,' Belinda observed.

'So I should jolly well hope,' Kay laughed. 'All that open-air living.'

'Wish *I* could go camping,' Sue pouted, pulling Kay towards the house. 'We never get to do fun things like that.'

'The parents have been foul all holidays,' Belinda confided in a hoarse whisper. 'We're not allowed to go anywhere without a police escort.'

'Don't exaggerate,' Kay said.

She was trying not to stare at the house, looming over her like a huge bird. What had she expected? That it *wouldn't* overwhelm her? Photographs could lie, she knew that, but the ones she'd seen in *Fine New Zealand Homes*, and in the snap Geoffrey carried in his wallet, had told the truth. Lionel and Winifred Grieve lived in a mansion, a blue and white stucco mansion with Ionic pillars, a Victorian conservatory, and a flagpole flying the Union Jack in the front garden.

'Welcome home, darlings,' Winifred, cool in white linen, cooed from the top of the steps. 'How well you look,' she complimented Kay. 'Marriage obviously suits you.'

Kay, who knew the drill by now, let her mother-in-law kiss her on both cheeks. 'Welcome to the family, Elizabeth,' Winfred said.

Elizabeth? Was that, along with the twins' version, to be her name now?

'Take the car round to the back, will you, dear?' Winifred

instructed her son. 'I don't want all that junk coming in through the front door.'

'You've got the pink room,' Belinda shrilled from inside the house. 'It's got the hugest double bed.'

19

'For God's sake, Mother, can't we eat in the family room?'

Winifred cast a doleful glance in her son's direction. Geoffrey registered the blue eye shadow, which may or may not have accounted for the film of moisture over his mother's eyes. Winifred Grieve was a practised weeper. Geoffrey had lost more arguments than he cared to remember through his mother's tears. Was she going to cry now? 'Not that we don't appreciate . . .' he amended lamely, waving at the platter in his mother's hands.

'It was your father's idea,' Winifred informed him, as she headed for the seldom-used dining room, with its mahogany table and seating for twenty. 'Starting off on the right foot, he called it.'

'You've gone to a lot of trouble.'

'You mustn't worry about your wife,' Winifred sang over her shoulder. 'She's not nearly as fragile as you seem to think.'

But Geoffrey did worry about Kay. He'd brought girlfriends home before. He knew how this place affected them. The only person not to be intimidated was Amanda.

'Why would your mother call me Elizabeth?' Kay had asked, when her tour of the house and garden was over. She'd not said much till then. A remark about the tennis court, that was all.

'She didn't.'

'She did. You just didn't hear.'

'A toast,' his father announced, when they were all seated. 'To the newly-weds.'

Geoffrey winked at Kay. He wanted to convey that he didn't feel at home here either. He wanted to reassure her their life would be different. Not for the first time he wished he could have introduced her to Daisy Mountford. Daisy would have taken Kay under her wing.

'This is delicious, Mrs Grieve,' Kay gushed.

'Winifred, *please*.'

'I'm afraid I'm not much of a cook.'

'Mum has a girl to help her usually, don't you, Mum?' Belinda piped.

'Not with the cooking. I do that myself.'

'Only she's gone to have a baby.'

'Who has?' Kay asked.

'Merle. The girl who was helping.'

'I guess you'd need help in a place this size,' Kay acknowledged.

'All the girls who come here are pregnant,' Belinda smirked.

Geoffrey clattered his fork on to his plate. Belinda was a little devil, bringing this up on their first night. Kay would be sure to take it the wrong way. 'You better explain, Dad,' he muttered.

Lionel gave a hearty laugh. 'There's no mystery,' he asserted. 'It's a perfectly good scheme, of benefit to both parties.' He turned to Kay. 'As you correctly diagnosed, my dear, my wife needs help to run this place. After going through the usual channels, finding and losing housekeepers the way most people find and lose sixpences, a friend of mine came up with the solution to the problem. The girls who come here are all in need of a home. A temporary home till their babies are born. They've got themselves into trouble, you see. You'd be surprised at the numbers. We give them bed and board in return for help around the house.'

Kay glanced at Geoffrey, then turned back to her father-in-law. 'This friend of yours,' she said, 'would he be a gynaecologist, by any chance?'

'How did you know?'

'What happens to the girls afterwards?'

'Afterwards?'

'When they've had their babies.'

'I imagine they get on with their lives.'

'And the babies?'

'They're adopted. That's part of the deal.'

'Even if the mothers don't want it?'

'Why shouldn't they want it? They're in trouble, aren't they? This is a way out for them.'

Geoffrey didn't often have reason to be grateful to the twins, but when Sue began to choke on a fishbone he almost thanked her for the diversion. 'Poor old Sub-two,' he comforted.

'I wish you wouldn't call her that,' Winifred scolded.

'Tell you what, Mother, if they stop calling Kay Lilibet, I'll stop calling them Sub.'

By the time the meal was over Geoffrey had revised his estimate of how long he could bear to live with his parents. Two days was his current reckoning, at the most.

'Good to have you back, old man,' Lionel beamed when, as was the custom, father and son retreated to the study for a nightcap. 'What'll it be? I've an excellent whisky. Single malt.'

'Whatever you're having, Dad, thanks.'

'So,' Lionel began, when they were settled in their chairs, 'married life up to your expectations?'

Geoffrey grinned.

'Good show.'

'And what about you, Dad? Keeping busy?'

Lionel stretched out his legs and rested his feet on the fender, a gesture which used to unnerve Geoffrey when he was younger. Father and son talks which began in this relaxed fashion almost always ended badly. 'Actually, I've just landed a corker of a brief,' Lionel confided. 'You know Richie Palin? Well, unbelievable as it may sound, the poor bastard's being done by the Serious Fraud Squad. According to them he's been shipping large amounts of illegal money out of the country. Now Richie's no boy scout, as we both know, but you can take it from me he'd never do anything so stupid.'

Geoffrey nodded, though more to encourage his father than to indicate agreement. His opinion of Richie Palin was not one he was willing to share.

'Want to hear how I'm going to handle the case?' Lionel asked.

Geoffrey, listening to his father's voice, tried to imagine the conversation his mother and Kay would be having in the kitchen. What did women talk about when they were on their own? He simply couldn't imagine.

'It's all there in the documents,' Lionel concluded.

'Sounds pretty water-tight, I agree.'

'So, twelve-thirty all right with you?'

'What for?'
'Tomorrow. Lunch at the club.'
'I'm not sure, Dad. Kay and I were . . .'
'It was Bunce Goodbody's idea. Break the ice. You know.'
'But I don't start work till January the 20th.'
'Never too soon to make a good impression.'

Geoffrey bit back the reply he'd have liked to make. He should tell his father the truth, shouldn't he? That this job with Goodbody and Sutch was not a career move, but simply a way of earning money. 'Kay and I are taking off at the end of the year.' That's what he should be telling his father. But when he thought of the effect this revelation would have, he balked. Better to keep his own counsel; play along, for the time being. He could always present the idea later, as if it had just cropped up.

'Kay and I were going to go flat-hunting,' he said, 'but I guess . . .'
'They do an excellent silverside on a Tuesday.'
'Twelve-thirty, you say?'
'Kay can potter round with Winifred. Give them a chance to get to know each other.'
'She'll want to look at flats. She's marked a couple already in the paper.'

His father jerked his legs back from the fender. 'Ready for a second?' he asked, indicating his own empty glass.
'No, thanks, Dad.'
'Well, since varsity didn't make a drinker of you, maybe marriage will. And while I'm on the subject,' he continued, from the other side of the room, 'there's no need to look for a flat. You can have Sunnydell.'
'It's let, isn't it?'
'Not anymore. Tenants moved out at Christmas.'
'You'll find someone else.'
'I'm offering it to *you*, Geoff. I won't charge you rent. So long as you pay the rates, and keep the place in order.'
'That's generous of you, Dad, but I think we'd prefer to find our own place. Thanks all the same.'
'You won't find anywhere to match Sunnydell. Not on what you'll be earning.'
'It won't be just me. Kay'll be working too.'
Lionel grinned over his shoulder. 'Not for long, I imagine.'

20

Kay was never able to pinpoint the exact moment when she knew she was wasting her time, but it was somewhere around the sixth day. She'd arranged to meet Geoffrey late in the afternoon, to go and look at a flat on the North Shore. Geoffrey had been tied up in the earlier part of the day, arranging various memberships – Law Society, Public Library, Chamber Music Society, some ski club he was keen to be admitted to. Kay had spent an exquisitely boring morning being lectured on the value, historic and monetary, of her mother-in-law's collection of china: a pair of Dresden vases, a Wedgwood tea set, a Royal Doulton dinner setting for twenty, assorted condiment containers from Delft, a copy of a Meissen shepherdess. 'You should take up a hobby too, Elizabeth,' Winifred had advised. 'You'll find you'll need something, later on.'

The drive across the bridge to the North Shore was punctuated by Geoffrey's account of his day's activities, and Kay's exclamations of delight the further they travelled from Remuera. But the flat, when they eventually located it, was not to Geoffrey's liking. It was shabby. It was over-priced. The drive in and out of the city would make the day too long.

'But it's only for a few months,' Kay protested. 'And we can soon make it nice. A coat of paint, and you won't recognise it.'

The journey back took place in silence. 'You know something,' Kay said, as the Union Jack fluttered into view, 'I don't think you want to find a flat at all. I think you want to stay here, with your parents.'

'Don't be ridiculous!'

'Why are you always so critical then? We must have looked at over twenty places. They're not going to get any better.'

'Can we talk about this later?'

'After your bedtime chat with your father, you mean?'

'Aunt Pauline's coming to dinner.'

Kay plunged her index finger into her mouth. She'd been wrestling with the urge to chew its broken nail all day. 'Who's Aunt Pauline?' she asked sulkily.

'My father's sister. I've told you about her. Actually she's his only relative apart from us.'

'The lady who keeps birds.'

'You'll like her, Kay. She's not like the rest of us.'

Geoffrey was right. The moment she was introduced to Pauline – small, dark, dressed in slacks and a man's jersey – Kay's humour improved. Over drinks and then dinner Pauline chatted happily, about her birds mainly, while Winifred sighed and yawned, and Lionel nodded dutifully, and refilled his glass.

'Hardly a day goes by without my finding a wounded creature to care for,' Pauline informed Kay, in her gravelly voice. 'Wax eyes, tits, sea birds, fantails, whiteheads. I even had a morepork for a while. Till his wing mended. People keep bringing them to me, you see. One old man brought me a cat with a sparrow in its mouth. He seemed to think I'd be able to persuade the wretched moggy to let go of it.'

'Was the sparrow dead?'

'Of shock, poor darling. I told the man he should keep his cat locked up in future.'

'That's cruel,' Sue piped.

'Not as cruel as killing,' Pauline answered serenely.

By the time the meal was over Kay knew all about the habits of the kereru, New Zealand's native pigeon, and why it was prized as a delicacy by the Maori. 'Lives on a diet of berries and leaves, you see,' Pauline had recounted. 'Makes for very tender flesh.'

No sooner was Pauline out of the room than Winifred, with Kay as audience, launched into a litany of complaint. Retreating to the bathroom was the coward's way out, but Kay had come to rely on it as a technique to avoid argument. If it weren't for the fear of discovery she'd have hidden a sherry bottle in the cupboard by now.

Later, in bed, Kay returned to the subject of the flat on the North Shore.

'OK,' Geoffrey conceded. 'We'll look at it again tomorrow. Now, can we please go to sleep?'

But when Kay phoned next morning, the flat had gone.

'Never mind,' Geoffrey comforted, 'we'll find something today, I promise. First decent place we see.'

At the end of the day he took her to see Sunnydell. 'I know, I know,' he acknowledged, when she protested, 'but the places we've seen today have been the dregs. I just thought . . .'

'So your father has an income from this as well as from his practice?'

'It's not against the law, Kay.'

'I can see why you brought me here. It's lovely.'

'We'd have it rent free. Did I say that? Imagine the money we'd save.'

'Is that why your father's offering it to us? So we can save money?'

'I think he just wants to help.'

'How would you describe it?' Kay asked, as she moved from sitting room to verandah. 'It's not a typical New Zealand house, is it?'

'It's a colonial cottage. Dates from the 1860s. Dad bought it to stop it being pulled down.'

'Very philanthropic.'

'He reckons places like this'll be worth a fortune one day.'

Kay moved her hand up to her head and tested the spots she suspected would one day be bald. Her terror of losing her hair was equal, at this moment, to her fear that if she said yes to this cottage – to its cosy living room with open fireplace and wall-lights shaped like lanterns, to its lacey bedroom overlooking the garden, to its tiny, shell-pink bathroom, and its kitchen, with scrubbed wooden bench and cupboards made of kauri, the trap would spring, and she would never have a place that was hers, hers and Geoffrey's, *theirs*. She would turn imperceptibly into the kind of person her in-laws wanted her to be, dressing as Winifred dressed, cooking as she cooked, travelling only when Geoffrey's career dictated.

'No!' she said. 'Absolutely not. Tell your father, thank you but no. Why did you bring me here, Geoffrey? Did you think I'd be tempted?'

One week later Geoffrey and Kay moved into Sunnydell. Helping with the move, exclaiming with delight at the cottage's many charms, were Harold and Esme Dyer.

It's because of you I'm here, Kay thought, as she listened to her parents extoll the virtues of open fires – 'You'll save a fortune on electricity bills' – and the advantages of a shower (recently installed by Lionel) over a bath. Esme had already volunteered to embroider a cover for the fireguard. 'Mr Grieve won't mind, will he?' she'd said to her daughter. 'Something along the lines of those cottage scenes you see on chocolate boxes. You know, with roses framing the doorway.'

Kay had said what her mother wanted to hear. She had no wish to hurt her, but neither did she want to remember the visit she'd made to her parents three days ago, when the horror returned, and she understood that she'd married Geoffrey not because she loved him, though she did, she was certain, but to escape. To escape as finally and completely as her brother had.

'I've changed my mind,' she'd announced, on her return to Remuera. 'I'd like to live in Sunnydell after all.'

Geoffrey's astonished face had made her laugh.

'I know, Mum,' she said now, 'you don't have to remind me. I know how lucky I am.'

21

'Life,' Geoffrey said aloud, 'is settling into really quite a nice pattern.'

Six weeks had passed since the move to Sunnydell. Kay had landed a job at the University Library. He was cutting his teeth on some interesting industrial work. The car was running like a dream. And summer showed every sign of being neverending.

He leaned over to the radio, turned the volume up, and lit a cigarette. Kay had gone to the railway station to meet her brother. Poor fellow was off to Malaya. Well, Borneo, to be exact. To fight in one of the nastier of the world's current wars.

'The Reverend Martin Luther King was today sentenced to six weeks in gaol for his part in the recent disturbances in Marion, Alabama. The Reverend King, addressing the court, vowed to continue the fight for equal voting rights for the Negro.'

Geoffrey got up from his chair and moved into the kitchen. The newsreader's voice followed him. There was to be a further house-to-house collection for the Churchill Fund Appeal. The amount collected so far had proved disappointing. If Churchill were still alive, Geoffrey thought, as the drum of water in the kettle briefly drowned the broadcast, he'd probably be calling for universal conscription. Defending the Empire against its enemies. Showing Sukarno who's boss.

Clive, Kay's brother, would be with them two nights. Apparently he had no wish to stay with his parents. 'I've invited Mum and Dad for dinner tomorrow,' Kay had informed him, as she was leaving for the station. 'They can say their goodbyes then.'

It had struck Geoffrey as odd that a man going off to fight in a war should choose not to visit his family home, but where Kay's parents were concerned he'd learned it was better not to ask questions. Besides, the little he'd seen of Harold and Esme Dyer had convinced him there wasn't much to be gained from a closer relationship. Esme was frankly boring, and Harold reminded him of a master at school whom he'd particularly disliked: a thin, humourless man, with a receding chin; a dead ringer for Kay's father.

'Russia has again called on the United States to get out of Vietnam,' the voice from the sitting room announced. 'According to Tass news agency, Moscow has issued its severest warning so far. Unless American bombing of North Vietnam ceases forthwith, the world will be faced with the prospect of global warfare.'

Geoffrey, coffee mug in hand, returned to the sitting room. He should be doing something about Vietnam. If he were still in Dunedin he'd be out on the streets at every opportunity. But there was something about this city that deadened political protest. He could imagine what Bunce Goodbody would have to say on the subject. Most of *his* legal battles were fought on the premise that all recalcitrant workers were either real or crypto communists.

Geoffrey didn't hear the car pull up. The first he knew was when the door opened, and the man he'd last seen vomiting into the gutter outside Wain's Hotel, marched into the room.

'You're early,' Geoffrey greeted, stubbing out his cigarette. 'Didn't expect you for half an hour or so.'

'I'll put the kettle on,' Kay volunteered. 'Darling, will you show Clive his room?'

'If you can call it that,' Geoffrey laughed. 'More like a cupboard.'

'There's sherry if you'd prefer,' Kay called over her shoulder.

'So, Sis, pretty neat set-up you've got here. I'd say you've done rather well for yourself.'

It was the next morning. Kay had taken the day off. It hadn't gone down too well, either with her employers, or with Geoffrey. 'You've only been working a month,' he'd reminded her.

'You sound just like the parents,' Kay answered her brother.

'Well, that has to be a first.'

Kay looked at the man sprawled in the opposite armchair, at his large feet and hands, and his enviable hair (cut short, but still with a recalcitrant wave), and the question she'd asked herself so many times before tunnelled out of her sub-conscious: DOES HE KNOW? She and Clive had never been good at talking. As children they'd exchanged practical information – Clive would teach her how to mend the puncture on her bicycle; or she'd instruct him in the art of forging her mother's signature to sneak a day off school – but that was more or less the extent of their communication. Perhaps, she thought now, he's as ignorant as I once was? Perhaps joining the Army was just his way of escaping the suburbs?

'What would you like to do today?' she asked. 'I'll have to be around later on to cook, but we could go somewhere if you want. Geoffrey's left me the car.'

'Decent fellow, your Geoffrey.'

'Glad you think so.'

'And you've got this place for nothing?'

'It's only for a few months.'

Clive ran his fingers over his recently shaved chin. Kay, watching him, remembered how, as a teenager, he used to lock himself in the bathroom every Saturday night, and come out smelling of after-shave and Brylcreem. Nothing's really changed, she thought. I still don't know what makes him tick.

'You don't fancy a spin out to Astley?'

'Hell, no!'

Kay laughed. 'That's a relief.'

'Wouldn't worry me if I never saw Astley again.'

When Harold and Esme arrived at Sunnydell, at six o'clock as invited, they found their son and daughter drinking on the verandah.

'Nice for some,' Harold quipped, nodding at his daughter's sherry glass.

'Mum. Dad. Grab a chair. What'll it be? Sherry? Beer?'

'You know we don't drink,' Esme replied curtly.

'Just thought I'd ask.'

'Lemonade, if you have it,' Harold instructed. 'Otherwise just water.'

'When's that nice husband of yours coming home?' Esme enquired when Kay returned with the drinks.

'He's been held up. He should be here by seven.'

With the four of them seated, conversation began to fail. This was how Kay remembered it: sitting silently at the table or round the radio, praying for the moment when she could escape to her room. What was it about her parents that froze speech? Was it because they couldn't speak to one another? Couldn't, wouldn't, didn't dare – it came to the same thing.

'Well,' she said brightly, 'this is something of a special occasion.'

'Don't see what's so special about it,' Esme protested. 'My only son going off to war.'

'Now now, Mother,' Harold soothed. 'We agreed. Remember?'

'Well, I think it's special.'

'It's a fine thing you're doing, son,' Harold stated solemnly. 'Your mother and I are proud of you.'

'What time . . . ?'

'Plane leaves at eight. You can wave a tablecloth, Mum. We fly out over Astley.'

'Another beer, Clive?'

'Wouldn't say no.'

In the kitchen Kay checked the meat roasting in the oven and refilled her sherry glass. Fifteen minutes past six. Three-quarters of an hour before she could expect Geoffrey. Men must enjoy killing each other, she thought, as she made her way back to the verandah. If they didn't, war would have ceased to exist centuries ago.

This was her third sherry of the evening. A mistake. She'd expected too much of the day with Clive, that was the trouble. The only time he'd opened up was when she asked him if he remembered Blair Wihongi, whose name had jumped out at her from a newspaper last week. Blair had been in her class at school. Now, on trial for armed robbery, he was in the headlines.

'I remember his sister,' Clive had answered. 'Beaut-looking Sheila.'

'I s'pose you're going to tell me you went out with her?'

'Not for want of trying.'
'Dad would have had something to say if you had.'
'Dad talks a load of bull.'

Geoffrey didn't get back till after eight. By that time the meal was ruined.

'You shouldn't have waited,' he whispered to Kay.

'You should have phoned,' she snapped back.

Listening to her mother's careful vowels, watching the way her head bobbed whenever Geoffrey spoke, Kay felt the old sense of shame well up inside her. She wished she could recover her unquestioning love for her mother, but ever since the night when the truth of her world was revealed to her she'd been unable to rid herself of the thought that her mother was an accomplice. An unwilling one, possibly, but an accomplice nonetheless.

'We ought to be going, Mother,' her father said when the ruined meal was over.

'So soon?' Geoffrey protested.

'Early start tomorrow.'

'Hope the roads are clear for you,' Geoffrey said, getting up a shade too eagerly, Kay thought, from his chair. 'There was a snarl-up near the new motorway extension on my way back tonight. It's the reason I was late. A petrol truck had broken down. Your people couldn't get through, Harold.'

'Ah, well, that's progress for you.'

The farewells were awkward. Neither Clive nor his parents was equal to the occasion.

'Is everything that goes wrong in the world to do with communication?' Kay asked Geoffrey, as they were getting ready for bed. 'Is that why we're fighting the Indonesians? Is that why the Americans won't get out of Vietnam? You're the lawyer. You tell me. Don't people want to understand each other? Or is it that they can't? Even if they try, they just can't.'

Geoffrey put on his owl face. She knew why he was doing it. It was impossible to be angry with him when he looked like that. 'Come here,' he said.

'You won't want me,' she answered.

'Wanna bet?'

'I've got my period.'
'Damn.'
'You can't sleep in the spare room. Clive's there.'
'It doesn't matter.'
'But it does. You practically fall out of bed when we have to share. You're so anxous not to touch me.'
'I don't want to disturb you, that's all.'
'Having my period doesn't make me an invalid, Geoffrey.'
'Let's not talk about it, darling. It's late.'

22

With the coming of winter the pattern of Kay and Geoffrey's life began to change. Instead of trips to the beach there were movies and dinners and parties, at some of which they encountered marijuana.

'You try it,' Kay urged her husband the first time they were offered a joint. 'I don't smoke.'

'It's illegal,' Geoffrey whispered. He didn't want to be overheard. Dave de Vere, who was offering the joint, was his oldest friend. Dave had always been a bit of a pioneer.

'You've done illegal things before,' Kay reminded him. 'Didn't you tell me you broke into a council meeting once? That must have been illegal.'

Geoffrey took off his glasses and rubbed his eyes. It was so dark he could barely see his own hand, let alone identify the shadowy figures circling around him. The record Dave had put on was an old one: 'I'm in the Mood for Love'.

'Breaking a law in the name of a higher, moral law is not the same as breaking a law in the pursuit of pleasure,' Geoffrey declared.

Kay let out a snort of laughter. 'Darling, you're a scream,' she exclaimed. 'Look around you. This isn't a courtroom.'

So Geoffrey smoked his first joint, and pronounced it very pleasant, and he and Kay danced with their arms wrapped round each other, safe in the knowledge that love, for them, was not a question of mood.

Towards the middle of the winter Geoffrey took up skiing. He was uneasy leaving Kay behind for whole weekends at a time, but she was adamant in her refusal to accompany him. Each time he returned and asked her what she'd been doing, her answers failed to satisfy. She'd been to a concert in the Town Hall. She'd read the whole of *Crime and Punishment*. She'd gone for a five-hour walk along the waterfront. Then, returning late one Sunday evening, she told him she'd joined the University Peace Group.

'You've done what?'

'You should join too. You're a graduate.'

'I'm not a pacifist, Kay.'

'Neither are most of the members. It's specific wars they're against. Vietnam principally, but Malaya as well, and Cyprus.'

'Quite the little United Nations.'

Geoffrey knew he was reacting badly, but he couldn't help it. The weekend had been a disaster. Hardly any snow, and Trixie de Vere flirting too openly for comfort. Not that he didn't fancy her, any man with eyes in his head would, but Dave was his friend, for God's sake. Kay should have come with him. Things like that didn't happen when you had your wife along.

To cap it all, he'd almost had an accident on the ski tow. The woman ahead of him had come to grief, but he was so busy looking round he didn't see her. By the time he heard the chap behind shouting a warning, it was almost too late. 'I'd get my ears tested if I were you, mate,' the chap advised when they'd made it safely to the top. 'I was yelling my bloody head off.'

'What's the matter with you?' Kay asked now. 'I thought you'd be pleased. You were the one who got me protesting in the first place, remember?'

'I'm sorry, darling. It's just that I think you need to choose your forum.'

'And what would that be? The Labour Party? The Methodist Church? They're against the war too, you know.'

'You're right,' Geoffrey conceded. 'I've been feeling guilty about it, if you must know. I could see myself turning into an armchair protester.'

To his relief, Kay laughed. She didn't want to quarrel any more than he did.

'Tell you what,' he said, 'we'll go to the next meeting together.

Give me a chance to vent my spleen about the French. You know they're planning to explode a hydrogen bomb in the Pacific? When I think of those bastards fouling up our ocean . . .'

But when the next meeting happened, Geoffrey had to work late. When Kay got back to Sunnydell she found him lying on the sofa, listening to *La Bohème*.

'Come here,' he called out softly. 'Don't say anything,' he urged, as she crouched beside him. 'I just want to hold you.'

Our world, Kay decided, is a mirror reflecting back the image others have of us. She was sitting with Geoffrey by the fire. It was rare for them to have an evening together. Either she was working the late shift at the Library, or Geoffrey was back in the office preparing a case. Some days they spent no more than a few minutes together.

People *like* us, Kay acknowledged, returning to her line of thought. We get more invitations than we can cope with. So why do I feel like tearing all my clothes off and running, screaming, down the street?

'What do you mean, you're only in Auckland temporarily?' people would react when she revealed their travel plans. 'Geoffrey's never said anything.'

'You know,' he said now, frowning at her over the edge of his *Law Review*, 'I don't think you should smoke pot anymore. You didn't sleep a wink after that last party of Dave's.'

'What's brought this on?'

'Just thinking aloud.'

Kay chewed the corner of her thumb. Should she say what was on *her* mind? She'd been waiting for the right moment for days now. 'Geoff?'

'Yep?'

'When are we going to make our bookings?'

'What bookings?'

'For England. We've got enough saved. If we leave it much longer we'll . . .'

'Have you any idea what it costs to live over there?' Geoffrey interrupted crossly.

Kay shook her head. That wasn't the point. The point was . . .

'I know what you're going to say. We'll get jobs. Any old

job. But what you don't appreciate is the miserable pittance we'll earn.'
'So you don't think we've saved enough?'
'What?'
'Geoffrey!'
'Sorry. Can you repeat . . . ?'
'You never seem to hear me these days.'
'It's wax. I need to get my ears syringed.'
'Thought you said it was an old rugby injury.'
'That's what causes the wax.'

One week later Kay was arrested. The occasion was a sit-in at the United States Consulate to protest New Zealand's involvement in the war in Vietnam. The long struggle of the Labour Party to keep Kiwi troops out had failed. A Battery unit from the 16th Field Regiment was already on its way. Prime Minister Holyoake, echoing the sentiments of what was still the majority, announced the decision with the words, 'New Zealanders hide their heads in the sand if they believe they can help Malaysia and leave others to worry about Vietnam.'

For Kay there was never any doubt. Not with a brother in the Army. When the Peace Group called for volunteers, she was the first to raise her hand. Where there *was* doubt, was when she tried to explain, to herself, and later to Geoffrey, why she didn't tell him what she was doing.

Otherwise she had no regrets. The insults that were hurled at her as she carried her placard ('No New Zealand Guns. No New Zealand Sons') only strengthened her conviction that what she was doing was necessary, and right.

'Geoff, sorry to disturb you at the office . . . No, no, I'm fine. It's just . . . Look, I'm at the Central Police Station. Can you come and get me? . . . No, there hasn't been an accident . . . No, I'm fine, really. I've been arrested.'

The best thing to do, Kay decided, while waiting for Geoffrey, is apologise. He's been looking so washed out lately. I'll tell him I'm sorry. Explain I didn't want to worry him, and miss the next couple of meetings. We've made our point anyway. It'll be in the papers.

But publicity, Kay quickly realised, was the last thing Geoffrey wanted. 'You know, you amaze me, Kay,' he said, as they drove in angry mood back to Sunnydell. 'Sometimes I think you're two people.'

'What's that supposed to mean?'

'Doing something like this behind my back.'

'I've explained that. And I've said I'm sorry.'

'Do you want notoriety, is that it? Is the life we live not exciting enough for you?'

'I wasn't protesting about our life,' Kay retorted. 'Anyway, they're not pressing charges. My name may not even get mentioned.'

But it did. And there were repercussions. Lionel, struggling to keep his temper, called her 'misguided', and warned her to steer clear of political activity in the future. 'You young people think you know everything,' he complained tetchily. Winifred, echoing her husband, accused her of being 'unladylike'. 'What does your mother think?' she pouted. 'Really, Elizabeth, it's so undignified. That could have been you in that awful photograph.'

Nor was that the end of it. At the Library she was told, if she ever lied again (she'd told Reg Lane, her boss, she had a dentist's appointment) she would be asked to leave. 'Your political opinions are your own business,' Reg fumed, 'but what goes on in library hours is *my* concern. If you must protest, do so in your own time.'

So Kay stayed away from the Peace Group, and went to the pictures with Geoffrey instead. They saw *Zorba the Greek* and *Pillow Talk*, *Tom Jones* and *Doctor in Distress*. They watched, without comment, the newsreels which preceded the main features; gazing with disbelief on the scene in New York when 4,000 protesters burned their draft cards; averting their eyes when a peaceful demonstration in Alabama was broken up with tear gas; gasping with horror when 10,000 National Guardsmen charged rioters in Los Angeles; weeping silently as women and children fled their burning villages in Vietnam.

Geoffrey promised to come home earlier in the evenings. Kay promised to be a better wife. Every Sunday they had lunch with Lionel and Winifred, where the talk, when it ranged beyond the personal, centred on the performance of the Springbok rugby team, currently touring New Zealand.

'What do you think?' Geoffrey asked, on the way back from what he considered a particularly mellow lunch. 'Shall we have a party? It's our turn.'

'You just want a chance to flirt with Trixie,' Kay teased.

'Ah, so you've noticed.'

'So long as you don't expect me to flirt with Dave.'

'Poor old Dave. Not exactly God's gift, is he? Beats me how he ever landed a doll like Trixie.'

'Oh, that's easily explained, darling. She's come up in the world. Like me.'

23

By the end of the year Kay had decided on just the one name for Auckland: City of Traps.

'I'm sorry, darling,' Geoffrey said when she challenged him, again, to set the date for their trip to England. 'I can't think about it right now. This case I'm working on is an absolute pig.'

'The man who was injured?'

'Blinded. By a shower of flying metal. Horrible. Absolutely horrible. But an accident, I'm sure of it. The employers are not liable.'

'If I'd thought, when I first met you, that one day you'd be acting for employers against workers . . .'

'Don't be naive, Kay. This isn't communist China, where all workers are heroes by definition. Employers have rights too, you know.'

Kay, clutching her glass of sherry, was tempted to hurl its contents at her preoccupied husband. In four days' time it would be Christmas. Everything had been arranged. Christmas Day with the Grieves. Boxing Day with her parents. The prospect was almost too horrible to contemplate.

'I can get you all the pot you want,' Dave had said to her at his last party. 'Just say the word.'

For Geoffrey, the thought of Christmas and Boxing Day, while hardly calculated to increase his pulse rate, aroused no particular anxiety. He was more practised than Kay at navigating the hazards of Grieve family gatherings. Especially the kind that demanded displays of the party spirit. He knew how to pacify his mother when she was becoming dangerous; and how to flatter his father when he was becoming bored. The twins he could manage with his hands tied behind his back. Deflection was the key where they were concerned. They were selfish little brats. They weren't interested in anyone but themselves. All they wanted from him were salacious titbits about his marriage.

But he *was* anxious about Kay. Ever since her resignation from the Peace Group (he assumed she had resigned: the subject was never mentioned) she'd been at a loose end. She read avidly, and went to concerts with a Polish woman she'd met at the Library, but she was restless, anyone could see that. It had even begun to affect their sex life. Except for those occasions when they'd been to a party, and she was particularly mellow, he'd observed what he could only describe as signs of impatience. She never refused him. She wasn't one of those women who claimed to have a more or less permanent headache. But she wasn't the sexy girl he'd proposed to on the beach either.

Twice, in recent weeks, he'd found her wandering through the house in the dead of night. Since she didn't respond when he called out to her he assumed she was sleep walking. 'I used to sleep walk as a child,' she told him when he questioned her about it, 'but never since, so far as I know.'

He was worried on another account too. This obsession of hers with going to England: how could he be sure it came from a genuine interest in travel, and not, as he suspected, from the very restlessness he'd been observing? He didn't deny that they'd planned to go. Nor was he ready yet to say they *weren't* going. So far as he was concerned the trip was still on, but only when he was satisfied as to Kay's motives.

Not for the first time Geoffrey found himself comparing his wife, unfavourably, to Daisy Mountford.

'Don't you think you've had enough?' he said, seeing Kay head for the sherry bottle.

'No.'

Geoffrey glanced at his watch. Almost time for the BBC news. He leaned over to the radio and turned the dial. 'The war in Vietnam,' he heard, 'is not a war in the usual sense, but a series of violent actions, some of them like Al Capone gang raids, some like frontier skirmishes in the Indian wars, others like savage encounters . . .'

He switched it off irritably.

'It only takes two sherries,' Kay had said the other day.

'What does?'

'To get that feeling.'

'What feeling's that?'

'Geoffrey!'

'Sorry, sweetheart. I heard most of what you said.'

'Aunt Pauline would approve. I bet she wishes she was a bird sometimes.'

'Why do you want to be a bird?'

'Why do you think?'

24

Astley, as the crow flies, is not much more than ten miles from Remuera, but the journey, through mostly dreary suburbs, took Kay and Geoffrey the best part of an hour. Afflicted with an unexpected nervousness, Geoffrey (incredible as it now seemed, this was his first visit to Kay's home) kept up a running commentary for most of the way. The ancient volcanic hills, towards which they were headed, prompted him to speculate about Auckland's fiery past, and when, rather than if, molten rock would again be hurled into the sky, and lava flow through suburban valleys.

'I thought they were extinct,' Kay argued.

'Dormant. It's not the same thing.'

When he'd done with volcanoes, he turned his attention to the harbour. 'People prefer the Waitemata,' he remarked, 'but give me the Manukau any day. I *like* mangrove swamps.'

'You're a romantic,' Kay accused,' with a very poor sense of smell.'

'The other thing I like,' Geoffrey said, as they climbed out of New Lynn and headed for Titirangi, 'is the fact that this part of Auckland was populated by working people. That bloke your suburb's named after – Theodore Astley – he started out as a bushman.'

'Thought he was a mill owner?'

'From Bushman to Mill Owner in One Generation! Auckland Man Astounds World!'

Kay laughed. 'How come you know so much?' she asked.

'Don't you ever wonder about the past?'

'Not if I can help it.'

Geoffrey frowned at his wife. It annoyed him when she was being enigmatic. 'It wasn't just the English who came here,' he went on. 'There were Irish, Welsh, Scots, Dalmatians, Germans, Italians. Anyone determined enough to carve a living out of the bush.'

'You sound like my Social Studies teacher.'

'Imagine how they must have felt. Ferried from their ships by tattooed Maoris in canoes. Nothing but bush and mangroves everywhere they looked.'

'I used to work for a German family,' Kay surprised him by saying. 'Well, they were Austrian actually. If you can call fifth-generation Kiwis Austrian.'

'You never told me.'

'I did. Lassmann's Vineyard. Remember?'

'Lassmann's . . .'

'I worked there the summer before we met.'

For the last part of the journey Geoffrey was silent. It was Kay who was noticing things now. Not that she said much. Something about an abandoned graveyard; and a brief exclamation when they passed a neglected wayside shrine.

'Astley, Gateway to the Secondhand Car of your Dreams!' Geoffrey declaimed, as they free-wheeled down the hill.

Kay's laugh almost cured him of his nervousness.

'"Kauri Avenue",' he read. 'That's yours, isn't it?'

'It's the cream house on the left. With the AA van in the drive.'

Geoffrey glanced at his watch. 'Twelve minutes late. Not bad.'

'You know there'll be nothing to drink.'

Geoffrey pulled the car up at the kerb. 'We had more than enough yesterday,' he reminded her.

As he walked up the path he realised the house and garden were exactly as he'd imagined them. Kay hadn't exaggerated any of it. Not a blade of grass out of place.

His mother-in-law was waiting at the door. When he saw her fingers flutter nervously to her hair it occurred to him that that might be where Kay got her mannerism from. Women, he'd read somewhere, were supposed to be obsessed with their hair.

'Welcome, welcome,' Esme gushed. 'Happy Christmas. Happy Boxing Day, I suppose I should say. Come in, come in . . . Your father's waiting,' she said sternly to Kay.

Inside, Geoffrey encountered the same stifling tidiness. The sitting room had the appearance of an exhibit in a museum. A floral sofa with symmetrically arranged cushions: matching floral armchairs; a glass cabinet full of silver spoons and china ornaments, marshalled neatly into rows; a vile orange fireplace, whose function had been usurped by a three-bar electric heater, chosen, Geoffrey assumed, for its guarantee of cleanliness. The only picture was a painting on black velvet of a woman in a blue dress. Geoffrey had used it once in a capping sketch, to symbolise suburban life.

He was no sooner seated than Kay and her mother disappeared. This was his father-in-law's cue to launch an attack on the latest moves to isolate South Africa. Geoffrey listened to his fulsome praise of Verwoerd, and the doctrine of white supremacy, but refused to be drawn into an argument. Words were wasted on men like Harold Dyer.

When Kay came back to announce that lunch was served, Geoffrey flashed her a sympathetic smile. He'd never really tried to imagine her childhood before. Now he felt guilty about his lack of curiosity.

Over lunch Geoffrey tried to steer the conversation into less troubled waters, but Harold was not a man to be deflected. A friendly enquiry about Clive led to another rant, this time about 'slant-eyed' communists. Geoffrey, struggling with his shredded lettuce, avoided Kay's eye. Yesterday may have been a trial for *her*, but at least the food was good. He hated to think what would follow the lettuce and mashed potato. Custard and prunes?

At last the ordeal was over. 'Fancy a trip to Piha?' Geoffrey whispered in Kay's ear, as they were taking their leave. 'There's enough of the day left.'

'What did you and Dad talk about?' Kay asked when Kauri Avenue was behind them.

'This and that,' he answered. 'Mostly he was trying to persuade me if Labour gets in at the next election, we'll be overrun by communists within the year.'

'That old chestnut.'
'In which case, he intends to shoot your mother first, then himself.'
'Good old Dad,' Kay said.

25

There was never any question as to how Kay and Geoffrey would spend New Year's Eve. They'd received six invitations in all, but the one they accepted was from Trixie and Dave.

'Actually, it's a bit of a ritual for me,' Geoffrey confessed. 'Dave and I go back a long way.'

'I know. You told me.'

'We used to spend holidays together. Our parents are friends.'

'I've never been sure what a stockbroker does exactly. Dave hates talking about his work.'

'That's because he doesn't want to give away any secrets. A good stockbroker is a man who listens, but keeps his own mouth shut. And Dave's good. The best there is. Wish I earned what he does.'

As they were dressing for the party it struck Kay it was two years almost to the hour since she and Geoffrey met. Everything about that night she remembered with absolute clarity. She could even recall what she was wearing: a short green skirt and pale blue cardigan, buttoned down the back. 'Blue and green should never be seen,' her mother would have sniped, if she'd been there. 'Now that's what I call elegant,' she'd simper, if she could see tonight's outfit. She'd register, probably unconsciously, that grey was a colour that didn't suit her daughter, but she'd guess, accurately, that the dress had come from Winifred. 'They're cast-offs,' Kay had explained when her mother commented on the additions to her wardrobe. 'Most of them don't even fit properly.'

'You know, Elizabeth, you really must stop perming your hair,' Winfred had advised some months ago. 'It's not doing it any good.'

So Kay had let the frizz grow out, and gone to Winifred's hairdresser and had it cut in the pageboy style. People said it suited her, but that didn't stop her hiding it beneath a scarf most days.

'Ready?' Geoffrey called from the sitting room. 'You look great,' he complimented, as they headed for the car. 'That's new, isn't it?'

'The latest thing,' Kay replied.

Dave and Trixie's house, The Cedars, was not featured in *Fine New Zealand Homes* for the simple reason that when the book was published it was still at the drawing-board stage. But its place in all subsequent editions was guaranteed. Built to Dave's specifications on a promontory overlooking the Waitemata, it was the kind of house that infected visitors with discontent. It wasn't that the place was flashy. Its charms were too discreet for that. But if, as a first-time visitor, you were to wander from one level to another, pausing to admire a stained-glass window here, or a piece of statuary there, wondering all the time if those rays of golden light could possibly be natural, the feeling that this was how human beings *should* live would gather strength, so that when lunch or dinner or the party was over, you would return to your own home in irritable mood, your eyes opened to its imperfections, your heart heavy with envy. Your only recourse then would be to find fault with your generous hosts. Dave's voice was too soft; his flesh too flabby. There was something spineless about the man, for all his success with money. As for Trixie, she was blonde, brassy, and one of these days, with her high-pitched giggle and her habit of embracing everyone in sight, she'd fall flat on her face.

But none of this would alter the fact that at The Cedars you could hear the clock of the future ticking. Trixie worked in television. Dave made pots of money. Both of them took risks. As their guests, you could listen to the latest Rolling Stones album on a stereo system imported from America. You could drink Australian wine, and smoke good quality pot. And if none of these things appealed, you could stand on one of three balconies and gaze across the harbour to the rising towers of the city.

The party to welcome 1966 was to be the largest Dave and Trixie had ever held.

'Who'd have thought, two years ago, that we'd be doing this?' Geoffrey said to Kay, as they drove through the warm city streets.

'So you remember?'

'Course I remember.'

'Let's dance when we get there. Let's dance together all night.'

But they were no sooner through the door than Trixie claimed Geoffrey as *her* partner. 'You don't mind, do you, Kay?' she pouted. 'You have him all week.'

'Be my guest,' Kay grinned.

'What d'ya think of the outfit?' Trixie mouthed over Geoffrey's shoulder. 'Dave dared me to wear it.'

Kay signalled her approval. Trixie's white mini dress was made of organdie. The fact that she was wearing no underwear was plain for all to see. 'I gave up wearing knickers when I married Dave,' she'd confided to Kay. 'You've no idea what a turn-on it is.'

'You look as if you could do with something to make you fly,' a voice whispered in Kay's ear.

Kay smiled. 'Dave,' she said.

'Follow me,' he ordered.

He led her up a flight of stairs to the room he called his 'eerie'. Kay had been here several times before. It was where he kept his supply of dope, but that wasn't the only reason she followed him. The eerie was where she and Dave talked. That she looked forward to these conversations was something she still found surprising. Dave, when she first met him, had seemed an unlikely candidate for an exchange of confidences. But ever since she'd told him about her habit of imagining she was a bird, and he'd looked, not alarmed, like Geoffrey, but interested, she'd known she could trust him.

'Close your eyes,' she'd instructed when he asked her how it felt. 'Feel the air lift your wings, up, up above the ground. See the sky filled with creatures like yourself, wheeling in harmony with one another. Watch the city dwindle into insignificance. Who can see you now? No one. No one but God.'

Gradually a pattern had been established. Kay and Dave would retreat to the eerie, while Geoffrey and Trixie listened to records. Sometimes the four of them climbed the stairs to share a joint, but mostly it was just Kay and Dave.

One night, curled up on the window seat, savouring a delicious feeling of serenity, Kay saw a falling star. It seemed to hover above her head for several seconds, before plummeting to earth. 'Did you see that, Dave, did you see it?' she called out. 'Are there mermaids in heaven?'

'Mermaids?'

'I've just seen one. Well, it was a star really, but it had a tail like a mermaid. It left a trail of phosphorescence behind it. Look, you can see where it's been. Above those trees. Look!'

'Sounds to me like a comet.'

'It was a mermaid.'

Dave laughed. 'You've been reading about Ikeya-Seki.'

'Who's he?'

'Not he. It. A comet. Due to pass over New Zealand any day now. Sounds like you've just given yourself a sneak preview.'

But Kay didn't want an explanation. She preferred her falling star.

'Happy New Year, Kay,' Dave said now. 'Hey! We should be passing this round.' He waved the joint at her. 'New Year's Eve and all that.'

'I like it up here,' Kay said.

'Me too.'

'Why do you do it, Dave? It's not really your scene.'

'Smoking?'

'Parties. You and Trixie seem to have them every second week. I bet you don't know who half those people are down there.'

'Trixie knows who they are. She keeps a little black book. Names, addresses, phone numbers, occupations. She even writes down her opinions. This person is fun, that one's a dead loss, another is boring but knows a lot of interesting people so has to be put up with. You're in there. "Kay Dyer, married to the gorgeous Geoffrey", it says. I sneaked a look.'

'Is that all it says?'

'Can't remember.'

'Liar!'

'Oh, well . . .' Dave pulled a face. 'You probably know anyway. She doesn't like you much. Thinks you're stand-offish.'

Kay drew the smoke deep into her lungs. Ah, but it was good. Pure goodness streaming through her veins. 'What Trixie means,' she remarked lazily, 'is that I'm not good enough for Geoffrey.'

The minutes ticked away in companionable silence. Kay trailed her fingers through her hair, and marvelled at its luxuriance. When had it grown so thick? And Dave. Where had he learned to smile like that? People dismissed him as unattractive, but they were wrong, he was beautiful. His head was bathed in a soft pink light.

'*Hello Dolly*,' he announced suddenly.

'What?'

'That's what's playing right now, as we speak, in Saigon. *Hello Dolly*.'

'The film.'

'The musical. Entertaining the troops.'

Kay giggled.

'D'you know what I think? I think it's great. Just the thing to cheer a guy after a hard day in the jungle. Get the napalm out from under his fingernails. And you know what else? I don't think anyone makes any difference to anything. It's like that comet. Inevitable. Preordained. Take Trixie now. Great little woman, bundle of energy, and clever, oh my God, yes, not to be underestimated, my Trixie. Don't be taken in by the blonde curls and the squeaky voice. You're not taken in, are you, Kay? Good. Didn't think you were. But Trixie, you see, Trixie . . .'

'Are you all right, Dave?'

'Inevitable,' he muttered.

'What did you mean about making a difference?'

'Ah . . .' Dave swung his legs over the side of his chair. 'Funny thing that,' he answered. 'Bit of a laugh all round really. Money. That's what it's about. I've always wanted it, you know. Usual reasons. Expect Billy Bunter wanted it too, poor sod. Ha ha! Kay, you're not laughing.'

'I'm listening.'

'Thing is, thing was, I didn't want money for all this' – he flapped his hand, as if swatting a fly – 'I wanted to make a difference.'

'Who to?'

'Not who, what. Or do I mean, where? I wanted to make a difference to the world.'

Kay scratched her arm vigorously. Had she been bitten? There were no marks that she could see.

'What I wanted to do, you see, Kay, was charter a yacht and sail up to French Polynesia and show those bastards what I thought of their bloody hydrogen bomb. Now don't you think that's funny? Trixie did. She laughed like a drain.'

After that the conversation seemed to fizzle out. Later, when she tried to piece the evening together, Kay remembered feeling itchy, and Dave staring for a long time at his watch before announcing that it was nearly midnight. She imagined she must have followed him down the stairs because the next thing she recalled was standing on the balcony that led off the living room, protecting her ears from a prolonged burst of shouting. 1966 had arrived.

The realisation brought her thudding back to earth. She must find Geoffrey. Starting the year without him could bring bad luck.

She tried the living room first, but the crush was so great she was forced out into the hall. From there she was swept along on a tide of singing people till, in desperation, she pushed open a door and found herself in a bedroom. Alone, she assumed, till she heard Trixie giggle in the dark. Unmistakable that giggle. As unmistakable as Geoffrey's English vowels, which she heard next.

'There's someone in the room,' he whispered.

'Happy New Year, darling,' Kay said. 'Happy New Year, Trixie. It's a great party.'

26

To say that life returned to normal after New Year's Eve would be to describe only the surface of things. Geoffrey went back to his office. Kay went back to the Library. Sunday lunches with Lionel and Winifred were resumed as soon as the sailing season was over. But between Geoffrey and Kay there was now an unacknowledged conspiracy of silence.

Kay had accepted Geoffrey's assurance that nothing other than cuddling had taken place in that bedroom. It might even have been true. Geoffrey was miserable enough for her to *want* it to be true. So she forgave him that same night, and told him nothing had changed, and admitted, because he seemed to need it, that yes, she was jealous, not anymore, not now that she knew it had all been harmless, but at the time, standing in that doorway, listening to her husband whispering to another woman, yes, of course she was jealous, she wanted to strangle Trixie de Vere.

But words weren't enough. Geoffrey's misery went too deep. So she undressed him, and then herself, and did things to him that she'd only ever read about, and cried out when he cried out, and pledged her love again. Only later, when he was peacefully asleep in her arms, did she let herself remember. It wasn't jealousy she'd felt, it was something altogether more shameful. She'd felt her wings lift, as first the room, then the house, then the city, sank into the earth beneath her.

How could she tell him these things? She didn't understand them herself. How could she expect him to?

Geoffrey's part in the conspiracy of silence, a source of guilt and anguish over the following weeks, was, he convinced himself, every time he felt tempted to confess, something only a man could understand. Five more minutes in that bed and he'd have been guilty of adultery. He could blame Trixie, of course. She'd made all the running. But he was more inclined to put the blame on the *zeitgeist*, the spirit of the times. Sex was in the air. It was in the streets, in the shops, in the coffee bars and cinemas. It was the spark that ignited dinner conversation and fuelled, more effectively than alcohol, the regular round of parties. Girls wore skirts that barely covered their thighs. Their eyes shone out of painted circles. Their lips tasted of peppermint or cherries. They laughed at dirty jokes. They even told them. Little wonder he thought of Trixie in ways that constituted a betrayal of both wife and friend. Little wonder, when he thought of Daisy Mountford these days, it was to imagine her in bed with a stranger who, when he turned his head, looked just like him.

None of it had anything to do with love.

So Geoffrey and Kay kept their thoughts to themselves, and embarked on a second honeymoon. The only obvious source of tension between them was the question, regularly raised by Kay, of when they were going to England. Geoffrey felt the pressure as a pain in his gut. There were times when it even affected his sexual performance. Yet he couldn't deny Kay's right to ask. In the end he broke his own rule, and discussed the matter with his father.

'If only I could be sure,' he said when he'd explained the situation.

'Of what?'

'That it would be good for us. For Kay and me, I mean.'

'What's good for you is good for Kay,' Lionel asserted.

'That's not a very enlightened view, if I may say so, Dad.'

His father grinned. 'Don't let yourself be persuaded by all this feminist nonsense, Geoff. Women don't like it really. Not if they're honest. Friend of mine, she has a handle on these things, she spelled it out for me years ago. You'd be surprised. What women want is to be mastered. That's how it works for them. Forget equality. That's for nuns and university students.'

Geoffrey forced out a laugh. His father in bullish mood reminded him uncomfortably of Harold Dyer. What would the old boy say when he found out, as he would, that he and Kay were no longer seeing the de Veres? 'Never let a woman come between you and a buddy, son.' Something of that sort.

'Look, Geoff,' his father said now, 'it's simple really. Where do you want to live your life? Here or in England? Because that's what's at stake. If you and Kay go gallivanting off with no plan in your head but seeing the world, you can give up any idea of succeeding here. Doors close, you know. They don't stay open forever.'

It was those words that clung, like flies to fly-paper, Geoffrey thought, every time he tried to shake them loose. He'd decided long ago, in the misery of exile, that he was going to live and work in New Zealand. No half measures, no regular escapes. His children would be raised, without apology, as Kiwis. They would grow up proud of their accent and their way of life. They would neither seek, nor need, any other passport.

'You want my advice?' his father said, at the conclusion of their talk. 'Get your wife pregnant. That'll put a stop to all this nonsense. Can't travel with babies. Can't run about protesting either,' he added, for good measure.

Two weeks after that conversation Geoffrey was offered a partnership in Goodbody and Sutch. The occasion was a lunch at the Northern Club. Geoffrey, flattered to have been invited by the Senior Partner, remained unsuspecting till the moment the bombshell was dropped. Which, he persuaded himself later, was probably why he reacted as he did.

'I would be honoured to accept,' he said. No doubts, no queries, no hesitations. The words spoke themselves.

'Of course we're aware, the other partners and I, that you've been hoping to break into criminal work,' Bunce Goodbody remarked when he'd got over his own surprise. Lionel had led him to believe the boy would raise all kinds of difficulties. 'We'll discuss this, naturally, when we draw up terms, but in the meantime, if you're happy, I'd like to leave the question of your area of specialisation to one side.'

Driving back to Sunnydell at the end of that day Geoffrey easily convinced himself it would be a mistake to tell Kay right away. Things were still a little shaky between them. There was that awful scene the other night when Dave phoned and Geoffrey, instead of making the usual excuses, did what he thought Kay would want, and told him the friendship was over. Dave had been pretty cut-up, but it was nothing to the way Kay reacted. She lost no time telling him he'd behaved like a prat.

'You're very quiet,' Kay remarked, after they'd sat for some time in front of their television set, a Christmas present from Winifed and Lionel.

'I'm enjoying the programme.'

'*The Dick van Dyke Show*? I thought you hated it.'

'It's mindless. Which is just how I want to be tonight.'

'Bad day at the factory?'

'I've known worse. How was yours?'

'Chaos. It always is when the students come back.'

'No one forces you to go to work, you know. You could . . .'

'Could what?'

Geoffrey grinned. Kay was wearing a housecoat. She'd be naked underneath. 'You could stay at home and take care of me,' he said.

27

April Fool's Day. Kay had always hated it. A licence for cruelty, in her experience. Pulling a smelly fish out of her bed; spluttering from a bucket of water upturned on her head; if she didn't laugh her brother would call her a spoil-sport, and devise even more horrible ways to make her suffer. Even her father used to get in on the act, telling her a boyfriend had called when he hadn't, guffawing when she raced to the phone to call back.

But none of that compared to April Fool's Day, 1966. Only a God with a malicious sense of humour, Kay decided in retrospect, could have planned that one.

The first thing that happened was that her mother phoned. Geoffrey had already left for work. Kay wasn't due at the Library till noon.

It was rare for her mother to phone. Kay was immediately suspicious. But there was a good reason for the call. Clive was coming home. Captain Clive Dyer, he was now. He was returning from war covered in glory.

For the best part of an hour Kay wandered round the cottage, too happy and relieved even to flick a duster. Then the post arrived. When she saw Clive's handwriting she tore open the envelope, and fell on the letter inside. He was coming home all right. And he *had* been promoted to Captain. But it wasn't glory he was covered in, it was blankets.

Haven't told Mum, you know how she fusses. And the old man'll be sorry it's not a war wound. Can't you just hear him? 'Let me get this straight. A worm has burrowed into

149 •

your foot, and you're to be holed up indefinitely in hospital? Have I got that right?'

Actually, Sis, I don't mind admitting, the pain's pretty grim.

The rest of the letter Kay read through a blur of tears. When Clive was twelve he fell from a tree and broke his arm. It was a bad break, a double fracture. Kay, who'd been playing in the tree with him, yelled twice as loudly as he did. When their mother arrived on the scene, the look on her face confirmed Kay's fears. The accident was her fault.

The pages fluttered from her hand. It was the longest letter Clive had ever written to her. The house, she saw, as she looked dully around, was a mess. Geoffrey complained every day about her untidiness. She'd planned to have a clean-up before she went to work. Pleasing Geoffrey was as good a way in as any to the subject of England. 'We *have* to talk, darling,' she was going to insist. 'It's April. If we want to be in England for the summer . . .'

She slid open the french doors, and took in a long gulp of air. The canna lillies which bordered the lawn stood in bright yellow clusters against the dark green of the neighbouring bush. Geoffrey was always telling her how lucky they were, living next to a reserve. 'Means we'll never be built out,' he'd say. It puzzled her, that use of 'we'. It wasn't as if it was *their* house.

Clive would be home in three days. A special room was being prepared for him in the Auckland Hospital. Leptospirosis was a common enough disease among soldiers fighting in the jungle, but what Clive had was not conforming to the usual pattern. There was the lethargy and the nausea, but there was also, more worryingly, a persistent high fever. The army doctors couldn't say for certain whether the fever was caused by the original infection or by some subsequent contagion. What *was* known was that the level of pain was unusually high. Clive, who never winced when splinters were pulled from under his finger nails, who barely cried when his arm was crushed, had described it as 'grim'. 'Please God,' Kay begged, 'please make it go away.'

So fervent was her prayer that when the phone rang a second time she felt certain it was her mother, calling to say there'd been a mistake, she'd had a letter too, and there was no fever, and no hideous worm. Clive was fit and well. But it wasn't her mother, it was Stuart Sutch, one of the younger partners in Geoffrey's firm.

'I'm afraid I've got some bad news,' he began.

Kay's heart stopped beating. When it started again she tried to speak, but a faint click in her throat was the only sound she produced.

'Thing is, Geoffrey's been taken ill. I'm sure it's nothing serious, but he collapsed, you see, and . . .'

'When?'

'What?'

'When did he collapse?'

'Ah . . . I'm not sure. This morning some time. He was in court.'

'Collapsed. What does that mean? He faints sometimes at the sight of blood.'

'I don't think there was any blood.'

'Where is he? Can I talk to him?'

'They've taken him to Auckland Hospital.'

'Why?'

'Well, because he collapsed . . .'

'But if it was only a faint . . .'

'I think it's a little more serious than that.'

Kay took the receiver away from her ear, and stared at it as if it were the dead fish her brother had planted in her bed. Stuart's voice drifted back to her. 'Are you still there? Kay, are you all right?'

'I'm fine,' she said. 'Thank you for telling me.'

When she picked up the phone again, it was to order a taxi. While she waited for it to arrive she thought of Winifred. She should phone, shouldn't she? But there was no answer from the Grieve mansion. She tried Lionel next, but he wasn't in his office. He'd been called out, his secretary told her.

'Where to, lady?' the taxi driver asked.

'Auckland Hospital.'

'You'd have been quicker to walk.'

'Why?'

'They're tearing up the streets, haven't you noticed? It's all motorways and skyscrapers now. Might as well be living in New York.'

Kay found Geoffrey in a private room, doped in preparation for surgery. Winifred and Lionel were at his bedside.

Kay's first words were addressed to her mother-in-law. 'I tried to phone you,' she said.

Winifred's face was streaked with mascara. 'We thought you'd be at work,' she mumbled.

Lionel, who'd at least managed a smile when she arrived, glanced at his watch. 'What's keeping him?' he grumbled.

'Who?' Kay asked.

'Peter Glass. The surgeon. He's looked after Geoff before.'

Kay's eyes slid over her husband's ashen cheeks and closed eyes. Stuart was wrong. There *was* blood. Two tell-tale stains on his neck.

The nurse who'd escorted her here told her an abscess had burst in Geoffrey's ear. She hadn't been able to take it in. 'What are they going to do to him?' she asked now.

No one answered. When she put the question again Lionel turned to his wife, as if it was she who'd spoken. 'Depends how far the infection's travelled,' he said.

'Travelled?' Kay repeated. 'I don't understand.'

'If it's reached the brain or not.'

Kay laid her hand against her husband's cheek. 'Geoffrey?' she whispered. 'Can you hear me?'

'Good mind to tell Glass what caused this bloody abscess,' Lionel muttered behind her.

'You mean he's had it before?' Kay asked.

'Why don't *you* answer that, Winifred?'

Kay glanced at her mother-in-law. The look on her face was the kind her own mother would have described as 'fit to curdle milk'.

'What we have to hope for,' Lionel said, 'is that it's only the ear that's affected.'

'But he'll get better, won't he? It is just an infection?'

'Better? He'll be lucky if he has any hearing left in that ear at all.'

* * *

The operation lasted four hours. In that time Kay drank eight cups of coffee, and learned from her mother-in-law that Bunce Goodbody had phoned to tell her about Geoffrey an hour before she herself was contacted. She tried to make sense of this, but couldn't. All she could do was listen dully to Winifred, and be grateful when she was silent.

'I blame that awful school,' Winifred said when her husband was out of earshot. 'I never wanted him to go there, but Lionel insisted.'

'Geoffrey told me he was injured in a rugby game.'

'Did he?' Winifred gestured vaguely. 'That's right, yes, rugby. Awful game. So violent.'

Kay folded her hands round her cup, and stared at the treacly remains. She was not so numb as to be indifferent to the taste of the stuff the hospital served up as coffee. Since going to work at the Library she'd become something of a coffee addict. This, that she'd been drinking all afternoon, was really chicory essence, strong and black and sour-tasting. Just for a moment she was tempted to phone Dave. He ground his beans in an electric mixer then brewed them in a percolator. The smell was one of the many things she missed about The Cedars.

Winifred had started up again. Geoffrey didn't appreciate her, that was the complaint now. Sons never appreciated their mothers. They took after their fathers, who were no sooner married than they began taking their wives for granted. Not that the girls were much better, but at least they were loyal. When Lionel came home late, or not at all, as happened sometimes, they were as disgusted as she was. She just hoped, when Geoffrey had children of his own, he'd realise how much women sacrificed for their families. No one ever thought to ask her if she'd like to be doing something else with her life.

Kay listened, responding when she had to, and prayed for Lionel to come back so that the monologue would end. There was really only one person she could bear to talk to right now, and that was Sandra Grajawaska. Her friendship with Sandra had begun six months ago, over coffee at the University. Since then it had developed into a close and – for Kay at least – challenging relationship.

Geoffrey had never met Sandra. Every time Kay thought about

• Elspeth Sandys

bringing them together she hesitated, not because she feared her husband's reaction, but because she was afraid of what her new friend might say. Sandra was a 'free soul'. She was as opposed to the bourgeois life as she was to the Vietnam War. War, she maintained, like suburbia, was a product of the capitalist system. 'Not that I'm political,' she'd been careful to explain. 'Politics is dead. It's the personal life I'm talking about. The realisation of potential. We're only half alive most of the time. You, Kay, are only a quarter alive. Buried under a mountain of books all day, rushing home to hubby at night. When I look at you, do you know what I feel? Angry. You could *be* someone, really *be* someone. You have so much potential.'

What would Sandra say if she could see her now, huddled on an ugly plastic seat, listening to her mother-in-law?

'You can't just walk away,' Kay had argued. 'The people in your life *are* your life.'

'So you're happy, are you?'

'I will be,' Kay had answered.

It was after six when the surgeon came to inform them that the operation was over, and so far as he could tell at this stage, successful. 'If all goes well post-operatively, he should be in the clear within a week or ten days,' he assured them.

'And his hearing?' Lionel asked.

'Ah, well, that's not so encouraging, I'm afraid. The damage was pretty extensive. Of course there's a lot he can do. Hearing-aids are very sophisticated nowadays. But the harm had been done so far as that ear is concerned. Luckily he has around 90 per cent hearing in the other ear so he shouldn't be too handicapped.'

'*If* all goes well . . .' What am I to make of that? Kay thought. And the thing about hearing-aids. That's bad, isn't it? Winifred's mascara was running again, but her tears had no effect on Lionel. His muttered, 'Pull yourself together,' struck Kay as cruel.

'Can I see him?' she asked.

'He won't come round till the early hours,' the surgeon answered. 'I suggest you all go home and get some rest. You can come back first thing in the morning.'

28

It was taken for granted by Winifred and Lionel that Kay would spend the night with them. Kay, who felt in urgent need of a sherry, protested she had nothing with her. 'You can borrow a nightdress of mine,' Winifred said. 'And if you're worrying about your silly work, you can phone them in the morning.'

Arriving at the house Kay was surprised, and pleased, to find Pauline in residence. 'I've been telling those two little madams a few home truths,' she whispered in Kay's ear.

'I'm glad you're here,' Kay responded warmly.

They were a sombre group round the table. The latest girl engaged to help in the house had gone off to marry her boyfriend, much to Winifred's disgust. 'I'd just got her trained,' she complained bitterly. 'I had no idea there was anything else in the wind.'

On her way upstairs Kay looked in on the twins. Their unhappy faces at the table had distressed her. This family was more fragile than she'd imagined.

'OK, you two?' she enquired from the door. 'Not asleep, are you?'

'Aunt Pauline tells lies,' Belinda's muffled voice declared from under the sheets.

'Now now,' Kay protested.

'I don't want her looking after us again. We're fourteen now. We can look after ourselves.'

'Your brother's going to be all right, you know,' Kay said. 'That's what's really worrying you, isn't it?'

'Anyway, she stinks,' Belinda asserted.

'I'll see you in the morning,' Kay said.

'G'night, Lilibet,' Sue called out. 'Wish you could be here always.'

Rising early next morning, Kay found she wasn't the only one unable to sleep. Lionel was sitting on the back verandah, smoking a cigar. In the pale dawn light the smoke, drifting towards the tennis court, scrawled an indecipherable message.

'Kay, my dear,' he greeted.

'Don't get up,' she said quickly, moving to sit beside him.

'There's tea in the pot.'

'Don't suppose there's been any news?'

Lionel glanced at his watch. 'Thought I'd ring about seven,' he said.

'What's the time now?'

'Six-fifteen.'

They lapsed into an anxious silence. Not that Kay felt uncomfortable. On the contrary, her father-in-law's presence was curiously soothing. His face, she noticed, had undergone a change. Where it had been round and oddly smooth for a man his age, it was now a map of deep, interconnecting lines. She used to think he looked like Winston Churchill ('You wouldn't think that if he didn't smoke cigars,' Geoffrey had countered), but he didn't resemble anyone famous this morning. Anxiety had made him ordinary.

'Do you believe in God, Kay?' Lionel asked.

The question startled her. Apart from the odd curse, God was not a name you heard in this house.

'Yes,' she answered. 'Well, I think so. ('God?' Sandra had mocked, over a cup of cappuccino. 'If you mean the God of the Catholic Church, the church I was raised in, then I have to tell you, my innocent young friend, God is dead.') Though I don't go to church,' Kay amended lamely.

Lionel's eyes, so like Geoffrey's, held a brief smile. From the bank that rose behind the tennis court Kay could hear the faint chattering of birds.

'*I* go to church,' Lionel said. 'But I'm not sure I believe in God. I wanted to very badly at one time. But wanting, as I'm sure you've discovered by now, is no guarantee of getting.'

Kay thought better of the answer she'd been going to make. This was not the moment to tell her father-in-law how the world saw him. 'A man who gets whatever he wants, that's Lionel Grieve.'

'Forgiveness,' he said. 'That's what I was after.'

'Forgiveness for what?'

'Trouble is, how do you know when you've got it?'

Kay's instinct, at that moment, was to touch her father-in-law's hand. She even went so far as to reach out to him. But then she drew back. Perhaps when she knew what he was talking about . . .

'Nothing happened, you see,' he went on. 'No blinding light, no voice from the mountain top. Do you know the play *Hamlet*, Kay?'

'I can recite great chunks of it.'

'Then you'll know what I mean when I say I'm a bit like Polonius.'

Kay, digesting the idea, decided her father-in-law couldn't know the play very well. Polonius was a murderer. What Lionel must be thinking of was the prayer scene. He, like the usurping king, had prayed for forgiveness, but it would hardly have been for the crime of fratricide.

'"The sins of the fathers",' Lionel quoted. 'Do you believe in *that*, Kay?'

''Course not. Nobody does. If you believed in that you'd have to believe in an eye for an eye.'

'Just so. But can you imagine a better way to punish a man than through his only son? I can't.'

Kay risked a hand on her father-in-law's arm. 'I'm not sure I understand you,' she said, 'but if you're thinking Geoffrey's illness is your fault, then you're wrong. You're a much better father than most. When I think of my own . . .' She drew her hand back. Careful, she warned herself. Confessing can be catchy. 'I'll tell you something,' she said instead, 'when Geoffrey gets better I'm going to take him away for a long rest. You know we've been planning to go to England? Well, this illness clinches it. We'll go by sea. Five weeks with nothing to do but eat and sleep and read. I wouldn't be surprised if at the end of that time he finds his hearing has come back.'

• Elspeth Sandys

Lionel turned to her. The expression on his face caused her heart to miss a beat. 'Hasn't Geoff told you?' he said. 'There's no question of going to England. He's accepted a partnership.'

29

When Geoffrey opened his eyes and saw his wife staring down at him, he wanted to shout with relief. God, but she was beautiful! Those eyes, which in the nightmare he'd just woken from had looked at him with disgust, were gazing at him with so much tenderness, the urge to kiss them was overwhelming. The bad dream was fading; the dream in which she drew back from him in horror at his wounds; drew back so far he could no longer see her.

'I thought I'd lost you,' he muttered.

'Oh, darling . . .'

'It's all right, you can touch me. I won't break.'

'All these tubes . . .'

'They'll be gone soon.'

'I've been so worried, Geoff.'

'Come on, old thing. No tears. I've been lucky. It could have been much worse.'

He watched her struggle to regain control. She wasn't a crier. A few tears when her brother left for Malaya, a couple of episodes on their honeymoon, that was about the size of it. Actually, he probably had Clive to thank for her stoicism. Kay had told him about his 'cry-baby' taunts, as much a part of her childhood, apparently, as her mother's lettuce and Vegemite sandwiches.

'Are you in pain?' she asked, from behind her handkerchief.

He tried to grin, but his lips wouldn't stretch that far. His mouth felt as if it were full of sand. 'I've felt better,' he admitted.

'Your parents are here. Your father suggested I come in first. I think he thought . . .'

'Bit of a romantic, my dad.'

'We've had a long talk.'

'You and Dad?'

'This morning. He told me . . .'

'Have *I* told you how beautiful you are?' Geoffrey interrupted.

Kay's hand, which had been resting on his, shot up to her head. She was wearing the scarf he'd given her for Christmas. She had a thing about scarves. Last time he asked she told him she had over thirty.

'Because you are, you know,' he persisted. 'I don't deserve you, and that's a fact.'

'Don't be silly.'

'Listen, darling, before the parents come in . . .'

'You shouldn't be talking.'

'Lying here, I've had time to think. You know you asked me, that awful night after Dave's party, if sex was what it was all about? I've forgotten your exact words, but you asked me if I thought it was the source of everything. Of life. D'you remember?'

'Vaguely.'

'I didn't answer because I thought you were asking me about, you know, about Trixie, and I had to convince you, I was desperate, that that meant nothing, nothing at all.'

'We've been through all this, Geoff. You shouldn't be . . .'

He moved his head on the pillow. His teeth ached as if each one had been painfully drilled. There was a strange smell too. Anaesthetic probably.

'*Please*, darling, don't talk.' His wife's face hovered above him. She looked frightened. That's what he was trying to tell her, that there was nothing to be frightened about. 'Your bandage,' she whispered. 'It's . . .'

'Thing is,' he said, 'I can answer you now. This operation, God knows how, but it's made me *see*.'

'I think I should call a nurse.'

'Sex *is* what it's about. The meaning, the fountain, whatever. But not sex in the gratification sense. Whether the earth moves, all that garbage. I mean sex in the fullest sense there is. Love, loving someone. Sleeping with her. Eating with her. Talking, laughing, touching, fighting. Am I making sense? . . . What are you doing? There's no need to call anyone. I *want* to talk. It's important. Kay, listen to me. I'm talking about us. Us committed to each other, body and soul . . .'

Geoffrey stayed in hospital two and a half weeks. At the end of that time he was pronounced clear from infection. Convalescence, Kay was told, must last for at least a month. The danger of reinfection was real.

Kay, whose daily visits to the hospital had had to be extended to include time with her brother (still in pain, but beginning to respond to treatment), foresaw a difficult period ahead. She still hadn't confronted Geoffrey about the partnership. She would have done so that first day had he not made that extraordinary speech. Since then he'd been so loving, so grateful, she hadn't had the heart to accuse him. He would explain it himself, in time. He'd explain it, then he'd make it go away. A man who read the *New Statesman* did not become a partner in a commercial law firm.

In the meantime there was the problem of Geoffrey's convalescence. She was already in trouble at the Library. The day of Clive's arrival she'd phoned to say she was sick. She hadn't been believed. There'd been too many requests for changes in the roster, for hours off. Between her pale husband, with his foul-smelling bandage, and her brother with his unshaven chin, and lips flecked with saliva, she felt like a rubber band, stretched to breaking point.

'You're making a martyr of yourself,' Sandra had scoffed, last time they'd managed a coffee together. 'Why do you let them do it to you?'

If Sandra knew what she was contemplating now – the abandonment of her job – she'd give up on her in disgust.

'You better come to us,' Winifred had said to Geoffrey, in Kay's hearing. 'Your wife can't take care of you. Away at the Library all hours.'

But Geoffrey had been unexpectedly firm. 'No, thank you, Mother,' he'd said. 'Sunnydell is where I want to be.'

The day Geoffrey was to come home Kay rose early, resolved to clean the cottage from top to bottom. *Spring* cleaning, her mother called it. Well, this was autumn, but what did that matter? Clive was to be in hospital another week at least. His fever was down, but until they were certain he was free from infection he was to be kept under observation.

It was impossible, Kay saw that as she moved the sofa from its accustomed place, and looked with horror at the accumulation of cigarette butts, scraps of food, and pieces of paper, strewn across the carpet. Her schedule at the Library changed from week to week. Around that she would have to fit in the twice-daily changes of Geoffrey's dressing; the shopping, cooking, and cleaning; plus her visits to Clive. However she organised it, Geoffrey would be left alone for long stretches of the day. And that was wrong, wasn't it?

She glanced at her watch. Geoffrey wasn't due till after lunch. She'd write her letter of resignation now, and finish the cleaning later.

But the words were slow coming. She loved her job. She loved the look and feel and smell of books. Even though she had little time to read she felt surrounded by knowledge. And there was another thing. Now that she no longer had Dave to talk to she'd come to depend on her conversations with Sandra. Sandra was five years older than her, but you'd never know it to look at her. She was a tutor in the Psychology department. She dressed like a gypsy, smoked pot openly, and talked about her sex life as if it was an adventure that would go on forever. Occasionally, when Geoffrey was working late, Kay would go with her to a concert or a play. The thought of giving all that up brought on a spasm of resentment. Why should she have to? And why did she feel this tearing of loyalties, as if she must choose – Sandra or Geoffrey?

To ease her task she poured herself a tumbler of sherry. It was disgustingly early to be drinking, but this was no ordinary day. Her working life was coming to an end. As, more than likely, was the one friendship she valued in this city. If she'd been a better correspondent she could have written to Lynne or Judy: shared her troubles with friends of longer standing than Sandra. But they'd given up on her. 'This is positively my last letter till I hear from you,' Judy had written. She had a job teaching in a rural primary school. She was happy, she said. Phil Muir's name was never mentioned. As for Lynne, her letters were full of her baby son. Nothing else, it seemed, was happening in her life.

Kay was still struggling with the letter when it struck her that giving up this job didn't really matter all that much. They would still be going to England. She was certain of that. This partnership thing of Geoffrey's was an aberration. Probably something to do with his illness. He must have agreed to it just before he collapsed. He'd have told her about it otherwise. Once he was home they'd talk it through, and he'd put the whole process into reverse. He was an adventurer, Geoffrey. 'The most radical student of his generation.' He wanted to change things, not confirm the status quo.

Her optimism restored, Kay picked up the phone and informed her boss of her decision to quit. The reaction was hardly flattering. 'I see,' he responded. 'Well, we'll be sorry to lose you, of course.'

There was nothing for it then but to finish the cleaning. The sitting room first, then their bedroom. She emptied drawers, cupboards, wardrobes, obsessed, now that she'd started, with the need to get rid of things. Jettisoning Winifred's cast-offs almost persuaded her she was enjoying herself.

At the back of one of the drawers in Geoffrey's desk she found a puzzling object. It looked like a belt of some kind, though it was too narrow to go round any but a child's waist. An elastic belt with hand clasps at either end. She turned it over, searching for an explanation. 'Mr Sandford's Chest Expander', she read. She pulled on it experimentally. The muscles of her chest expanded to accommodate the stretch. Was this the reason Geoffrey took so long in the bathroom each morning? Did he secretly exercise there, hoping to add vital inches to his chest measurement?

Kay leaned against the desk, cradling Mr Sandford's invention in her arms. The discovery had unnerved her. If Geoffrey had kept that secret from her, what else did he have hidden away? I don't really know you, Kay thought. Then, remembering her own secrets, acknowledged, reluctantly, that he didn't know her either. It's all a game, she decided. A game we're forced to play because the alternatives are so much worse.

30

'Darling, have you seen my diaphragm?'
 'It's in the bathroom cupboard, isn't it?'
 'That's what I thought.'
 'Have you tried the other cupboard?'
 'It's not there either.'
 'Well, I don't know, darling. It's your diaphragm.'
 'I thought it was ours.'
 'Not much use to me.'
 'You didn't take it to hospital with you, did you?'
 'Now, there's a thought.'
 'Some of those nurses were very sexy.'
 'All part of the service.'
Kay smiled at her wounded husband. His first night home. 'Perhaps we should wait a day or two?' she suggested.
 'If I wait any longer I'll burst!' Geoffrey exclaimed.

Geoffrey cupped his hand over his wife's breast. He wanted to talk, but for the moment he was out of breath. Had it ever been this good before? If it had, it was so long ago he couldn't remember. 'I love you,' he breathed into Kay's hair.
 'I love you too,' she responded.
 A steady rain was falling. It made a muffled drum-roll on the roof. Geoffrey listened to it with the same attention he brought to opera. There was a common quality, he decided. The persistent beat of the rain, like a great aria, contained within it the quality of silence. After the busy, sleepless nights in the hospital, the sheer delight of such listening induced in him the kind of happiness he used to imagine for himself on those other sleepless, English nights.

'Kay?'
'Hmm?'
'Are you asleep?'
'Not quite.'
'You make me very happy, you know.'

She turned to him. Her eyes shone in the dark. 'How's it feeling?' she asked, touching the plaster that covered his ear.

'Better than that ghastly bandage.'
'You don't think I should change it?'
'Morning will do.'
'You know I have to work tomorrow.'

Geoffrey winced. It wasn't pain he was feeling, it was guilt. When Kay told him she'd resigned from her job he knew from the way she dismissed his protests that she still believed they'd be going to England. He *must* tell her about the partnership. He'd tried a couple of times in the hospital, but lost his nerve. Then he tried again when he got home this afternoon. When that attempt failed he went into the bathroom, took her diaphragm out of the cupboard, and hid it in his dressing-gown pocket. He didn't plan it. It just happened. Tomorrow he'd replace it. It would turn up, and their life would go on as before. They'd always said they wouldn't start a family till they'd been married five years. 'Wherever we are in the world by then,' Kay used to add.

'I want you to know,' Geoffrey said, not without difficulty, 'that I appreciate ... I wish you hadn't, really, but I do appreciate ...'

'I only have to work out the week,' Kay interjected cheerfully.

'Tell me about Clive. You reckon he'll be out in a few days?'
'That's what they say.'
'He's welcome to come here, you know.' The look on his wife's face convinced Geoffrey he was right, despite his reservations about his brother-in-law, to have made the offer.

'That's sweet of you, darling,' Kay answered. 'If you'd said something a week or two earlier ... But he's already arranged to go to this place the Army have. Didn't I tell you?'

'He wouldn't go to your parents?'
'He'd rather sleep in the park!'

Geoffrey, disguising his relief in a laugh, found his wife's breast again. Spent though he was he felt a faint stirring in his groin. Kay had beautiful breasts. Not the bee-stings most slim girls seemed to sport. When she let him suck on her nipples, as he had tonight, he longed for the feeling of lust and safety – heady combination – to go on forever. How could he ever have allowed himself to be led on by Trixie?

'Sometimes I wish you were my mother,' he confessed lazily. 'Joking, of course, but you're so different from her I can't help fantasising . . .'

'She's been very upset about you,' Kay said.

'You know she burned all my Biggles books when I was a kid, did I tell you? I don't think I've ever forgiven her.'

'Why would she do a thing like that?'

'It was soon after the twins were born. I suppose she was suffering – what's it called? – post-natal depression. Anyway, I was just about to sail for England, my first time, when we got into an argument about what I was to take. I wanted to pack my Biggles books. She said there wasn't room in the trunk. I guess we were both on edge.'

'She told me she was against your going to that school. She hated the whole idea of it. Perhaps the person she was really angry with was your father.'

'Yes, well, that's been true for most of their marriage.'

'Geoffrey?'

'It wasn't long after that she was prescribed valium.'

'There's something I have to ask you.'

'She's still on it, as a matter of fact. How many years does that make? Twelve? Thirteen? You see now why I'm not keen on you smoking pot. Once these things get a hold . . .'

'I didn't know.'

'What?'

'About the valium.'

'You can't talk to her about it. She used to have a temper. A real bobby dazzler. She'd hurl anything within reach. Saucepans, books, records, the telephone . . . My father called it her black dog. It still makes an occasional appearance.'

'Geoff . . .'

'When I was at school – I don't think I've told you this, stop me if I have – I used to lie on my back in my lumpy bed, and imagine my life as a man. Why is it that time in childhood passes so slowly? A day can seem like an eternity. A whole term . . . Perhaps that's why we keep returning to it. Once you're an adult everything speeds up. There's no time to make sense of anything.'

Kay's breast rose and fell deliciously beneath his hand. Suddenly he wanted very much to confide in her. It was how he'd felt in the beginning. Now, of course, there were things he could never tell her, but his boyhood dreams could be shared. He might even tell her the truth about his mother.

'You never went to boarding school,' he said, 'so perhaps you can't imagine the peculiar misery it induces. Everyone is miserable, every pupil that is, yet that, instead of bringing you closer, acts as an abrasive. You're hurting, so you strike out. It's as if you know you all come from this same tribe, a tribe famed for its cruelties down the generations. You suffer terrible bullying, and when your turn comes, *you* become the bully. It's an infallible system. Designed, so one enlightened master told me, to produce leaders of Empire.'

'It didn't turn you into that.'

'Ah, but I had a different dream, you see. I told myself the misery would vanish as soon as I got back here.'

'But it didn't, did it?'

'What?'

'You weren't happy at home.'

'*You're* my home.'

'I don't mean now, I mean then. When you came back.'

'I was happy at university. 'Specially once I'd met you.'

'Geoffrey . . .'

The way she said his name put Geoffrey on the alert. His hand slid off her breast. 'Yes?' he answered.

'Will you tell me something, honestly? When are we going to England? According to your father . . .'

'That's what I've been trying to tell you. We're not going. We can't. Least not for a year or two. I've accepted a partnership.'

It had come out all wrong. He'd been going to put the whole thing in context. Describe his lunch with Bunce. Lead up to the moment when the trap was sprung. 'I was an idiot,' he was going to say. 'I fell right into it.'

'I know,' Kay reacted. 'Your father told me.'
'What?'
'The day of the operation.'
'You've known all this time?'
'I kept waiting for you to explain.'
'Jesus, Kay, I'm sorry, what on earth must you think of me?'

She didn't answer. The rain had eased a little. He could hear her quick, sharp breathing.

'I meant to, please believe me, I meant to tell you straight away. It's just that . . .'

Kay propped herself up on her elbow. The expression on her face was discouraging. 'What are you going to do about it?' she demanded.

'Do about what?'
'The partnership.'
'What *can* I do? I've said yes. You can't go back on a thing like that.'
'You said yes to me too. About England.'
'I know, and I'm sorry, really I am. But it's not the same.'
'You said yes, Geoffrey.'

He lifted his hand to his damaged ear. The pain had returned. 'Where did you put my pills?' he asked.

'You're not due one till morning.'
'I need one now.'

Kay's mouth contorted angrily. It occurred to him that there could be a temper behind that sweet exterior. He waited to see what she would do. He really was in pain. It wasn't a ploy.

She turned away from him, and slid out of bed. He watched her naked body glide across the room. When she returned with his pills he thanked her humbly. 'I'll make it up to you, darling,' he vowed. 'I promise.'

31

In the middle of June Kay learned she was pregnant. When she began to laugh her gynaecologist, Wilfrid Halsey (*Sir* Wilfrid he was now; knighted in the recent Queen's Birthday Honours), frowned and made a note in his pad. His friend, Lionel Grieve, had once or twice hinted that all was not well in his son's marriage, but nothing specific had been said. 'She's been 100 per cent over this illness of Geoff's,' he'd acknowledged recently. 'Gave up a good job to take care of him.' Well, Lionel would be pleased about the pregnancy. He'd made no secret of his desire for a grandson.

'Not often I see such a demonstration of delight,' Sir Wilfrid remarked. 'I take it this is what you and your husband have been hoping for?'

'It's not that,' Kay spluttered.

Sir Wilfrid arched his bushy eyebrows.

'Are you a gambling man, Doctor?' Kay asked. She couldn't get used to calling him 'Sir'. She'd met him a couple of times at Lionel and Winfred's. He'd been plain Mister then.

'One night, one shot at it, you might say. What would the chances have been, d'you reckon?'

'If you're referring to . . .'

Kay stood up. She felt mildly hysterical. It had been a mistake to come here. Sandra had told her about a clinic in Ponsonby run by and for women. She should have gone there. 'And if it's what you suspect,' she'd urged, 'you'll have someone sympathetic to talk to.'

Sandra had assumed Kay would want an abortion.

'You should make an appointment with my secretary,' Sir

Wilfrid instructed Kay's retreating back. 'A month from now will be fine.'

'Thank you,' she said.

It was a relief to be outside. Sir Wilfrid's rooms had reminded Kay uncomfortably of her first meeting with her in-laws'.

She headed down the hill towards the Public Library. She could have gone up to the University, but she wasn't ready yet to confront Sandra. Sandra had been urging her to study Psychology. Kay had admitted she was tempted. With Geoffrey back at work the days were long and empty. What would Sandra say now there was to be a baby? She knew what Geoffrey's parents would say. 'Just as well you didn't go back to work, dear. No question of that now.'

She reached the Library, hesitated at the door, then turned towards the park. What would happen if she didn't tell Geoffrey? If she kept the information to herself, as he had done when he accepted the partnership? She needed time to get used to the idea. To work out what it meant. But of course that was impossible. Wilfrid Halsey was probably on the phone to Lionel at this very moment.

The park was deserted. The cold wind from the harbour had seen to that. A flock of seagulls scavenging round a rubbish bin took off in a noisy flurry as she approached.

She chose her seat carefully. Out of sight of the university buildings, and at a distance from the two students kissing inside the band rotunda. Her heart was beating with a heavy, persistent thud. What would happen over the next weeks? Would she be sick? Her stomach would swell, and her breasts. Would her hair fall out? She'd heard of that happening. If her hair fell out she'd never be able to look in a mirror again.

Further up the path there was a statue of a Boer War soldier. She only needed to turn her head to see it. There were names carved in stone in every town in New Zealand. In some districts there were memorials with twenty or more names, and almost no evidence, in the surrounding countryside, of population. What if the baby inside her were a boy? There would always be wars. That's what Clive believed. Geoffrey too, she suspected. These days he did little but wring his hands over the horrors in Vietnam.

She pulled a handkerchief from her bag, and blew her nose. Her eyes were stinging with cold. A man was executed recently in a public square in Saigon. She could see his terrified face as the gun was put to his head. In the same square another man, a holy man, set fire to himself.

Suddenly it was as if she were drowning, and all the images she'd been trying to obliterate flashed in front of her eyes: burning villages; maimed children; flag-draped coffins; the faces of protesters; the faces of police . . . A voice started up in her head. Father Someone speaking on the radio. 'Aucklanders care for nothing but chasing a fast buck . . .'

She turned her head in a slow circle. Neat botanical borders, a floral clock, tall English trees, birds, a statue of Queen Victoria, the lovers in the rotunda, an old man drinking meths . . . and me, Kay thought, staring in astonishment at her belly, me and my baby.

That night, at Sunnydell, there were tears of happiness. Please let it be a girl, Kay prayed, as Geoffrey ran to the phone to call his parents. Dear God, if you're there, and you're listening, please let it be a girl.

32

Over the next seven months almost everything about Kay changed. Her skin became translucent; her hair (oh, miracle of miracles!) grew thick, and even began to curl; her belly swelled; her breasts pushed out of her bra; her walk became languid as winter turned to spring, and spring dissolved into a humid summer. She gave up biting her nails, stopped (to Geoffrey's relief) sleep walking, read Simone de Beauvoir and Graham Greene, listened to Sandra's recording of Timothy Leary, went to concerts, swam in the open-air baths, cooked for Geoffrey, and studied Dr Spock. Winifred had enrolled her in Plunket classes. There she learned how to bath a baby, and wrap her in muslin like a Christmas cracker. She learned how to fold a nappy, sew the regulation gowns, feed, burp, and sterilise. For today's busy mothers, bottle feeding was advised.

But the real change in Kay was not physical. For the first time in her life she was content; deeply, smugly content. Every time she stood in front of a mirror and touched her swelling body she felt sorry for anyone who wasn't her. What greater meaning could there be than the child growing inside her? No more loving connection could be imagined. For this small, unknown person, she would perform all manner of miracles. The world could be safely ignored; newspapers unread, television news unwatched. National elections, centred, in the wake of a visit from President Johnson ('Hey, Hey, LBJ, How Many Kids Have You Killed Today?') on the issue of New Zealand's involvement in Vietnam, were dismissed as irrelevant. Though she did stir herself sufficiently to vote for the party that would pull out of Vietnam if it could. When she asked

Geoffrey how *he* voted, he laughed and reminded her the ballot was secret.

Six months into the pregnancy Kay invited Sandra to dinner. The evening was surprisingly successful. Sandra smoked Geoffrey's cigarettes, and laughed at his jokes, and managed not to say anything too outrageous. When she phoned next day she congratulated Kay. 'Your husband's a dish,' she conceded. 'I see now why you put up with him.'

Geoffrey's opinion of Sandra was almost as flattering. 'An interesting woman,' he granted. 'Unusual.'

'They call her the pocket battleship at Varsity.'

'Why are tiny women so fierce? Is it nature's way of making up for lost inches, d'you think?'

'She's not fierce. She's passionate.'

'If it weren't for her name you'd never know she was Polish.'

'She was only five when she came here – 1944. The year I was born. A whole bunch of them, kids from four to thirteen, were shipped out from Siberia. They'd already been thrown out of Poland. God knows what they must have been feeling. They'd lost parents, country, everything.'

'And they were the lucky ones.'

'She doesn't remember much about her arrival. Grass, she remembers that. How slippery it felt; its astonishing greenness.'

'Well, I'm glad to have met her at last.'

She doesn't think of herself as Polish anymore. She learned very quickly to pass herself off as a Kiwi. They all did.'

'Understandable.'

'Not that she calls herself a Kiwi now. Nationality is at the root of most wars, she reckons. That and religion.'

On 30 January 1967, the following notice appeared in *The Herald*:

> GRIEVE. To Geoffrey and Kay, a daughter, Nina Joy, at National Women's Hospital on 28 January. Sincere thanks to Sir Wilfrid Halsey.

That it was a daughter was a disappointment to both Geoffrey and his father. Winifred had no feelings either way, so long as no one called her 'Grannie', or expected her to babysit. As for the other grandparents, when Kay phoned to tell them the news they expressed relief that all was well, and sent their best wishes to Geoffrey and his parents. 'No need to rush in,' Kay told them. 'Plenty of time to get acquainted.'

What she didn't tell them was how beautiful their granddaughter was. The nurse put this down to the fact that she was slightly jaundiced. 'Most new babies look as if they've been boiled up with the beetroot,' she joked.

But jaundice, Kay knew, had nothing to do with Nina's looks. She had fine fair hair and china blue eyes, and little fingers that grasped Kay's and held on so tight she could feel the tiny nails biting into her skin. No one would ever persuade Kay those new moon lips weren't smiling, not when the eyes were gazing so deeply into her own. And the smell. Why had no one told her how delicious that would be? The smell of her daughter's skin carried Kay away on a bubble of enchantment. Every time she felt that little snub nose press into her neck, and heard the gurgling sounds that were their first words of communication, she felt her heavy, aching body grow light with love.

'Six pounds six ounces,' Geoffrey noted with satisfaction. 'A good weight.'

Poor Geoffrey. He looked harassed. Fear, relief, disappointment that he hadn't fathered a son.

After she'd been in labour for twelve hours Wilfrid Halsey had sent Geoffrey home. 'You'll only get in the way,' he'd told him. But then labour had stopped altogether, and Wilfrid had gone home himself. By the time he returned Nina was born. 'You should have delayed things,' Kay heard him growl to the intern who'd handled the delivery. How ridiculous! How crazy! As if anyone could delay such a momentous force.

'Who is she like, do you think?' Geoffrey asked.

Kay smiled blissfully. 'She's not like anyone,' she answered. 'She's just herself.'

Kay stayed in hospital ten days. During that time she read copiously and planned her new life. Nina would go everywhere with her. To the baths, to the beach, to the park. She was such a good baby, drinking eagerly (Kay had elected to bottle feed), burping to order, sleeping six hours at a stretch, there was no reason why she shouldn't be taken to concerts; even to lectures. For Kay had decided to take Sandra's advice and study again. Nine months of full-time domesticity had begun to rot her brain.

When she shared her plans with the other mothers in the ward, those with children already looked at her pityingly and advised her to wait a few years. Kay smiled at the predictability of their responses. Nina wasn't like other babies. She didn't scream and puke all day.

'I want her to sleep in our room,' Kay announced, on her return to Sunnydell.

'She'll only be through the wall,' Geoffrey protested. 'You'll easily hear her.'

'Just for the first few weeks.'

Geoffrey put his arm around his wife. He didn't like to tell her what he was thinking: that they couldn't make love if Nina was in the room with them. It had been four months now. Kay would have been happy to keep on love-making till the very end, but he'd found her large hard belly, not repellant exactly, heaven forbid, it was beautiful in its way, but not sexy, oh no, definitely not sexy. Wilfrid had already had a word with him about what he'd called, 'the resumption of marital relations'. 'Give her six weeks,' he'd advised. 'We can put her on the pill then.'

'It's you I'm thinking of, darling,' Geoffrey said. 'You'll need your rest. And, of course, I still have to go to work in the mornings.'

'She's only ten days old, Geoffrey.'

'Tell you what, let's see what Dr Spock has to say on the subject. I seem to remember you reading me something about the need to reassure the husband. Me, in other words. Aren't I supposed to be feeling jealous at this point?'

Kay giggled. 'You're not, are you?'

Geoffrey adopted a comic pose. It was one Kay remembered from his student revue days: the chain-smoking journalist. '"Jealous Husband Insists on Conjugal Rights,"' he drawled. '"Angry Scene in Parnell Bedroom."'

'You are joking . . .'

'Course I am. But not about wanting you, time alone with you. I'm not joking about that.'

In the end it was easier to do what Geoffrey asked. And since he slept so deeply there was nothing to stop Kay spending as much time as she wanted with her daughter, singing to her till she fell asleep, marvelling at her beauty, troubled by one thought only: how, in this confusing world, was she to keep her safe?

33

A week after Kay's return from hospital, Clive arrived on a visit. He was due for a check-up at the hospital, but Kay chose to believe he'd delayed the appointment in order to meet his niece. He'd never say so, of course. That wasn't his way. But something in the tone of his letter encouraged her to think of him as a loving uncle.

Because there was no room at Sunnydell, and Astley was too far from the hospital, Geoffrey agreed to ask Winifred if Clive could stay with them. It would only be for two nights. Kay could see no reason why her mother-in-law should object.

But Kay, in her new love affair with human nature, had forgotten that she'd once compared Winifred (in answer to a question of Sandra's) to an iceberg: one-tenth dazzle, nine-tenths submerged danger. Clive might be a captain, with a bright future in the Army, but he was not, absolutely not, the kind of person Winifred had to stay in her house.

Geoffrey never did tell Kay how hard he had to lean on his mother to get her to agree. Clive was too big, too clumsy, too uncouth. He'd corrupt the girls with his army slang. He'd get drunk, as he did at the wedding. 'For God's sake, Mother, the man's been ill,' Geoffrey protested. 'And he's come up to see Nina. You can't object to that, surely?'

'I don't object to anything except having him in my house.'

'Two nights. And he'll be with Kay all day. You won't even see him.'

At least, in this argument, there were no tears. Winifred conceded with a bad grace, but with mercifully dry eyes.

'Just this once,' she grumbled. 'I'm very fond of Kay, as you know, but I've no intention of turning my house into a hostel for her relatives.'

The visit began well. Clive pronounced Nina 'cute', and confessed, under pressure from his sister, that he would like to be married himself.

'Anyone in mind?' Kay probed.

Since his illness Clive had been stationed at Trentham near Wellington. His duties – instructing new recruits in the hazards of jungle warfare – were designated 'light'. As for his personal life, it remained as big a mystery as ever. None of the questions in Kay's letters had been answered.

'There are one or two candidates,' Clive acknowledged grudgingly.

'Don't suppose Patricia Wihongi's one of them?'

'Christ, no! She's probably married with a brat of her own by now.'

Kay lifted Nina on to her shoulder. The sweet smell filled her nostrils. 'There's no question of your being sent to Vietnam, is there?' she asked. 'I mean, they wouldn't, would they, not after . . . ? You've done your bit,' she persisted when her brother failed to respond. 'Surely to goodness . . .'

'I'll tell you something,' Clive interrupted, 'this war would have been won by now if it weren't for people like you. Protesters. Ho Chi Minh sympathisers. If I had my way I'd round up the whole lot of you and stick you in prison.'

Kay laughed. She knew when she was being baited. 'I haven't been near a protest for over a year,' she informed him.

'Glad to hear it.'

'Nor am I likely to be. Not with Nina in tow.'

'Yeah, well, see you keep it that way.'

That evening, after a leisurely dinner, Geoffrey drove Clive to his parents' house. Kay had told her brother not to hurry in the morning. Geoff had promised her the car. She'd fetch him about ten after Nina's bath. But Clive was on the doorstep before eight. She didn't need to ask if he'd walked. It was obvious from the sweat stains on his shirt.

She let him in silently, and poured him a cup of tea. She knew that look in his eyes, just as she knew there was no point asking what had gone wrong. As a boy, when his pride was wounded – an insult at school; a tactless comment from a relative – he would clam up so tight, Kay would feel the muscles of her throat tensing in sympathy.

Over his second cup of tea he announced he was going to book into a hotel.

'Why?' Geoffrey asked. 'The parents'll be expecting you.'

'I don't think so.'

'But surely . . .'

'Let's leave it, eh, mate?'

Clive's departure triggered a dramatic change of mood in Kay. 'Ask your mother,' she snapped when Geoffrey tried to discover the cause of the reversal. 'Ask her what she said to Clive.'

'What on earth are you talking about?'

'He came all this way just to, just to . . .'

'Don't cry. Please, Kay, don't cry.'

'You think he's insensitive, don't you? Soldiers aren't like other people. They don't have feelings to be hurt.'

'I wish you'd tell me what you're talking about.'

'You wouldn't understand if I did.'

At the beginning of March Kay enrolled in the Anthropology class at the University. She made the decision without consulting Geoffrey. She knew what he'd say. Nina wasn't even three months old. How could she think of leaving her?

But I'm not, she answered him silently. Three lectures and two tutorials a week That's hardly a full-time job.

'Anthropology!' Sandra shrieked. 'What brought that on? I thought it was to be Psychology.'

Kay laughed. Nina was asleep in her carry cot on the floor. People kept coming over to admire her. 'God, it's good to be out,' she confessed. 'This coffee tastes divine.'

'Anthropology,' Sandra prompted.

'You won't like it.'

Sandra spooned up the froth from her cappuccino. Her tongue darted over her lips like a little red snake.

'I think it goes further, if you must know. Not just what motivates individuals, what motivates whole societies.'

Sandra leaned back in her chair and contemplated her friend through a fringe of dark lashes. Kay considered Sandra beautiful. Her hair, which was the colour of ripe wheat, grew to her waist. Sometimes she wore it loose, tossing it about as she spoke in the same way she tossed her beads and bracelets. Mostly though she coiled it in a knot on top of her head, a golden knot from which tiny curls strayed enchantingly. 'You're coming on, aren't you?' she remarked.

'Does that mean you approve?'

'Why do you need my approval? If it's what you want to do . . .'

'Actually,' Kay admitted, 'Nina's so good I'm sure I could manage French too. Make a start on my MA. But Geoffrey would have a fit.'

'Geoffrey, Geoffrey . . .'

'I haven't told him about Anthropology yet.'

'And what do you imagine he's going to do? Lock you up in a tower?'

'You don't understand. You live on your own. You don't have to consider anyone else.'

'That's the first stupid thing I've heard you say.'

'Sorry.'

'And don't apologise.'

'I *want* to be with Nina, Sandra. This isn't about wanting to escape from her.'

'Second stupid thing,' Sandra muttered.

'Geoffrey isn't the problem really, it's his parents.'

Sandra rummaged in her overflowing bag for a cigarette. The coffee bar was filling up. Students with loud voices and greasy hair, and badges emblazoned with 'MAKE LOVE NOT WAR' jostled at the counter. One student, bolder than the rest, sported a badge proclaiming the message, 'ALL THE WAY WITH LBJ'.

'I've found somewhere for Nina to go, did I tell you?' Kay went on. 'It's a creche for infants up to the age of five. Handy too. I can walk there.'

Sandra took in a deep draught of smoke, exhaled, and yawned. 'What's that husband of yours up to anyway?' she asked.

'I hardly ever see him. His firm have opened an office in Hamilton. He has to stay over two nights a week.'

'Not much use as a baby-sitter then.'

'He adores Nina. But he's hopeless at anything practical. I asked him to change a nappy the other day. Just a wet one. He couldn't cope with the other sort. It ended up around her ankles.'

'Shrewd fellow, your husband.'

'Pardon?'

'Never mind.'

'He's making quite a name for himself in court these days. That ICI case? You must have read about it.'

Smoke streamed from Sandra's nostrils. Her eyes darted to right and left. She's bored, Kay thought. I'm beginning to sound like Lynne.

'Thought you said he'd given up court work?' Sandra drawled.

'He did for a bit, after the operation. But then he got this dinky little hearing-aid fitted.'

'So, you're on your lonesome two nights a week?'

'I'm not lonely. I've got Nina.'

Sandra flicked the ash from her cigarette on to the floor, narrowly missing Nina's cot. 'Well, all I can say is, your sex life must be pretty good. Since there's fuck-all else for you in this marriage.'

'Don't start, please.'

Sandra grinned. 'You've always been cagey about sex, haven't you? Not a good sign, in my book. Sex is to be enjoyed, loudly, publicly, and often . . . Did you get that?' she challenged the fascinated group at the next table.

The eavesdroppers grinned sheepishly, and buried their faces in their coffee cups.

'One of these days,' Sandra went on, to Kay, 'if you go on looking so hangdog, I'm going to drag you back to my place, and put you in bed with me and my current lover. It's still Mike, by the way. You've never experienced an orgy, have you? No need to look so shocked. You'll find, if you do your Anthropology homework, that it has a place in a number of societies, ancient and modern. As do drugs. Life's for living, sweetheart. If you hadn't sussed that by now we wouldn't still be friends.'

34

Geoffrey couldn't remember when he'd felt so happy. No. That was wrong. He'd never been this happy before. There was nothing to compare it with. The only cloud in the sky was the fear that, if he thought about it too much, it would come to an end. Define yourself as *unhappy* and the condition will go on as relentlessly as ever. Define the opposite, and you risk destroying the mood completely.

It was the middle of winter, yet here they were, he and Kay and Nina, lying in the sandhills at Piha. That in itself was cause for celebration. Where else in the world could you have a mid-winter picnic on an almost empty beach? He'd stripped down to his shirt. Kay had jettisoned sweater and slacks. Nina was lying on her stomach on the rug, kicking her bare legs and laughing at her mother, who was dangling a wooden puppet in reach of her grasping fingers.

The picnic had been his idea. There was something he needed to discuss with Kay and he had the feeling Sunnydell was not the place to bring it up. Kay had been quiet lately. Not moody exactly. *Broody* would be more accurate. Though he didn't think she was ready for another child anymore than he was. Nina was the best thing that had ever happened to them. Any guilt he might have felt about the stolen diaphragm (notoriously unreliable things anyway) had long since been subsumed in their mutual delight in their daughter. Looking at Nina now he could hardly believe he'd had any part in creating such a perfect creature. How could he object to Kay's studying when Nina demanded so little of them? His father had kicked up a fuss – 'I warned you, didn't I son? Clever women are never satisfied.' Geoffrey's answer to that had been to remind his father of the pitfalls of being a housewife. An interest outside the home would keep Kay happy (keep her off the valium was what he'd meant).

'You ought to get Nina christened, you know,' his father had said recently. 'How old is she now? Six months?'

'But we don't go to church.'

'That's not the point.'

'I don't think Kay would want . . .'

'You were *married* in church.'

When, a couple of days later, Geoffrey raised the subject with Kay, it had started a conversation which lasted the entire evening. Kay had just finished an essay on the initiation ceremonies of the Inuit people. 'They're no more primitive than us really,' she'd insisted. 'When we baptise babies we ask the godparents to renounce the devil. I don't see the difference between that and . . .'

'It's just words, Kay. No one believes it. Not the bit about the devil anyway.'

'Then why do it?'

In the end, in exasperation, Geoffrey had demanded to know if Kay believed in God. 'Your father asked me that once,' she told him.

'What did you say?'

Waiting for her answer he'd watched her gnaw the side of her thumb, a habit he'd hoped she was cured of. When she announced she was an agnostic, he laughed. Only later, going over the conversation in his mind, did he discover he was annoyed. Why *shouldn't* Nina be christened? It wasn't as if they were planning to indoctrinate her.

But he hadn't suggested this picnic in order to rehash the pros and cons of christian baptism. He was reasonably confident of bringing Kay round. She'd called herself an agnostic, not an atheist. If he put it to her that Nina had a right to that particular start in life he was sure she'd agree. Her devotion to her daughter was absolute.

No, what he wanted to talk to his wife about was buying a house. He'd been working up to it ever since Nina's birth. Sunnydell was way too small for them. That disastrous business with Clive would never have happened if they'd been living in a decent-sized place. Besides, he still owed Kay for her disappointment over England. He hadn't forgotten he'd promised to make it up to her. What better way than to buy her a place of her own?

'I think I might swim,' Kay said. 'Will you watch Nina?'

'You'll freeze,' Geoffrey protested.

'Not in the water I won't. It's virtually the same temperature, winter and summer.'

'You don't have togs, do you?'

'I'll go in in my knickers.'

Watching her run, half naked, into the sea, Geoffrey's mood took a brief nose-dive. The beach was still more or less deserted – a woman walking a dog at the far end; a couple of surfers in wet suits – but that didn't mean she should make an exhibition of herself. It wasn't that he was prudish, but he'd noticed a change in her since she'd taken up with Sandra Grajawaska. The adjective that sprang to mind was *immodest*.

Geoffrey had spoken the truth when he told Kay, after that first meeting, that he liked Sandra, but he'd altered his opinion since then. Her views were little short of bizarre. All that garbage about personal fulfilment, and the need to 'draw back the veil'. As for her behaviour, well, last time she'd visited Sunnydell she began chatting him up the moment Kay was out of the room. He didn't tell Kay about it. Why revive the memory of that awful business with Trixie? But he stored the information for possible use later. Sandra Grajawaska might think of herself as a sexual pioneer but what she was, in Geoffrey's book, was an adventuress.

'What do you think, Nina?' he whispered to his daughter. 'Will Mummy be happy if I buy her a house?'

Two things had happened to make Geoffrey's dream of home-ownership possible. One was that he was now, thanks to his work in Hamilton, earning a considerable sum of money. When he was first approached to oversee the new office he said no. He didn't relish the idea of time away from his family. But then Bunce told him what the pecuniary advantages would be, and he reconsidered. Eventually, after discussing the matter with his father, he agreed. To Kay he simply said he'd not been given a choice. 'I'm still the new boy on the block,' he'd joked. Her distress had fuelled his determination to buy her a home of her own. She'd never been happy at Sunnydell.

The second thing that had happened was that his father had offered to lend him the deposit. This had so startled Geoffrey – his father was not a generous man – he'd felt an immediate obligation to accept. He and his father had been getting on a great deal better since the operation. It helped that Lionel assumed (wrongly) that their political differences were over. But the real cause, of course, was that Geoffrey was doing what his father had always wanted: carving out a career for himself in the fastest growing city in the country.

'I've only one stipulation,' Lionel had said. 'I want the house to be in your name.'

Protesting had proved a waste of breath. Those were his father's terms, take it or leave it.

Geoffrey craned his head above the fringe of tall grasses that hid the sea from view. His wife was bouncing up and down in the waves, arms above her head, breasts white against the limpid blues of sea and sky. Nina, beside him, was asleep. He reached round for a blanket and tenderly covered her. Suddenly he wanted very much to be making love to his wife. Not since those heady, frustrating days on the Otago Peninsula had he felt such a sense of urgency. It wasn't that his love life had become routine exactly, it was more that he'd been feeling for some time now that Kay's mind was elsewhere. It was partly Nina, of course. He'd read enough of the literature to know that first-time mothers were often preoccupied with their babies to the exclusion of all else. But it was also, he was sure of it, the people she was mixing with at Varsity, people like Sandra, without family responsibilities. So far as he knew she hadn't rejoined the Peace Group, but as she seldom volunteered information about her activities he couldn't be sure. It distressed him to think he'd become the kind of husband who was only content when he knew his wife was safely tucked up at home.

But there was another possible explanation for Kay's remoteness. Like his father she believed he'd turned his back on his radical past. Lionel had even begun to joke about it. 'Must say, you saw the light quicker than I did, old boy. Let me guess. You voted for Holyoake?' When Geoffrey laughed the question away, his father went on, 'Dodgy chap that Norman Kirk. Touch and go though. Hate to think where we'd be now if Labour was at the helm.'

In the past Geoffrey would have argued, but these days he tended to take the coward's way out. It would have surprised his father to learn that he'd regretted his vote almost as soon as he'd cast it. Norman Kirk had integrity. If *he* were the Prime Minister he'd be doing everything in his power to end the war in Vietnam.

I *have* changed, he acknowledged, dismissing his father and addressing his absent wife, but not in the ways you imagine. It's hard to put into words, that's why I've not talked about it.

What Geoffrey was struggling to articulate was the ongoing process of his thinking about Vietnam, and New Zealand's official support of American policy. His opposition to nuclear weapons was as strong as ever, but he was more sanguine these days about the Americans. OK, so they weren't the wisest of people. They lacked the European instinct, an instinct born of a terrible history, for what was possible. They believed in solutions. When they saw something wrong, something 'rotten in the state', they rode in, uninvited, to put it right. Johnson and his advisers clearly believed democracy was what all Vietnamese wanted, even if not all of them knew it. It was naive. It was ignorant. But it wasn't wicked, as Stalin's purges were wicked.

The problem, as Geoffrey saw it, lay not in the now worldwide protest against American policy, but in the manner of that protest. When he first started to organise demonstrations the spur that drove him on was the self-righteouness of governments who believed, with no real mandate to justify that belief, that they alone knew what was best in matters of defence. The American people had never been asked if they wanted nuclear weapons. Nor had the British. As for New Zealand, though she possessed no nuclear arsenal of her own, she was nevertheless linked by treaty to nations that seemed altogether too likely to deploy weapons of mass destruction whether their peoples agreed or not. The issue, in Geoffrey's mind, had been clear. Nuclear weapons were not a defence, they were a threat, the worst ever mounted against the human race.

But then things started to change. The protest movement began to take on the very mantle of self-righteousness Geoffrey had originally fingered as the principal crime of government. He'd detected it first in Dunedin. It was there in the choice of words, and the willingness, the eagerness even, to confront police. Bloody noses attracted far more attention than polite words from the podium.

For a time he went along with it. Civil Disobedience was the way of virtue after all. Look at Martin Luther King. But one night, arguing with Alistair, the suspicion that he had become a mirror image of his friend began to take hold. Language, which had at first liberated him, had sprung its trap. He and Alistair preached different creeds, but the language they used was the same.

That had been the start of it. Coming to Auckland had merely completed the process. There had to be another way. The violence that was now an inseparable part of the protest movement was a sign, not of its rightness, but of something rotten at its core.

He glanced at his sleeping daughter. If Kay came back now they could make love quietly without disturbing her. They were well hidden in their sandhill. Perhaps, so absurdly happy did he feel today, they might even start talking, really talking, to each other again. Kay was the most fair-minded person he'd ever come across. She gave everybody the benefit of the doubt. If she heard what he had to say she might stop thinking of him as a backslider, a betrayer of promises, and see him as the complex, hedged-about man he now understood himself to be.

He was tempted to call out to her, but that might wake Nina. God, but she looked lovely out there in the waves. She'd had her hair cut short. He'd hated it at first, but now he admitted it suited her. He wanted to tell her that. She'd been upset at his reaction. He wanted to tell her she'd always be beautiful in his eyes.

'How can I be interested when all your clients are rich?' she'd retorted the other night when he accused her of being indifferent to his work.

'That's not true. Many of the firms I act for are struggling just to stay afloat.'

'How can they afford *you* then?'

Her assumption that he was guilty by proxy of crimes against the poor had infuriated him. He was damned if he'd justify himself. If he told her he frequently adjusted his fees to help those on low incomes she'd find something else to lambast him with. He had enough trouble with Bunce and the other partners on that issue without having to listen to his wife.

What he did tell her, because it had the advantage of moral clarity, was that he'd recently turned down a lucrative brief on the grounds that the company involved could not honourably be defended. It was the closest he'd come to open warfare with his partners. The chairman of the company was an ex-cabinet minister. The understanding was that he would bring a lot more work into the firm. But Geoffrey wouldn't budge. The company, Eden Properties, had been involved in some dodgy land deals. There was even a suspicion they'd cheated the Maori of land on the waterfront that should have been returned to them after the war. Harry McSkimming, as Minister of Housing, had been in a position to know exactly what the status of that land was. Now, thanks to Eden Properties, who'd made over half a million from the sale, it was in private hands. It reminded Geoffrey of the Tuwharetoa case, which he'd studied as a student. Both, in his opinion, left the government, and its business advisers, smelling distinctly rotten. 'It'll backfire on you,' he warned Bunce. 'One day the Maoris'll organise themselves and start looking at these deals. There'll be hell to pay then.'

Kay had heard him out in silence. He'd anticipated questions, praise even, but all she'd said was, 'Someone else'll take the case though, won't they? With all that money involved.'

Geoffrey rummaged in the basket for the latest *New Statesman*, already three months out of date, made himself comfortable on the rug beside his daughter, and lay back to wait for his wife.

Moments later her voice was in his ear. 'Time to go, darling,' she was saying.

'Wh . . . what?'

'You've been asleep.'

'Is Nina . . . ?'

'Both of you. Babes in the wood.'

'I didn't hear you come back.'

• Elspeth Sandys

'You're not wearing your hearing-aid, that's why.'
'What time is it?'
Kay smiled serenely down at him. 'Time we went home,' she said.

35

The house was in St Heliers: a good suburb, almost on a par with Remuera. Built in the 1950s of alternating red and yellow brick, it was described, accurately, in the land agent's brochure as 'a desirable residence'. The section it was built on measured just over a quarter of an acre. Previous owners had established a delightful rose garden at the top of a sloping lawn. The rest was laid out in shrubs – camellias, daphne, hypericum, lavender.

The house had three and a half bedrooms. Geoffrey had already earmarked the 'half' as his study. The living area was light and spacious, and opened out on to a paved patio with a built-in barbecue. From there the view over lawn and garden widened to include a section of the street, a panorama of red and grey roofs, a pleasing number of trees, and a glimpse of the harbour.

'What d'you think?' Geoffrey asked.

Kay gestured absent-mindedly. For no reason she could think of she was close to tears. 'It's a long way from Varsity,' she said.

'Look how private it is. You can't see the neighbours on that side at all.'

'We're being watched from the other direction, in case you hadn't noticed.'

'We'll plant a hedge. Way things grow in this climate, she'll be out of an occupation before you can say, "Jack Robinson!"'

Kay turned a slow circle. There were daffodils growing under the shrubs. An earthenware pot by the patio doors was filled with sweet-smelling hyacinths. From the curious neighbour's garden came the throaty cry of a tui. 'I don't know,' she said.

Geoffrey fished in his pocket for his cigarettes. He'd imagined this scene so differently. Kay excited; grateful. Nina crawling happily beside them. But Kay had left Nina at the creche.

'Look,' he said, 'if you don't like it . . .'

'It's not a question of not liking it.'

'What then?'

Kay trawled her fingers through her hair. Since she'd had it cut short she'd almost stopped worrying about it. After Nina's birth it had returned to its former straightness, but to her huge relief it had showed no signs of falling out. It was Sandra who'd persuaded her to cut it like a boy's. The salon she patronised these days was called 'The King's Road'.

What she had to do was tell Geoffrey about her plans for next year. She'd intended to wait till Nina was walking. She had the feeling, if Geoffrey could see his daughter running around, he'd accept that she was ready to spend more time with other children. Nina adored going to the creche. Her face lit up the moment she heard the squeals from inside the house. She was a great favourite too, not just with Auntie Bet who ran the place, but with the three and four year olds who queued up to look after her. If only Geoffrey would come and see for himself. But he was away three days a week, and too busy the rest of the time.

'I want to start my MA next year,' Kay said. 'I've worked it all out. I'll do it over two years. That way Nina won't have to be at Auntie Bet's much more than she is now. I'll do four papers in my first year, then I'll write a thesis, most of which I can do at home. I've already talked to the Head of Department. He doesn't foresee any problems.'

Geoffrey was silent. The smell of his cigarette mingled headily with the perfume from the hyacinths. He smoked regular cigarettes these days. He'd given up his Turkish brand at the time of the operation.

As Kay waited for his response she had a vision of herself standing in the rain at the St Heliers' bus stop, burdened with pushchair and books and Nina's bag of nappies, reassuring her fretful daughter that the bus would come *soon*. Public transport in Auckland was a joke. 'This city specialises in punishing its poor,' was how one of Sandra's friends had put it.

'If you had the car, would that help?' Geoffrey said.

Kay looked at her husband in astonishment.

'You could have the car,' he repeated.

'What about you?'

'I'd buy another one.'

'Can we afford that? I thought we could barely afford this house.'

Geoffrey laughed bleakly. 'Needs must,' he said.

In spite of herself, Kay smiled. Geoffrey's woebegone look never failed to move her. He was doing all this for her, wasn't he? The house; the offer of the car; the tacit acceptance of her study plans. If only she could talk to him the way she used to. Something had changed in her with Nina's birth. Her mother would say she was growing up at last, but then her mother didn't know the direction her thoughts were taking! Half the time Kay didn't know herself. She just followed whatever trail opened up for her, whether it was through her reading or her anthropological research or just listening to Sandra and her friends. She'd never realised before what an adventure thinking was. It was as if, having given up the struggle to see the world through other people's eyes (Nina's gift to her), she was looking at *everything* for the first time.

'You're not angry then?' she said.

'Angry?'

'About the MA.'

Geoffrey raised an eyebrow, another of his endearing habits. 'If I think about it, I'll probably get jealous,' he answered truthfully.

Kay linked her arm in his. There was so much she wanted to tell him. Why did she hesitate? He was always so tired when he got home at night, and the weekends he wasn't away skiing were taken up with work and Winifred's Sunday lunches. There were no absolutes, that was what she wanted to say. Absolute good, absolute evil, these were constructs of institutions with a vested interest in defining the way the world is. Of course, he'd realise at once where these ideas came from. Comparing one culture to another, like comparing religions, was bound to bring on an attack of scepticism. But she had her answers ready. The most real thing in the world, she would tell him, is power. Personal power, group power, political, religious, moral. Before you can change anything you have to recognise that fact. Once you do, the veil lifts, and you begin to understand that the absolutes of your own culture – christianity, democracy, capitalism, the nuclear family – are not God-given but historically arrived at positions, whose 'rightness' and 'goodness' are not the cause of their existence, but the justification.

'So,' Geoffrey said, in the clipped voice he used when irritable, 'd'you want the car or not?' He was thinking of what his father would have to say about this new scheme of Kay's. 'What's the matter with you, man? Get her pregnant! It's time you had another baby.' Something subtle like that.

'You still haven't told me if we can afford it,' Kay reminded him.

Geoffrey hardly ever talked to her about money. She didn't even know what he earned. They had a joint account on which she drew for household expenses, but there were other accounts of which she had no knowledge. Occasionally he'd question her about her household spending, but he always accepted her explanations. She was not extravagant by nature. Frugality had been drummed into her from birth.

'We can afford it,' Geoffrey stated flatly.

'Then yes, thank you, I would like the car.'

The look he gave her then made her suspect it wasn't money that had been worrying him after all. Once she would have felt confident she knew what he was thinking, but not anymore.

'So,' he joked, 'we'll buy a house, *and* a car, and eat bread and water for six months. Now, say, "Thank you, Geoffrey", and give me a kiss!'

Three weeks after the move to St Heliers Nina was christened. The ceremony took place in an atmosphere of argument and recrimination. Kay had wanted Sandra to be a godmother. Geoffrey had flatly refused. When Winifred got wind of the disagreement she spiked both their guns by announcing she'd already indicated to the twins that *they* would be godmothers. 'Well, naturally,' she pouted, 'I assumed . . .'

As for god*fathers*, Kay insisted on her brother, while Geoffrey insisted on Alistair Glendinning. Neither was happy with the other's choice (Kay had secretly planned on Philip Muir, and

Geoffrey had earmarked Stuart Sutch), but at least the compromise was theirs, and not something forced on them by Winifred.

The ceremony was held at St Saviour's in Remuera. The priest, the Reverend Theodore Meddings, had visited the young parents several times, impressing on them the importance of church attendance, not just in the run-up to the baptism, but in the years to come. 'We'll expect to see little Nina at Sunday School,' he'd said. 'Of course I realise St Saviour's isn't your local church, but it's no distance by car.'

Kay, uncomfortable in a linen coat-dress, waited outside the church for the guests to arrive. Clive had written to say he couldn't make it. The hurt she'd felt was hedged with anger. He would have stayed with them in the new house. He needn't have had anything to do with Lionel and Winifred.

First to arrive were her parents. Kay, seeing the lengths her mother had gone to to 'dress up', felt a tug of love for her. She was wearing the outfit she'd bought for the wedding, a full-skirted pink nylon dress that might have looked passable on a teenager, but looked ridiculous on a grey-haired woman with 42-inch hips. Over the top of the dress she wore a brown woollen jacket with an astrakhan collar. Not only did it belong with another outfit, it belonged in another era. Her hat was the inevitable white straw.

'Lovely to see you, Mum,' Kay greeted, kissing her warmly on the cheek.

Kissing her father didn't come so easily.

By the time everyone was seated Kay's head was aching, and Nina, frustrated by the restrictions on her movement, had started to grizzle. Geoffrey, whose hands she observed with dismay had begun to shake, looked at her gravely, as if she alone were responsible for the deteriorating atmosphere. Nina wasn't used to being hemmed in. Kay would have nothing to do with the playpens other mothers set so much store by. *Her* daughter was allowed to roam freely.

'Do you have children, Mr Meddings?' Kay had asked, during one particularly uncomfortable session.

It had been the wrong question to put. Not only did the Reverend Theodore have no children, he had no wife. All he had were answers. Attend church every week, send Nina to Sunday

School, give generously to the Church Missionary Society, and all your troubles will vanish.

My father made me go to Sunday School, Kay had been tempted to reply, but he never went near a church himself. Would you like to know about my father, Mr Meddings? Now, that would make an interesting confession. Not that *he*'d ever tell you. The walls of his world would come tumbling down if he did.

The church was not particularly full. The Reverend Theodore was no crowd-puller. The usual small congregation was augmented by Nina's family and friends, but even so there were several empty pews.

'You do have a stand-in for your brother?' Mr Meddings checked, as the ceremony was about to start.

Nina, responding to a sudden groan from the organ, threw her arms up in the air, clocking the hapless vicar on the chin. 'Car,' she urged. 'Car, Mum-mum.'

'Later, darling,' Kay soothed. Nina's first recognisable word, apart from 'mum', was 'car'. Going in the car meant going to Auntie Bet's, and that meant smiles all round.

'My partner is standing in,' Geoffrey explained, coming to his wife's rescue.

Kay smiled at her husband. Perhaps it was as well Clive had stayed away. Lunch was to be at Winifred's. Kay had protested, but her mother-in-law, whose manner of asking about her studies – 'How *do* you manage? All that reading, so bad for your eyes' – never failed to produce feelings of inadequacy, had worn her down. 'Your exams are quite close, aren't they, dear?' she'd said, demolishing argument in a final, telling swoop.

'"Dearly beloved, forasmuch as all men are conceived and born in sin . . ."'

It'll soon be over, Kay reassured herself. Tonight, when everyone's gone, I'll put on a record, and you and I'll dance, she silently promised her daughter. 'I Can't Get No Satisfaction'. You like that one.

'"They brought young children to Christ, that He should touch them; and His disciples rebuked those that brought them . . ."'

Now that was more like it. If Jesus were alive today would He wear a badge saying, 'Make Love not War'? What form would His civil disobedience take? Jesus the First Hippie.

'"Dost thou, in the name of this Child, renounce the devil and all his works . . . ?"'

The twins' faces were a study. Winifred had drummed into them what a serious occasion this was. Not even Nina, busy pummelling her mother's neck, distracted them.

'"I renounce them all,"' the godparents chorused.

'"Nina Joy, I baptise thee in the name of the Father and of the Son and of the Holy Ghost."'

Kay's heart gave a sudden lurch. If only it were true, she thought. If only there *were* a God to keep her safe.

Then it was over, and they were outside again, and the sun was pouring down on them, while Nina basked in universal admiration. Even Pauline, normally impatient with small children, expressed approval of the child's good humour. 'Take my advice,' she whispered to Kay. 'Keep her out of Winifred's clutches.'

'Winifred's seen to that herself,' Kay whispered back. 'She refuses to babysit.'

Pauline's eyes sparked. There was a large white stain on the shoulder of her jacket. Her hat, a shapeless woollen object, looked suspiciously like a tea cosy. 'You and my nephew,' she went on, 'I like what I see. But you need to watch out.' She looked round pointedly. Kay's eyes followed, taking in the bright wooden church, the lines of parked cars, the vicar dispensing goodwill, the well-dressed people talking in the sunshine. 'These are shark-infested waters,' Pauline warned.

36

The day the last exam ended a series of small riots broke out on the campus of the University. Waves of students in jeans and jandles and loose-fitting Indian shirts burst out of the exam rooms, filling the quads and gardens with shrill voices, and volleys of books tossed into the air. Beer bottles were produced from satchels; cigarettes lit; tins of marijuana passed, with packets of cigarette papers, from hand to hand. Exams were over. The long summer holidays were beginning. It was the end of 1967. What a time to be young!

In the middle of this maelstrom two young women stood arguing. One was small, golden-haired and fiery. The other was taller than average, slim, with large eyes and pale cheeks framed by a boyish haircut.

'But I don't *want* to come, Sandra. I've been looking forward to a weekend on my own.'

'I'm not inviting you for the weekend.'

'Besides, there's no one to look after Nina.'

'What about the famous Auntie Bet?'

'She's not a casual babysitter.'

'A neighbour, then.'

Kay plunged her thumb into her mouth. The truth was her neighbour, the nosy one, was always offering to babysit. It was tempting to accept, but something about Mrs Bettina Cantwell stopped Kay each time. For one thing, she was a paid-up member of the 'yoo-hoo' brigade. Once she got her foot inside the door there was no shifting her. In the run-up to exams Kay had several times moved the car out of the garage, just to give the impression she wasn't at home.

'I'll see what I can do,' she conceded.

'Cheer up,' Sandra laughed. 'I'm not inviting you to a funeral.'

But it'll be *my* funeral when Geoffrey finds out, Kay thought, as she hurried off in the direction of her car. Geoffrey had changed his mind about Sandra. If her name came up, which it didn't anymore if Kay could help it, he'd call her a 'pot head', and urge Kay to look for a more suitable friend. 'You're a mother now,' he'd remind her. 'I'd have thought you'd want to share that experience with others in the same boat.'

If you were home more often, Kay answered her husband, as she climbed into the car and started the engine, I wouldn't need to see so much of Sandra.

'That was Dad,' Geoffrey had said when he came off the phone two nights ago. She'd known by the way he looked at her that something unpleasant was brewing.

'What did he want?'

'He's invited me to go on the boat with him this weekend.'

'You said no, didn't you?'

'He's never invited me on my own before.'

'Does that mean you're going?'

'That kind of invitation, it's really a summons.'

Arriving at the creche Kay found Auntie Bet waiting for her on the doorstep. 'I've got the sherry glasses out,' she announced. 'It's unwind, time. You do like sherry?' she laughed, over her shoulder.

'I used to drink rather a lot of it,' Kay admitted.

When Nina spotted her mother she squealed and reached up her arms, only to wriggle away seconds later, and return to her game.

'I hope that hubby of yours is taking you out tonight,' Auntie Bet said. 'A nice dinner somewhere. You look washed out.'

'We're going to a party,' Kay lied. 'A celebration for the end of exams.'

'Well, you make sure you enjoy yourselves.'

Mrs Cantwell, as Kay had predicted, was only too keen to babysit. 'Sorry about the mess,' Kay apologised, seeing the look on her neighbour's face. 'I've been rather busy lately.'

'Mr Grieve away, is he?'

'Sailing. With his father.'

'Well, it's nice you have a girlfriend to keep you company. A woman needs her friends.'

'Nina's all ready for bed. There's a bottle if she wakes, but she almost never does.'

'Little angel she looks in her nightie.'

'I usually wait till she's sleepy. I think bed should be a place children *want* to go to, don't you?'

Mrs Cantwell smiled stiffly.

'I'm sure she'll settle early,' Kay rushed on. 'She's had a very busy day. If you have any trouble just put on a record. She loves music.'

Twenty minutes later she was at Sandra's door.

'You made it,' Sandra greeted. 'Hey! What's with the dress? I like it.'

Kay grinned. She was wearing a maroon cotton shift dress and strappy sandals. She didn't often feel confident about her looks, but tonight she did.

She followed Sandra into the flat. Most of the guests were known to her, but there were one or two strangers. Mike, Sandra's lover, was leaning against the chimney breast, smoking.

The room smelt of pot and incense. Kay felt the old tug in her gut. Just for once she'd like to relax, really relax. She'd told Geoffrey she didn't smoke anymore and it was true, near enough. She'd shared the occasional joint with Sandra, but she'd always been careful to stop before she got high. If Geoffrey were here she wouldn't even be considering it, but he was on the harbour with his father.

She moved to the other side of the room, found herself a drink and a cushion, and sat on the floor. Someone put on a record. A melancholy wail filled her ears. Indian music, Sandra's favourite. When a joint was put into her hand, Kay smiled gratefully and drew the smoke deep into her lungs.

Sandra's walls were covered with posters. There was one from her Easter trip to Haight-Ashbury, another advertising a Bob Dylan concert. But the one that dominated was a huge photo of Timothy Leary, with the words, 'Tune in, turn on, drop out' coming out of his mouth in a flowery bubble.

With a part of her mind Kay began looking for Dave. Not that he was likely to show up at a party like this. He and Sandra inhabited different universes. Kay had heard a rumour that Trixie had left Dave, but there was no way it could be true. Trixie would never turn her back on all that money.

The joint came back to her. She was beginning to feel the buzz now. Tomorrow, Sunday, she would go to church. The Reverend Meddings had been on the phone again. 'Haven't seen much of you and your good man lately,' he'd accused. She might even phone Winifred and suggest they go together. Two 'yachting widows' keeping each other company.

'Hi! Have we met? I'm Roy.'

Kay smiled at the figure hovering above her. She was still sober enough to realise that the effect he was having on her was as much to do with her relaxed state as with his undeniable attractiveness. He was tall and slender, with long fairish hair tied back in a pony tail. But it was his eyes that were making Kay's heart race. Or rather, the *look* in his eyes. I know you, they signalled. Don't think you can escape. 'I'm Kay Grieve,' she said.

'Ah, so you're Kay.'

'D'you want to sit down?'

He smiled. Goodness, Kay thought, as he lowered himself on to her cushion, that stuff must be stronger than I realised.

'Sandra and I are old friends,' Roy volunteered.

'Then why haven't I met you before?'

There was a flash of white teeth, and that look again in his eyes. Why had Sandra never mentioned him? He wasn't the kind of man you forgot. 'We could dance,' he suggested.

'You'll need to change the record.'

'Something tells me you're good dancer.'

It didn't seem to concern Roy when, a few moments later, they found themselves the only people dancing. Kay hoped no one was watching. Her cheeks were flaming: her body, leaning into Roy's, reacting in ways she couldn't account for. She fixed her gaze on the string of beads hanging round his neck. If she looked at those, and not at the drifts of pale hair visible through his open shirt, she'd resist the temptation to kiss him.

'Sandra didn't do you justice,' Roy said when the record, the latest Ray Columbus, came to an end.

'Oh?'

'Don't get me wrong. She thinks a lot of you. But she neglected to mention how sexy you are.'

'You do know I'm married?' Kay muttered.

'Don't worry about it,' Roy answered.

'*And* I have a daughter.'

Roy took her hand. Kay wondered how a heart could beat as hers was beating and not jump right out of its cage. 'You and Sandra,' she said, as they made their way back to their cushion. 'How long have you been friends?' An unwelcome thought had entered her head. Mike was not Sandra's only lover. Could it be that Roy . . . ?

'Sandra said you were bright,' he remarked cheerfully.

'So, you are more than just friends?'

'Past tense, dear lady. History. *You're* the person I want to go to bed with.'

Kay's laugh verged on the hysterical. She snatched at the joint, which was being passed her way, and sucked on it eagerly.

'Maybe not tonight, maybe not for a week or a month, but we will go to bed together. I'd bet my life on it.'

Later that evening Kay found herself sitting next to a girl with stained teeth and stale-smelling breath, listening to Roy sing to his own accompaniment on the guitar. Roy Blade, his name was. He was a singer by profession. He could be heard most nights in a coffee bar called The Devil's Kitchen, which Kay knew by reputation. Roy's father, she'd learned, was a Methodist minister.

'He's trouble,' her unfortunate neighbour confided. 'I'd give him a wide berth if I were you.'

Kay waited till the music had stopped; then, taking advantage of the general movement in the room, she slipped out of the door. She glanced at her watch. It wasn't even ten o'clock.

'My, you *are* back early,' Mrs Cantwell gushed. 'I've only just got the little madam to bed. Six o'clock on the dot mine always went. Regular as clockwork. Children need to know what's what.'

'I'm very grateful to you, Mrs Cantwell. Did you manage to watch *The Plane Makers*?'

Mrs Cantwell's lips puckered. 'I'll have to ask my friend to fill me in,' she sniffed. 'Pity. It's my favourite programme.'

When Kay woke the next morning her mouth was dry, and her head ached as if she were about to succumb to the 'flu. Her mind was clear though. Everything about the evening, including her good intentions, she recalled in vivid detail. But in the harsh light of day the thought of Winifred and church was too daunting. She'd clean the house instead. That would please Geoffrey. And Nina would think it was a game. Just come home, she urged her absent husband. Come home quickly.

'What's all this then?'

Kay tightened her grip on her husband's neck. 'I'm glad you're back,' she said fiercely.

'I've only been gone one night.'

'Well, it was one too many. You can tell your father from me, next time I'm coming with you.'

37

Over the three months of the university holidays Kay worked hard to obliterate the name Roy Blade from her mind. She avoided Customs Street, site of The Devil's Kitchen was. She all but broke off the friendship with Sandra. She buried herself in her reading, devouring great chunks of Molière, Rimbaud, Verlaine, Stendahl, Flaubert. For the first time she took an obvious pride in her home, working (to Geoffrey's amazement and Nina's delight) long hours around the house, painting window frames, weeding, washing curtains, cleaning out cupboards.

Occasionally, for no particular reason, she would burst into tears. Then Nina would run to her (she'd started walking the week before Christmas), and throw her little arms around her neck, and demand to know where it hurt.

The day she read in the paper that The Cedars was for sale, she wept inconsolably. If she could have kept Dave as her friend she need never have had Sandra in her life, and the name Roy Blade would have meant nothing. Dave, like Sandra, might be a pot head, but he was a decent human being who loved his wife, and dreamed of a better world. Now he was heading overseas. The rumours about his marriage were true. Trixie *had* left him. All of which must have been known to Geoffrey, yet not once had Dave's name been mentioned.

When another fit of weeping overcame her two days later, Kay, feeling Nina's damp cheeks pressed against her own, hearing her angel voice, 'No, Mum-mum, no cwy,' felt sick with shame. The occasion of this particular collapse was a letter from Lynne. Brian had been kicked out of medical school. He'd failed one too many exams. It was what Kay, and everyone else in their circle at Otago, had expected, but now it had happened Kay was filled with despair. She'd just written to Lynne to congratulate her on being pregnant again. 'In case you're wondering,' Lynne had explained, 'this baby is planned!'

What would they do? How would they live? Was nothing good ever to be allowed to last?

At the beginning of March Kay enrolled for the first part of her MA course. The Head of the French Department, Professor Nathan Bute, went out of his way to welcome her. 'You should have been on board last year,' he scolded, 'not wasting your time with Anthropology.'

At the end of the year she would sit four papers: Language and Translation, Symbolist Poetry, the Plays of Molière, and the Nineteenth-century Novel. Driving back to St Heliers she felt, for the first time in months, that she could manage her life. She was on track again. Her heart had stopped bouncing up and down like a juggler's ball. She would have to see Sandra. That couldn't be avoided. But if Roy's name came up, which it would, she'd enquire casually about him and leave it at that. For all she knew he wasn't even living in Auckland anymore.

So the term began. Kay had coffee with Sandra, and endured her sarcastic remarks about domestic bliss, and discovered, without having to ask, that Roy *was* still around, still singing at The Devil's Kitchen, still wondering, like Sandra, what had happened to a certain woman he'd been very much attracted to, but whose life, sadly, was not her own.

And in due course, as was inevitable, Kay turned a corner and there was Roy, sitting on the park bench where she herself often sat, idly strumming his guitar. There's nothing to be afraid of, she told herself, as she obeyed his invitation to join her. You have a lecture in twenty minutes. This will fill in the time nicely.

More encounters followed: in the park, in the coffee bar, outside the Library. They were never arranged. It's a small world, Kay told herself each time. And all I'm doing is talking.

She never consciously looked for him, not until the day in April when Martin Luther King was shot. Geoffrey would be as appalled as she was, but it wasn't Geoffrey she wanted to be with, it was Roy. He'd let her cry, not try and stop her. He might even cry with her. And he'd remind her the world was changing, she only had to look around. 'Our generation is different,' he'd insist. 'We believe in love, not war.'

It was late in the afternoon when she found him.

'You know, we're not so different, you and I,' he said when they'd done with weeping. 'We both come from dishonest families.'

'You don't know anything about my family.'

'Don't I?'

'Not unless you're psychic.'

He took her hand. 'My father is a hypocrite and a coward,' he announced.

'I thought he was a Methodist minister?'

Roy's laugh sounded uncomfortably like a sneer. Kay turned her head. Queen Victoria stared smugly down at her from her pedestal.

'Two years ago,' Roy explained, 'my father was arrested and charged with indecent exposure. My mother had just died, lucky for her. I was the one who had to bail the old pervert out.'

Kay nodded. Either Roy was psychic or what he'd just said came under the heading of coincidence. Not that their histories matched: but if she ever told anyone *her* story, she suspected it would come out in much the same bitter way. 'You don't sound as if you've forgiven him,' she said.

Again Roy laughed. 'He thinks I have,' he answered.

'What does that mean?'

'It means, my lovely, that I'm not going to tell you anymore until you agree to sleep with me.'

38

Geoffrey was worried about his wife. When he tried to put his anxiety into words it sounded absurd. She's being too nice. She's trying too hard to please. I'd be happier if we were having the occasional quarrel...

Take last night, for instance. He'd told her he was going to forego skiing this year. Nina was growing up so fast he didn't want to miss out on her. But Kay had argued him out of his sacrifice. 'You know how much you love it,' she'd said. 'Besides, it's good for you. Helps you unwind.'

'You used to want me to stay at home.'

'And you used to say it was me you missed, not your daughter.'

She'd become secretive too. He knew, for example, that she'd started going on demonstrations again, but she never talked about it. If he questioned her, she'd shift the goal posts, subtly, so that he became the one doing the justifying. 'If you approved of the Tet offensive,' she'd challenged recently, 'you must approve the use of nuclear weapons. The argument is the same. Whatever it takes to finish the war.'

The night they learned Robert Kennedy had been shot he offered to come with her on the inevitable demonstration. Robert Kennedy was the peace candidate. On him, as on Martin Luther King, the hopes of millions had been focused. But Kay didn't want her husband to march with her. 'It'll interfere with your work,' she argued. 'You'll get into trouble with the partners.'

She was lying, of course. Those weren't her reasons. He remembered, with some bitterness, the question mark he'd put beside the word 'Truthful' on his list of Negative Qualities.

He should have realised then that Kay Dyer had problems with the truth.

There were other changes as well, physical ones. Sometimes he wondered if she were taking something. His mother had changed in just the same sort of way when she started swallowing valium. It wasn't anything he could put his finger on. She was thinner, anyone could see that, and her eyes seemed to be permanently enlarged; but the change he was talking about had more to do with the way she moved. She walked round the house like someone in a trance.

He'd expected, of course, that her studies would preoccupy her, but he hadn't imagined it would be to the exclusion of almost everything else in her life except Nina. So far as Nina was concerned he couldn't complain. She was running everywhere now, cheerful as a sandboy, chattering nineteen to the dozen. No one could describe her as neglected.

So what was it that was bugging him? Was it Kay's success? She'd got an A in Anthropology last year, and seemed headed for the same sort of triumph this year. Recently he'd gone to see her in a Molière play. It was all in French, but he didn't need language to identify her talent. She was a born actress. Why had that never come out before?

If only there was someone he could confide in. All this speculation was beginning to wear him down. But he knew what his parents would say. Their disapproval of their daughter-in-law was close to the surface these days. As for society's other licensed adviser – the vicar – he'd rather talk to a stranger in the street. Theo Meddings's visits had been something of a joke at first. Now they were plain irritating.

Perhaps he should take Kay away on a holiday. Without Nina. A week in Fiji, perhaps? But how the hell was he supposed to do that? He could afford it. That wasn't the problem. But he couldn't afford the time away from work. And then who would look after Nina? That was the other problem. His mother was a non-starter, and he couldn't see Kay agreeing to leave her beloved daughter with *her* parents. No, it was out of the question. He would just have to put up with the anxiety, and hope for the best.

Kay stood at the door of The Devil's Kitchen. She knew what

she was doing. Roy had kept up his pursuit of her through one and a half terms. 'The day you decide you want to *live*,' he'd said to her last week, 'come and hear me sing. You won't need to say anything. I'll know.'

For one and a half terms she'd endured a fickle heart beat, sleepless nights, a barrage of encouragement and contempt from Sandra, and the recurring delights of being Nina's mother. She had also experienced, in the company of Nathan Bute and others in her class, the joys of a language and literature she loved above her own. It should have been enough. The voice in her head had been shouting that for weeks. You love Geoffrey, the same voice kept reminding her. Just because you had doubts in the beginning doesn't excuse . . . But I haven't done anything, she'd argue back. I can't help the way I feel . . . And how is that? . . . Trapped, I feel trapped . . .

She pushed open the door. A gust of warm air clutched at her face. For a second or two she couldn't see. Then her eyes made out, among a blur of faces, Roy, sitting at a table with a girl in a red mini dress. She turned to go. 'When I look into your eyes,' he'd said to her yesterday, 'I feel I'm looking into a bottomless lake. Come to think of it, Lake is a good name for you. I'm going to call you that from now on.'

She'd laughed, though more from irritation than amusement. 'Why does everyone feel this need to change my name?' she'd complained.

'I'm not changing, I'm recognising.'

'Kay!' she heard. 'Lake!'

Her hand was on the door. So long as she didn't look back she'd be safe.

'People,' Roy's voice rang out. 'I want you to meet my friend Lake. The most beautiful woman in Auckland.'

It was Kay's impression then that the whole place fell silent. Well, it would, wouldn't it? she thought, as she slowly turned.

'Lake and I are in love,' Roy announced.

Kay giggled. Then, as the audience began to clap and whistle, she felt herself blush. Next moment Roy's hand was on her arm, propelling her through the door.

'Have you got your car?' he asked.

'Yes.'

'Then let's go.'

She took it for granted they would be going to his place. Geoffrey was in Hamilton, but Nina was at home with the baby-sitter. 'You'll have to direct me,' she said, as she started the engine.

'Will it shock you to discover I live in Remuera?'

Kay didn't answer. She would scarcely have registered if he'd said he lived in Buckingham Palace. She was a bird flying high above the city.

He started undressing her the moment they entered his flat. Apart from her name, her new name, which he shouted twice, he didn't say anything. She'd assumed they would go to his bedroom, but instead he lowered her on to the floor, pausing only to prop a cushion under her hips.

It was all over very quickly. Lying in his arms, Kay told herself this wasn't the real world. Real was driving home to Nina, and Geoffrey returning from Hamilton.

'I love you,' she whispered.

'Yes,' he answered.

'Do you love me?'

'I love swimming in your lake,' Roy said.

39

Lionel stared at the newspaper in front of him, and tried to ignore the sound of the twins quarrelling outside his window. The first warm day of spring. After weeks of rain the air smelt like a chemist's shop. 'Why don't you play tennis?' he'd suggested, in exasperation. 'I spend all this money getting a court put in and you hardly ever go near it.'

You'd think, at sixteen, they could amuse themselves without squabbling.

His hand reached for his whisky. Winifred was lying down upstairs. She had another of her headaches. His one attempt to convince her the headaches would stop if she knocked off the valium had ended in disaster. 'I took your advice once, if you remember,' she'd spat back at him, 'and my reward was your floozie with the pound signs in her eyes. How is she, by the way? Still working in that *divine* little dress shop?'

How his wife had discovered his secret was a mystery to Lionel. Other men seemed to get away with it. But Auckland, as he knew now to his cost, was a city with a genius for scandal.

'The Chief Justice, in a judgement delivered in the High Court, has advocated surgery for the treatment of hardened criminals. "In these surgically enlightened times," Mr Justice Cornelius said, "it should be possible to disable a criminal by the removal of a hand or limb, thus ensuring an end to his criminal activity . . ."'

The man's off his rocker, Lionel thought. And to think *he's* Chief Justice, whereas I can't even make it to the District Court Bench.

Today had not been a good day. Over lunch with Bunce

Goodbody at the club it was as good as spelled out for him that he would never make Judge. What hurt most was the knowledge that the entire profession must have known for years that his hopes were futile, yet *he'd* gone on believing his elevation was inevitable. He'd done everything according to the book: grabbed the high-profile cases; cultivated the right people; taken silk at the right moment. He'd only made one mistake but that, he acknowledged, in the bitter aftermath of today's lunch, had cost him everything. In that one moment of weakness he'd lost his marriage, his hopes of a Judgeship, and his peace of mind.

'We've been friends for nearly four decades,' Bunce had said. 'I think it's time I came clean with you.'

'So this lunch isn't about a replacement for Judge Davidson?'

Bunce shook his head.

'I'm not in the running then?'

Another denial.

'Since you seem to have the ear of everyone from the Prime Minister down,' Lionel had persisted, probing for a truth he dreaded to hear, 'you presumably know *why* my name is never on that list?'

'If it's any comfort,' Bunce had replied, after the kind of pause that spoke more than words, 'your son's name came up in discussion recently. He's been making quite a splash, as you know. If he plays his cards right . . . In fact, that's the reason I suggested this lunch. I wanted to check with you that there's nothing I should know, of a personal nature. You understand what I'm saying?'

Bloody cheek! Lionel reacted now. As if I didn't know what you were on about. 'We don't see much of Kay these days,' Bunce's wife had simpered when he found himself standing next to her at a recent cocktail party. 'Though I did see her a week or so ago on one of those ghastly anti-American marches. Don't you just hate the way everyone attacks the United States now? Bunce and I can't understand it. Not after what they did for us in the war. She had little Nina with her too. I was surprised to see that. Not really the place for a toddler, I would have thought.'

Lionel got up to refill his glass. The twins had stopped fighting, thank God. The thwack of ball on racquet, and their intermittent squeals prompted an attack, rare for Lionel, of self-pity. His life wasn't supposed to have worked out like this: thwarted ambition; unhappy wife; spoiled daughters; his only son saddled with a dodgy marriage. He'd been born with the proverbial silver spoon in his mouth. He should have made better use of it. He had, until that wretched business fifteen years ago.

He returned to his chair. There were other, more immediate things to think about. Geoffrey was decades away from being made a Judge, but that didn't mean Bunce's warning should be ignored. Trouble was, he couldn't talk to his son anymore. Not about Kay. Whenever her name was mentioned he clammed up tighter than a nun's arse. 'Bring your wife to heel,' he might have said, a year ago. 'Cut off her allowance. There are always ways.'

But someone had to talk to him. It wasn't just this business of demonstrating, though that was bad enough. It was something he saw himself, last Tuesday night. If Bunce had been in the car with him he wouldn't have needed to invite him to lunch today. He'd have known the rumours surrounding the wife of his Junior Partner were true.

What happened was this. Lionel was taking Diane ('She has a name,' he'd shouted, in a recent quarrel with Winifred) to dinner. For thirteen years they'd been going to the same place, a restaurant in a hotel at the bottom of Queen Street, patronised almost exclusively by overseas tourists. Not once in all that time had Lionel seen anyone he knew. Till last Tuesday that is, when he spotted his daughter-in-law coming out of a seedy-looking place in the street behind the hotel, called, if memory served, The Devil's Pantry.

'Good God!' he'd exclaimed when he realised the identity of the young woman in the short skirt and leather jacket.

'What is it?' Diane had asked.

'It's Geoff's wife.'

Diane's request that he slow down was ignored. Too risky. Besides, he didn't like mixing Diane up with his family. He'd worked hard over the years to keep the two parts of his life separate.

Another drink was what was needed. It usually took three for his head to clear. The problem was, how to approach Geoff without betraying his own situation. He couldn't stop Winifred throwing Diane in his face, but he sure as hell didn't want to give his son the chance. That Winifred had kept his secret he never doubted for a moment. She may have stopped loving him, but she had her pride and she was loyal. He'd staked a lot on that loyalty of hers. Whoever blew the whistle on him over that business fifteen years ago, he'd swear an oath it wasn't his wife.

Theo Meddings. The name came to Lionel as he drained the last drop from his glass. Of course. He should have thought of him before. Theo kept a pastoral eye on Geoff and Kay. Who better to sound out the situation, alert Geoff to what his wife was getting up to, than the man who'd christened Nina?

'I'd like to see you as soon as possible,' he said when Theo answered the phone. 'It's a matter of some delicacy.'

'Come in, come in. Good to see you.' Theo Meddings shook Lionel's hand, and ushered him into the sitting room. A delicate matter, the man had said. That suggested sitting room rather than office. 'Whisky?'

'Don't mind if I do.'

'Been a while since you and I . . .'

Lionel nodded. Fifteen years to be exact. He'd come here on that dreadful night. Seeking, what? Absolution? But to qualify for that he'd have had to tell the truth.

'Family all right?' Theo enquired when they were both seated.

Lionel smoothed his few remaining hairs across his scalp. There were times, in the past, when he'd wondered about Theo. Was the man a fairy? He didn't, thank God, have any of the mannerisms, but he'd never shown any inclination to get married either. Probably, if they talked about it, which they never would, he'd make a joke of it; say he'd not met the right woman yet. That any man, not a Roman Catholic priest, would choose to be celibate, was beyond Lionel's comprehension.

'You know, you're a lucky man in many ways,' Lionel said. 'Children aren't all they're cracked up to be. My daughters will probably bankrupt me, and my son . . .'

'Yes. How *is* Geoffrey?' Theo asked. It must be three months since he last visited the young couple. He'd never say anything to Lionel, of course, but they were far from being his favourite parishioners. In fact, if it weren't for the baby, he'd have given up on them by now. 'My wife has declared herself an agnostic,' Geoffrey had said, at their last meeting. What on earth was he supposed to make of a remark like that?

'It's Geoffrey I've come to talk to you about,' Lionel said.

'I see.'

'Well, not so much Geoffrey as Kay.'

Theo waited. His own view of Kay Grieve was not one he was prepared to share. Short skirts, bare legs, hair shaved above her ears. The latest thing was that she'd become an actress. He'd read a review of some French play she'd been in. 'A dazzling performance,' the reviewer had written. 'Like most other members of the audience, I couldn't take my eyes off her.'

'Thing is,' Lionel was saying, 'I caught sight of her the other night, coming out of a rather dubious-looking coffee bar in Customs Street. I was driving Fred Mullins home from Rotary. He lives in Herne Bay.'

'Customs Street,' Theo said.

'You know the sort of place I mean. Waterfront dives.'

Theo nodded.

'Needless to say, she wasn't with Geoff.'

'I can understand your concern.'

'I don't want Geoff hurt, Theo. He's had enough of that in his life. If his wife's playing fast and loose, I think he should know about it.'

'And you want me to . . . ?'

'You're the obvious person. If it came from me, well . . .' Lionel spread his hands. 'Winifred and I have had our reservations about Kay from the start. Geoff knows that. He'd tell us to stop interfering.'

Theo rocked his glass in his hand, watching as the light danced over the surface of the whisky. Sometimes he thought he was in the wrong profession. Having to justify God's ways to men like Lionel Grieve was an exhausting occupation.

'Don't suppose you noticed the name of this place?' he enquired casually.

'What?'

'Where you saw Kay.'

'Devil something. Devil's Pantry?'

• Elspeth Sandys

'The Devil's Kitchen.'
'You know it?'
'By reputation.'
'And what's that when it's at home?'
Theo flicked the dandruff from his collar. Should he offer another whisky? Four, the man had drunk on that other night. 'Let's just say, you're right to be concerned,' he said.

40

'Stop it! Stop doing this. Jesus . . .' Sandra turned to the two other people in the room. 'Do something, Roy,' she commanded.

Roy smiled his miraculous smile, and ambled towards the woman he'd been fucking every Tuesday and Wednesday night for the past three months. She wasn't the only woman he was fucking, but until something better turned up she was still Number One. He just wished she wouldn't go in for these crying jags. This particular one had started when she turned up on his doorstep tonight. He couldn't make sense of her jabbering. Something about a Reverend someone or other threatening to tell tales to her husband. He'd given her something to calm her down, and waited for Sandra and Mike.

'Now now, Lake,' he soothed, pulling her into his arms, 'you're getting things all out of proportion. We agreed about this, remember? You wanted it as much as we did.'

'I want to go home,' she sobbed.

'You are home. *We're* your home. Me, Sandra, Mike. How often do we have to tell you?'

'Please, Roy. You don't know what's happened.'

'Who got you out of that trouble with the police, eh? Not once, but twice. Who gets pills for you when you have to stay up all night to write an essay? We're your family, Lake. Your *real* family.'

'I know, and I'm grateful, but . . .'

'We're talking about love, Lake. Love is what it's all about. Now come on, get your clothes off. Why should we be the only ones who are naked? No one's going to hurt you. How can four people who love each other do any harm?'

• Elspeth Sandys

The pill he'd given her earlier was having an effect. She was like a rag doll in his arms. But that would change with what he planned to give her next: a mixture of Methadrine and Drinamyl, known as a purple heart.

He sat her on the end of the bed, and helped her pull her dress over her head. He couldn't help wishing it was Noeline sitting there. Noeline wouldn't need a pill to get her going. For a sixteen year old she was extraordinarily knowledgeable. Sixteen going on fourteen, he suspected. The moment he spotted her outside The Devil's Kitchen, trying to pluck up courage to walk in, he knew he had to have her. In her navy gym slip and black lace-up shoes, she was irresistible.

'Christ, you look awful,' he said when all Kay's clothes were off. 'Your eyes are like little redcurrants.'

'All right, young lady, you've got some explaining to do.'

Kay looked from her father-in-law to her husband, and tried to make sense of the fact that they were both sitting in her house on a Tuesday night when Geoffrey was supposed to be in Hamilton. Her head felt as if it had been hit by a hammer. As for the rest of her body, if she thought about that she'd throw up.

'Where's Karen?' she asked.

'Karen?' Lionel directed the word at his son.

'Baby-sitter,' Geoffrey answered.

The way he said the word forced Kay to look at him again. When had his eyes become bloodshot? And where were his glasses? He must have sensed her staring because he turned to face her. What passed between them then was worse than any words. *I've* made him look that, Kay thought.

'Perhaps you'd care to tell us where you've been tonight?' Lionel said.

'With friends,' Kay answered.

'These friends, you met them at The Devil's Kitchen, did you?'

'No.'

'Don't lie!'

'Dad,' Geoffrey protested.

'Leave this to me, son.'

'I'd rather . . .'

'Leave it to me!'

'Would you like a cup of tea?' Kay couldn't believe she'd just said that. What did she think this was? A Tupperware party?

'I'm surprised you still know how to make it,' her father-in-law replied. 'Or do you throw other things in with it? Pills of one sort or another.'

'Dad, this isn't getting anywhere.'

'Have you looked in on Nina?' Kay asked her husband.

'She's asleep,' Geoffrey muttered.

'I think I'll just . . .'

'You're not going anywhere till we hear what you've been up to,' Lionel scowled, pushing her back into her chair. 'We know about The Devil's Kitchen, and we know about the police raids. So there's no point lying to us. What in God's name possessed you to get tied up with a place like that?'

Kay leaned her head on the back of her chair. If they would just let her sleep, then she'd answer their questions. She couldn't remember how she'd got home. All she could remember was standing on Roy's doorstep, blubbing. Roy's flat, where she'd experienced the best and worst moments of her life. Roy's flat, paid for by his father. 'Guilt money,' Roy had explained. 'Stroke of genius, don't you think? Making the poor bugger pay for my silence.'

'I'm sorry, Geoff,' she whispered. 'I'm so very sorry.'

'So, you don't deny . . .'

'Dad, I think you'd better go.'

'I'm not going till we have the truth.'

Kay slid forward in her chair. For the first time she looked, really looked, at her father-in-law. What a sad sack of a man he was. She couldn't think why she'd ever been afraid of him. 'The truth?' she mocked. 'Oh, yes, let's have that by all means.'

'Darling . . .'

'No, Geoff, your father's right. Truth or Dare. Which will it be?'

'You're sick . . .'

'Yes.'

'You've been taking something.'

'Yes.'

'You've been smoking?'

Kay laughed.

'Ask her if she's been unfaithful?' Lionel intervened fiercely. 'Go on. Ask her that.'

'Leave it out, Dad.'

'Don't you want to know if your wife's been sleeping with another man?'

'Why don't you ask me yourself?' Kay challenged.

'All right, I'm asking. Have you committed adultery?'

Kay threw back her head. The ceiling rippled drunkenly above her. Where was Roy? She was having a bad trip. Roy knew what to do. Hold the right wrist and the trip will be good. Hold the left . . .

'What are you doing?'

'Take my hand,' she begged. 'No, not that one. Hold it by the wrist. Please, Roy . . .'

'Who's Roy?'

'Help me.'

'What do you want me to do?'

'Hold me.'

'Christ . . .'

'OK,' Lionel snapped. 'That's it. I'm calling a doctor.'

Two weeks later Kay and Nina moved into a flat in Grey Lynn, a suburb of Auckland seldom visited by people from St Heliers. They took almost nothing with them: Nina's cot and toys, one of the spare beds, a couple of chairs from the basement. In the note Kay left for her husband she apologised for taking the car, and promised to return it as soon as she was earning and could afford to buy one of her own. 'You can see Nina whenever you want,' she wrote. 'I'm not taking her away from you.'

Three days after the move Kay started work as a proof-reader on *The Herald*. The job was dreary, but the hours were flexible and the pay enough to cover food and rent. The trouble was, she wouldn't be paid for a fortnight, and in the meantime she had no money. Geoffrey had closed their joint account the day she moved out.

Who could she borrow from? She must have food for Nina. Her first thought was Auntie Bet, but that would mean explaining her situation, something Kay couldn't bring herself to do. Auntie

Bet was one of the world's generous people. If she caught even a hint of Kay's circumstances she'd refuse to take money for Nina.

Her next thought was Sandra, but the prospect of explaining things to her was even more chilling. She'd already decided to throw in her studies. When she phoned Nathan to tell him she wouldn't be taking the exams, his reaction was curt. 'Your private life is your own affair,' he said, 'but if you want my advice, you'll reconsider this decision.'

No question of asking Nathan Bute for money.

So who did that leave? Geoffrey? 'You haven't told me anything,' he'd sobbed, the night before she left.

'I've destroyed our marriage,' Kay had answered. 'Why do you need to know more?'

'Then you *have* been unfaithful?'

The expression on his face, when she told him the truth, was part of her punishment now.

There was only one person she could ask, and that was her mother.

'You've done what?' Esme screeched down the phone. 'You're a wicked girl, Kay Dyer, a wicked wicked girl.'

Kay laughed. How could she have imagined it would be different? 'Yes, well, you know what they say,' she retorted, 'like father like daughter.'

'What's that supposed to mean?'

'Forget it.'

'Poor Geoffrey. Oh, that poor boy. What can he be feeling? And his parents. After all they've done.'

'This is hopeless.'

'You're not crying, are you? I'm the one who should be crying.'

'Will you lend me the money or not?'

The silence on the end of the phone lasted so long Kay thought her mother had hung up. But then the saving words came. 'Not a word to your father, mind. This is between us.'

So a new life began for Kay A life of work and looking after Nina that slowly, day by plodding day, began to seem normal.

At first Nina asked repeatedly where her daddy was, but then she too began to accept the new pattern, chattering to Geoffrey most evenings on the phone, seeing him every Sunday, unaware of the anguished glances her parents exchanged as she ran from one pair of arms to the other. Kay, watching anxiously for signs of secret unhappiness, was reassured. Nina, her joy, her pride, her reason for living, was as much in love with life as ever.

There were new friends for Nina too, neighbourhood friends, something she hadn't had in St Heliers. There was Winston Nene, whose family lived in the adjoining flat; and Ruta Ta'ase, from the house across the street. For the first time in her life Kay felt she wasn't being judged. Her story was just one among many.

About two months after the move to Grey Lynn, Sandra turned up on her doorstep. Kay never thought to ask how she'd discovered her address. These days she saw no one from her old life.

'Everything that happens is meant to happen,' Sandra informed her cheerfully, as they sat on the verandah drinking coffee. Kay, who just wanted her old friend to go, rejected the notion, but was surprisingly comforted by her next words. 'Separation is like a death,' Sandra remarked, 'only no one lets you grieve. Everyone assumes you've got what you want.'

When Roy's name was spoken, Kay shook her head fiercely. 'I never want to see him or hear his name again,' she said.

Six weeks after the meeting with Sandra, Kay was served with divorce papers.

'Grieve v. Grieve', it said on the title page. Inside, in a language Kay found more foreign than French, she understood it to say that the petitioner, Geoffrey Ayrton Grieve, was suing for divorce on the grounds of her adultery with Roy Michael Blade. The hearing would take place in the Supreme Court of Auckland on 20 April 1969.

'So,' Kay said aloud, 'it's come to this.'

Divorce

41

The night Geoffrey discovered his wife and daughter had gone, he sat down and wrote out, in longhand, his opening address for the case he was to take next day in the Supreme Court. It shocked him that he could think so clearly. He even felt mildly inspired.

The case had already attracted considerable attention. Geoffrey's client was a well-known chemical company, caught up in an action for wrongful dismissal. But as the pages began to fill with his busy writing, it struck Geoffrey that what this case provided was a unique opportunity to defend the company's – any company's – right to dismiss an unsatisfactory worker. In this particular case the worker had joined the company not in the usual 'good faith', but in order to pursue an agenda of his own: namely, to expose the company's secret production of chemicals, destined (according to the complainant's paranoid theory) for Vietnam. This latter assumption, which the company had strenuously denied, was to be a key point in Geoffrey's defence. But even without it the evidence was strongly in his client's favour. Whatever the moral issues, the law was on the company's side.

Here Geoffrey stopped. Kay's voice, condemning his action, had begun to interfere with his thoughts. As if *she* had the right to condemn anyone.

He got up from his desk and read her note again. Massey Street, Grey Lynn. He didn't know it, but he could picture it. Crumbling wooden villas badly in need of paint; neglected gardens; broken pavements heaped with uncollected rubbish; brown faces; Nina running amok in Maori backyards . . .

He screwed the paper into a ball, and hurled it across the room. 'You can see Nina whenever you want'. What was that meant to do? Comfort him? In his rage he began to stumble through the house. *This* was Nina's home. The study; the living room; the patio where she played; the kitchen with its waste disposal unit and its tasteful green and white tiles; the nursery . . .

Here Geoffrey stopped, and leaned against the door. He was in urgent need of a cigarette. 'You forgot the mobile,' he said out loud. It was the only thing left in the room.

Next moment he was on all fours hunting for Kay's note. He'd ring and speak to Nina. He wouldn't talk to *her*. What was there to say? She'd told him she no longer saw this Roy person, but how could he believe her when she'd proved, beyond all doubt, that she was a liar?

But he couldn't phone, could he? Not at half-past midnight. All he could do was wait till morning.

It was after three when Geoffrey finally collapsed, exhausted, into bed. He couldn't imagine what the next days and weeks would bring. The only thing of which he could be sure, was that he couldn't endure this torment on his own.

'What you do, son,' Lionel said, 'is divorce the woman. Get her out of your life. You've got what you need, an admission of adultery. I can't think what's stopping you.'

'There's Nina,' Geoffrey said.

'You'd be doing it *for* Nina. For Christ's sake, Geoff, you can't spend the rest of your life moping. There are other fish in the sea, you know.'

But Geoffrey was paralysed. The more his parents tried to spur him to act, the more passive he became. He accepted their offers of help – meals, dinner parties in his honour, sailing trips, a week's holiday in Fiji – but the lethargy clung to him like a second skin. The only time it lifted was when he visited Massey Street. What he felt then, as he watched his wife move around the poky living room, profoundly shocked him. He wanted to hurt her. He wanted to make her beg for mercy. Most of all he wanted her to know what it was like for him.

'Managing all right, are you?' (Conversations usually began this way.)

'Fine, thanks.'

'You know, I don't understand you, I really don't. You have a first-class degree, yet you settle for a dead-end job.'

'I like it. It suits . . . it fits in with things.'

'What will you do today? I'm taking Nina to Aunt Pauline's by the way.'

'She'll like that.'

'I'll be back about six.'

'No need to hurry.'

'So, what will you do with yourself?'

'I've plenty to occupy me.'

'You should get someone to help you tidy this place up. Your friend Roy, can't he lend a hand?'

Somehow they always got to this place, which was where the conversation would end. But it would start up again a week later. We're on a treadmill, Geoffrey concluded, after one particularly bitter exchange. And soon Nina will be on it with us.

'You're not paying her anything, are you?' his father asked.

'Don't worry, Dad. I took your advice. Three pounds a week till things get settled.'

'That's why you've got to get cracking on this divorce. Put things on a proper footing.'

But divorce wouldn't stop Geoffrey feeling as if he were walking round in a straitjacket. It wouldn't take away the rage he felt at Massey Street, or free him from the shame of his recurring dreams.

'Geoffrey? I am speaking to Geoffrey Grieve, aren't I?'

'Who is this?'

'Sandra Grajawaska.'

Geoffrey adjusted his hearing-aid. The name was not one he'd expected to hear again. 'Just a moment,' he said. He got up from his desk and closed the door. In the four months since Kay moved out he'd been treated with extraordinary delicacy by the people in his office. Responsibility for the Hamilton operation had been handed to one of the other partners, leaving him free to attend to things in Auckland. These days, if he disappeared without explanation, no questions were asked. He didn't think his work had suffered, but he was aware that the time had come for him to separate his private from his professional life.

'Sorry,' he murmured into the phone.

'Would you rather I called you at home?'

'What's this about, Sandra?'

He thought he heard her laugh, but with his dodgy hearing he couldn't be sure. 'You don't like me much, do you?' she said.

'I don't see what that has to do with . . .'

This time the laugh was unmistakable. 'Poor old Geoffrey. You wouldn't know a good turn if you fell over one.'

'Listen . . .'

'No, you listen. I was going to suggest we meet, but I can see you couldn't handle that.'

'I'm perfectly willing to meet you if there's a valid reason . . .'

'His name's Roy Blade. He lives at 56a Rata Street, and he's about to flee the country.'

Geoffrey cleared his suddenly constricted throat. With his spare hand he took off his glasses and laid them carefully on the desk. The file he was working on concerned an accident on a fishing boat. He'd been looking forward to a spin out to West Auckland to see the damage for himself. 'Why should you imagine I have any interest . . . ?'

'Difficult to prove adultery without a co-respondent, I would have thought.'

Geoffrey's hand, on the receiver, was sweating. He was having difficulty ridding his mind of a picture of Sandra, naked but for the necklaces and bangles that were her trademark. These days he seemed to see sex in everything.

'If you're wondering why I'm doing this,' she said, into the silence he'd created, 'I'll tell you. There are two reasons. One is Roy. I don't hold with morals, as you know. I consider them an obstacle to happiness. But Roy Blade has moved into a category of his own. He wants to play adult games with children. Now that's not on, not in my book anyway.'

'And the other reason?' Geoffrey prompted. He was trying to ignore the earthquake in his stomach. Since Nina's birth he'd been better able to cope with the unpleasant side of life. Blood, mucous, facial deformities – he didn't like them, but he could be reasonably sure of holding on to the contents of his stomach.

'The other reason is your wife,' Sandra said.

'Go on.'

'I went to see her yesterday.'

'Is she still seeing this Roy person?'

'No.'

'Are you certain?'

'Positive.'

Geoffrey's internal eruptions began to subside. Kay had told the truth then. About that, anyway. Of course there could be other men. Bound to be. An attractive woman living on her own. One of these Sundays Nina would let slip that she had a new daddy. He'd been braced for it for weeks.

'Your wife is a lost cause,' Sandra informed him.

'What's that supposed to mean?'

'I think you know.'

'Is that why you want me to divorce her?'

It was Sandra's turn to be silent.

'That is what this call's about, isn't it?'

'Look, I don't care what you do. It's your funeral. I just thought you should know . . .'

'Funny. I would never have imagined you making common cause with my father.'

'Kay has to hit bottom before she can start living again.'

'Is that what they teach you in Psychology?'

'I don't expect you to understand.'

Geoffrey twisted round in his chair. Through the open window he could hear, above the noise of traffic, a ship's horn. Three long blasts as a liner pulled away from the wharf. 'Did Kay put you up to this?' he demanded. 'Does *she* want a divorce?'

'Kay doesn't know what she wants.'

That night Geoffrey lay on the floor of the living room and listened to the whole of *La Traviata*. When it had ended he phoned his father. 'All right, Dad,' he said. 'You win. I'll file for divorce in the morning.'

42

When terrible things happen, Geoffrey had concluded, there are no words. Cliches were the nearest he could get to describing the torrents of despair that every day threatened to engulf him. His heart was broken. His life was ruined. He was a shadow of his former self.

'You better move in with us, son,' his father said, as the day of the divorce hearing neared. 'Staying on in that house is only going to remind you.'

In the conversation he'd had with Kay after she'd been served with the papers he'd told her she should get herself a lawyer. 'Why?' she'd protested. 'I'm not denying anything.'

'Your friend Roy Blade will be subpoenaed. A lawyer would tell you what that means.'

'Why can't *you* tell me?'

'Just get yourself a lawyer, OK?'

In the end a lawyer was appointed by the court. Not that there was much for him to do. Kay's only concern was to keep custody of her daughter. Her financial rights, impressed on her by her young and eager solicitor, were of little interest to her. 'Geoffrey loves Nina,' she insisted. 'He'd never let us starve.'

When Kay learned she wouldn't have to appear in court her relief was such she threw her arms round her solicitor's neck. 'Hang on a minute,' he laughed. 'We haven't won any victories here.'

But Kay *had* won a victory. She wouldn't have to see Roy Blade, or listen to his voice.

The day of the hearing, like the days immediately preceding and following it, dawned hot and humid. Cicadas buzzed in Lionel's garden. The tar on the tennis court glistened. From the front of the house came the sound of water running. These days the gardener started work early.

'You're not wearing that tie, are you?' Winifred complained to her son, over breakfast.

'What's wrong with it?'

'You look as if you're going to a funeral.'

Geoffrey shot a warning glance at the twins. He was in no mood for their questions. It had been a mistake to move back here. The expression on Kay's face, when he'd told her, had made that abundantly clear.

'Listen to this,' his father said, from behind his newspaper. '"The value of residential property in Auckland has gone up by over 20 per cent in the last financial year. The rise has been steepest in the suburbs of St Heliers and Kohimarama. Houses with a view of the harbour . . ."'

'OK, Dad. I get the message.'

Lionel folded his paper. 'Waste of time letting that place of yours,' he said. 'You should sell.'

The hearing was due to start at 11 a.m. Stuart Sutch, acting for Geoffrey, was confident it would all be over in fifteen minutes. It wasn't as if Roy Blade was refusing to co-operate. On the contrary, he seemed eager to give evidence.

'Is that him?' Geoffrey hissed, as he followed Stuart into the courtroom.

'Colourful-looking character, isn't he?'

Geoffrey took off his glasses. Reducing the man to a blur was the only way he knew to control his obsessive interest. This hippie, this *pervert*, had robbed him of wife and child.

'Oh, yes,' the fellow said, in answer to a question from the Judge, 'it was a full-blown affair. In fact, full-blown describes it nicely. Lake – Kay as she's called in your world – is an inventive lover.'

'*Is?*' the Judge queried.

'I don't imagine she's taken a vow of celibacy, do you?'

'I think you know what I mean, Mr Blade.'

'You're asking me if Lake and I still see each other?'

'Do you?'

'Nope. She and I are history.'

'Thank you, Mr Blade. You may sit down.'

Stuart's prediction was right. It *was* all over in fifteen minutes. Custody of Nina was awarded, on an interim basis, to Kay, with Geoffrey being granted regular access, and consultation in all matters relating to his daughter's moral, spiritual and intellectual upbringing. Costs were ordered to be paid by the co-respondent. Geoffrey, whose last, clear-sighted glimpse of Roy Blade confirmed his undying hatred, grabbed Stuart's arm and said, 'You know he's planning to leave the country?'

'Is that a fact?'

'Perhaps the court should be informed?'

'Consider it done.'

That night a dinner party was held at the home of Lionel and Winifred Grieve. Present were Bunce and Aileen Goodbody, Stuart and Muriel Sutch, and a young woman named Penelope Christmas, who was a member of Geoffrey's ski club. It wasn't difficult for Geoffrey to guess how his father had got hold of Penelope. A couple of phone calls enquiring as to who was the most eligible female in the club would have done it. Geoffrey couldn't help wondering if Trixie de Vere's name had come up. Now that would have made for an interesting evening!

The atmosphere around the table was determinedly jolly. Winifred had excelled herself in the cooking department. Vichyssoise, duck à l'orange, Spanish chocolate pudding. As for Lionel, his contribution to the feast was three bottles of prize-winning Australian claret, and an excellent late harvest Riesling. Geoffrey might have appreciated it more if he could have expunged the image of Roy Blade from his mind; but each time he tried to engage the undoubtedly attractive Penny in conversation, Roy's face, and that absurd mane of long fair hair he sported, got in the way.

Nina belongs with me, Geoffrey found himself thinking as the night wore on. It's not just her mother she needs to be rescued from, it's her mother's friends. Beatniks and nymphomaniacs. What kind of society is that for a growing girl? And who's to say Kay, with her naive trust in other people, won't choose another

• Elspeth Sandys

Roy Blade? The word to describe *him* caused Geoffrey to choke on his claret.

'So, what do you say?' Penny's voice intruded. 'Are you on?'
'What? I'm sorry, I . . .'
'You haven't heard a word I've said, have you?'
'Sorry. I'm a bit preoccupied.'
'It's all right, I understand.'
'You were saying something about the regatta?'
'It was your father's idea.'
'What was?'
'That we should sail with him. The two of us.'
'When?'
'Next Sunday.'

Geoffrey pushed his plate away. He'd have to risk offending his mother tonight. Either that or throw up. 'It's OK with me,' he said. 'So long as I can bring Nina.'

Over the next seven months a strange normality settled on Geoffrey's life. He began once again to put in long hours at the office, just as he had when he'd imagined himself a happily married man. Most Saturday nights he saw Penny, and eventually, at her suggestion, they began sleeping together. Sundays – the one day when he felt himself to be alive – were given over to Nina. He'd pull up outside the house in Massey Street at nine o'clock on the dot, and at the first sight of his daughter running down the rickety steps to greet him, his heart would (in the words of the cliche) give a leap, and he'd remember what the preceding days had almost made him forget – his reason for living.

He spoke to Kay only when obliged to. If anyone had asked him to describe how she was looking he'd have shrugged his shoulders. Kay, and this Auntie Bet person, had Nina all week. He only had her for one precious day.

Then, one Saturday towards the end of November, the façade of normality crumbled. Geoffrey, sitting over a late breakfast, reading the reports of the week's hearings in court, came across a brief description of a case against one Roy Michael Blade. His conviction for unlawful sex with a minor had earned him a two-year jail sentence.

Geoffrey folded the paper carefully, drained his coffee, and went to the telephone. Fortunately his mother and sisters were occupied elsewhere. His father was away sailing.

'Geoffrey Grieve here,' he said into the phone. 'Sorry to trouble you at the weekend, Mrs Gorman, but I need to speak to Wesley. Something rather urgent has come up.'

The Graveyard

43

It lay across the side of a hill. A strange place to have chosen, Kay thought, seeing, as if for the first time, the kaleidoscope of roof and chimneys; the thin grey roads specked with cars; the park, lying like a small green lake at the heart of the town; the mangroves framing the river in the distance; the vineyards splayed across the hill . . . St Joseph's church, where you would expect people to be buried, was out of sight, obscured by the banners and billboards of the suburb's second-hand car yards.

Perhaps there *was* a church here once? It was the sort of thing Geoffrey would enjoy speculating about. Don't you ever wonder about the past? he'd say, before launching into an explanation of how the graveyard came to be here, buried in the bush. The first settlers, he would guess, weary from their journey halfway round the world, chose this plateau in preference to what was then an impenetrably forested valley. From this vantage point you could see the river which had brought them upstream from the sea. Perhaps they needed that reminder. A river that had carried them to this place could also ferry them away.

27 JULY 1883
HANS WERNER BIEGELEBEN
Beloved son of ERICH and ILSE
Killed by a falling tree in his twenty-first year
THY WILL BE DONE

URSULA LASSMANN
Faithful wife and mother
Born Corinthia, Austria, 1844
Died Astley, New Zealand, December, 1878

Kay pushed away the long grass, and knelt beside the grave. 'Lassmann,' she murmured. She'd driven out west in her old Ford Prefect because she couldn't think what else to do on her first Saturday without Nina. She'd spent the afternoon wandering the streets of Astley, circling Kauri Avenue as if it were infected with the plague. Finally, as the sun was sinking low in the sky, she'd come here, to the graveyard she'd played in as a child.

She closed her eyes. Lights sparked in the sudden darkness. Cicadas screeched. Summer had hung on late this year. Birds that should have begun their migrations were still chirruping in the branches.

Her job at Lassmann's Vineyard had paid well. Only three days lost through rain, and the prospect of the work going on right through the summer. Her mother had seemed especially pleased. 'We'll be seeing something of you for a change,' she'd said.

Kay had liked her employers. Fedor Lassmann, her boss, was a large bewhiskered man who teased his female workers in a way that might have seemed offensive in a less good-natured man. His daughter, Sophie, worked alongside Kay in the vineyard. Their job, tucking and tying, required them to walk as a pair along the rows of vines, fastening the straggling branches on to the wires. It would have been tedious had it not been for the conversation. Sophie wanted to be a writer. She wanted to tell the story of her people. 'Everyone assumes we're German,' she'd said, 'but we're not, we're Austrian. My great-great-grandfather came to New Zealand to avoid fighting in Bismarck's wars.'

If I'd listened more closely, Kay thought now, I might have known who Ursula was. She flattened her palm, and moved it over the weedy stone. Ursula was born in Corinthia so she must have been one of the original settlers. Sophie's great-great-grandmother perhaps.

Only those with nothing to hide, Kay decided, answering the question Geoffrey had asked her a lifetime ago, can safely wonder about the past.

She got to her feet. The light was beginning to go. If, as part of her had seemed to want, her parents had spotted her this afternoon, what would she have done? Confronted them with what she knew?

I dare you! her brother's voice hissed in her ear. Go on. What are you waiting for?

Kay looked round sharply. She was alone, of course. No one in their right mind walked round an abandoned graveyard at dusk.

It was her brother who'd introduced her to this place. A permitted excursion to the nearby park had become, through his daring, an adventure into forbidden territory. Even then the place had been a mess. Tangled grass, fallen headstones, broken bottles, shards of pottery, chipped plaster flowers scattered like daisies among the weeds. Compared to the park, with its neat lawns, its swings and slides in full public view, it had seemed an Aladdin's Cave. The thrills it offered had been equal, in Kay's young mind, to the excitements of the ghost train at the Winter Show; or the Royal Maze, the thought of which could still induce flutterings of panic.

It had seemed large then too, though it wasn't much bigger than a school playground, Kay saw now. But otherwise it was as she'd remembered it: the rows of foreign names ('Huns,' Clive had called them); the memento moris of mysterious Catholic derivation. After that first magical exploration Kay had never needed persuading to come again. The grip this ruined garden had had on her imagination was one of the reasons she'd ended up here today.

'Nice time at the park?' Esme would sing out when the miscreants returned.

'Yeah, great,' they'd chorus in reply.

Kay and her brother had been friends then. Allies. Despite her reluctance to do as she was commanded, and scratch out the name of some poor 'Hun'.

'Cowardy custard!' Clive had taunted.

She'd heard that sarcastic note again, at Christmas, when she admitted to her brother that Geoffrey was suing for custody of Nina. 'Jesus Christ!' he'd cursed. 'Well, you've only yourself to blame. You should've played by the rules.'

VERGILIA YERKOVICH
Dearly loved daughter of Milan and Maria
Born April 1904
Died July 1904
Our little angel safe in the arms of Jesus

Kay sank to her knees. A sound that seemed part of the secret language of this place escaped her lips. She could have been a bird falling to the ground, or a rabbit scurrying through the grass. In all her years of truancy she'd never once noticed a child's grave. Such a small plot, tucked among the fallen masonry, its message weathered to a hazy scratching.

Her hands reached out to the tablet of stone. 'Poor wee love,' she moaned, cradling the broken headpiece in her arms. 'Oh, you poor wee darling. Were you sick? Was there no doctor to make you better? Shhh . . . It's all right. Mummy's here. It's all better now. That's right, sweetheart. Sleep . . .'

But this wasn't Nina's grave, this was a stranger's. Would she be crying like this, choking on her sobs, if Nina had died? Was the loss she was enduring now harder to bear than death?

Sandra, the last time Kay talked with her, had assured her *divorce* was worse than death. 'Everyone assumes you've got what you want,' she'd said. 'No one lets you grieve.'

You should have stuck around, Kay answered her vanished friend. 'Everything that happens is meant to happen.' Wasn't that what you said? So I was *meant* to lose Nina.

'Our divorce laws,' Geoffrey had pronounced, in that other life, 'are draconian. They enshrine the medieval concept of blame. The idea that two people can decide to get married, but not decide to get *un*married, is insane.'

Why had she only remembered those words now? At the very least she could have thrown them back at him.

She reached up to her hair. One of the few things she could remember doing this week was taking down the mirrors in her flat. Now, when she wanted to comb her hair or put on lipstick, she used her compact. It would hardly surprise her if she woke up one of these mornings to discover she was bald.

What would Nina be doing at this moment? Would Winifred have taken charge? Winifred had never wanted to look after her grandchild, but that hadn't stopped her accusing Kay of shutting her out. Geoffrey was a busy lawyer. He'd want to get home to his daughter, but most days there'd be something to keep him late. As for the twins, it was safe to assume they'd be viewing Nina as a threat. Baby-sitting didn't feature on their teenage agendas.

Kay's hands slid down the stone. It was cold to the touch, as if the day's heat had passed over it. What if this was her own grave, and not Vergilia Yerkovich's? What would the headstone say?

ELIZABETH KAY . . .

Her fingers dug into the mossy recesses. Elizabeth Kay what? Dyer? Grieve? Who would erect the monument anyway? Her parents would be too embarrassed; her husband too angry; her daughter too young . . .

ELIZABETH KAY
30 December 1943 – 17 March 1970

('There, you see! Wasn't hard, was it? A decent Kiwi name instead of all those Huns.'

'They're not Huns, Clive. They've been here since forever. They fought on our side in the war.'

'They've got Hun names.')

Mother of NINA, aged three.
A beautiful angel whom she couldn't keep safe

Kay let go of the stone. If she went on thinking this way she'd go mad.

Get with it, Lake! What are you doing in a graveyard anyway?

No! She shielded her eyes from the shape that had risen in front of her. *Not you. You have no right.*

You always did have a morbid streak.

Get away from me! Haven't you done enough?

Come on, Lake, this isn't like you. Loosen up. Go with the flow. You should forget your kid, you know. She's not your property.

'If you were here, and I had a gun, I'd shoot you,' Kay said out loud.

The sound of her voice made her feel better. Roy Blade couldn't harm her or anyone else now. He was in prison.

She stood up, and brushed the moss and leaves from her trousers. As she picked her way through the maze she began counting the days till she would see Nina. Twenty-one. They would pass. Just as the days of this week had passed. I must plan carefully, Kay thought. Think of a way to persuade Pauline to let us have time alone. It could have been worse, she saw now. She could have had Winifred as chaperone.

- Elspeth Sandys

Reaching the gate, Kay stopped and looked back into the darkening graveyard. There was no one there. The only voices were the ones in her head.

She put out her hand to lift the catch, at which moment she noticed a headstone standing by itself to the left of the gate. It was not like the other stones. It was new, for one thing, and its colour was a dark mottled grey. Elsewhere the stones, cream-coloured originally, were covered with greeny-brown stains.

Curious, Kay approached the grave. It was well cared for. She did a quick calculation. None of the other headstones was dated later than 1914. Clive said that was because they were all Huns, and when the First World War started no one wanted to be buried with Germans. But someone must have wanted to. At the base of this stone was a jam jar full of fresh carnations.

Then she registered the dates: 1845–1872. So it wasn't a recent burial.

She looked closer. '**Of your charity pray for the repose of the soul of Patrick Brendan Kierin. Unjustly cut down in the bloom of his youth.**

She did another calculation. The man was her age when he died. 'Unjustly cut down.' What did that mean?

She looked over her shoulder. Now it was not ruin she saw, but design. The pines that surrounded the graveyard had been deliberately planted. Within their borders the plots were neatly marshalled in rows. Even what remained of the headstones seemed to conform to a pattern: a broken angel here; a jagged pillar there. When she lifted her eyes and saw a crescent moon hanging on the horizon, the transformation was complete.

But you're not German, she argued, turning back to the headstone.

So? (Kay smiled. The voice in her head was Clive's.) *What does that prove?*

But Clive could make no more sense of it than she could. Patrick Kierin had been dead since 1872. Who would be mourning him in 1970?

The question insisted on an answer. Which didn't make sense either. There were enough unanswered questions in Kay's life without taking on any more.

Patrick Kierin, she mused, as she made her way back to her car. *Who were you?*

44

'Well, young man, I hope you're satisfied?'

Geoffrey pulled his owl face and marched past his aunt into the house. He'd come to fetch Nina, not listen to a lecture. The day had been quite stressful enough without Pauline adding her penny's worth.

'She's out the back,' his aunt informed him.

'It should have been *this* place we were selling,' Geoffrey couldn't resist remarking. 'One of these days it's going to fall down round your ears.'

He found Nina crouched over a shoe box, feeding a clutch of baby birds from a pipette. As always, when he visited his aunt, he wondered at the origin of her fascination with wings and feathers. Three tall wire cages, home to a variety of pigeons and parrots, filled the back yard. Nina, in frilly pink shorts and top, looked like an exotic flower in a jungle.

'Shhh,' she cautioned her father, as he approached.

Geoffrey grinned, and sat down on one of the two frayed wicker chairs to wait. *Kay* had a thing about birds too. Maybe that was why Pauline liked her. Only Kay didn't want to keep birds, she wanted to *be* one.

It had occurred to Geoffrey that Nina's enthusiasm for coming here might have more to do with Pauline's connection with Kay than anything else. But watching his daughter now he could see he needn't have worried. As a child he'd loved visiting this house himself, and for many of what he imagined were the same reasons. The place might be, as Winifred constantly complained, a health hazard, fit only to be condemned, but for a child it was a paradise where the boundaries between the adult world and the child's were mysteriously blurred, and all manner of shared adventures became possible.

Six months had passed since the custody hearing. Geoffrey had worked hard to erase the memory of that day, but every time he looked at Nina and saw Kay the images would come flooding back: Kay in her pathetic fake fur jacket; Justice Barrett peering, like some sharp-nosed savant, over his gold-rimmed spectacles; Wesley Gorman disguising his yawns behind a hairy fist.

Did he regret his action? Yes and no. Nina *was* better off with him, he was sure of it. But there were times – when the twins lost patience, or Winifred's voice rose – that he doubted. Most of the time Nina seemed happy. She'd settled into her kindergarten; made new (and far more suitable) friends. If she wasn't quite the chatterbox she'd once been people still commented on how bright she was. Looking at her now, absorbed in her task, he couldn't think why he should be worried. She'd be four in January. Almost ready to start school.

'Finished, darling?' he asked.

'Shhh,' she said again.

'How many are there in that box?'

She held up five fingers. 'They've lost their mummy,' she explained. 'They're vewy hungwy. And they're sad,' she added.

Geoffrey nodded. He didn't believe in shielding children from the truth. When Nina asked him why her mother wasn't with them he explained, as kindly as he could, that Kay had done something wrong. Not being allowed to look after her daughter was her punishment. 'But she does love you, sweetheart,' he'd been quick to add.' And you can talk to her on the phone whenever you want.'

He took out a cigarette and lit it gratefully. It had been a long day. Cleaning out the house at St Heliers had proved even more of an ordeal than he'd anticipated. Every cupboard he opened seemed to spring a trap: an album of wedding photographs (that had been the worst); Kay's favourite teapot (why hadn't she taken it with her?); a rattle that had been Nina's when she was a baby; the forgotten chest expander . . . Winifred had come along to help, but her presence had only made things worse. 'Did Kay choose these?' she'd demanded at one point, brandishing a pair of candlesticks in the shape of bananas.

Enemy Territory

When he didn't answer, she smiled smugly and sashayed out of the room.

But it was done now. The house sold for a handsome profit to a couple from Wellington. It troubled Geoffrey that Kay wasn't to have a share of the proceeds. Had it been a joint family home she would have stood to gain a tidy sum. He could make reparation, of course, but the thought of Kay's inevitable refusal dissuaded him. Besides, she wasn't badly off. She was working full-time now, with only herself to support.

'There,' Nina sighed. 'That's better.'

'Righto,' Geoffrey said.

'I'm the best at feeding the babies,' Nina informed him solemnly, as they walked, hand in hand, into the house. 'Aunt Pauline spills everything.'

'I'm sure you do it brilliantly,' Geoffrey agreed.

'I wish *I* was a bird,' Nina said.

Pauline was waiting for them in the sitting room. When Geoffrey saw her pick up the sherry bottle, he waved a hand in protest. 'We really must be off,' he said.

'Sit down!' Pauline commanded. 'I've something to say to you.'

Geoffey frowned, and flicked his head in his daughter's direction. He knew his aunt in this mood. 'Time you heard a few home truths,' she'd say, before launching into what usually amounted to an attack on his parents.

'Don't worry about Nina,' Pauline reassured, as she poured liberal amounts of sweet sherry into two far from clean glasses. 'She'll have heard worse in her time.'

'Listen, sweetheart,' Geoffrey said, turning to his daughter. 'Why don't you go and see how those babies of yours are doing? You could sing them a lullaby. They'd like that. Or tell them a story.'

'Can I take them home with me?'

'Oh, I think they'd be happier here, don't you? With all Aunt Pauline's other birds.'

Nina's departure sent Geoffrey scrabbling for another cigarette. Two weeks had passed since Nina last saw Kay, so this couldn't be about that. Pauline, as Nina's chaperone, was nothing if not discreet. Each month Geoffrey had to fight the temptation to quiz her. He wanted to know how Kay was looking. He wanted to know what her job entailed, now that it was full-time. Most of all he wanted to know who her friends were.

'There,' Pauline said, handing him his sherry. 'Get that inside you.'

Geoffrey lifted his glass to her. In her grubby overalls and unravelling cardigan she looked a mess. Just like this room, he thought, eyeing the lopsided prints on the wall, the forgotten tea cups, the *Birdwatch* magazines scattered over the floor.

According to Nina the days with her mother were pure magic. Trips to the beach, to the gardens, to the zoo; rides on the ferry. Two weeks ago she'd come back with a tale of having tea with some old Maori woman. 'She let me brush her hair,' Nina had said. 'It were long as long, Daddy. It went all the way to her bottom.'

'So,' Pauline said, when she'd settled into her chair, 'tell me about her.'

'Tell you about whom?'

'Penny. I believe that's her name. Don't you think it's time I met her?'

'You'd frighten her, Aunt Pauline. She's a radio technician. She doesn't meet many eccentrics.'

'Is that what you think I am, an eccentric?'

Geoffrey grinned.

'It's always seemed to me to be the other way round,' Pauline remarked.

'I know that look of yours,' Geoffrey observed gloomily. 'You're plotting something, aren't you?'

'It's for you own good, dear.'

'I really do have to go, Aunt Pauline.'

'Penny waiting for you, is she? Got yourself a date?'

'None of your business.'

'You better watch out, Geoff. Now that you've sold the marital home . . .'

'I'm not about to set up house with Penny, if that's what you're thinking.'

'So what *are* you going to do? Stay on with your parents?'

'In the meantime, yes.'

'Is that wise, do you think?'

Geoffrey sloshed his sherry round the sides of his glass. Whatever germs were lurking there should die in the alcohol.

'Because it seems to me,' his aunt sailed on, 'young Nina, whom I happen to dote on, as you know, is not entirely safe in the bosom of your family.'

'What on earth are you talking about?'

'How's your memory, Geoff? D'you remember much of your childhood? The "accident" that caused your deafness, for instance, d'you remember that?'

You old witch, Geoffrey thought, eyeing her over the top of his glass. So this is what you're on about.

'I've noticed you Grieve men tend to have convenient memories,' Pauline said.

'What's that supposed to mean?'

'Ask your father.'

'Look, Aunt Pauline, you've been very kind to Nina, to all of us, and I appreciate . . .'

'Fiddle dee dee! This has nothing to do with kindness.'

'No harm will come to Nina,' Geoffrey stated firmly. 'Do you think I'd stay in that house a single day if I thought . . .'

'How old were you when it happened? Five? Six? Not much older than Nina, as I recall.'

'It was an accident,' Geoffrey muttered.

'Oh, so you think Winifred didn't *mean* to throw the telephone at you. Is that it? She just happened to pick it up, and it flew out of her hand. I see.'

'She didn't mean to hurt me,' Geoffrey corrected.

'Ah . . .'

'You've never liked my mother, have you?'

'Not much, no.'

'Well, that's honest anyway.'

'Doesn't mean I don't have sympathy for her.'

'You could have fooled me.'

Pauline squeezed her lips between her thumb and forefinger. Her nails, Geoffrey noted with disgust, were filthy. 'Lionel is my brother,' she said. 'I feel a certain atavistic loyalty. But he's been a bad husband. Quite how bad I'm not sure, but I have my suspicions.'

'I don't see what all this has to do with Nina.'

'Don't you?'

'Look.' Geoffrey pulled out the cushion he was sitting on, and tossed it on the floor. Pieces of grey wool hung down in a beard from its seams. 'Nina is at kindergarten all morning,' he said. 'She's only with Mother for the afternoons, and the twins are around for much of that time. If you're suggesting . . .'

'Oh, Geoffrey, Geoffrey, what am I going to do with you? You should have done what Kay wanted. Put half a world between you and your parents.'

'Is that what you and Kay talk about? I've often wondered. Wait a minute.' Geoffrey slid forward in his chair. 'Did Kay put you up to this?'

His aunt smiled serenely at him. 'Don't change the subject,' she said. 'We were talking about Penny. You say you're not going to set up house with her. I'm not sure I believe you.'

'Kay's behind this, isn't she?'

'Your ex-wife and I have better things to talk about than your sex life,' Pauline said.

Her tone of voice, saccharine where it was normally guttural, annoyed Geoffrey almost as much as her words. 'I'm very fond of Penny,' he conceded irritably. 'Very grateful too. I haven't exactly been the best of company these last months. But I have no plans to marry her. Or anyone else for that matter.'

'You still love Kay, don't you?'

'Hardly.'

It was his aunt's turn to be annoyed. She cocked her head, and frowned at him. He felt like one of her birds, being scrutinised by a cat. Come to think of it this whole house, with its winding staircase and its tower nestling on the roof, was like a giant aviary. No wonder he felt caged.

'Who *do* you love then?' Pauline asked. 'Apart from Nina.'

Geoffrey's grin was both involuntary and guilty. The name that had come into his mind would take some explaining. Daisy Mountford, or Daisy Dutton as she must surely be by now, was as much a romantic fiction as Pauline's belief that he still loved Kay. He could recall all too clearly Kay's words on hearing about his meeting with Daisy. 'I can see I'm going to be compared to this paragon for the rest of my life,' she'd complained.

'There was a woman I *could* have loved,' he confessed now. 'If she'd been free and twenty years younger.'

'That's the trouble with men,' Pauline grumbled. 'They love what they cannot have.'

To Geoffrey's relief the conversation stopped there. Nina's appearance in the doorway brought it to an end.

But Pauline hadn't finished with him. As they stepped out into the hall she dropped another bombshell. 'You know what your trouble is, don't you?' she said. 'You can't cope with the idea of Kay's sexuality. Just because she was once your wife . . .'

'Leave it out, Aunt Pauline,' Geoffrey snapped, pushing Nina on ahead of him. What he felt like saying was, What do *you* know? You've never even been married.

'The Virgin-Whore complex, I believe it's called,' Pauline went on obliviously. 'Once a man's wife becomes the mother of his child . . .'

'You don't know what you're talking about.'

'Don't I?' Pauline's eyes twinkled shamelessly. 'You'd be surprised, young man.'

That night the usually sanguine Penny was driven to criticise the man she was determined, sooner or later, to marry. 'You're a cold fish, Geoffrey Grieve,' she accused. 'You don't know how to give.'

45

Kay's house in Massey Street, like most of the other houses in the neighbourhood, was really only half a house. A wooden villa, divided into two flats, with a shared backyard and rotary clothes line, and a strip of front garden which Kay had filled with agapanthus and daisies.

This evening, at the end of the first really warm day of spring, Kay had come out on to the verandah to read. The Nene children were playing in the garden – a local version of cops and robbers so far as she could make out. Winston, Nina's special friend, had long ago stopped asking where his playmate was, but his eyes still lit up on the rare Sundays when Kay brought her daughter home. 'Can she play?' he'd plead, standing legs apart, hands on hips, in the doorway. 'Hey, Nina! Wanna see my new bike?'

For Kay it was always a struggle to let Nina go. Every second of their day together was precious. But her reward was seeing Nina's face, smudged with mud and happiness, tearing past the verandah in pursuit of one of Winston's siblings, screaming in assumed terror and delight.

Winston could never understand why Nina had to leave at the end of the day. 'She don't like it here anymore, eh?' he'd reflect sadly.

There were two more weeks to be got through before Kay could see Nina again. Try as she might not to count the days, it was what she did, obsessively. At least her job on *The Herald* was more interesting now, and that helped the time to pass. She still did her share of proof reading, but most weeks she was allowed to write something of her own. Occasionally she was asked to fill in for the film or book reviewer. When that happened several hours might go by before she remembered to count the days.

Kay had already decided what they would do for Nina's next visit. Exactly what they did the last time: have tea with her friend, Makere te Tuhi. Perhaps Winston could come as well? Makere wouldn't mind, and Pauline had taken a real shine to the button-nosed Maori boy.

The book Kay had brought with her to read sat invitingly in her lap. It was not one of her usual books, the Margaret Drabbles and Simone de Beauvoirs she devoured to distract herself. This book was hand-written and leather-bound. It had been loaned to her by Makere. 'You're not to read it when you're tired,' her friend had commanded. 'This is no bedtime story.'

Kay was still puzzling as to why she'd been lent it. 'When you told me about your daughter I knew you were the one,' Makere had said.

'THIS BOOK IS THE PROPERTY OF PATRICK BRENDAN KIERIN, 5 THE QUAY, ARKLOW, IRELAND,' Kay read on the front page. She'd already flicked through it, of course. Her curiosity had been too great. But she'd kept her promise to Makere; waited till now when she knew she wouldn't fall asleep.

The street was full of the noise of children. Across the road Eve Ta'ase, mother of Nina's friend, Ruta, was chatting over the fence with Bert, an elderly widower loved by everyone in the street. Like Kay, Eve had no man in her life, though she'd managed to acquire five children along the way. Eve worked as a cleaner, driving her rusty old Standard to Remuera every morning, to clean the houses of the rich. Kay could hear her laughter now, as she regaled the old man with the dramas of her day.

It was at the grave of Patrick Kierin that Kay first encountered Makere. After her earlier visit, when she'd wept for little Vergilia Yerkovich, she'd vowed never to go back. She had a year to prove herself worthy to be Nina's mother again. Hanging round graveyards wasn't going to help her case.

But the following Saturday, driving away from Massey Street, she found herself heading once again for Astley. This time she kept well clear of Kauri Avenue. She'd had a letter from her mother earlier in the week. 'Sometimes we have to accept the most terrible things,' Esme had written. 'Things we can't ever see a way of recovering from. But if you can accept, and move on, you'll find you do still have a life to live . . .' Kay had been both astonished and moved. Whatever ideas she may have had about confronting her parents had been utterly changed by that letter. When – if – she spoke of what she knew, it would be to her mother alone, and it would not be to attribute blame.

So, with no particular purpose in mind, Kay had wandered past her old school, pausing to listen to remembered voices, wondering what had happened to her classmate, Blair Wihongi, to turn him into a criminal. But then it had struck her people were probably asking much the same question about her. What ever happened to that nice girl to turn her into a . . . what? Slut? Drug addict? Unfit mother?

If I could get back to the beginning, Kay had thought, I might be able to unravel the tangle. I don't feel like a bad or even a weak person, but I must be, to have let this happen. A 'just punishment', her father had called it. Was that why she'd felt the urge to confront him? To put the blame on *him*?

Turning away from the school, Kay had found herself heading along wet Saturday streets for the hills. Once or twice she'd recognised faces, but she couldn't put names to them. She wasn't part of the human race anymore. That was how she'd felt.

Which, she thought now, running her finger along the frayed edge of Patrick Kierin's book, was how I felt on that other day, when the streets shone with rain and passing cars splashed my nylon stockings. She was standing on the Karangahape Road, waiting for the bus to take her back to Astley. It was a Friday evening. The shops were open late. Having just turned sixteen she'd been allowed for the first time to meet a friend in the city. She wasn't supposed to be on the Karangahape Road. Things went on there that respectable folk weren't meant to know about. But it wasn't the sight of the girls in their short skirts and high heels that had catapulted her into exile, it was the glimpse she'd had of her father . . . It was more than possible, she saw now, returning to the question that had continued to haunt her, that the tangle began there. The decision to tell no one what she'd seen could have been the first step on the road that led to Justice Barrett's courtroom. She must ask Makere next time she saw her. Makere was the only person she knew who could answer such a question.

Kay glanced at the book in her lap. She didn't have to read it today. 'It's yours to keep for as long as you want,' Makere had said.

Kay grinned. 'Yours to keep' meant 'yours to do something with', didn't it? She'd grown used to Makere's elliptical way of speaking.

Whenever Kay thought how nearly she didn't go into the graveyard on that wet Saturday afternoon she felt the urge to thank someone, or something, for her good fortune. The last six months would have been so much harder to bear with no Makere to comfort her. Walking up the hill from the town, finding herself outside the graveyard, she'd almost turned back. Her car was parked near the school, a couple of miles away. She'd never intended to walk so far. But then she'd remembered the name Patrick Kierin, and curiosity had taken her in through the gate.

Approaching the new headstone it had occurred to Kay she might find fresh flowers on the grave. When she spotted the dead carnations she felt peevish with disappointment. What had she been hoping for? Proof that love could last more than a century?

'Good afternoon to you,' a voice had called out from the direction of the gate.

Kay was still staring at the dead carnations.

'Or should I say good evening? I like this time of day, don't you?'

Kay had been uncharacteristically tongue-tied. Not that the woman approaching her had looked intimidating. On the contrary, she was comfortably built, with long grey hair and eyes that seemed both shrewd and kind.

'I'm Makere te Tuhi,' the woman had announced. 'I've seen you here before.'

'Really?'

'Last Saturday.'

Kay had pointed to the flowers in the Maori woman's hand. 'Are those for this grave?' she'd asked.

Makere had nodded.

'Was he a relative of yours?'

'You could say that.'

'It's just that I've noticed, well, it seems to be the only grave that's looked after.'

Makere's laugh had sounded reassuringly normal. 'It's only been here a couple of years, that's why,' she'd answered, picking up the jam jar and tossing the dead flowers into the grass. 'Had the devil's own job getting permission to bring the poor boy home at all. You'd have thought, wouldn't you, after all these years . . . But then you Pakeha believe punishment should go on beyond the grave. Even when you're wrong.'

'I'm sorry,' Kay had said.

'Not your fault you were born white,' Makere had retorted cheerfully.

'What did he do? You said he'd been punished . . .'

Makere's answer had been to invite Kay back to her place for a beer. 'We can pick your car up on the way,' she'd said, as if she'd known all along where it was parked.

'You were going to tell me about Patrick Kierin,' Kay had reminded, on reaching their destination.

'Was I?'

'You said he was some sort of relative.'

Assuming her questions were about to be answered, Kay had followed Makere into her house. But Patrick's name was not mentioned again. The Maori woman's home, which was unlike any Kay had ever been in, echoed with the noise of half a dozen grandchildren. When, two hours later, Kay got up to go, the stars were blazing, illuminating the river which ran by the house, but mysteriously eclipsing the suburb of Astley.

'You know where I live,' her new friend had said as she was climbing into her car.

'You still haven't told me about Patrick Kierin.'

'Plenty of time.'

Kay smiled as she recalled those words. Six months it had taken. Six months of regular visits to the house on the river, in the course of which Makere had learned all there was to know about her, while the only things Kay had gleaned were that her friend had seventeen grandchildren, most of whom came to live with her at one time or another, and that her people were the

Kawerau, a tribe she herself had described as 'virtually extinct'. 'We were defeated twice,' she'd explained. 'Once by the Ngata Whatua, then by the Pakeha.'

Kay, until her visit two Sundays ago with Nina and Pauline, had all but forgotten Patrick Kierin.

That Makere would love Nina, Kay had never doubted for a moment. 'So this is the little princess,' she'd greeted, stooping to stroke Nina's hair.

'I'm not a princess,' had been the indignant response. 'I'm Nina.'

'Don't you want to be a princess?'

'No, thank you.'

Kay's anxiety, that Nina would be overwhelmed by Makere's noisy brood of grandchildren, had been quickly dispelled. Within minutes of their arrival Nina was playing happily among the mangroves.

'This place was our Garden of Eden,' Kay heard Makere say to Pauline. 'We had pigeons, pukeko, eels, ducks, mussels, pipis, taro, kumera. Enough to feed all our people.'

'What happened?' Pauline had asked.

'*Your* people came,' Makere had answered. 'They cut down the trees and drove away the birds.'

'You should never have let them,' Pauline had scolded.

'How were we to stop them? They had the muskets.'

Listening to the two old dowagers – for in Makere's house Pauline too had seemed venerable – Kay had asked herself why she'd waited so long to bring Nina here. Was it for fear of what might get back to Geoffrey? Or was it Pauline she'd doubted? She should have known better. Pauline and Makere were birds of a feather.

'I've something for you,' Makere had announced as they were leaving.

'What is it?' Kay had asked.

'You said you wanted to know about Patrick Kierin.'

'Who's Patrick Kierin?' Pauline had interjected.

'That's for your niece to find out,' Makere had answered, placing a worn, leather-bound volume in Kay's hand. 'Now, you're not to read it when you're tired,' she'd admonished. 'This is no bedtime story.'

'Do I have to go back to Grannie Winnie's?' Nina had whined all the way home. 'Why do I? Why?'

'Not for much longer, darling,' Kay answered her now.

She took up Patrick's book and began to read.

46

February the second, 1863
Today is my eighteenth birthday. This book is the gift of my mother, Bridie O'Neill Kierin. My father's gift was the honouring of his promise made to me when I was a boy. 'I give you my word now, Patrick,' he'd said, 'if God and the blessed Virgin spare me, you'll come with me to New Zealand when you're a man.'

So here I be, a man at last, facing the prospect of a voyage round the world. We leave the first week in March. My mother is all tears at the thought of waving me goodbye but I tell her it's a great thing I'll be doing. I'll be learning my father's trade.

'You'll not come back, I know it,' she answered. 'You'll find yourself a lass and that'll be the end of it.'

There are one hundred pages in this book so I will write only when I have something of import to say. I thank God for my dear parents, for this book, and for the adventure that awaits me.

March the fifth, 1863
Truly I could have been filling these pages every day since my birthday. The vessel my father is to captain is a brig named, after my mother's village in the mountains, *Camaderry*. It has already made three trips to New Zealand, ferrying tools and other manufactured goods to the colonists and returning with cargos of flax and kauri spars. The kauri, my father has told me, is a tree like no other in the world, growing straight and tall to heights

of one hundred feet and more. The native people call it
Tane Mahuta, Lord of the Forest.

What wouldn't I give to see those trees up close!
One of the officers, a talkative fellow by name Daniel
O'Malley, boasted he'd seen one that measured forty feet
in girth. 'Ah, go on,' I answered him, ''tis not possible.'
But he swore it were true. 'Tis a great thing to see the
world, so it is,' he assured me solemnly.

My task, this last hectic week, has been to supervise the
loading of the cargo. Several heavier than usual trunks
attracted my curiosity. 'Guns,' my father explained, when
I enquired as to their contents. 'You might as well know
now, Paddy, there's a war going on in New Zealand.'

March the sixth, 1863
Today the *Camaderry* sailed from Arklow on the first stage
of its ninety-day journey to New Zealand. My mother
clung to me on the wharf so that I thought she would
never let go. My own eyes, I don't mind admitting, were
more than a touch moist. 'Let the boy be, Bridie,' my
father scolded. 'You want his shipmates to think he's soft
in the head?'

My sister Molly cried too, but I don't think she knew
well what was occurring.

Fortunately we were so busy once the ropes were
cast off I had no time to dwell on private griefs. The tug
pulled us out into deep water where we were to wait
for a favourable wind. But even as we were engaged in
the exercise to correct the compass the wind got up, and
my father ordered the tug to be cut free. Now, at almost
midnight, we are skimming down the Channel under a
full press of sail. I have said my rosary, adding a prayer
for my dear mother and for wee Molly. I don't imagine I
will sleep.

March the twenty-first, 1863
I cannot believe more than two weeks have passed since
I wrote in this book. At this rate I will be an old man
before I reach the last page!

I hardly need explain that I have been busy! My duties are not onerous but circumstances have conspired to make them so. Two days into Saint George's Channel we struck a storm the like of which my father swore he'd never encountered in these waters. I was glad we were carrying but twenty passengers, since they are my particular responsibility. One poor woman, Mrs Gallagher from County Cork, mother of two small boys, was so hysterical I had to ask the ship's surgeon to administer laudanum. The rest managed to make themselves useful slopping out storm water. Mrs Gallagher's two boys were particularly adept at this task. I suspect they were glad of the excuse not to do their schoolwork.

We are free of the Channel now and, God be thanked, of the storm. I miss my dear mother greatly, and my Arklow friends. I have no doubt, if I'd stayed in Ireland, I'd have done what my mother feared (and Father Donovan secretly hoped for), and joined Seamus and the others in the Fianna. The taste of injustice was growing sour on my lips. But now that we are on the open sea, out of sight of land (Father says we catch only occasional glimpses – the west coast of Madeira should be next) it's hard to remember how passionately I wanted to rid my country of the English. Perhaps, when I return from New Zealand, there will have been an uprising and the English will be gone. I used to say such things to my mother, to rile her, and she would clip me round the ears and call me an eejit!

The person I miss most, though, is my baby sister. I wasn't expecting that. Molly will be four next birthday. A regular pest I used to consider her. 'Get along out of here,' I'd yell, if she showed her face at my door. Now I'd give a week's rations to see her perky face.

Kay let the book fall into her lap. She could only have been reading a few minutes, which didn't account for the fact that the light appeared to be fading. She closed her eyes and tried to picture Patrick Kierin. The face that rose in front of her had high cheekbones, grey eyes, a long patrician nose and a shock of fine straight hair. Geoffrey.

She opened her eyes. Tallulah Nene, Winston's older sister, was crawling past the verandah, her body twisted into a corkscrew in the effort to make herself invisible. She looked up at Kay and signalled her to play dumb. Kay waggled an understanding finger.

'What's lost can always be found again,' Makere had said, the day Kay told her about Nina. Kay had felt a stab of disappointment. She'd expected more. At the very least she'd thought Makere would comfort her.

'Dry your eyes, young lady,' Makere had scolded. 'You and I have work to do.'

April the seventeenth, 1863
Today we sighted the Saint Paul's Rocks which means we are now very near the Equator. The last two weeks have been hot and still with activity reduced to a minimum. Poor Mrs Gallagher has been confined to her cabin with a fever. Mrs Gallagher's husband is an officer with one of the Imperial Regiments in New Zealand. Apparently, when this present war is over, and the Maoris are subdued, Mr Gallagher is to be rewarded with a gift of land. Several hundred acres, according to his wife. The Gallaghers are Protestants. They do not attend my father's daily services.

I confess I am heartily sick of both sea and ship. We move at a snail's pace. My father remains cheerful, but I fear I'm not cut out for a life at sea.

May the twenty-third, 1863
Today I kissed my Cross of Saint Brighid and said a prayer to God the Father and the Blessed Queen of Heaven. We have picked up the westerlies which will carry us to New Zealand.

'If you've got a brain in your head you'll let this wind carry you to your fortune,' Daniel said to me today.

'Ah, go on with you,' I answered him. 'You're always yammering on about fortune.'

'You're no seaman, Patrick Kierin, for all you're your father's son.'

'What am I then?'

'You're a man of the trees. I hear it in your speech. You should come away with me when we get to Auckland. Let me show you the mighty kauri.'

'No harm in looking.'

'You'll not go back to Ireland once you've seen it.'

'You're wasting your time, Daniel.'

'Ah, don't be like that now. Wait till you meet my friend the mill owner. He's set himself up in the heart of the kauri forest. It's going to make him a very rich man.'

'Well, ain't he the lucky one?'

'Luck's got nothing to do with it.'

'Does this Midas have a name?'

'Theodore Astley.'

Kay looked up from the page. The street had gone quiet. Freed from occupation by its tribe of children it was once again the domain of birds. Only the occasional car broke the illusion of peace.

She put a hand to her hair; tested nervously for bald patches. She knew who Theodore Astley was. She'd had to do a project on him at school. Her own street, Kauri Avenue, was testament to his destruction of the forests that had once graced the hills and valleys of West Auckland.

'Go home,' she wanted to shout to Patrick across the years. 'Don't you know what awaits you here?' *Unjustly cut down in the bloom of youth*. Those words had begun to haunt her.

47

'Kay? It's Geoffrey. Is this a bad moment?'
'Has something happened to Nina?'
'Nina's fine. Tucked up in bed, I imagine.'
'Where are you phoning from?'
'The office.'

The silence on the other end of the phone disconcerted Geoffrey. It was eight o'clock in the evening. He'd wondered if he'd find Kay at home. Her life, these days, was a mystery to him. Pauline was singularly unenlightening, and Nina's chatter only succeeded in rousing his curiosity further. 'Listen, can we meet?' he said. 'I hate talking on the phone.'

'There is something wrong with Nina, isn't there?'
'I told you, she's fine. You'll see for yourself.'
'I don't see her for another ten days, Geoffrey.'
'I assure you, Kay, there's nothing wrong with our daughter.'
'So why do you want to meet me?'

It was Geoffrey's turn to be reduced to silence.

'I'm sorry,' Kay said. 'I didn't mean to sound unfriendly. It's just that it's easier if I don't see you. I, um, I've made a new life, you see, and . . .'

'I'd like to take you to dinner,' Geoffrey announced.
'What?'
'This Saturday. Are you free? There's a new Indonesian place in Lorne Street.'
'Saturday . . .'

Geoffrey held his breath. If she wasn't free he'd know there was a man.

'Won't your girlfriend object?'

'What girlfriend?'

'Pauline told me you were serious about her.'

Geoffrey ground his teeth together. What did that interfering old busybody think she was doing? 'There *was* someone,' he admitted curtly, 'but it's over.'

'I see.'

Kay's response left Geoffrey none the wiser. Was she relieved or merely indifferent? 'Well?' he said. 'Do we have a date?'

Kay laughed. It was the only normal moment in the entire conversation. 'What time Saturday?' she asked.

'Pick you up at seven?'

'No need for that. I'll meet you there.'

After he'd hung up Geoffrey sat for several minutes staring at his hands. He really must stop smoking. Or do something about those stains. Now that the date with Kay was fixed he was having second thoughts. He'd persuaded himself she had a right to know what was going on. Not about Penny, that was his business. Though he'd told Kay the truth, the relationship *was* over. No, what had prompted him to pick up the phone was his decision to move out from his parents' house. Two things had happened to bring him to this pass. One was that Nina had started sleep walking; the other was that Winifred had begun to lose control. 'She hits Nina, did you know?' Sue had confided at the weekend. 'She uses a wooden spoon.'

'What? How long has this been going on? Why didn't you tell me?'

'It only started a couple of weeks ago.'

'Jesus Christ.'

'I don't think she hurts her or anything.'

Sue's face, as Geoffrey recalled it now, had looked as if it had been punched. He must make it up to her. She was not a natural tell-tale.

'I wouldn't have said anything,' she'd mumbled, 'but Aunt Pauline told us once . . . I mean, I'm sure it was a lie, but I kept thinking about it, and . . .'

'What did Aunt Pauline tell you?'

'That Mum hurt you when you were a boy. Really hurt you.'

'Jesus . . .'

'Is it true, Geoff?'

'Oh Christ . . .'

'It's true, isn't it?'

Tonight he would tell his parents he was going to be moving out. He'd already phoned a land agent and asked him to look for a flat. As for Nina, he'd think what to do about her later. After he'd talked to Kay.

'You're late tonight,' Stuart Sutch remarked, as he made his way out of the office.

Geoffrey patted his briefcase. 'If there's anything I hate,' he said, 'it's a dispute involving a will. Ask me, we should do away with inherited wealth. Save a lot of unnecessary work.'

'Don't let Bunce hear you talk like that,' Stuart cautioned. 'He'll think you've had a relapse.'

48

When Kay, with Patrick's diary in her hand, walked inside from the verandah, she intended to carry on reading. The name Theodore Astley had startled her. Was *he* the reason Makere had given her the book? But she'd no sooner settled herself on the sofa than she was overcome with weariness. She couldn't explain it. She was no busier than usual at work, and the only late nights she'd had in the last week were those she'd spent reading.

Aware of her promise to Makere not to read the diary when she was tired, she put it aside and ran herself a bath. Half an hour later, at a ridiculously early hour, she was in bed, asleep.

Several days passed before she opened the book again. Then it was Geoffrey's phone call which acted as the spur. The prospect of having dinner with him in three days' time was guaranteed to keep her awake.

June the sixteenth, 1863
If I were to describe my first sight of Auckland as we sailed into the harbour I would fill the rest of this book. And since I am determined to write sparingly I will confine myself to impressions only.
  O Mary of the Graces, what a country this is! I don't know well whether I've landed in Paradise, or the other place! The first glimpse of land persuaded me of the former, but on closer inspection I am more inclined to the latter. Clearly God intended this country to be inhabited by angels. The sea is a miraculous turquoise blue; the hills are garlanded with trees, some mighty

like the oak, others knotted and gnarled like old men's hands. The waters teem with fish; the air is filled with birds; there is a perfume (Daniel tells me every land has its own particular smell) which filled me with the kind of longing my mother predicted would keep me here. But as we drew nearer to the shore the perfume faded, and other less appealing smells filled my nostrils. The birds were silenced too. Instead there was a low rumbling, as if the earth were growling, which gradually separated out into a number of distinct noises: the screech of the windlass from a ship at anchor; the clattering of wheels as a carriage raced along the waterfront; shouts and curses; a distant band (military, Daniel informed me); barking dogs; a volley of gunfire. *Satan's* land, I concluded, reversing my earlier opinion.

We weighed anchor, and those of us with permission to leave ship were ferried to shore by canoes. Daniel and I travelled with Mrs Gallagher and her boys. Our guides were fearful-looking creatures, covered in strange blue markings which Daniel told me denoted their standing, or *mana*, in the tribe. They spoke good English though, and seemed to find my visible apprehension amusing.

Mrs Gallagher's reunion with her husband made my eyes moist, for all he looked a sorry character, with his scarred cheeks and his cap all awry.

'It's a great thing to have a wife, so it is,' Daniel remarked, seeing me wipe my eyes.

I wonder sometimes if that man can read my mind!

The city is a place I cannot recommend. It lies in a swampy hollow, under a permanent pall of smoke. The houses are mostly ramshackle, though there are one or two elegant buildings. I noticed a bank with fine Greek columns, and some pleasing features on the Courthouse. There was, in addition, a generous scattering of churches, all (so far as I could ascertain) of the Protestant persuasion. The streets are little more than mud tracks. No one here seems to have heard of enclosed ditches. As for the inhabitants, with the exception of the soldiers (who seem to make up the bulk of the population) they are a rum-looking lot. The sight of men lolling about in broad daylight, some with bottles of cheap liquor in their hands, others with that look men get in their eyes when they've lost all hope, reminded me of how it was at home in the days of the famine. I saw natives carrying firewood on their backs, and children begging for pennies, and women whose occupation was written in the manner of their dress and on their ravaged faces. The soldiers, many of whom were anything but sober, roamed the streets in twos and threes, their bandoliers of bullets tossed casually over their shoulders. When I looked back at the harbour and counted the gunboats anchored there I wondered if any of us would live to see the *Camaderry* set sail again. 'Aren't we the unlucky ones?' Daniel complained. 'The war has spread to the Waikato now. That's a deal too close for my liking.'

My father had given me permission to be away three days. Daniel's doing, I have no doubt of it. He has an influence with my father, for all his rough ways. Within half an hour of our stepping ashore (a giddying experience after so long at sea) Daniel had hired horses and we were making our way through Auckland's putrid streets to the highway known as the Great North Road. At the junction I turned for a last look at Auckland and was reassured by the sight that greeted me. Church spires rose white and clean against a brooding sky. Could it be that this is a land of angels after all? Have I been too hasty in my opinion?

June the eighteenth, 1863
My name is Patrick Brendan Kierin. I am from Arklow in the county of Wicklow in the land of the saints. So why do I feel as if I will never see my homeland again?

I must endeavour to understand the last two days. Daniel and I arrived at what looked at first sight like a military camp: a cluster of tents in a clearing in the bush, inhabited by rough-looking men in whose company we were to spend the evening. Two makeshift huts built of ponga logs and roofed with a flax-like material known as nikau (Daniel is making sure I learn the native words) gave the camp a more permanent air.

Having been introduced as a 'new chum' I found myself sitting between two men of my own country, one who calls himself The Pope, the other known to everyone as Paddy Boots. Over the course of the evening we drank a goodly quantity of gin, passing it, in the manner of the mass, in a bowl from hand to hand. 'You mind yourself now,' I could hear my mother warn. 'These people are heathens.' But after a meal of wild pork and the native potato known as the kumera, I was more inclined to think of them as my friends. 'They're bushmen,' Daniel had told me. 'They work for Mr Astley.'

The following day we rode on to meet the man himself. It is not in my power adequately to describe the sights that greeted me as we trotted down the hill to the settlement (already named for its founder). Suffice it to say Daniel did not exaggerate when he told me Mr Astley was a man of vision. The township has literally sprung out of the bush. (I'm learning to say 'bush' not 'forest', though the word seems puny when faced with the reality it denotes.)

The first thing you notice is the mill. With its huge water wheel and vast iron roof, it towers over the other buildings. Not that these are inconsequential. There's a barracks for single men, cottages for married couples, a manager's house, a school (unfinished), a church (Protestant), a forge, a bakery. There's even the beginnings of a tramway, part of a network, Daniel explained, intended to travel deep into the bush.

We walked our horses through this metropolis, amid clouds of sawdust, and the music of a community hard at work.

Mr Astley was no disappointment. A tall, well-proportioned man, with thinning hair and side whiskers, he greeted Daniel with enthusiasm. His manner with me was almost as friendly, but I could sense him sizing me up. 'You must take your young friend to see the king,' he instructed Daniel.

Enemy Territory

I had the feeling, from the way the two men looked at one another, that I was being set some kind of trap.

The next thing I knew we were riding along a frequently invisible track, through dense bush. Several times we had to dismount, and cut back the tangled fronds that blocked our path. By the time Daniel called a halt it was past noon. This being mid-winter we had to watch the light, though in the midst of that vast forest (I could no longer describe it as bush) there was little enough light even at midday.

The trees that surrounded us were magnificent specimens. Tall, virtually stripped of branches, they stood like so many giants, proud and straight. Their trunks invited caressing. Though by no means as smooth to touch as in appearance there was nevertheless something sensual about their nakedness. I did not need to be told I was looking at kauris.

'Eight hundred years,' Daniel said, as I stood, in silent admiration. 'That's what it takes for one of these little beauties to reach maturity.'

'How can you bear to cut them down?'

'How can you bear not to? You're looking at a perfect ship's spar.'

I assumed we had reached our destination; that these upstanding soldiers of the forest were what I had been brought to see. But there was a greater wonder in store. Obeying Daniel's instruction to tether my horse, we set off on foot, Daniel brandishing his sickle as if it were a cutlass, me following, like the busy fantails that accompanied us, at a safe distance. After about twenty minutes of this we came to a small clearing. I thought I could hear water running, though from what direction I couldn't tell. Through the branches, high above us, thin sunlight trickled down, reminding me of the way the light spills from the high windows in our parish church at home.

''Tis a great thing I am about to show you,' Daniel said, 'so do as I say, and close your eyes.'

I was sceptical, but did as he asked, allowing him to

lead me by the hand for several treacherous yards. The moment I opened my eyes I fell to my knees. Had I not been a Catholic I would probably have uttered some kind of obeisance. God help me, I thought, what I'm seeing cannot be.

'Aye, and it's a grand sight, sure as God's in Heaven,' Daniel pronounced.

'This is the king?' I whispered.

'Tane Mahuta,' Daniel answered.

'How old is it?'

'How old is God?'

'You'd never cut this one down,' I said. 'It would be a crime.'

June the thirtieth, 1863
God stand between me and all harm, for I've decided to throw in my lot with Daniel O'Malley and Theodore Astley. I cannot explain my decision except to say that something about this land has struck the hidden part of my soul. My father fears I will become a heathen if I stay. He has no time for my descriptions of the ways of the Maori people, or my feeble tributes in verse to Tane Mahuta. He believes I am already half damned. 'And how are you to receive the mass,' he challenged, 'when there is not a priest to be seen for miles?' I was able to reassure him I would be taking mass with a community of German Catholics who have settled not far from Astley. 'They are engaged in planting a vineyard,' I explained, 'so you need not fear their hasty departure.'

I wish I could say I had my father's blessing on the life I have chosen, but I fear his heart is too hurt. Only when I told him about Mr Astley, whom the newspaper here describes as a 'coming man', did he appear to comprehend my decision. 'Sure, and I can see how you might be persuaded,' he acknowledged sadly. 'And when I think of what could have been your destiny at home . . .' I knew what he was thinking. A patriot himself, he has lived in fear that I, his only son, would die in Ireland's cause.

> So, here I be, equipped with an axe, a crosscut saw, a paling knife, a jack, a mattress made from the teased out fronds of the mingi mingi fern, a pair of half-knee boots, two flannel shirts, two singlets, two pairs of baggy bushmen's trousers, a wide-brimmed hat, a large quantity of tobacco, and a packhorse to transport me and my strange new belongings to the bush. I will be working with Daniel in a team of ten men. Our job is to fell, cut and transport kauri from the bush to the mill. Eleven shillings and sixpence per one hundred feet of sawn timber is what we will be paid. If Daniel is to be believed we will be rich men by next Easter!
>
> It will be hard to part from my dear father. Harder still if I think of Mam and wee Molly waiting for me on the Arklow wharf. But the die is cast. This land, where the rain sheets straight from a warm sky (so unlike our missling rain at home) is where I will find, or lose, my life.

Kay's sudden gasp was occasioned, not by Patrick's words, but by a loud knocking on her door. She glanced at her watch: 10.30. Who would be visiting at this hour?

Moments later she was following Eve Ta'ase across the street. Bert had fallen and cut his head. Kay was needed to sit with Eve's children while she drove the old man to hospital.

For the time being Patrick Kierin was forgotten.

49

The restaurant was a disappointment. Geoffrey, arriving ten minutes before the appointed time, took in the black linoleum, the black and white tiled walls, the plastic-topped tables and chrome chairs, and cursed himself for not choosing the Italian across the road. If it wasn't Saturday he'd risk cancelling and trying elsewhere, but going out on Saturday night was as much of a national institution as rugby football or betting (till recently, illegally) on the horses.

Waiting for Kay was a nerve-wracking experience. He hadn't seen her for over six months. It was Pauline who came, every fourth Sunday, to collect Nina.

'Hello! How are you? You look . . .' Geoffrey's arms went up and down like a marionette's. How do you greet an ex-wife? Is it all right to tell her she looks beautiful?

'Hello, Geoffrey,' Kay said, kissing him on the cheek. (I've missed you, oh God, I've missed you, he thought).

They sat down, studiously avoiding each other's eyes. After a few moments of excruciating silence, they both started talking at once. When Kay laughed, Geoffrey felt a surge of confidence. He turned to summon the waitress. For three days he'd been asking himself why he'd set this meeting up. Now he knew the answer. He wanted Kay back.

'Talk to me about Nina,' she urged when he'd filled her glass with wine. 'Tell me what your days are like. I want to know everything, however trivial.'

It was easy to oblige. Stories about Nina came readily to his lips. When he'd satisfied her craving he announced that he and Nina would be moving into a flat in two weeks' time.

Kay's expression suggested she hadn't heard him. Then, screwing up her face in exactly the way Nina did when puzzled, she asked him why.

'It's a lot of things,' he hedged. 'Mother for one. She gets tired, and . . .'

'How will you manage?' Kay interrupted. 'You work twelve hours a day.'

He didn't care for the sharp note in her voice. But she's Nina's mother, he reminded himself, she has a right to ask. 'I've spoken to her kindergarten,' he told her. 'They're prepared to have her there till three o'clock. It'll be good training for school.'

'And after three o'clock?'

'I'll hire someone. Don't worry,' he added, seeing Kay frown again, 'Whoever it is will be thoroughly vetted.'

'I could do it.'

Geoffrey, in the act of lighting a cigarette, froze. He stared at the woman sitting opposite him. Why hadn't he anticipated this? And why was he feeling, suddenly, as if he didn't trust her? He couldn't ask the questions that tormented him. Do you sleep with men? Do you take drugs? But how, without answers, could he be sure of her? 'What about your job?' he muttered.

'That could be arranged.'

'I thought . . . I understood from Pauline that you were working full-time?'

'If Nina were living with me I wouldn't be working at all.'

'You mean if Nina were living with *us*,' Geoffrey said bitterly.

Fortunately, at that moment the food arrived. Geoffrey, stepping back from the minefield they'd strayed on to, enquired casually about Kay's position at *The Herald*. Perhaps he would get his answers by going round the subject. He was reasonably sure she no longer used drugs. She'd sworn as much in court. And he only had to look at her to see she was leading a healthy life.

The questions tumbled out of him. What sort of people do you work with? Who are your friends these days? Who's the Maori woman Nina keeps talking about?

To his surprise Kay seemed perfectly willing to supply answers. 'I don't have a lot of friends,' she admitted. 'But those I have are – what's that saying? – "worth their weight in gold".'

Geoffrey laughed. 'What about your Dunedin pals? Do you still hear from Lynne?'

'I'm afraid I never sent her my new address.'

Geoffrey chewed his food. He was beginning to feel like a private detective. Did men figure among these friends who were "worth their weight in gold"? 'How are your parents?' he asked. 'I hope they're being . . .' He bit his lip. No one would ever associate Harold and Esme with gold. 'I've been meaning to take Nina out to see them,' he lied.

'That would be nice.'

'I should have done something about it before.'

'Acutally, I'm going to see Mum tomorrow. Dad's away at a Rotary conference.'

'Tell me more about Makere te Tuhi. You obviously think a lot of her.'

'She's the great-great-granddaughter of a Kawerau chief – Patara te Tuhi. You've probably heard of him.'

Geoffrey shook his head.

'He and his tribe sided with the Waikato people during the wars of the 1860s. Their villages were burned in retaliation.'

'So, Makere's got you interested in history at last.'

'Oh, it's more than that. She's got a plan for me. Don't ask me what it is, but it's something to do with a book of hers, a diary. I'm reading it at the moment actually. It's from that time, the 1860s.'

Geoffrey tried to ignore the whine in his hearing-aid. He didn't like enigmas, especially ones that involved Kay. He wondered if he should tell her his real reason for moving into a flat. But then he thought she'd be bound to create a fuss. There'd never been much love lost between Winifred and her daughter-in-law.

'Listen,' he said, over coffee, 'there's something I want to talk to you about.'

Kay's eyes widened.

'The issue of custody will be coming up in a few months. I want you to know . . .' It was painful watching the changes in Kay's face. Whether there was a man in her life or not there was no doubting her love for her daughter. 'I want you to know,' he repeated softly, 'I won't oppose, well, some easing of the original order. Perhaps even . . .'

'Nina's being punished as much as I am,' Kay cut in fiercely.
'Oh, I think that's an exaggeration.'
'Why don't you ask *her*?'
Geoffrey lunged for a cigarette. How could he ever have imagined he could get his wife back? She hated him, didn't she? He could hear it in her voice.
'Anyway, it won't be up to you, will it?'
Conversation faltered after that. Geoffrey, in a further blunder, brought up Sandra Grajawaska's name. Kay's response was icy. 'Why don't you just ask me if I'm sleeping around?' she said. 'That's what you really want to know, isn't it?'
When she announced she was going he felt only relief. 'Thank you for the dinner,' she said.
There was no farewell kiss. Geoffrey watched her till she was out of sight; then he paid the bill, and drove home.

50

July the eleventh, 1871
The most extraordinary thing! Clearing out the hut today I found this diary. God help me, but I'd forgotten its existence. Now here I be, on the eve of my marriage, confronted with the raw young man I was eight long years ago. Ah, but it's a cruel thing to think back on what is gone forever. My dear friend and comrade, Daniel, killed in the fighting that broke out a mere three weeks after we started work for Mr Astley. Cruel times indeed those were. Gunboats prowling up and down the Manukau, firing volley after volley into the Maori settlements. Daniel, may God and the Good Mother of Mercy rest his soul, would take it upon himself to run ahead of the boats, calling on anyone foolish enough to have stayed behind to take refuge in the bush. When he didn't return I went with Paddy Boots and Seagull Jack to search for him. He must have been killed at once. There was barely enough of him left to identify him. We buried him in the new graveyard at Astley. In the absence of a priest a Methodist minister officiated. I tucked his rosary in beside his poor broken body and said the Hail Mary, which he would have wanted. I miss him still. He would have stood beside me when I marry Hinemoa. But he'll not be forgotten. My first son will be named Daniel. Hinemoa has agreed. Daniel Taumanu Kierin.

How can I fill in those eight years? If I try to recreate them, sure as my name's Patrick I'll write a lot of blether. Hard physical labour makes a plum duff of the intellect.

• Elspeth Sandys

> I only have to look at my hands, browned and gnarled like old nuts, to mind how it's been for me since I came to this land. Strange, but I do believe, if I'd returned to Ireland, I would be languishing in an English prison by now. Or dead. The Fianna did what they'd always boasted they'd do: organised an uprising. But with most of their leaders in prison it was doomed to failure from the start. I still have the letter my father sent four years back, telling me of these events. 'All your old friends – John O'Leary, Jeremiah O'Donovan, Thomas Luby – all behind bars,' he wrote. Later that year another letter came, telling me of the death of wee Molly. That one I destroyed. Some griefs are too hard to bear.

Kay twisted her head on the pillow. She'd taken the diary to bed with her, determined to finish it. The meeting with Geoffrey had not been a success. Driving back to Massey Street she'd not known whether to be angry or sorry.

She did a quick calculation. Molly would have been eight when she died.

> I worked for Mr Astley for five years. I didn't become rich, as Daniel had predicted, but I was able to put aside enough money to buy the land on which I now live. I've called this place Sean Bhean Bhocht which is one of the ancient names for Ireland. Hinemoa teases me, insisting it sounds more like a curse than a name, but the sweet creature indulges me in this, as in so much else.
>
> My mind is racing backwards and forwards over the years: the meeting with Hinemoa which, so long as I draw breath, will continue to fill me with wonder and gratitude; the Sundays (alas, few and far between) when I walked ten miles to receive the mass; the kindness of my Austrian friends; the visits of little Nina . . .

The book fell from Kay's hand. What was Makere up to?

She flicked through the remaining pages. The word 'murdered' jumped out at her. Then, on the same page, 'arrested'. Her heart contracted painfully. She'd asked Makere once if she knew what

Patrick looked like. Makere's reply had been enigmatic. 'That's for you to decide,' she'd said.

But I need more, Kay argued silently. She wasn't thinking of Patrick now, she was thinking of tomorrow's visit to her mother. That was Makere's doing too. 'Tell her the things you've told me,' she'd advised. 'I think you might be surprised.'

Sometimes, Kay accused her friend, in a rare flash or irritation, *you ask too much*.

She picked up the diary again.

But Nina comes later. Before that there was my life as a bushman. Selecting the next tree to be felled; working the saw; the moment when the shout, 'Under below!' went up, and the tree shivered like a huge sad child, swaying and creaking till it fell. Such a commotion there would be then as the tree's cargo of birds flew, shrieking, into the sky, and the trunk tore like a lion through the undergrowth, tossing ferns and twigs and the bright petals of orchids high into the air. I mind so well those days, and the ones that followed, working in the sawpit, marking up the logs to be cut, splitting off the shingles. When the creek was full we'd start the drive, guiding the logs on their slow journey to the mill.

Then there were the days when mist filled the gullies and we sat about in our hut drying our clothes by the fire, playing blackjack and gin rummy, sharpening our saws, taking bets as to when the packhorse would arrive with fresh supplies from town, writing letters home . . . Till the day came when I could bear it no longer, and I walked through the bush to tell Mr Astley I was quitting. 'But for heaven's sake, man,' he protested, 'why quit now? I've four ships tied up at the wharf, and more orders coming in than I can ever hope to meet. China, America, Chile, Australia, the Home Country, they all want our kauri. We can't get the logs out fast enough. Is it more money you're wanting?' He couldn't seem to understand that I had become possessed with the spirit of Tane Mahuta.

How do I explain that now? Supposing my son Daniel

were to read this diary, what would he make of his
father's decision to turn his back on a generous wage,
and take up the uncertain life of a homesteader? Would
he accuse me of wilfulness? Or would he understand
that I could not be a witness to any more destruction?
Though, inevitably, I had to clear this land of mine before
I could plant grass seed. I chopped manuka and rimu and
rewa rewa, but not, God be thanked, the kauri. The stand
that grows behind the house I have built for Hinemoa
will be there forever, if my wishes count for anything.
Hinemoa agrees with me. It was the kauri that brought us
together.

But I run ahead of myself again. Before Hinemoa there
was Nina. Little Nina Lassmann . . .

Here, for the second time, Kay stopped. She'd told Makere about her job at Lassmann's. You could see their vineyard from Makere's back garden. 'I used to work for them too,' Makere had told her. 'The old man, Fedor's father, hired me to scare away the birds. I was only a kid.'

. . . Little Nina Lassmann, who has been coming here
every week for the last two years, bringing fresh bread
and pickled cabbage and the strong wine her father
makes. I encountered the Lassmanns in my first weeks in
New Zealand. They were camped with two other families,
the Schroeders and the Biegelebens, in a valley not far
from Mr Astley's mill. Their kind offer to join them in the
mass was instrumental in persuading my father to accept
my decision to make a life here. Little did I know, when
we spoke that morning on the *Camaderry*, that no priest
would come near Astley for almost a year. And then it
would be another six months before I saw his like again.
Even now, eight years later, I can count the number of
times I've taken mass on the fingers of my hands. But
I've not become a heathen! I read my prayer book, and
say my rosary, and I can still recite most of the catechism.
And when I marry Hinemoa it will be before Father
Zangerl, an Austrian, like the Lassmanns. (I had assumed,

at first, they were German. It was Nina's mother, Ursula, who enlightened me. 'We are here for escaping the wars,' she told me, in her broken English. 'And on account of the potatoes.' That had puzzled me till I realised she was talking about the blight. Ireland, I learned that day, was not the only land to suffer famine.)

While I was still a bushman I saw little of the Lassmanns and their compatriots. The walk through the bush was too long and arduous to encourage me to visit other than to attend the mass. But once I'd bought these acres (closer to the Lassmanns by several miles) I became a regular visitor. In return for pigeon and wild pig, which I would carry out from the bush, they would supply me with vegetables and wine. 'We an arrangement could make,' Paul, Ursula's husband, proposed one day. 'You bring us timber for the building. We send Nina to your hut one time a week for the bringing of supplies.'

That was how it started. Since then, every Friday afternoon, I have waited to hear the merry voice that never fails to call to mind my own wee Molly. 'Herr Kierin! I come to you. Herr Kierin!' And I put down my axe and hold out my arms, and the little pig-tailed sprite from Austria drops her parcels and throws herself at my chest. On summer days, when she can linger, I teach her the games I used to play as a child, or read to her from the books I have borrowed from Mr Astley's library. But on winter days she must return quickly. The path through the bush is narrow and can be treacherous. Not for all the gold in the world would I have Nina come to harm.

Tomorrow will be her last visit. It is my only sadness in this time of so much joy. We will talk of the wedding, which will take place in ten days' time in the church of Saint Joseph, which I helped build myself. These days there are four families living near the vineyard. The Schroeders moved on to the gum fields of the north, but their place was taken by two Dalmatian families, who came to the rescue during the first harvest, and stayed on to buy land of their own. The wedding day will see them all in their traditional clothes, dancing their polkas and schottisches before the assembled company of Hinemoa's people. How can I hope to describe what my mind already presents to me as a gathering so colourful and generous that words must surely fail, or be reduced to blarney? Hinemoa, my raven-haired beauty, who has become a Catholic (more to please me than from conviction, I suspect), has assured me, amidst giggles, that I will be pleased with her appearance as a bride. I told her I would be happy if she wore sackcloth and ashes, a joke she failed to appreciate!

I have Tane Mahuta to thank for bringing Hinemoa and me together. I had got into the habit of visiting what I secretly thought of as a shrine, on the days when rain confined us to camp. Had Daniel been alive I might have taken him with me. He at least understood, even if he did not share, my sense of awe at the sight of that majestic tree. The others, I felt certain, would think me soft in the head. 'God help us, but he'll be seeing leprechauns next,' Paddy Boots would taunt.

The day of our meeting was wet and windy, so that even I, pushing my way through the bush, began to doubt the wisdom of the exercise. The air smelt of decay; the wind was a blade in my face; creeping tendrils grabbed my legs, pulling me down into a stew of rotting bark and leaves. The stumps of the felled kauri, sticky with gum, depressed me. The work of centuries destroyed in a day.

Imagine my astonishment then, when I saw, as I approached Tane Mahuta, that I was not alone. A figure in a long cape – I could not at that stage tell whether it was a man or a woman – was standing close to the tree, looking up at its crown. In some trepidation I made my presence known. I felt sure the intruder (for so I regarded the stranger) was Maori. As bushmen we were dependent on the Kawerau people for much of our food. Relations were cordial enough, but the military action of 1863, and the subsequent retreat of all but a few of the tribe, had soured the Kawerau's view of the white man. Had it not been for Daniel, whose heroism I'd heard celebrated in a *waiata*, it's doubtful they would have agreed to trade with us at all.

'Good day to you,' I called out.

The figure turned. Though I could see but little of her face, I sensed her beauty at once. She was tall, almost as tall as I, with bright brown eyes and skin as smooth as the skin of a pear. When she smiled, my heart did a somersault. In that instant, I fell in love.

''Tis a grand sight,' I said, into the silence her beauty had created. Though I could speak a little of her language I could not, at that moment, recall a single word.

'I am Hinemoa Taumanu,' she informed me.

'Patrick Kierin.'

She giggled.

'You have come to pay homage?' I hazarded.

'Homage?'

'To Tane Mahuta.'

Her smile became a frown. Both were equally enchanting to me. When she turned away it was as if the sun had gone behind a cloud. I edged closer, determined to discover where she lived.

'You are from the coast?' I enquired.

She nodded.

''Tis strange I've not seen you.'

'I've seen you,' she responded coyly.

'Oh?'

'You came last week for fish.'

After that it was as if we had always known each other. It's not something I can explain. She took me back to her village, and I met the old people who were her guardians, and she explained that she had come from the north, where the rest of her family lived, to visit her relatives.

Two weeks after my meeting with Hinemoa I resigned my job with Mr Astley and took up this land. Hinemoa's promise to visit me here was the trigger to my new enterprise. A year later, with the land cleared and the first seed planted, she agreed to marry me. Since that day I have worked as hard as any man can to turn this hard volcanic soil into pasture, and build a house fit for my heart's love.

The candle is guttering. If I don't stop now I will be feeling my way to my bed in the dark. God bless my sweet Hinemoa and all her people, and may the Blessed Saint Brighid look kindly upon our union.

July the twelfth 1871
The day has been sour with rain and I am in a bother about Nina. It is long past her usual time of arrival. I've searched the path, and called her name till I'm hoarse with shouting. I've even blown the bullock horn, a favourite 'toy' of hers, which I've promised to give her when I have no further use for it. Ah, but surely Ursula would not have let her come out on so bitter a day? That must be it, for all that I cannot remember a time in the past when such a thing occurred.

I have lit the lamp and placed it near the door. I sleep in the house now. The hut where I have lived for the last three years has been relegated to a storeroom. Tomorrow I will finish butchering the pig I killed this afternoon. The meat will make a useful addition to the wedding feast.

I have said the rosary and prayed to Saint Christopher to keep wee Nina safe. The wind has an eerie sound tonight, as if this house were being tossed on the sea. I swear I can hear ships' timbers creaking, and the groans of sailors as they struggle to keep the heaving vessel afloat.

July the thirteenth, 1871
I can scarce bring myself to put these words down: Nina is missing. I woke this morning with a premonition of disaster. So powerful was it I abandoned my daily chores and set off at first light along the track that leads to the vineyard. It seemed to me, as I walked, that the bush gave off a particularly pungent odour, causing my nose to itch uncontrollably.

I found the settlment in uproar. Paul Lassmann and his two sons had spent the night searching for Nina. Now the other families were to be involved. Erich Biegeleben was to search the area to the south. The Yerkovich brothers would take the track to the north, while Paul and the Puharich men would go back along the path I had just travelled.

'When she failed to appear yesterday I told myself, sure, and you would have forbidden her to come,' I said to Ursula. 'With the rain and all.'

'If only I had,' she wailed.

'What can I do?' I asked Paul.

'Return to your house,' he instructed. 'She may still her way find to you. It is best you wait there.'

'At least it's a fine day,' I observed miserably.

But Nina has not found her way to me, and now darkness has fallen, and there is a pain in my heart which cuts my breath in two.

O Blessed Virgin succour this lost child, and bring her safely home again. Holy Mary Mother of God and all the company of Heaven, watch over our dear Nina, and protect her from harm.

July the eighteenth, 1871
I have been arrested for the murder of Nina Lassmann. May God and all the saints defend me.

The book slid from Kay's hands. 'Do you know what Patrick looked like?' she'd asked Makere. She knew the answer now. When he wrote those lines he would have looked like Geoffrey, the night she told him the truth about Roy.

Patrick was innocent. That was the reason Makere had wanted her to read the book. But what was she supposed to do with the knowledge?

Tomorrow she would visit her mother. 'Only God knows the truth of the human heart,' Makere had said.

Wrong, Kay answered her now. *You know. You look at the past, and you read the future. If I didn't love you I'd be afraid of you.*

51

The drive from Massey Street to Astley was one Kay, since knowing Makere, had come to enjoy. But her destination today was not Makere's house on the river, but her parents' home in Kauri Avenue.

She wasn't looking forward to the visit. Her mother's letter ('Sometimes we have to accept the most terrible things'), which had once seemed to hold out an invitation, struck her now as no more than coincidental. That Esme Dyer knew what her husband was had been an article of faith with Kay ever since the Christmas she'd fled to Dunedin. Now, suddenly, she doubted. What if her mother didn't know? Clive, she was certain, was ignorant of the whole sordid business. It was possible (though unlikely) that that was true of her mother too. People who didn't *want* to know things could always find explanations.

Approaching Astley Kay stopped the car at the top of the hill, and got out. Saint Joseph's church was clearly visible from this side of town. It wasn't the church Patrick had helped to build – that had long since gone – but there might be some trace of him left, a name from that time, a reference to the original church. Presumably the present-day Lassmanns, if they were still Catholics, worshipped there. She might even see Sophie.

Patrick Kierin was tried before a Grand Jury in the Supreme Court in Auckland, and found guilty of the murder of Nina Maria Lassmann. The principal evidence against him was the large amount of dried blood discovered at the back of his house. Patrick's defence, that the blood was from a pig he'd slaughtered that same day, was not believed. He was sentenced by Judge Prendergast to be hanged on New Year's Day, 1872.

• Elspeth Sandys

I met *Geoffrey* on New Year's Day, Kay had thought, as she read those words.

That entry, like the others covering Patrick's last terrible months, was brief and unemotional. Only when Hinemoa's name was mentioned did a hint of the condemned man's suffering emerge.

> Hinemoa visited me today. She brought me lemons
> from our tree, and a basket of salt fish. She was wearing
> the cloak she wore that first day when we met by
> Tane Mahuta. Truly I have never seen a more beautiful
> woman, nor loved anyone more.

As Kay coasted down the hill towards St Joseph's, Patrick's words played over in her mind. A line of cars was parked outside the church. She took that to mean there was a service going on.

She pulled up on the opposite side of the road and wound the window down. A faint sound of chanting reached her from inside the church's closed doors. The only prayer she knew was the Lord's Prayer. It wouldn't achieve anything, except to make *her* feel better, but she said it anyway. Patrick was innocent. When she thought of his suffering hot tears sprang into her eyes. Only Hinemoa had gone on believing in him. To everyone else he had been a child-killer.

Minutes later she was parked outside the house in Kauri Avenue.

'Goodness!' her mother exclaimed. 'You're early.'

Kay took in the outsize apron, tied at the neck and waist, the protecting plastic sleeves, the scarf tied round the head, and for the second time that morning forced back tears. 'It's good to see you, Mum,' she said.

'Yes, well. How long has it been? Anyone'd think you lived at the other end of the country.'

Kay followed her mother into the kitchen. The familiar smell of baking had her diving for her handkerchief again. 'Is all this for me?' she asked, waving a hand at the plates of scones and pikelets and shortbread.

'Don't imagine you do much cooking in that place of yours,' her mother snapped.

'Well, I'll live like a king this week. Thanks, Mum.'

Over the next hour, while Esme finished her baking, and Kay repeatedly checked the state of her hair, conversation stopped and started, drying up when either Nina's name or Geoffrey's was mentioned, flowing more easily when it came to Clive (promoted to Major now), only to dam up again when Esme began to talk about Harold.

'Excuse me a sec, will you, Mum?' Kay interrupted.

'Where are you going?'

'The loo.'

Hurrying down the corridor, Kay accused herself of cowardice. She'd come here to talk about her father, yet here she was, at the first mention of his name, scurrying away like a rat from a sinking ship.

When she'd finished in the bathroom she walked, unaware of any conscious purpose, into her parents' bedroom. Everything was as it had always been: the ugly oak bed; the green candlewick bedspread; her father's tallboy; her mother's vanity table with its immaculate frilly hem; the cheap floral curtains. The only thing that was different was the framed photo of Nina hanging on the wall.

Back came the tears. Kay shook her head vigorously. She had the same photo hanging in her own bedroom. She should be able to look at it without blubbing.

She turned her back on her daughter and walked across the room to the built-in wardrobe her parents shared. Last time she looked inside – on her first visit after her marriage – she fled the house. She would not be so impulsive today.

Sliding open the doors, she stood back to examine the contents. The dresses were there in full view. The same ones she'd seen on the clothes line the summer she worked at Lassmann's. Three long satin frocks, one red, one gold, one emerald green. The red one she'd seen for the first time that night in Karangahape Road. She'd had to stare for several seconds before her mind would accept that the person wearing the dress was her father.

'Yes, your life is a tangle,' Makere had agreed, 'but you won't sort it out by attributing blame. It's your mother you must talk to, not your father. Maybe, when you've done that, you'll see things more clearly.'

'So,' her mother's voice said from the doorway. 'I see you know.'

Kay spun round so fast she lost her balance. Her mother smiled. For a second Kay was a child again, twirling in her mother's arms, dizzy with laughter. Could the world ever be that safe again?

'I somehow thought you did,' Esme said.

'I've known since I was sixteen.'

'That long?'

'I saw him on the Karangahape Road.'

Esme nodded. Then, without warning, she threw back her head and screamed.

Kay, when she'd recovered from her shock, hurled herself across the room and folded her mother in her arms. She couldn't remember when they'd last hugged each other. A cool kiss on the cheek had long been their only sign of affection.

'I'm sorry,' Esme gasped. 'Oh, my darling, I'm so sorry.'

'It's not your fault,' Kay said.

'I should at least, since I couldn't protect you, have tried to talk to you. I mean, I could see . . . well, it was obvious, wasn't it? That Christmas when you dashed off to Dunedin . . .'

'Shhh,' Kay soothed. 'It doesn't matter.'

'But it does. Ten years of your life. What can you have been thinking all that time?'

As if her mother were blind, Kay led her to the bed and sat her down. 'How long has it been going on?' she asked. She still couldn't bring herself to say her father's name. 'Have you always known about it?'

'I didn't know when I married him, if that's what you mean.'

'And you never thought of leaving him?'

Esme gave an odd little laugh. 'Oh, I thought about it all right. When I first found out, I wanted to take you and Clive, and run away to Australia.'

'Why didn't you?'

'Because I could never have managed on my own. My generation, we're not like you, Kay. We were never taught, most of us anyway, to survive in the world. I married your father when I was eighteen. The only job I'd ever had was working in a chemist's shop. Besides, I couldn't have divorced him, not for the real reasons. You and Clive would have had to live with that knowledge for the rest of your lives.'

'I'm living with it anyway, Mum.'

'Yes.'

'After I saw him that time, my periods stopped for over a year.'

'Oh, darling . . .'

'I was afraid to tell you. I thought you might think . . .'

'You didn't trust me,' Esme said, her voice quavering unhappily. 'Well, you wouldn't, would you?'

'It wasn't you, Mum. I mean, it wasn't because of you, or even of what I'd seen. It was how it was then. None of my friends confided in their mothers.'

'At least I protected Clive. At least he didn't suffer.'

'How can you be sure?'

Esme dropped her face into her hands. 'Don't say that,' she pleaded.

'I've wanted to ask him so many times. The only reason I haven't . . .'

'But it would be so much worse for him. Don't you see? He's a man.'

'Why should that make a difference?'

'Sons model themselves on their fathers.'

Kay smiled. 'I don't think you need worry about that,' she said. 'Clive is as different from Dad' (There, I've said it, she thought) 'as any man could be.'

Esme's sigh bordered on the theatrical. Kay tried to speak, but her mouth had gone dry. She had no idea how often Clive wrote home, or even if he wrote at all. Now that he was a major, being sent to Vietnam was a distinct possibility.

She reached out and took her mother's hand. Why had she never realised before how much she loved her? The hand felt warm and surprisingly soft. There were spots like gravy stains all over the skin. 'You don't have to stay with him any longer, you know,' she said. 'Clive and I aren't children any more.'

'Where would I go?'

'You could live with me.'

Esme's eyes filled with tears.

'Think about it. I'm going to get Nina back, I know I am. You could help. For God's sake, Mum, the man's sick. Why should you stay with him?'

'Perhaps that's why.'

'Now you're being a martyr.'

'I don't hate him, Kay. I've never hated him.'

'But you don't love him . . .'

'Love?' Esme laughed. 'Do any of us know what that word means? You thought you loved Geoffrey . . .'

Kay released her mother's hand. But I do know something about love, she wanted to protest. I know for an absolute certainty that I love Nina. And this morning, sitting on this bed, I've been reminded of my love for you.

'Your father has always been a good provider,' Esme said.

The predictability of the remark made Kay smile. She'd heard those words so many times before. 'I'm starving,' she announced. 'Do you think we can have one of your scones, or are they just for show?'

'There's no call to be cheeky.'

'I love you, Mum,' Kay said.

For a moment it seemed Esme might dismiss the protestation. But then her frown became a smile and she reached out her arms. 'My darling,' she said.

It was almost dark by the time Kay reached Makere's house. She'd wondered about going at all. The day with her mother had left her exhausted. But then she'd remembered the diary, and she'd known she had to go, if only to discover what Makere had in store for her.

'You find me alone for once,' Makere said, as she opened the door. 'The *mokopuna* have gone north for a *tangi*.'

'You didn't want to go yourself?'

'I was expecting you,' Makere said.

Over the first of several cups of tea, Kay launched into an account of the conversation with her mother. She knew she'd get no answers to her questions about Patrick until she'd told her own story. This time the reaction did not disappoint. Makere's smile widened until it seemed to cover the whole of her face. 'You've done well, Kay,' she said. 'You are beginning to unravel your tangle.'

'Is Patrick part of it?' Kay asked. 'Is that why you lent me his diary?'
'You've finished it?'
Kay nodded.
'And what did you think?'
But Kay, ambushed again by tears, couldn't answer.

52

On balance, Geoffrey thought, pouring himself a second cup of coffee, I feel pleased with my new way of life. The flat was large and airy, with a glimpse of the harbour at the front, and just enough garden at the back to prevent claustrophobia. Nina's room, next to his, was furnished with a bed, a desk and chair (in preparation for the schoolgirl she would soon become), a bookcase, a chest full of toys, and the doll's house he'd bought for her as a surprise when they moved in.

It hadn't been easy extricating himself from his parents, but he'd managed it. There had even been a small breakthrough with his father. Faced with Winifred's hysterical reaction to her son's decision to move out, Lionel had taken Geoffrey aside and urged him to make allowances. 'Your mother has a lot to put up with,' he'd said. 'More than you know. In many ways she's an astoundingly generous woman.'

Geoffrey had assumed his father was referring to his affair, and his wife's supposed tolerance of it; but thinking back on the conversation now he wasn't so sure. 'She once did something for me,' Lionel had said. 'Put herself at risk, for my sake. I should never have let it happen. It was my fault. But the harm's done now.'

Somehow he hadn't sounded as if he was talking about a mistress.

Today was Nina's day with her mother. Since the moment she woke she'd been jumping up and down like a jack-in-the-box. Geoffrey had suggested to Kay that she come and fetch Nina herself. If she came early enough they could have time together before meeting up with Pauline.

Things were going a little better with Kay. She'd phoned him earlier in the week, not to talk about Nina – he'd already reassured her as to the workings of the new regime – but to ask his advice. If she could have seen his face she would have realised the effect just hearing her voice had on him.

'You remember that Maori case you worked on when you were a student?' she'd said. 'Something to do with a land deal that went sour.'

'The Tuwharetoa case. What about it?'

'It went back a long way, didn't it?'

'Turn of the century.'

'How do you go about re-opening a case like that?'

'Well, that depends. With the Tuwharetoa it was . . .'

'I'm talking about a murder trial.'

'Cripes!'

'It's a long story.'

That was when he'd suggested she come to the flat. He wanted her to see it anyway. He was hoping she might compliment him on his housekeeping skills!

'Eat up, darling,' he urged, seeing his daughter pile a slice of buttered toast on top of two already uneaten ones. 'Aren't you hungry?'

'It's for Mummy,' Nina said.

'I think Mummy will have had breakfast.'

'Can I wait outside? She might get lost. Is Auntie Pauline coming too?'

Geoffrey drained his coffee. 'Come on, sweetheart,' he said. 'We'll both go and meet her.'

Minutes later Kay's car pulled up at the gate. Nina let out a whoop of joy and catapulted into her mother's arms. Geoffrey hung back. He didn't want Kay to think he'd been waiting for her. She was wearing a long Indian skirt and pale blue jumper. She didn't look like a lawyer's wife, but she looked pretty good all the same.

'You should get yourself a decent car,' he said, waving a hand at her rusted Ford Prefect.

'Don't knock it,' she laughed. 'It hasn't let me down yet.'

Once inside it was Nina who took upon herself the responsibilities of proprietorship. Taking her mother's hand, she escorted her from room to room, proudly showing her 'Daddy's big bed', and 'my very own house', and the bathroom 'where Daddy scrapes his whiskers off with a knife'. Kay's responses were all Geoffrey could have hoped for. When he heard Nina confide that she wanted a piano, he mouthed the word 'Christmas' to Kay.

'I've been thinking about your murder case,' he said when Nina could be persuaded to leave her mother alone. 'When did you say the original trial was?'

'1871.'

'And you're convinced this fellow is innocent?'

'Absoutely. I know a diary isn't sufficient evidence. And I know instinct means nothing to a lawyer . . .'

'Oh, I wouldn't say . . .'

'But I'm *certain* Patrick is innocent. It's as plain to me as you are, sitting in that chair.'

'May I ask what makes you so sure?'

Kay tucked her feet underneath her. Geoffrey couldn't remember when he'd last seen her looking so animated. Her hands, as she launched into her story, made a constantly changing pattern in the air. 'I can't explain it,' she said when she'd finished, 'but it's as if Patrick is asking me, *ordering* me, to clear his name.'

'I would say it's your friend Makere who's doing the ordering.'

'Can you imagine anything worse than being innocent and having everyone believe you're guilty? To die knowing that?'

Geoffrey busied himself with a cigarette. She was talking about herself, wasn't she? She might not know it, but this obsession of hers had more to do with losing Nina than proving the innocence of some long-dead Irishman.

'You know he never got a proper burial? He was just thrown into a hole in the ground.'

'What is Makere's interest in him? It all sounds a bit unlikely to me.'

'Hinemoa, the woman he was to have married, is her great-great-grandmother.'

'I see.'

'Two years after Patrick's death she married Patara te Tuhi, the rebel chief I told you about.'

Geoffrey raised a quizzical eyebrow. 'And now Makere wants his name cleared,' he said.

'That isn't why I'm doing it.'

'But she's encouraging you.'

'She's my friend, Geoff. If she wants me to do something, you can be sure it's for my own good.'

Geoffrey drew deeply on his cigarette. 'Are you in a hurry?' he asked, through a cloud of smoke. 'We could put Pauline off for an hour or so.'

'Makere's expecting us for lunch.'

'I'd like to talk this thing through with you.'

Kay glanced at Nina, busily drawing at her feet. 'OK,' she agreed, 'if you're sure it's not holding you up?'

Geoffrey grinned. It could be months before he had another opportunity like this.

'To be frank with you,' he said when he'd made the call to Pauline, 'you don't stand a chance unless you can come up with some fresh evidence. The diary's no good to you. Patrick could have written anything he liked in it. It's not unknown for guilty men to go to the gallows protesting their innocence.'

'He's not guilty.'

'I'm just trying to explain how the law works.'

'That's lovely, darling,' Kay said, as Nina thrust a piece of paper under her nose. 'Is that Daddy?'

'It's you and Daddy in the car,' Nina said.

'Of course it is. Clever girl. Now, why don't you do one for Makere?'

'Tell you what,' Geoffrey said, 'I'll have a word with Eddie Wihongi. He's making quite a name for himself these days. He might . . .'

'Did you say "Wihongi"?'

'D'you know him?'

'There were Wihongis at school with me.'

Geoffrey got up from his chair. 'Better still,' he said, 'I'll give you his phone number. You can talk to him yourself.'

'What shall I say?'

'Tell him the Maori part of the story first. That'll get him interested. He's had a run of successes lately in cases involving Maori land disputes. I'd say he's starting to ruffle a few highly placed feathers.'

'Can I mention your name?'

'You can do more than that,' Geoffrey said. 'You can tell him I was delighted with the judgement in the Eden Properties Case.'

After Kay and Nina had left, Geoffrey sat for several minutes staring at what the land agent's brochure had euphemistically described as 'an enchanting sea view'. 'A strip of water glimpsed between roof tops' would have been more accurate. But it wasn't the view Geoffrey was seeing. It was Kay's face as she talked about Patrick Kierin. 'Isn't ignoring injustice the same as ignoring a traffic accident?' she'd asked. 'You'd stop if you saw someone injured on the side of the road, wouldn't you? Well, that's all I'm doing.'

Had she ever talked about *him* with that degree of enthusiasm? he wondered.

When he could stand the unanswered questions no longer he jumped to his feet, grabbed his car keys, and strode out of the door. It didn't do to be late for one of Winifred's lunches.

53

Eddie Wihongi's office was on the seventh floor of one of Auckland's ugly new skyscrapers. Kay, travelling up in the lift, went over what she'd been told of the man she was about to meet. He was a barrister in his mid-thirties, with a reputation for taking on, and often winning, impossible cases. It was he who'd successfully defended the Ngati Whatua people in the case against Eden Properties which Geoffrey had suggested she mention. 'I refused to handle their business, if you remember,' he'd said. 'So when I heard about the case I contacted Eddie to wish him well. That's how we got acquainted.'

'Ah, Mrs Grieve, come in.'

Kay blushed. The man holding out his hand in no way resembled the person she'd imagined. He was dressed in jeans and a loose shirt, and his hair hung down to his shoulders. But it wasn't his casual appearance that had made her blush, it was his looks. Eddie Wihongi was a knockout!

'Grab a pew,' he instructed.

The office was unexpected too. There was the usual desk and chairs, with a bookcase stuffed with legal tomes, but the guitar propped in the corner, and the cloak made of feathers spread over one wall, suggested a life far removed from the law. Kay, seated now, struggled with the impulse to gnaw at her thumbnail.

'Hey!' the Adonis sitting opposite her said. 'Forgive me for asking, but are you Geoffrey Grieve's wife?'

'We're divorced,' Kay said.

'Whoops.'

'It's all right. We're good friends.'

'Decent chap, Geoffrey. Working for the wrong people, but a decent chap for all that.'

'He thought you might be able to help me.'

Eddie grinned. The effect on Kay was catastrophic. Since leaving Geoffrey she'd led a chaste life. She hadn't set out to, it had just happened. Every time a man made overtures to her she backed off. Now here she was, blushing like a schoolgirl just because this man was smiling in her direction.

'Fire away,' Eddie encouraged.

Inevitably, given the effect this interview was having on her, Kay's story came out in a muddle. Makere, Patrick, the diary, Astley, her childhood, Nina, they all got into the narrative. She finished by asking Eddie if he was related to Blair Wihongi.

'The wicked cousin,' he responded. 'Poor blighter. He won't be seeing Astley again for a while.'

'Do you visit him in prison?'

'Someone has to.'

'And you know Makere?' she asked, though she already had the answer. Everyone knew Makere te Tuhi, Eddie had told her, everyone Maori that is.

'You betcha,' he confirmed. 'Tell you what, let me know when you're going to see her next, and I'll tag along. If we're going to do anything about Patrick Kierin, I'll need to talk to her.'

'You think we *can* do something?'

Eddie took hold of the *taonga* around his neck and rubbed it between his fingers. Kay watched him with the fascination of a child learning a new game. He had nice hands, she observed: strong-looking, like the rest of him.

Kay looked down at her own hands. Never before had she been so aware of her white skin.

'I won't bullshit you,' Eddie said. 'The chances of getting this case reopened are minimal.' He jumped up from his desk. 'We'd be applying for a free pardon, and that's something that's only ever attempted if some pretty compelling new evidence comes up. Ah, here we are' – he grabbed a volume from the bookcase, and thumbed through the pages – 'we'd be petitioning the Governor General in Council for a free pardon "in exercise of the prerogative of mercy",' he quoted. 'What that means, in plain English, is that we'd have to have exhausted all other legal means of redress, the Court of Appeal, in this instance, but still have enough ammunition to persuade the Attorney General to advise the Governor to exercise his prerogative. Interesting, when you think about it. If we didn't have a monarch as our head of state, this last resort, as it were, would be denied us. It's not really to do with the law, you see, it's to do with the symbolic power of the monarch. Listen to this. "Mercy and pardon are not the subject of legal rights. They begin where legal rights end."'

'But Patrick was innocent,' Kay protested.

'So was Christ, but that doesn't mean he wasn't legally executed.'

'Are you saying it's hopeless?'

Eddie sat down again. The *taonga* swung across his chest. 'Tell you what,' he said, 'leave the diary with me and I'll get back to you.'

Assuming she was being dismissed, Kay handed over the precious journal and stood up. It was Eddie's grin which halted her.

'Don't forget to set up that meeting with Makere,' he reminded her.

'When would suit you?'

'Sooner the better.'

'I assume you're tied up during the week?'

'My evenings are free.'

'I'll call you.'

'Good.' He got up from his desk and walked her to the door. Their parting handshake brought on another blush. 'And don't, for God's sake, get your hopes up,' he called after her.

From the outside, Makere's house looks ordinary enough: a wooden villa, built in the thirties, with a lemon tree in the front garden, and neat rows of potato and kumera running down to the river. Clumps of untidy pungas and a straggly banana tree complete the picture. But inside the effect of ordinariness is quickly dispelled. A large square room with smaller, practical rooms opening off it, covers almost the entire area of the house. On Kay's first visit she compared the room to the meeting house she'd seen as a child in the museum. There was no conventional furniture. The floor was covered with rush matting; the walls lined with mattresses and cushions. By the end of that first visit Kay had learned the purpose of this arrangement. Makere's *whanau* was large and fond of visiting. The only time Kay ever found her friend alone was the day she came to talk to her about her mother.

Tonight there were three of them sitting on the brightly woven cushions: Kay, Makere and Eddie. Makere had prepared a feed of mussels and Maori bread, which they'd washed down with beer. Now, as Kay's contribution to the evening, they were eating chocolates. Makere had a notoriously sweet tooth.

Kay had driven out here with Eddie. It had been his suggestion. His arrival at Massey Street had caused quite a stir. Winston had wanted to come with them, not because he had any interest in the evening, but because he wanted to ride in Eddie's sports car.

'Bit of a mystery woman, aren't you?' Eddie had remarked, as they took off in a roar down the street. 'The lone white face in a street of coconuts.'

Kay had laughed. 'Now, if *I'd* used that word . . .'

'Anyway, you seem to have got yourself pretty well fixed up.'

'Actually, I'm not the only white face. There's Bert. When he's not in hospital, that is.'

The journey was over all too quickly. Kay, in an impulsive gesture, removed her head scarf. She didn't care how she looked. She didn't even mind when she blushed. She had to shout to make herself heard above the noise of the engine. That too was a source of delight.

Eddie and Makere greeted each other in the Maori fashion, pressing their noses together for a long, thoughtful moment. They had met before, but this would be the first time they'd exchanged more than casual words. Kay, aware of their respect for one another, tried not to feel left out. Makere was fond of her, she knew that, but *respect*? That was something you had to earn.

Patrick Kierin's name was not mentioned till well on in the evening. Six months ago Kay would have been alarmed by so relaxed an approach to something she regarded as urgent; but one of the many things she'd learned from Makere was patience. 'There's always a right moment to speak,' her friend had told her. 'The secret is to recognise it.'

'This diary,' Eddie said, taking Patrick's book from his briefcase and handing it to Makere. 'I agree, it's a compelling read, and the guy is almost certainly innocent, but it's not evidence, or at least not sufficient evidence. We need something more. Don't suppose you've got anything tucked away, have you, Makere? Something of Hinemoa's maybe?'

'The diary came to me from Hinemoa.'

'And you say the girl's body was never found?'

Makere shook her head.

'I've just had a thought,' Kay said. 'What if we were to find the body ourselves? I mean, it has to be out there somewhere, doesn't it? Would it help if we found it?'

'Only if it proved beyond all doubt that Patrick couldn't have murdered her.'

Makere caught her mane of grey hair in her hand and twisted it into a ball. Her lips moved eagerly round the chocolate in her mouth. 'When I first read that diary,' she said, 'I conducted a little experiment. I measured the distance from the vineyard to where I was reasonably sure Patrick's house must have stood. Well, when I say measured the distance, I paced it out. It took me just under an hour.'

'You mean the path is still there?' Kay asked.

'For part of the way. Then the bush takes over.'

'How did you know where the house was?'

'I worked it out from Patrick's description of the kauris. There aren't many of the old trees left, as you know.' Makere helped herself to another chocolate. 'Eddie,' she said, between chews, 'you asked me if I had anything tucked away. Well, as a matter of fact, I have.' She rolled over on her side, and stood up. Kay had given up speculating as to how old Makere was. Some days she seemed no more than forty; others she looked seventy at least.

As Makere moved towards the verandah, Kay looked across at Eddie. He smiled at her and said something she didn't understand, in Maori.

When Makere returned she was holding a weather-beaten board in her arms. Gesturing to Kay to join her, she laid it at

Eddie's feet. Kay, peering over Eddie's shoulder, made out the letter 'S' and what looked like a 'B'. 'Sean Bhean Bhoct,' she whispered.

'What?' Eddie asked.

'Patrick's house.'

'Ah . . .'

Kay shivered. She felt as if invisible fingers had just brushed her skin. Patrick had painted that sign. His hand had rested where hers was resting now.

'How well do you know the people who own the vineyard?' Eddie asked Makere.

'*I* know them,' Kay interjected eagerly. 'I used to work there.'

'D'you think they'd let us mount a search?'

Kay looked at Makere, who spread her hands. 'They've always been decent neighbours,' she said.

'Why don't I ask Sophie?' Kay suggested. 'Sophie Lassmann,' she explained. 'We worked together.'

'We couldn't do it on our own, of course,' Eddie pointed out. 'We'd need, oh, thirty people minimum, to make a thorough search.'

Makere smiled. 'That's no problem,' she assured him. 'I can get you double that number.'

'I have a friend in the police who could be useful,' Eddie said. 'I imagine there's a right way to go about these things. What would be good would be a map.'

'I think I can help with that,' Makere offered.

'So it's down to you then, Kay. You and your friend Sophie.'

The way Eddie was looking at her, head to one side, a teasing smile on his face, caused Kay's stomach to lurch.

'But I must remind you,' he went on, 'even if we do find the body, it might be no help to us at all.'

'It's our only hope though, isn't it?' Kay said.

'Oh, I don't know. You're a journalist. Nothing to stop you writing up the story. I'm sure, with your gifts, you'd have no trouble convincing people of Patrick's innocence.'

On the way back into town Kay brooded on what Eddie had said. Away from Makere's she felt less confident of her influence with Sophie Lassmann. Nina had been a member of the Lassmann family. They might not want old wounds reopened.

'You'll give me a call then, will you?' Eddie said, as they turned into Massey Street.

'I just hope Sophie remembers me,' Kay worried.

Eddie leaned across her to open the car door. 'No one could ever forget *you*,' he said.

54

Geoffrey had just had the oddest conversation. It was Friday evening. The partners had met, as was their custom, for a drink in Bunce's office. 'Putting the week to rest', was how Bunce described these gatherings.

The only possible explanation for Bunce's burbling tonight was that he was drunk. He'd scored a major victory in the courts that day with a verdict in a road accident case in his client's favour. It could explain why he'd downed more than his usual two whiskys. But it didn't explain the things he'd said. 'Every driver, you see, Geoff, is a potential murderer. Only way to look at it. Take your father now. He killed a man. Did you know that? Ah, I see you didn't. You were away in England possibly. Now, that was a case and a half. Judge Mossman presiding. He managed to keep it out of the papers, but word got around. Word always does.'

'You mean, it came to a trial?'

'Came and went, dear boy. More lies told in that courtroom than in a schoolgirl's dormitory.'

'I don't understand.'

'It's all there, in the record. Poor old Lionel. Biggest mistake he ever made.'

Driving home to Herne Bay Geoffrey puzzled over what Bunce had said. Drunk or not, his words had had the ring of truth.

The following Monday, in his lunch hour, Geoffrey took himself off to the Law Library. It didn't take him long to find what he was looking for. Only it wasn't his father who'd killed a man, it was his mother. Judge Mossman, in his summing up, concluded that, in the absence of any witnesses, the collision between Mrs Grieve's car and the dead man's motorbike had been an accident. That particular stretch of road was poorly lit for one thing. For another, Mrs Grieve, a woman with a hitherto unblemished driving record, had tested negative for alcohol.

'Case dismissed,' Geoffrey muttered, as he returned the file to the desk.

But the case wasn't so easily dismissed from his mind.

'Ah, there you are, Mother,' Geoffrey said, pushing open the door of the conservatory. 'Is that new?' he asked, indicating the piece of china in her hand.

Winifred held up a small, exquisitely painted jug. 'Perfect, isn't it?' she said. 'I found it in Sydney last time we were there.'

Geoffrey sat down in one of the cane chairs and lit a cigarette. His mother often sat here on summer evenings. Especially on Tuesdays when her husband ate out. While the twins watched television, or played an irritable game of tennis, she would sit cleaning her precious pieces of china, till failing light drove her back inside.

'The new girl seems nice,' Geoffrey remarked. 'We've been having a chat.'

Winifred tossed her head. 'She's a hopeless butter fingers,' she complained. 'I've told her she's not to touch any of the ornaments. I don't know what it is about pregnant girls. I'm sure *I* was never so accident-prone.'

'Mother . . .' Geoffrey puffed nervously on his cigarette. It had been many years since his mother had raised a hand to him, but that didn't mean he was indifferent to her anger. He'd made it a rule, since moving into the flat, to visit his mother every Tuesday night. He didn't want her to think he'd moved out because of her. Usually he brought Nina with him, but tonight he'd arranged a baby sitter. What he had to say couldn't be said in front of a child. 'There's something I want to ask you,' he said.

'I wish you'd put that wretched thing out,' Winifred whined. 'You're as bad as your father.'

'Sorry. I'll make this the last.'

'Not that either of you take a blind bit of notice of anything I say.'

'Mum . . .'

'This isn't about Christmas, is it?'

'No.'

'Your father wants us to have it on the boat.'

'I was in the Law Library the other day, looking up a case from a few years back. August 1953, to be exact.'

Winifred returned the jug to the table and plaited her fingers together. Geoffrey eyed her nervously. Was this the calm before the storm? 'Yes?' she prompted.

'I came across *your* case,' Geoffrey said.

'Just like that.'

'It happens.'

Winifred smiled. 'What a liar you are, Geoffrey. So like your father.'

'I'm not lying, Mother.'

'Let me see. Someone told you, I imagine. It was never the well-kept secret Lionel intended it to be.'

'Bunce said something at Friday's meeting. But only enough to make me curious.'

'So you went searching.'

'Was that wrong?'

Winifred's hands fell from her lap. For a few moments she looked straight ahead of her, as if determined to ignore the young man at her side. Then she said, '*I* didn't kill anybody. I wasn't driving the car. Your father was.'

Geoffrey stared at her. He had no doubt she was telling the truth. What was it his father had said? 'Your mother is an astoundingly generous woman'. He leaned forward and carefully extinguished his cigarette. 'What happened?' he asked.

'We'd been to the club for dinner. Your father had drunk rather a lot of whisky. We'd been hobnobbing with some of the legal bigwigs and it had given him ideas. He saw himself rising to the very top that night. "Chief Justice Grieve, Winnie," he said, as we drove away. "What d'you reckon to that?"'

'Go on,' Geoffrey encouraged.

Winifred turned to her son. In the fading light her face looked uncharacteristically vulnerable. Geoffrey had hardly ever seen his mother without make-up. She was the kind of woman who got up before everyone else in order to apply her mask.

'I'm sorry if this is painful for you,' he said.

'Actually, it's a relief,' Winifred confessed. 'When you've bottled something up for seventeen years . . .'

'What I don't understand is why I've only found out about it now?'

'You'd just sailed for England. By the time you came back . . .' She shrugged.

Geoffrey surreptitiously turned up his hearing-aid. His mother's voice, unusually for her, was little more than a whisper. He took out another cigarette, remembered what he'd promised, and shoved it back in the packet.

'Your father is out with his fancy woman,' Winifred said. The announcement was made so calmly Geoffrey wondered if he'd heard correctly. 'That's where he goes every Tuesday night.'

'I know.'

'What?'

'Well, I guessed.'

'I see.'

'I'm sorry, Mum. I should have said something, but I wasn't sure if you knew.'

'Is that what you two talk about when you creep off into the study? It's what men do, isn't it? Boast about their sexual conquests.'

'As a matter of fact, we've *never* talked about it. I found out purely by accident. If he *had* ever mentioned it, I'd have told him what I thought.'

'And what's that, when it's at home?'

'I think his behaviour stinks. I think you've had a really lousy deal.'

'I'm supposed to be comforted by that, am I?'

'Finish what you were telling me,' Geoffrey urged.

Winifred fanned out her fingers and stared at her rings. It was something Geoffrey had seen her do many times before. Should he get her a drink? he wondered. The glass on the table was empty.

'Have you ever been in an accident, Geoff?' she asked. 'The shock of the impact is something you never forget. I didn't see the motorbike. It was on the driver's side. All I remember is the noise, a sort of wrenching scream, then the car stopped, and there was this awful silence.'

Geoffrey tried to push back the images that were forming in his mind. What would he have done if he'd been the driver? One look at the mangled body on the road and he'd have passed out.

'Your father was the first to get out of the car. I don't remember whether I had the passenger door open, or whether I was still shaking in my seat, but I do remember Lionel telling me not to go round the front. He was quite calm. I've always admired that about him, his presence of mind. He helped me out of my seat, and walked me a few paces, and told me very gently that the motorcyclist was dead. There was absolutely no doubt, he said. I think he called it a "tragic accident", something of that sort. No one was to blame, he said, what with the road being so badly lit, and there being no other traffic. I reminded him we would have to get the police, and he agreed. That was when he asked me if I would say I was the driver. "Nothing will happen," he assured me. "They'll ask a few questions, that's all." I must have looked blank because he went on to explain that if *he* was known to be the driver there'd be all sorts of consequences. "I've been drinking," he pointed out. "They'll say my reactions were slow. Or I was driving too fast. Once they've established alcohol as a factor they can say whatever they like."'

Geoffrey reached for his mother's hand. He could imagine the rest of her story only too well. His father's skills of persuasion were legendary in the profession. He could turn a jury to his way of thinking even when the evidence was stacked against him. 'So you took the rap,' he said.

'Poor Geoffrey,' his mother soothed, 'this wasn't what you expected, was it?'

'Why?' he asked. 'Why did you do it?'

'Because I loved him.' She smiled. 'Does that shock you too?'

'And he never, not even when it came to a trial, offered to come clean?'

'He would have, if I'd let him, but I was inspired by then, you see. There was a point to my life, a purpose. I wasn't just a housewife. I was a worker of miracles. My husband would go on to be a Judge, and the victory would be mine as much as his.'

Geoffrey ran his hands through his hair. If his father walked in through the door now, what would he say? Was it possible both to love and despise another human being?

'And then, of course,' his mother went on, 'he loved me very much through that time. More even than at the beginning.'

'Yes,' Geoffrey said.

'When it was over, the trial I mean, he changed. I think he felt ashamed.'

Geoffrey took off his glasses and wiped them on his handkerchief. Shame was something he understood. 'He said to me once, well, implied, that you didn't want . . . after the twins were born . . . you more or less lost interest, he said.'

Winifred gave an angry twist to her wedding ring. 'More of his lies,' she muttered.

'Mum, I'm so sorry, I'm so very very sorry . . .'

'Then Diane came on the scene, and that was the end of that.'

'You know her name?'

'Mrs Diane Grey. She's a divorcee. A good-looking woman. Works in a dress shop. I believe she has a son.'

Geoffrey slumped back in his chair. In a moment he'd fetch them *both* a drink. He could hear the whine of the television from inside the house. If Nina were here she'd be watching with her aunts.

'I'm glad you know,' Winifred said. 'I don't care about protecting your father any more. I'm too tired.'

'You should leave him,' Geoffrey advised.

'Maybe I will,' Winifred answered.

Driving away from the house Geoffrey found he was heading, not towards Herne Bay, but in the direction of Massey Street. This is not a good idea, a voice in his head warned.

Fifteen minutes later he pulled up outside Kay's house. The light was on in the living room so she hadn't gone to bed.

He took the front steps two at a time and rang the bell. The look on Kay's face as she opened the door was not encouraging.

'Geoffrey! Is something wrong?'

'No. That is, yes, but it's nothing to do with Nina.'

'Where is she?'

'In bed asleep. Mrs Driscoll is with her.'

'It's after ten, Geoffrey.'

'I need to talk to you, Kay. I'm sorry. I should have phoned first. Can I come in?'

Kay motioned him to follow her. That was when he realised she was not alone.

55

When Kay heard the doorbell ring she assumed it was Eve, coming to ask her to babysit. Bert had taken a turn for the worse. Eve had been expecting a summons all day.

Discovering Geoffrey on the doorstep, Kay's stomach did a nosedive. Only Nina could have brought him out so late. When he'd reassured her, she almost asked him to leave. He couldn't have chosen a more inopportune time to visit.

'I think you two know each other,' she said, as she led him into the living room.

Eddie Wihongi jumped to his feet. 'Hey!' he greeted. 'Good to see you, man.'

'Eddie!' Geoffrey's astonishment was written all over his face. His owl face, Kay thought, torn between irritation and affection. 'Look, if I'm interrupting . . .' He glanced at the maps strewn across the floor.

'Other way round, I think,' Eddie said, looking at Kay. 'You two obviously have things to talk about.'

'No!' In her agitation Kay put a hand on Eddie's arm. The evening had been spent poring over Makere's maps. Kay couldn't remember a time when she'd felt so happy. Makere's eldest grandson worked in the Ordnance Survey Office. With his help they'd acquired detailed maps, both recent and historical, of the area where Nina Lassmann had gone missing. By comparing the earlier maps with the current one, Kay and Eddie had worked out where the original buildings were, and the exact route Nina would have taken to visit Patrick. When they realised the bush around Patrick's house (thanks to the kauris, subject of an early preservation order) had been virtually undisturbed for a hundred years, they'd hugged each other in excitement. It had lasted only a moment, but it had sent the blood racing into Kay's cheeks. 'You remember I told you about Patrick Kierin?' she said now, to Geoffrey. 'Well, we think we've found a way to prove his innocence.'

Geoffrey looked at Eddie, who gestured noncommittally. Kay, registering the exchange, had to fight back a sense of betrayal. Eddie's enthusiasm had been as great as hers. When she'd phoned to tell him she'd made positive contact with the Lassmann family, he'd whooped with delight. 'What are you doing tomorrow night?' he'd asked. 'We could start working on the maps.'

'Look . . .' Eddie's smile, directed at Kay, signalled his predicament. He was uncomfortable in Geoffrey's presence, but whether because Geoffrey was her ex-husband, or because he was a fellow lawyer, Kay had no way of knowing. 'I really should be on my way,' he said.

'We haven't settled the date,' she reminded him.

'I'll call you,' Eddie promised.

Kay walked out of the room with him. She didn't care what Geoffrey thought. Ridiculously, she felt close to tears. Things had been going so well. 'Goodnight then,' she said, at the door.

He put his hand under her chin. Back came the rush of blood. When he leaned down to kiss her cheek, she flung her arms around his neck. 'Goodnight,' he said softly.

'So,' Geoffrey said, as she walked back into the room, 'you and Eddie are in cahoots.'

Kay moved past him to the sofa. She was suddenly very tired. The last two weeks had delivered a bewildering mixture of joy and anguish. That first meeting with Eddie; the evening at Makere's; the reunion with Sophie, a married woman now ('Don't worry about Father,' she'd reassured. 'He'll do whatever I tell him'); a chance meeting with Eddie at the theatre, she in her capacity as a reviewer, he as a theatre buff; walking along the Karangahape Road with him after the show, untroubled by ghosts; Makere's words to her at the weekend: 'If you love your mother, as you say you do, you'll try and make things right with your father. He'd be home now, wouldn't he? Why not strike while the iron's hot?'

Joy and anguish. At least, Kay thought now, tucking her feet underneath her, I don't count the days till Nina's next visit as obsessively as I used to.

She looked up at Nina's father. 'Why have you come?' she asked.

Geoffrey moved towards the sofa, hesitated, then sat down on one of the large cushions scattered about the room. What was going on between Kay and Eddie Wihongi? Was he more than just an ally in this crazy project of hers? Would she tell him if he asked?

'These maps,' he said, pointing at the floor. 'I take it you're organising some kind of search?'

'That's right,' Kay answered.

'If you need money . . .'

Kay sat up sharply. Geoffrey didn't like the expression on her face one little bit.

'What I mean is, you should have had something from the sale of the house, it's been bothering me . . .'

'I don't want your money, Geoffrey.'

'Strictly speaking, it's yours anyway.'

Kay plunged her thumb into her mouth. Geoffrey fumbled for a cigarette. Sometimes he thought she deliberately misunderstood him.

'Eddie isn't charging for his services,' Kay said. 'In fact, nobody is. Makere's organising the people for the search.'

'I wish you well,' Geoffrey said.

Kay curled into the corner of the sofa. She didn't want to be in love with Eddie. It was too painful. She wanted to prove Patrick's innocence, and get on with her life.

Geoffrey shaped his lips to blow a smoke-ring. He should have known better than to seek sympathy from Kay. By the look of her, *she* was more in need of it than he was. 'I've just had rather an odd experience,' he said. 'I wanted to tell you about it.'

Kay's feet slid to the floor. 'D'you want some coffee?' she asked.

'That'd be nice.'

He followed her out to the kitchen. Clearly housekeeping was still a low priority with her. The kitchen was a mess.

While they waited for the kettle to boil he told her about his conversation with Winifred. Once he'd got started the words just tumbled out. Kay rinsed a couple of mugs, and ground the coffee, and when it was brewed she handed him his drink and led him back into the living room.

'I suppose you could say my father is a murderer,' he concluded.

Kay bent down to retrieve the maps from the floor. He could tell nothing from her expression. That flush in her cheeks could mean anything. 'Aren't you being rather harsh?' she said when the maps were stowed.

'The charge was manslaughter,' he responded bitterly. 'A man who could stand by and allow his wife . . .' He broke off. Disgust was making a dam of his throat. He didn't love his father, he hated him. What he had done *was* as bad as murder.

'You have to talk to him,' Kay said. 'You have to hear his side.'

'Side? What possible side could he have?'

Kay sipped her coffee. She was pale now, with just two spots of red remaining in her cheeks. It was agony to be so separate from her. If he could just put his arms around her everything would fall into place.

'Geoffrey . . .' Kay pulled at a piece of broken nail with her teeth. The look on Geoffrey's face reminded her of the way her father had looked at the weekend. She didn't want to tell his story, but she knew she had to. 'I harm no one,' he'd sobbed. 'Please remember that when you judge me.'

'This has been a horrible blow for you,' she said. 'I'm sorry.'

'Bastard,' Geoffrey muttered.

'Yes, I thought that too, at first.'

'You mean, you knew?'

'About Lionel? No. Though I guessed there was something. Pauline had dropped hints.'

'Don't tell me *she* knows?'

Kay gestured her ignorance.

'What is it about men like my father? Why do women cover up for them?'

Kay smiled. 'Oh, I don't think you should take it personally. If it's any comfort, my mother has been covering up for my father for over twenty years.'

'What do you mean?'

'If I answer that, you have to promise me you'll let your father tell his side of the story. You'll never get past this if you don't, Geoff. I'm not saying you have to approve or even forgive. Just open the door a little.'

'You sound like a psychologist.'

'Blame Makere,' Kay laughed. 'It was she who made me hear my father out. She was right too. It didn't make me like what he's done, but it helped me understand why my mother has "covered up for him", as you put it.'

'I can't imagine Harold doing anything shocking.'

'That's where you're wrong,' Kay said.

It was after midnight when Geoffrey finally got up to go. He'd had to phone Mrs Driscoll to beg her to stay late. Kay walked out on to the road with him. When he leaned over to open the door she put her arms around him. They hugged each other silently. Then he climbed into the car and drove home through the deserted streets.

Kay lay in bed and listened to the faint patter of rain on her roof. That Geoffrey was awake too, listening, if not to the rain then to one of his beloved operas, she had no doubt. In the room next to him Nina would be dreaming of Christmas, or of Pauline's birds, her arms splayed above her head in a gesture of confidence and trust. The image of her daughter sleeping was one Kay carried with her everywhere.

Would Nina one day have to face terrible truths about her parents? ('If I could stop what I do, don't you think I would have by now?' her father had cried out. The words, and his tears – the first Kay had ever seen him shed – had drowned her anger, leaving in its wake only an exhausted sorrow.) How do you break the cycle of discovery and blame? More than anything in the world, more than her dream of loving Eddie, or her now abandoned fantasies of flying, Kay wanted to free her daughter from that doomed inheritance. Perhaps, with Geoffrey's help, she might manage it. It was too soon to say what effect Winifred's confession would have on her son, but that he was changed, jolted out of his old certainties, had been obvious from the moment he started his story.

'Sleep well, my darling,' Kay whispered into the darkness. But the face she kept seeing was not Nina's, but Geoffrey's.

56

After much discussion the date agreed on for the search was the first weekend in December. Kay had wanted it to be later. Her reasons were not ones she was prepared to admit to. She was afraid, once the search was over, that she would lose contact with Eddie. If they failed to find the body, his involvement would come to an end. She was reasonably confident Eddie was attracted to her, but so far he'd made no move. When she tried to pump Makere on the subject all she got for her pains were the words, 'Eddie knows what he's doing. I wonder if you do?'

It was Fedor Lassmann who put the final spoke in Kay's plans. Supportive though he was, he didn't want his Christmas sales of wine interrupted. Having dozens of people running round his vineyard with spades was not his idea of a sales pitch.

Over the week immediately preceding the Saturday, Kay's every spare moment was taken up with organisation. At the suggestion of Dave Winterbourne, Eddie's detective friend, the area to be searched was divided into sections and marked with luminous tape. These sections were then allocated among Makere's volunteers. Dave, who'd made a thorough examination of the area, had advised concentrating the search on the hill Nina would have had to climb before reaching Patrick's house. At the top of this hill lay a narrow plateau, with a steep escarpment falling away on one side into dense bush. 'Let's face it,' Dave had said, 'if she'd come to grief closer to the vineyard she would have been found by now. That ground has been dug over a thousand times. But down there' – he was standing on the edge of the plateau, looking across the valley – 'see for yourself, it's virgin country.'

Eddie had immediately volunteered to head that particular section himself. Kay had wanted to join him, but he'd persuaded her she would be more use elsewhere. 'Most of Makere's helpers are kids,' he'd reminded her. 'They'll need supervision if we're to get the area covered in the two days.'

Had Kay been religious she would have prayed for Saturday to be fine. Makere's confidence was not enough to stop her worrying. Through a sleepless Friday night she went over and over the details, terrified something vital had been missed out. Tomorrow's *Herald* would carry her story of Patrick's life, and death. Eddie had advised her not to wait till after the search. The more publicity their enterprise received the better.

Kay was up at five. She and Sophie had undertaken to make enough sandwiches to feed everyone for lunch. As the pile of buttered bread grew Kay found herself remembering her first venture into bulk sandwich-making, on the morning of Lynne's wedding. When all this was over she would write to Lynne. She just hoped her long silence would be forgiven.

Eddie was on her doorstep well before seven. Kay hugged him warmly. 'Makere was right,' she said. 'It's going to be fine.'

'Don't tell me you doubted,' Eddie teased.

They stowed the sandwiches in the back seat of his car, and set out on the familiar road to Astley.

'The early bird catches the worm,' Fedor Lassmann called out to them, as they pulled up in his driveway. In his large leather apron, jaunty cap and trousers tucked into his boots he looked, for all his Kiwi accent, the archetypical Austrian. These days he no longer sported whiskers, but his manner was as jovial as ever. 'There's tea on the go,' he announced.

Makere and her army of helpers were due to arrive at eight. While Kay and Sophie unpacked the sandwiches, Eddie organised the assortment of tools he'd borrowed. Spades, rakes, hoes, shovels – anything that could be used to turn the soil had been commandeered. By 8.30 most of the names on Makere's list had been ticked off. Any stragglers would be directed by Sophie to the relevant section.

Kay's feelings, as she set off down the path Nina Lassmann had travelled on the last day of her life, were so close to the surface she felt as if she had a bone stuck in her throat. She hoped her companions wouldn't expect her to talk; a hope she was almost immediately forced to abandon. Makere had roped in cousins from as far away as South Auckland. To them the weekend was a cause for celebration. It wasn't often the *whanau* got together in such numbers.

The section Kay had been allocated was the one immediately surrounding the site of Patrick's house. Once the path petered out the going was more difficult, but with the route clearly marked they were in no danger of getting lost. Crossing the escarpment Kay looked for Eddie, but he and his team had been swallowed up in the bush. She could hear them though. Someone had brought along a transistor radio. The sound of disembodied voices belting out the theme from *The Avengers* was just one of the many strange things about this day.

'Right,' she said when they'd located the kauris, 'this is where we get to work. And remember, stay within your markers, otherwise we won't know whether all the ground's been covered.'

For the first part of the morning the air was filled with good-natured banter. 'Seen any catepo spiders yet, Linda? You better watch out, eh? This bush is famous for them.'

'Hey, Rangi! Come and take a gink at this! Reckon I've found some buried treasure.'

But as the sun rose in the sky, the talk died down, and the only sounds to be heard were the trilling of birds, the thud of spade on soil, and the persistent hum of the cicadas. Eventually Kay called a halt for lunch. Most of the searchers had been told to return to the vineyard, but Kay and Eddie's teams, further away than the others, had carried their food in with them. It was frustrating to know Eddie was on the other side of the hill, yet not be able to talk to him. No doubt if he'd found anything he would have come to tell her by now. The only things her group had found were a few rusted nails and a piece of curved metal, part of an old scythe or sickle.

At half-past one Kay ordered her team back to work. With the sun high in the sky, and stomachs full, there were one or two backsliders, but Kay, using Makere's wrath as threat, persuaded them to keep going. She could see there would be absentees tomorrow, though. The novelty was beginning to wear off.

By five o'clock the ground around the kauris looked as if it had been hit by a tornado. Kay, her face streaked with mud and perspiration, felt a stab of dismay. They'd promised the council, who were responsible for this area of native bush, that they'd replant anything they dug up. How would they manage it? 'Sure you haven't bitten off more than you can chew?' her father had challenged last weekend.

'Any luck?' Makere asked, as Kay and her weary band emerged, like the seven dwarfs, from the bush.

Kay shook her head.

'Me neither,' Makere said.

'Is Eddie back yet?'

'He sent a message. He's going to work on till dark. He said not to wait. Plenty people heading back to town. You can take your pick who you ride with.'

Kay lowered her shovel and leaned disconsolately across its handle. She'd been looking forward to this evening. Though nothing had been arranged she'd imagined Eddie and she would have dinner together. Now she was trapped. If she waited, it would signal her feelings all too plainly. If she left, she might lose her last chance of being alone with him.

'I'll go with Linda,' she said.

'Cheer up,' Makere encouraged. 'It's not over yet.'

57

Geoffrey folded his newspaper and put it down among the breakfast things. Nina was watching a cartoon on television. He'd promised to take her to see Pauline later. As always, at weekends, his daughter had been pestering him about Kay. 'Why *can't* I see Mummy?' she'd whined. 'I think you're a meany boots.'

Nina, he was sorry to say, was becoming a bit of a grizzler.

Kay would be out on her wild goose chase with Eddie Wihongi by now. Her article in this morning's paper had given details of the search, and the reason for mounting it. 'Patrick Kierin is innocent,' she'd written, 'and I for one can have no peace until his name is cleared.'

The article was well written. The paragraph about justice and the law, and how the former was not always served by the latter, had made Geoffrey's hackles rise, but he had to admit her arguments were well presented. By the time he'd read it through twice he was half convinced of the man's innocence himself. But then Kay had always been good at finding redeeming qualities in anyone 'condemned by the system'.

What he should be doing today was going into the office. He was woefully unprepared for his case on Monday. But Mrs Driscoll was out of town, and Nina flatly refused to be looked after by her grandmother. Perhaps he could persuade Pauline to take over for an hour or two. The twins had already turned him down.

Directly lunch was over he got out the car and drove to his aunt's. 'You're an hour early,' she scolded, as he let himself into her house.

'Sorry. Were you resting?'
'Fat lot you care.'
'We can amuse ourselves for a bit, can't we, sweetheart?'
But Nina was already on her way to see the birds.
'Sit down then,' Pauline instructed, from her chair. 'If you want a drink, you'll have to get it yourself.'
Geoffrey did as he was told. He'd come to ask his aunt to babysit, but now he was here he had a better idea. He'd ask her about his father. He'd more or less promised Kay he'd give his father a chance to put his side of things. The only trouble was, when he tried to picture such a confrontation, his mind went blank. Lionel Grieve was a man other men (and that included his son) looked up to. Destroy that balance, and what would be left?
'Are you all right, Aunt Pauline? You don't look . . .'
'I'm fit as a fiddle, thank you very much.'
'You'd say, wouldn't you? If it was too much, us coming here, I mean? Nina gives me no peace till I promise she can see you.'
'She should be with her mother, that's why.'
'Yes, well . . .'
'Muck this one up and you'll be sorry for the rest of your days,' Pauline growled.
Geoffrey fought back the smart reply he'd have liked to make. Pauline would know all about Kay's current crusade. So far as he could tell the two women told each other everything. 'You know, it's strange,' he said, 'I often think about it, but Nina only exists because I cheated.'
'What?'
'I hid Kay's diaphragm. It was just the once, but I'm 99 per cent sure that was when Nina was conceived.'
Pauline slid to the front of her chair. She looked like a cat about to spring. 'Whatever made you do that?' she demanded.
'No idea really. Impulse. It was the night I came home from hospital.'
'Men,' his aunt muttered. 'What idiots!'
'Now, hang on a minute . . .'
'What was Kay's reaction when you told her?'
'I haven't. There didn't seem any point.'
Pauline hooked a straggle of hair behind her ears. Geoffrey

had been thinking she didn't look well, but what he was seeing now was not pallor but fury. 'You will tell your wife exactly what you've just told me,' she snapped. 'And if you've any sense, you'll say you're sorry.'

'I can't be sorry Nina was born. Neither, I imagine, can Kay.'

'This isn't about Nina. It's about you and your wife.'

'I wish you'd stop calling her my wife,' Geoffrey protested.

Pauline slapped the sides of her chair. '*You* may not need a drink, but I do,' she said. She got to her feet, and bustled across the room.

Geoffrey watched her over the top of his spectacles. She was right. He *was* an idiot. He'd have to tell Kay about that business with the diaphragm now. If he didn't, Pauline could take it into her head to spill the beans herself. While he was at it he should probably come clean about Amanda as well. Not that he'd lost much sleep over that. He'd only claimed to be a virgin bridegroom to make Kay feel better. 'Don't suppose you've got any brandy?' he asked hopefully.

'That bad, is it?'

Geoffrey made a self-mocking gesture. He'd asked Kay if she had any brandy when she'd come to the end of her story about her father. But Kay, it seemed, didn't keep alcohol in the house.

Harold Dyer – his father-in-law, Nina's grandfather – was a transvestite. It didn't bear thinking about. But the worst thought was what Kay must have suffered, bearing that knowledge in silence for so many years. When he tried to imagine *that* he forgot his disgust, and felt only sorrow. Sorrow and *love*, he acknowledged, as the brandy hit the back of his throat.

'Can I ask you something, Aunt Pauline?' he said.

'Fire away.'

'It's about my father . . .'

Geoffrey never did get to the office that day. Pauline, though she knew about the trial (how could she not?), was ignorant of the rest of the story. 'I always suspected something,' she said. 'Lionel was horribly cagey around that time. But then I heard about the "other woman", and decided *that* explained his caginess. Poor Winifred. She should leave him.'

'That's what I told her.'

'Be the making of her.'
'Aunt Pauline?'
'Yes, dear?'
'Can I ask you one more thing?'
'Not another shock, I hope. I've had enough for one day.'
'Do you think Kay still loves me?'

Driving back to Herne Bay Geoffrey turned his aunt's reply over in his mind, searching for the comfort he sensed lay buried in her words. 'Kay is not the woman you married,' she'd said. 'You'd have to work hard to win her back. She knows what she wants now. She wants to be a mother to Nina, but on *her* terms, not yours, and certainly not Lionel's. Beyond that, she wants to be free to explore whatever life throws at her. She knows better than to make Nina, or you for that matter, the meaning of her life. She'll never make that mistake again. Are you ready for such a woman, Geoffrey? I'll be disappointed in you if you're not.'

By the end of the day he'd made up his mind. As soon as Kay had got over her obsession with this Patrick Kierin fellow, he'd start on a campaign to win her back. He'd already indicated he was prepared to share custody of Nina. Now he'd go further. 'Name your terms,' he'd say. 'But come back to me, please.'

So long as no one else has got to her, he thought, as he bent to kiss his daughter goodnight.

58

Eddie Wihongi's shout was heard – according to one version of the story – from as far away as the park in the centre of Astley. 'I won't say I heard anything as specific as a shout,' Esme told her daughter next morning, 'but I was bringing in the washing, and something made me stop what I was doing, and listen. It was the sort of feeling people used to get during the war when someone they loved was killed. A kind of heightened awareness. I came inside and told your father, and for once he didn't pooh-pooh what I was saying. "I'm sure it's something to do with this search of Kay's," I said to him. "You may very well be right," he answered.'

Kay heard the shout as clearly as if Eddie were standing only yards away. It was the end of the day. An exhausting, frustrating day, with only half of Makere's volunteers turning up, and no chance at all of satisfactorily completing the search. As if to rub salt into her wounds, Kay had been virtually ignored by Eddie. He'd phoned the previous night but only to say he was going to stay over at Makere's, leaving her to find her own way to Astley in the morning.

'What the hell was that?' Rangi asked, as the shout died away.

'Come on!' Kay ordered. 'We're finished here anyway.'

Where yesterday there had been eight in her group, today there were only three. Gathering up their tools, Rangi, his brother Wiri, and Linda, followed Kay into the bush. At the top of the hill they downed their shovels and spades, and peered over the edge of the plateau. Eddie's team too was reduced, but not as drastically as Kay's. She counted six figures, congregated at the bottom of the escarpment. 'Eddie!' she shouted. 'Eddie!'

For a moment, so convinced was she that the search was over and her life, as a result, irreversibly changed, she was tempted to lift her wings and fly. Patrick would see she came to no harm. He was her friend, now and forever.

'Get Dave!' Eddie shouted up at her. 'We need Dave.'

'Where will I find him?'

'Makere knows.'

Kay looked round at her companions. It was agony to be so near and still not know what it was Eddie had found.

'I'll go,' Rangi volunteered.

Kay flashed him a grateful smile.

'Come on, Wiri,' Linda urged. 'We'll all go.'

'Don't come down,' Eddie called out, as Kay's team took off into the bush. 'You might disturb something.'

'Is it the body?' Kay called back.

'Looks like it,' Eddie answered.

While they waited for Dave to arrive, Kay and Eddie called out to each other in the dwindling light. Eddie was adamant Kay must stay where she was. The police would want to work out, from the position of the body, the exact line of Nina's fall from the plateau. 'Because that's what happened, I'm certain of it,' he shouted. 'It was wet, remember? An absolutely foul day. I'd say she fell and broke her neck.'

When they weren't exchanging words over the edge of the plateau, Kay listened to the whisper of wind in the bush and the trillings of tuis and bellbirds and bush warblers as they took their leave of the day. She was hearing what Patrick would have heard: feeling, as he *must* have felt, the beauty of the world, and the perplexity of human beings in the face of that mystery. Patrick, on an evening like this, might have taken out his Cross of Saint Brighid, and given thanks for what he saw and heard. There would be no distant traffic noise to distract him; but thoughts of Ireland and his dead sister might have intruded. But then he'd have remembered Hinemoa, and his heart, like Kay's, would have burned with gratitude again. I have so much to be grateful for, Kay thought: a beautiful daughter; friends like Makere and Pauline and Eddie; Geoffrey, whom I can think of again with love . . . This world belongs to us as much as it does to those tuis, shouting from the trees.

With Dave's arrival, Kay's vigil ended. In his careful company she made her way down the bank to where Eddie was standing guard. His team-mates, taking their cue from Rangi, had already made their way back along the valley to the vineyard.

'Well, I'll be jiggered!' Dave exclaimed as he beamed his flashlight past Eddie. 'Will you look at that?'

Kay turned away. Nina Lassmann was not much older than *her* Nina when she died. What if it were *her* child's bones she was being asked to examine?

'I'm no expert,' she heard Dave claim, 'but I'd say that was your girl, all right. A pathologist will be able to tell for sure whether that's a female pelvis, but you can see for yourself what we're looking at is the skeleton of a child. How old did you say she was? From the way the bones are lying I'd guess her neck was broken.'

'It was sheer fluke we found her at all,' Eddie crowed. 'There was a bloody great jungle growing on top of her. What led us to the spot was this button.'

Kay turned. The small brass object in the palm of Eddie's hand brought tears to her eyes. She turned a little further and looked at the bones. They weren't as she expected. They were greenish-brown, not white, and bore little resemblance to the human frame. She was getting to be as bad as Geoffrey, turning her back on life's horrors.

'What now?' Eddie asked Dave.

'Out of your hands,' Dave answered. 'Whether this is Nina Lassmann or not, the police will have to investigate. I'll take a quick photo now, then put a cordon round the area. Tomorrow we'll get the forensic people out. You should have some answers by the end of the week.'

They were a bedraggled threesome who made their way along the valley floor to the vineyard, but there was no disguising their grins of triumph. 'Well done,' Makere said, hugging Kay tight. 'I knew you'd do it. I told Eddie so last night.'

Kay looked over her shoulder. Eddie was opening a bottle of beer with his teeth. 'What else did you two talk about?' she asked.

59

Over the next week the story of Patrick Kierin was recounted in homes and bars up and down the country. Kay's article, well received in Auckland, was immediately syndicated, bringing her instant, unexpected fame. Reporters from both local and national newspapers, as well as from radio and television, flocked to Lassmann's Vineyard, eager to be the first to reveal the latest developments in the story. Fedor Lassmann, basking in the attention, made sure the name of his vineyard was imprinted on the mind of every journalist who crossed his threshold.

Not everyone who heard Patrick's story was convinced of his innocence. Lionel Grieve, discussing the sudden celebrity of his ex-daughter-in-law with his son, was of the opinion the whole enterprise was a waste of tax-payers' money. 'Work it out for yourself,' he grumbled. 'Police crawling all over the bush. Expensive laboratory tests. And for what? To prove some Irish peasant shouldn't have been hanged? God Almighty, if we were to take up every case of wrongful punishment, the country'd be bankrupt within a year.'

'You don't think miscarriages of justice should be put right then?' Geoffrey challenged.

'Not a hundred years after the event. Who does it benefit?'

'Oh, I see, there has to be a benefit.'

Lionel flicked the ash off his cigar. Usually he looked forward to these exchanges with his son, but Geoffrey was in a strange mood tonight. Christmas was approaching, it could be that. And then the last few days had been unpleasantly humid. 'Everything all right at the office?' he asked.

'As right as they'll ever be,' Geoffrey answered.

So it wasn't that then. 'And Nina?' Lionel prodded.
'She's fine.'
'Good-oh.'
'Dad?'
'Yes, son?'
'Can we talk?'
'I thought we were.'
'I mean, really talk.'
'What about?'
'You and Mum.'

Lionel coughed into his fist. If he'd been in court now he'd have played for time. Geoffrey must have found out about Diane. What other reason could there be for discussing his marriage? Well, it was bound to happen, sooner or later. It was a mean trick though, springing it on him like this. Gave him no time to prepare a defence. 'I don't see that my relationship with your mother is any business of yours,' he said coldly.

'Why did you do it, Dad? What possessed you?'
'Do what?'
'Let Mum take the rap for you.'

Lionel's eyes dropped. He lowered his cigar into the ashtray, took a deep breath and raised his eyes again. The young man he was staring at was a stranger to him. No, it was more than that. Those insolent features were the face of his enemy.

'I know all about it.' Geoffrey said. 'There's no point in denial.'

'I wouldn't waste my breath.'

'So why? You must have had a reason. Was it ambition? Did you think the publicity would wreck your career?'

Lionel smiled. 'Something like that,' he conceded.

'And Mum? She did it to please you, I suppose.'

'Why don't you ask her?'

'I already have.'

Lionel slammed his fist on the table. What he longed to do was pick his son up by the collar and hurl him out of the window. What did *he* know? He'd always kept his nose clean. Played the wounded husband when his wife went off the rails. What did he know about decisions made in the heat of the moment, and regretted ever after? The man was a prick. An idealistic prick, who knew nothing about marriage and the complex arrangements needed to keep it afloat. He'd sunk his own ship at the first sign of trouble, and serve him right too.

'I'm sorry if this has come as a shock,' Geoffrey said. 'It was a shock to me too.'

Lionel opened his mouth. The word he was trying to say was *forgive*, but his lips couldn't seem to shape it. What came out instead was a sob. His son watched him struggle; then, slowly, reluctantly, stretched out his hand. 'Forgive me,' Lionel said.

'I'm not the one you've wronged,' Geoffrey answered.

Dave Winterbourne's prediction that they would have some answers by the end of the week was to prove premature. Almost two weeks passed before the police were able to say for sure that the body in the bush was that of a seven-year-old girl who'd met her death sometime between 1870 and 1880. The cause of death was given as a broken neck.

'Is it enough?' Kay asked Eddie. They were sitting in Makere's garden on a scorching Sunday afternoon. Nina and two of Makere's younger grandchildren were playing by the river. In the two weeks since the search Kay had seen little of Eddie. Until the police had finished their investigations there was nothing more to be done. Kay had nursed her disappointment in silence, comforting herself with the thought that at least she and Geoffrey were getting on better. Last time they'd talked he'd as good as promised she could have Nina back after Christmas. 'So long as you take me back too,' he'd joked.

Eddie's face, as he considered her question, reminded her of the famous Rodin statue. If she put her hand out she would *touch* his thought. It wasn't hard to guess what that thought must be. Till now, most of the donkey-work had been done by Makere and herself, but the next stage could only be master-minded by Eddie. He would have to shepherd the appeal through the courts, at God knows what cost to his own work. Most people now believed Patrick innocent. Should she suggest they stop there? Was her attraction to Eddie blinding her to what was fair?

'I would say it's more than enough,' he answered her.

60

With only one week remaining till Christmas, and a mad scramble on at work, Kay was too preoccupied to torment herself with thoughts of Eddie. As soon as all the new evidence relating to Patrick Kierin was amassed he was going to send it straight to the Attorney General's office. This, with Christmas approaching, meant he would be too busy to see her anyway. He'd said as much when he drove her back from Makere's on Sunday. 'Tell you what,' she'd suggested cheerfully, 'why don't you come over on Boxing Day? You can meet my neighbourhood *whanau*.'

He'd grinned, and promised to be there if he could.

As for Christmas Day, Kay would have been dreading it had it not been for the miraculous change in Geoffrey. His proposal that she join him and Nina at his parents' house had left her momentarily speechless. 'I won't pretend it'll be fun,' he'd added, 'but the time'll pass a damned sight quicker if you're there.'

It had been tempting to accept. She'd be with Nina, and nothing mattered alongside that. But in the end she'd refused. She wasn't ready yet to see Lionel and Winifred, or to be in their house. Geoffrey had told her about his conversation with his father. Whatever had changed as a result of that confrontation, one thing was certain: Geoffrey had declared his independence. Even so, Kay was unwilling to expose her new and still fragile feelings for her former husband to the scrutiny of his family. When – if – she ever visited his parents again, it would be on her own terms.

'Don't suppose there's any chance of you and Nina getting away in the evening, is there?' she'd ventured hopefully. 'We could have tea or something.'

• Elspeth Sandys

Geoffrey's eager acceptance was another reason Kay wasn't allowing herself to indulge in impossible dreams. She would see her daughter on Christmas Day. What better gift could she have been given?

As things turned out, gifts were not the only surprises to come Kay's way. With the arrival of Geoffrey and Nina on Christmas night she found herself on the receiving end of something far more unexpected than a present. She'd spent the day with her parents at Astley. She wouldn't go so far as to describe the occasion as happy – the understanding the three of them shared was too new and raw for that – but there were moments (speaking to Clive on the phone was one) when her heart burned, just as it had that evening, calling out to Eddie.

Later she'd looked in at Makere's, and the burning sensation had returned. For the first time Makere had greeted her with a *hongi*. It was all Kay could do to hold back the tears.

'I've got something to tell you,' Geoffrey said when Nina had opened Kay's presents (a carved Maori doll; a box of paints; a battery-operated gramophone), and Kay had exclaimed suitably over hers. 'It's been rather a sensational day.'

Kay beamed at her daughter, squatting among swathes of torn wrapping paper. 'Mummy, Mummy, Mummy,' she'd screamed on arrival. 'Guess what Father Christmas gave me? Guess, go on, guess! A piano! My very own. I can play "Puff the Magic Dragon" and "Jesus Loves Me" and "The Yellow Submarine" and and . . .'

Kay had stopped her with a kiss. 'Happy Christmas, my darling,' she'd laughed.

'So, what's happened?' she asked now.

Geoffrey frowned in Nina's direction. Kay felt a flicker of irritation. Her daughter had only just got here. She wasn't prepared to dismiss her so soon. 'It's about my mother,' Geoffrey mouthed.

Kay raised an eyebrow. At which moment there was a burst of noise from Nina's gramophone.

'She announced at lunch that she was leaving my father,' Geoffrey said, over an ear-splitting drum roll. 'Talk about dramatic timing.'

Kay shook her head in disbelief. Winifred had never struck her as an actress. 'But she'd already told your father?' she assumed.

'Nope. Not a word. You could have knocked him down with a feather.'

'That doesn't sound like Winifred.'

'I told you it was sensational.'

'What about the twins? It must have come as a horrible shock to them. How did they take it?'

'Belinda burst into tears, but Sue seemed quite sanguine. They both wanted to know why, of course.'

'What were they told?'

Geoffrey pulled his owl face. '"Irreconcilable differences" was the phrase my father used. Must say, once the shock had worn off, he rose to the occasion magnificently. Went and stood by my mother and told her she could count on his support. Even thanked her for all she'd done for him. "The house is yours," he said. "There's no need for you to move out."'

'Wow!'

'At which point Aunt Pauline started applauding. I tell you, it was all very bizarre.'

Kay smiled to herself. She looked forward to hearing Pauline's version of events. 'Do you think your mother'll go through with it?' she asked.

'I don't doubt it for a moment.'

'What about your father?'

Geoffrey stroked his chin reflectively. His head was turned slightly so Kay was seeing him in profile. Her stomach gave a small lurch. Dressed casually, as he was tonight, he could still be taken for the radical student she'd fallen in love with.

'You know what?' he answered her. 'I think he's relieved. We only spoke briefly, but that was definitely the impression I got. He even hinted he might give up the law. God knows, he doesn't *have* to work. He could live very comfortably off his investments.'

'And how do *you* feel?' Kay asked.

Geoffrey took his time answering. Kay, watching Nina's absorbed face, her hands waving about in time to the music, decided her question had been tactless. Divorce was a painful subject where she and Geoffrey were concerned.

'I feel responsible,' he admitted. 'I brought this thing into the open. If I'd kept my mouth shut . . .'

Kay reached over and touched his cheek. 'I was the one who urged you to talk,' she reminded him.

Geoffrey's fingers locked themselves round her wrist. For a moment it looked as if he might be going to hurt her. Then he said, 'I love you, Kay. Please come back to me.'

Geoffrey's revelation about his mother set a pattern that brought, over the next twenty-four hours, two more, equally startling declarations. The first came, once again, from Geoffrey. The second took the form of an announcement by Eddie.

Waking early on Boxing Day Kay picked up the phone and invited Geoffrey and Nina for lunch. She knew Geoff had other plans – he'd mentioned a party at the Goodbodys' – but she was confident, after yesterday's confession, that he'd rather come to Massey Street.

She was right. He was on her doorstep before eleven. 'You realise what you've done, don't you?' he laughed, as Nina hurled herself into her mother's arms. 'I'm no longer the ogre in our daughter's life. She's seen you two days in a row. That makes me a hero!'

'Is she still sleep-walking?' Kay asked when Nina had taken off in search of Winston.

'She didn't stir last night,' Geoffrey replied.

'Are you telling me it happens every night?'

'She wants you back,' Geoffrey said. 'We both do.'

While Kay prepared salads in the kitchen, Geoffrey, perched on a stool, talked as if he'd only just discovered the delights of communication. Winifred's announcement, far from distressing him, seemed to have freed him. When he mentioned that he was considering resigning from Goodbody and Sutch, Kay, instead of slicing the tomato she was holding, sliced her finger.

Geoffrey leaped off his stool. 'Are you OK?' he asked.

Kay pulled a face. 'I'll blame you if lunch is a disaster,' she said.

'You should give me a task. I'm not entirely inept, you know.'

'You won't like it.'

'Try me.'

'That pot on the stove, it's full of cooked potatoes. Can you peel and dice them? It's for potato salad.'

'Who's coming then? You still haven't told me.'

Kay held her finger under the cold tap and waited for the bleeding to stop. Geoffrey was the most decent of men. He would be appalled to know what she was thinking. But the truth was, he didn't know people like Makere and Eve Ta'ase. He didn't even know people like Bert, home from hospital now, after a miraculous recovery. How would he cope in such company? The fact that she was asking the question at all annoyed her. She'd been looking forward to today, and the prospect of seeing Eddie. She didn't want to have to *think* about Geoffrey. 'Wait and see,' she said, smiling over her shoulder.

'I assume the family next door are coming.'

'They practically live here.'

Geoffrey cleared a space on Kay's cluttered table and proceeded to attack the potatoes. How am I doing, Aunt Pauline? he asked silently. Not mucking anything up, I hope.

Tell her what you told me, Pauline's gravelly voice instructed. You won't get her back if you don't.

It struck him as bizarre, the idea of discussing birth control with his ex-wife, while they both chopped and peeled, and their daughter rampaged noisily in the garden. He had to admit Nina was in her element here. Judging by the number of voices he could hear, it would seem she'd persuaded the entire Nene family to join in her game.

Kay didn't say anything when he reached the end of his confession. She went on chopping as if what he'd just told her had no more significance than the weather. Then, to his astonishment, she started laughing.

'You don't mind then?' he asked, in disbelief.

'You bastard!' she gasped.

'You *do* mind?'

'Are all men like you? Thinking they own their women; own their bodies.'

'I told you, I didn't *think* anything. I acted on impulse.'

'You're still a bastard.'

Geoffrey took the risk of pulling a face. Kay used to complain that he used humour to avoid confronting painful issues. Was he doing that now? And what was the issue anyway? He'd learned his lesson. The way he was feeling right now he'd be prepared to take Kay back even if she no longer wanted to sleep with him. He wouldn't like it, but if those were her terms . . .

Kay, meantime, had dried her hands and moved across to the table. He couldn't interpret the expression on her face. Was that laughter in her eyes, or rage? 'We're quits then,' she said.

'What?'

'Unless there are other betrayals I don't know about?'

Geoffrey shook his head. Kay's gaze had become alarmingly intense. Didn't she know the effect she had on him? He could smell her hair; smell, if he closed his eyes, her skin.

'I want Nina to grow up surrounded by ideas,' she said fiercely.

Geoffrey tried not to look disappointed. He'd been hoping that intensity was for him.

'Real ideas,' Kay went on, 'not just notions of how to behave. We're too small on our own, Geoff. Too frightened. We need ideas to enlarge us.'

'What if they're bad ideas?'

'Better than none at all.'

Geoffrey stepped back a pace. He couldn't think while she was standing so close to him. 'I take your point,' he said carefully, 'but surely, as parents, it's our job to exercise caution? Throw ideas at her by all means, but keep the bad ones out of it. Hitler had an idea. So did Stalin.'

'They were maniacs.'

'With maniacal ideas.'

Kay grinned. 'I somehow don't think, when you threw away my diaphragm, that we conceived a maniac, do you?'

It was the grin that finished Geoffrey. He had to have her in his arms. When she didn't resist, he gave up the struggle and let himself savour the stirring in his groin.

'That's my mummy and daddy,' Nina's voice sang out from the doorway.

Geoffrey dropped his arms and turned, with an embarrassed laugh, to his daughter. Two faces, one white, one brown, beamed back at him.

'We'd better get a move on,' Kay said.

There were over twenty people to lunch: the entire Nene clan; Bert and two of his grandchildren; Eve and her five; and Makere. Kay, alert to every car pulling up in the street, looked in vain for Eddie.

'I like your Geoffrey,' Makere confided when the two women found themselves briefly alone in the kitchen.

'He's not *my* Geoffrey,' Kay replied crossly.

'Isn't he?'

'He's coping, I'll say that for him.'

'He's doing more than that, my dear.'

At six o'clock, with Kay's living room looking as if it had been torn apart by dogs, and the children finally silenced by Eve's offer of television, a car pulled up at the gate. Kay, slumped on a cushion, registered the fact, but elected to ignore it. She'd had her hopes raised too many times for one day.

But it *was* Eddie, clutching a bottle of champagne, looking as if he'd just won the lottery. 'Sorry I'm late,' he said, addressing the bodies sprawled around the room.

Kay got up to welcome him. She was aware of Geoffrey watching her. Aware of Makere too, tracing her every move. What did they imagine she was going to do? Throw her arms round Eddie and declare undying love? 'You look pleased with yourself,' she remarked, as she kissed him chastely on the cheek.

'So I should,' Eddie answered. 'Where are the glasses?'

'They're all dirty,' Kay said, heading for the kitchen.

'What's the celebration?' she heard Geoffrey ask.

She was back in time to catch the overflow as Eddie, with an expert slow twist of his wrist, prised off the cork. 'I had a call today,' he announced when the glasses were filled. 'From the Attorney General's office.'

'What?' Kay shook her head in disbelief. 'How can that be?' she protested. 'No one works at Christmas.'

'My friend does.'

'What friend?'

'Didn't I tell you? I've got a spy working for me. She's part of the legal team down there.'

'What did this friend of yours say?'

Eddie smiled enigmatically. Kay could see how much he was enjoying himself. While she was impatient to hear what he had to say, she also felt irritated. Geoffrey was nothing to do with Patrick Kierin. Neither, for that matter, was Bert. Eddie's news, whatever it was, should have been revealed to her and Makere alone.

'We're in with a chance,' Eddie disclosed, parking himself on the sofa. 'The Big White Chief read your article, Kay. My friend overheard him talking about it. Apparently, you got through to him. So when our petition arrived on his desk . . .'

'I knew it!' Makere exclaimed. 'Thank you, God,' she added softly.

'We're not out of the woods yet, Makere. All we know is that our petition has been favourably received.'

'Isn't that enough?'

Eddie glanced at Geoffrey. 'I'm afraid there are a few more legal bridges to cross yet,' he said. 'Assuming the Attorney General thinks we have a case his next move will be to consult the Solicitor General. If *his* reaction is favourable the matter will be referred to the Governor General, who's more or less obliged to act on the advice he's given.'

'Home and hosed,' Bert concluded happily.

Eddie spread his arms wide. 'If only,' he said.

'But it does look hopeful,' Kay insisted.

'The police evidence is strongly in our favour,' Eddie answered her, 'but unfortunately that doesn't prove conclusively that Patrick is innocent. He could have pushed Nina Lassmann over that cliff.'

'That's ridiculous!' Kay exploded.

'I agree. Still, we shouldn't be celebrating too soon.'

'So why the champagne?'

Eddie raised his glass. 'It's Christmas, isn't it?' he grinned.

That night, when everyone had gone, instead of clearing up Kay got into her car and headed for Astley. She had no plan in her head; just this urge to drive west. But when she reached the familiar streets she found she was steering purposefully towards the graveyard. Crazy, she told herself, you're crazy! It's the middle of the night, and you don't even have a torch.

Her footsteps, magnified by the silence, sounded like small gunshots. She pushed open the gate, and found her way to Patrick's grave. At first she could see very little. There was only a narrow moon, and the stars seemed to have retreated to another galaxy, leaving behind a mere milky smudge. A sudden longing for Dunedin's skies, for their mysterious aurora lights, filled Kay. In six days' time it would be New Year. Anniversary of Patrick's execution. Anniversary of her first meeting with Geoffrey.

Draping her sweater round her shoulders, Kay sat down on the cold stones. Makere's flowers were there, a little bedraggled but still upright in their jar. Kay wished she'd thought to bring flowers herself; but to do that she'd have had to know she was coming here, and when she left the house all she knew was that she wanted to get away.

Eddie had stayed on after the others had left. Geoffrey, cradling a sleepy Nina in his arms, had been reluctant to leave at all, but his daughter's exhaustion had given him no choice. Kay, farewelling them, had felt a pang of distress on Geoffrey's account. Bert had already gone back to his house, and Makere was making noises about needing her bed. Eddie and I are just friends, she wanted to say. He's staying behind to discuss the case.

That Eddie was still ensconced hadn't seem to bother Makere. Kay was puzzled, till she saw the look Makere gave Eddie as she was walking out of the door. She's hatching something, Kay had thought, and Eddie's part of it. But that notion had quickly given way to another. I've got it wrong, she'd decided. Makere *wants* us to be together.

With that thought to encourage her she'd gone to sit beside Eddie on the sofa. When his arm strayed on to her shoulder, she turned to smile at him. Something horrible happened then. She couldn't explain it, then or now. For a split second the face she saw was not Eddie's but Roy's. Roy's smile, she'd remembered with bitterness, was one of the things that had drawn her to him. By what trick of nature was the devil able to smile with the same apparent artlessness as this man, this good, generous, beautiful man, sitting beside her on the sofa? She'd contrived over the last months to push the memory of Roy Blade away. For all she knew he could be out of prison by now. Good behaviour, in his own interests, would not have been difficult for him. Was she going to have to deal with the horror all over again? Did the past never lose its power to hurt?

'What are you thinking?' Eddie had asked.

'That I love you,' Kay had replied impulsively. 'And that it's hopeless. You don't love me.'

'Don't I?'

Kay had managed a laugh. 'Not in the way I want,' she'd answered.

'And what way is that?'

'You know perfectly well.'

As they'd talked, Eddie's fingers had stroked her hair. She was wearing it longer these days, almost as long as he wore his. She still fussed over it, but not with the same anguish as before. It would never be thick, like Clive's, but it seemed to persist. A less than crowning glory, but not something she need be ashamed of either.

'Tell me something,' Eddie had said. 'What made you get involved with Patrick Kierin? You didn't just do it to please Makere, did you?'

Kay had thought a while before answering. Pleasing Makere had become a major focus of her life. But while that was clearly part of the explanation, it wasn't the whole of it by any means. She'd been drawn to Patrick before she met Makere. Something about his grave – the grave she was sitting on now – had compelled her attention.

'I think,' she'd answered hesitantly, 'I think I felt, if I could put that wrong to rights, I could begin to deal with my own past. Does that make sense? Mine's so much murkier, you see, than Patrick's. His innocence is like the sun and the moon. It shines out of the pages of his diary. I'm not innocent like that, but I'm not guilty the way the court decided I was guilty either. You're a lawyer,' she'd gone on, looking at him without embarrassment, relieved, whatever the consequences, that he now knew how she felt. 'You have to deal with these confusions every day. How do you decide between half guilt and half innocence? I know you have to; someone has to. Society would collapse if there was no law and no justice. But it's so inadequate, isn't it? *We're* so inadequate.'

Eddie's laugh had made her smile. She knew she was being earnest. But these things mattered, they mattered terribly. 'Everything's relative, isn't it?' she'd continued. 'We can never know, when a crime is committed or a wrong done, what really happened. All you can be sure of is your own part, and even that . . .'

'Go on,' Eddie had encouraged.

But Kay had come to the end. Eddie knew her story. There was nothing more to be said.

One of the reasons, she thought now, that she felt so good in Eddie's company was that he seemed to have the formula to free her from guilt. It wasn't anything he did, or said; it was more in the nature of a silent healing. She didn't forget the past but it ceased, in Eddie's presence, to be a burden. Partly, she supposed, it was because of his own readiness to forgive; but there was something else, something about him and the way he lived his life. He took things seriously, his work and his culture in particular, but he never took *himself* seriously. If Eddie were in her life, she reasoned now, she could accept what had happened, and live in spite of it. Whereas if she went back to Geoffrey . . .

'Tell me what *you're* thinking?' she'd urged. 'It's not fair I should do all the talking.'

'I'm thinking how lovely you are,' Eddie had answered. 'And how much I'd like to go to bed with you.'

Hearing those words again, in this haunted place, Kay felt her heart twist. They were the words she'd most wanted him to speak, yet remembering them now she was conscious not of joy, but of a seeping sadness.

'You're going to be fine, you know, Kay,' he'd gone on. 'You don't need me to validate your life.'

How had he known that that was what she was seeking from him? Had Makere enlightened him?

'You've learned to interrogate the past. It's something my people do to excess, but you Pakeha . . .'

'Is that how you think of me, as a Pakeha? Do I really seem so different?'

'What's wrong with difference?'

'It separates you and me.'

That was when he kissed her. At least I have that, she thought now. Confirmation of our connectedness.

'Geoffrey used to tell me I had no sense of the past,' she'd admitted, when the brief embrace was over. 'And he was right. Then. It was Patrick who changed me. Reading his story, I knew there had to be a way of rewriting the past – not the events, those are fixed, but our understanding of those events. I suppose you could say Patrick got into my bloodstream.'

'That's because you fell in love with him.'

'Did I?'

'Tell me something, when you visualise Patrick, who do you see?'

I should have lied, Kay upbraided herself now. I should have told him I saw *his* face. But she couldn't lie, not to Eddie. 'I see Geoffrey,' she'd answered.

They were almost the last words they spoke. Eddie, holding Kay's hand, had got up from the sofa and walked to the door. He kissed her again on the verandah. Then, with a wave over his shoulder, he was gone.

Now she was here, with Patrick, interrogating not the past but the future. 'You'll get your pardon,' she whispered, running her fingers over the letters on the headstone. 'Thing is, will I?'

She laughed at the absurdity of the question. Geoffrey had already forgiven her. And tonight, thanks to Eddie, she knew she'd forgiven herself.

61

On 10 February 1971 a story appeared in newspapers throughout the country which relegated to second place the daily reports, with accompanying photographs, from Vietnam. 'MAN PARDONED AFTER ONE HUNDRED YEARS' the headline read. 'GOVERNOR GENERAL'S GROUND-BREAKING DECISION'.

The story of Patrick Kierin's life and death had been told before, but that proved no handicap when it came to recounting the tale of his pardon. In sometimes lurid prose Patrick's arrest and trial were recreated for an eager public. The moment when Judge Prendergast donned the black cap to sentence Patrick Brendan Kierin to be 'hung from the neck till he be dead' was dwelled on at length. As was the ignominy of his burial in public ground, without benefit of priest or mourners. From there, in a century-long leap, the narrative jumped to 1970. Enter Makere te Tuhi, Kay Grieve, and Eddie Wihongi.

Most newspapers carried photographs of these three 'crusaders', as they were now popularly styled. Eddie Wihongi was described as an up-and-coming lawyer, with special interest in Maori land claims. Makere te Tuhi, honoured with the title of *kuia*, was characterised as 'one of the last representatives of the Kawerau people'. Kay Grieve, already familiar to many readers, was variously referred to as '*The Herald*'s leading reviewer', 'a rising star on the Auckland newspaper scene', and 'one of the new breed of women journalists'.

There were various speculations as to how these three had come to be associated together, but mercifully the focus of the story stayed fixed on Patrick. One West Auckland paper suggested the park in the centre of Astley be renamed Kierin

Park, in memory of the wronged man. Another advocated the setting up of a fund – the Patrick Kierin Fund – to help correct other miscarriages of justice. 'It's time we began to examine our past,' the writer, a young Chinese journalist, a fifth-generation New Zealander, urged. 'Too much time has been spent repressing uncomfortable truths.'

For several days after the story broke Kay's phone hardly stopped ringing. Her editor called to offer her a job as a senior reporter. Makere called three times, always with the same message. 'Hold your head high,' she said. 'My people are proud of you.' Her father called, to tell her much the same thing. 'Your mother and I are full of pride,' he said. Even Clive called, from Trentham. 'Thank God you still call yourself Grieve,' he said, in mock despair. 'I'd never live this down otherwise.' Eddie called to discuss a celebration. 'We have to have a party,' he enthused. 'Do you know of a hall we can hire in Astley? It should be held there, I reckon.' Geoffrey called to congratulate her. 'Nina has cut out your photo,' he told her. 'It doesn't do you justice, but *she* didn't want to hear that.' Pauline called to bark her delight down the phone. Winifred called. Kay didn't recognise her voice at first. 'I'm afraid I can't bask in your reflected glory, dear,' she said. 'Since the separation I've been using my maiden name.' Sophie called to invite Kay to a ceremony in memory of Nina Lassmann. The dead girl's remains had already been interred next to those of her parents. These days the graveyard was unrecognisable as the one Kay had wandered into a year ago. The Lassmann family had paid for the restoration not just of their family graves, but of the entire cemetery.

The only person to call and not mention Patrick Kierin was Maria Cargill. 'I've got news for you,' she said.

Kay's stomach went into an agonising cramp. Nina's custody order was to be reviewed next month. Geoffrey had told her he was going to approach counsel for the child to inform her of his change of heart. 'I love Nina's mother,' he was going to say. 'I want her back.' But Kay hadn't said she'd go back. She'd been on the verge of it, half a dozen times, but something had always stopped her. Would her hesitation be held against her? Was promising to live with Geoffrey again the only way to secure Nina?

'The hearing's been brought forward,' Maria said. 'It's scheduled now for March the first.'

Geoffrey closed the door of Bunce's office, walked across the hall to his own desk, picked up his briefcase, had a quick word with his secretary and hurried out on to the street. He'd just taken what was possibly the biggest gamble of his life. He needed to be somewhere else.

He glanced at his watch. Forty minutes before he had to collect Nina. Time to drive somewhere and think. But where?

He climbed into his car, and joined the stop-start traffic heading out of town. Reaching the top of Parnell Road he made a sudden decision. The Cathedral of Saint Mary was on the other side of the street. He'd wait there till it was time to fetch Nina.

Geoffrey's first instinct, on entering the cathedral, was to walk on tip-toes. He couldn't remember when he'd last come in through these doors. Ten years ago, at least. His parents were married here, he recalled. Now, in impressively amicable fashion, they were getting divorced.

Tip-toeing self-consciously, Geoffrey made his way to the darkest corner, and sat down in one of the pews. The cathedral was one of Auckland's architectural treasures: the second largest wooden church in the world, if he remembered right. On this particular humid evening its dark timbers and Gothic shadows were both cool and comforting. The stained glass windows scattered jewels of light on to the panelled roof and walls.

Geoffrey, his self-consciousness increasing, knelt on an embroidered cushion and prepared himself for prayer. The trouble was, he wasn't sure to whom he was praying. The idea of God had never troubled him over-much. There'd been that business with Nina's christening but that, he acknowledged now, remembering Kay's arguments, had had very little to do with God.

What he was looking for, he admitted, as he stumbled over the words of the Lord's Prayer, was some sort of blessing. *If you could just intervene with Kay*, he added, after the Amen. *Up the ante a bit in my favour. I want her back so very badly, you see...*
It wasn't exactly the language of prayer, but it was the best he could manage. And he did *want* to believe, he was sincere in that. Kay was right about humans being too small on their own. The

• Elspeth Sandys

idea of a loving God had been horribly perverted throughout history, but that didn't mean it wasn't a *good* idea.

As he made his way back to the door, Geoffrey stopped to look at the altar. Some sort of acknowledgment seemed to be required of him. That he might be observed no longer troubled him. The important thing was to act.

He bowed his head. 'Thank you,' he whispered. Then, self-consciousness returning, he bolted out of the door.

The Celebration

62

Imagine a rectangular, wooden building with a corrugated iron roof, surrounded by a gravel car park. This is ASTLEY MEMORIAL HALL, hired by Kay for the party to celebrate Patrick Kierin's pardon. By no stretch of the imagination can the building be described as an 'architectural treasure'. 'An ugly hall in the middle of an ugly suburb,' is how Kay had depicted it to Eddie.

Across the entrance to the hall a list of the dead from two world wars enshrines the notion of sacrifice in the cause of the British Empire. What Patrick would have had to say about that, Kay can only speculate.

It's a warm, late-February evening. The car park is steadily filling with cars. A stream of women carrying plates of food head for the wide-open doors. Children swarm like so many bees. Men, acknowledging one another with shy smiles and nods, lift crates of beer from the boots of their cars, and follow their womenfolk into the hall.

Inside, the atmosphere is one of cheerful chaos. The women, offloading their plates on to wooden trestles, greet each other with hugs, and a crescendo of words. Some have brought flowers to add to the already festive appearance of the hall. The children eye the streamers floating above their heads, and wonder what would happen if they tried to swing from them. One child, lunging for a balloon, causes it to explode, and bursts into tears.

At the back of the hall, on the narrow stage, six long-haired musicians tune their instruments. The noise they're making attracts the attention of some of the teenagers. 'Sounds like cats fighting, eh?' one lad observes.

• Elspeth Sandys

At the front of the stage, Eddie Wihongi, wearing loose-fitting trousers and an open-necked shirt, shouts instructions to the men setting up the chairs. Already seated is Makere te Tuhi, her hands plaited together as she contemplates the bustle around her. Her job is done, she figures. For tonight she's content just to watch. Bending over to talk to her is Kay Grieve. Kay's been here since early-afternoon. Now, with the hall starting to fill, she wishes she could go home and freshen up. How is it that Eddie, who's been working every bit as hard as her, can look so cool, while she feels sweat pricking at her armpits?

Hanging on the wall above the now groaning trestles is a pencil sketch of Patrick Kierin. It was donated by a local artist who'd developed his own idea of what the Irishman would have looked like. Kay, on being shown this work of (in her opinion, indifferent) art, was relieved to discover the portrait bore no resemblance to Geoffrey.

Most of the people invited to tonight's party have been involved in some way in securing Patrick's pardon. The entire Lassmann clan have shown up, as have most of Makere's team of searchers. Dave Winterbourne and his wife are here, talking with one of Eddie's associates, a young Cook Island lawyer named Jimmy Marsden. Just arrived, and looking round for Kay, are a couple of journalists from *The Herald*. The rest of the party are here for personal reasons. Kay has invited her mother and father. Eddie is waiting for his sister to arrive. Makere expects at least another twenty of her *whanau* to turn up. 'In my world you don't leave anyone out,' she's told Kay.

By eight o'clock most of the invited guests have been accounted for. The band starts to play; children, taking their cue from the music, skate excitedly round the clusters of preoccupied adults. Beer bottles are opened. Sherry and orange juice are poured. Kay, standing with her parents, feels as if she has come home after a long absence. When her father pats her on the shoulder, and compliments her on the turnout, she is momentarily lost for words.

At half-past eight a small flurry at the door presages the arrival of Astley's mayor. Joining in the celebrations was not his idea, but as soon as it was put to him he saw the advantages. With local elections less than six weeks away a commitment to honour Patrick Kierin, Astley's dead *hero*, would go down well with the voters.

'Ladies and gentlemen,' Eddie shouts, as the drummer comes to the end of an attention-getting roll. '*Kia ora. Tena Koutou Katoa.*'

The Maori among his audience, and those, like Kay, who understand his words, respond to his greeting. The rest look sheepish.

'Don't worry,' Eddie reassures, 'there aren't going to be any long speeches. Well, certainly not from me.' He laughs. 'But I have to say, Patrick would have been tickled pink to see us all here tonight. And you know what would have pleased him the most? That the mayor of this town, which he helped to build, has come here with the sole purpose of paying tribute to him ... Ladies and gentemen, it is my very great pleasure to ask Mr Brian Fitzgerald, Mayor of Astley, to say a few words. Thank you.'

A thin, hawk-nosed man climbs on to the stage. As he fumbles for his notes, the younger children start to titter. His speech, which is mercifully brief, refers to Patrick as an 'assisted immigrant', but is otherwise free from error. 'Don't forget to vote for me,' he jokes, at the end.

With the departure of the mayor, Eddie takes the stage again. This time it is Makere he summons to speak. Her contribution is to be a *karakia*, a prayer for the soul of Patrick Kierin. Though only a handful of people in the hall understand the words, such is Makere's presence, and the power of her voice, even the children are silent. The *karakia* ends with a blessing on the evening and everyone present.

'What was all that about?' Harold whispers to his daughter.

With the formal part of the evening over, the band starts up again. People take to the floor, in all sorts of combinations, dancing a variety of new and old steps.

'Go on, Dad,' Kay urges. 'Bet you and Mum haven't danced together for years.'

'You call that dancing?'

Kay grins. 'Think of it as doing your own thing,' she says.

It isn't easy, following her parents' awkward progress round the dance floor, to banish the image of those frocks, hanging in the wardrobe. One day, Kay promises herself, I'll try and understand. But for the moment all she can do is acknowledge her bewilderment, and the persistence, in spite of everything, of love.

'You should be dancing,' Eddie's voice chides from behind her. '*We* should be dancing.'

Kay reaches for his hand. The warmth of his skin, and the faint woody smell coming from his body, fill her with the same sense of enchantment she experienced on first kissing her baby's neck.

Eddie is a graceful dancer. From time to time their bodies touch and they smile at each other. When the music ends, Kay keeps hold of his hand.

'What time is it?' Eddie asks, as they amble back to their chairs.

'Just after nine.' Kay looks at him curiously. Why hasn't he consulted his own watch?

He sits beside her but seems not to want to talk. Every so often he glances at the door.

The band is just about to start playing again when Eddie jumps up from his chair. At the same time Makere, seated opposite, begins to move across the room. Kay turns her head and sees Nina, wearing her Christmas dress, peering into the hall. She shouts her daughter's name. Nina catches sight of her and starts to run.

The next few moments fly past like scenes from a speeded-up film. First there is Nina, hooking her arms around Kay's neck, spilling warm words on to her cheek. Then Kay spots Pauline, standing beside Makere. The two women, one white-skinned (Pauline would describe her colour as pinky-grey), one brown-skinned, waggle their fingers at her. Later Kay will remember their expressions as 'just a tiny bit smug'.

Kay untangles herself from her daughter and stands up. That's when she sees Geoffrey. He's standing by the door, staring at the two people he loves most in the world. The reason his gaze seems fixed is because he's struggling to hold back tears.

Standing a few inches behind Geoffrey is Eddie. As Kay's eyes meet Geoffrey's, Eddie signals to the band. Then, unnoticed by anyone but Makere, he slips outside.

'Dance, Mummy,' Nina orders. 'Dance, *now.*'

Kay scoops up her daughter in her arms. Her body begins to sway. Geoffrey shifts forward a few feet, then stops. How is he to interpret the expression in Kay's eyes? Is it an invitation?

Kay, gliding backwards, moves slowly towards the dance floor. Nina's happy voice soars above the music. Soon they will both be lost in the crowd of dancers.

Geoffrey adjusts his spectacles. The portrait of Patrick Kierin stares sternly down at him. 'Do something,' he imagines that dark mouth shouting. 'Tell her you'll take her to England. Only do something!'

The music is intolerably loud. Whoever invented amplifiers, Geoffrey thinks, never had to wear a hearing-aid.

He moves towards Kay. Is it an illusion, or has someone just dimmed the lights? He reaches out his hands. Kay rearranges her grip on Nina and takes his left hand in hers. Just over a year ago, Geoffrey thinks, a man walked on the moon. Anything is possible.

Kay can feel Geoffrey trembling. His cheeks are pale. His eyes, behind their spectacles, are full of questions. He starts to talk. 'I've resigned from the firm,' he tells her. 'I didn't just do it for you, I did it for myself. From the end of March I'll no longer be working for Goodbody and Sutch.'

Kay doesn't say anything. Somehow she is not surprised.

'I can't tell you what I'm going to do,' Geoffrey admits. 'I still want to practise law, but I want it to be, well . . .' He grins. 'Useful,' he says. 'Helpful. Who knows? I might even go into partnership with Eddie Wihongi.'

'I love you, Mummy. I love you, Daddy,' Nina pipes up. Her parents laugh.

'Or we could go to England,' Geoffrey says, risking, at last, that 'we'.

'England,' Kay murmurs.

'I didn't play fair over that,' Geoffrey confesses. 'You had every right to feel betrayed.'

'You're not asking me to marry you again, are you?'

'Of course I am. Only it doesn't have to be marriage. Living together is fine by me.' Geoffrey's smiling now. Can't help himself. He'd forgotten what it was like to feel happy.

'And we'd go to England?' Kay asks.

'For as long as you want.'

It's Kay's turn to smile. The happiness she feels is not as intense as Geoffrey's, but it's real enough. She starts to look round for Eddie, then stops. Eddie must have invited Geoffrey, she's just realised. Eddie and Makere together. 'I bet I know what you're thinking,' she says.

'And what's that?'

'That the real challenge would be to stay here.'

Geoffrey brings his mouth close to hers. He can't remember a moment when he's wanted her more. 'But *I'm* not writing this story,' he reminds her. 'We're writing it together.'